SHAW CONNOLLY

LIVES TO TELL

Also by Gillian French

Sugaring Off

The Missing Season

The Lies They Tell

The Door to January

Grit

SHAW CONNOLLY
LIVES TO TELL

Gillian French

MINOTAUR BOOKS
NEW YORK

First published in the United States by Minotaur Books, an imprint of St. Martin's Publishing Group

SHAW CONNOLLY LIVES TO TELL. Copyright © 2025 by Gillian French. All rights reserved. Printed in the United States of America. For information, address St. Martin's Publishing Group, 120 Broadway, New York, NY 10271.

www.minotaurbooks.com

Design by Meryl Sussman Levavi

The Library of Congress Cataloging-in-Publication Data is available upon request.

ISBN 978-1-250-35851-6 (hardcover)
ISBN 978-1-250-35852-3 (ebook)

Our books may be purchased in bulk for promotional, educational, or business use. Please contact your local bookseller or the Macmillan Corporate and Premium Sales Department at 1-800-221-7945, extension 5442, or by email at MacmillanSpecialMarkets@macmillan.com.

First Edition: 2025

10 9 8 7 6 5 4 3 2 1

For my dad, Brent, in appreciation of all the years of love, laughter, and support, and for Christopher Shane French, the youngest of the bros, born on 5/2/2024

SHAW CONNOLLY

LIVES TO TELL

1

He calls her for the first time in almost a year, knowing she'll pick up just before voicemail, envisioning her staring at the phone in bitter debate. He hears, almost feels, the tight suck of breath between her teeth as she answers, "What do you want?"

"It's been a while. I thought we were due."

"Were we?" She's moving, maybe pushing covers back, swinging her legs off the edge of the bed, the tendons rippling across the tops of her bare feet. He feels a warm surge at the thought of waking her, embodying the rough start of her morning before more than a vague ribbon of light has streaked above the tree line beyond that washed-out old Wyeth painting of a farmhouse she lives in.

"You must've been wondering." He lets air trickle from his nose. "'Is he dead?'" His impression of her is soft, subtle, a near whisper: "'Is the bastard finally out of my life?'" Waits. In his own voice, flatly, "You must've prayed to whatever god County girls turn to. Patron Saint of Pabst Blue Ribbon?"

She clears morning phlegm directly into the speaker, making him wince and smile. "Never once."

"I'm flattered."

"My luck's not that good, is all." She coughs. "You ought to know. You've made a lot of it."

"No argument from me." He presses his forehead against the back of his hand as leans into the doorframe where he is. "Is Ryan there beside you?"

Where Shaw is, she's off the bed, in motion, tugging on an old plaid robe over the big T-shirt that was once Ryan's; she seized it for sleep so far back in their marriage that the origin no longer registers. Her pulse is up, but the recording app's saving all this, adding another audio file to her Anders Jansen collection. "Damn, are you behind the times."

She goes down the hall on autopilot to the coffeemaker, kicking Beau's stray Nike out of the way. It bounces off the dog's dish and spills some of yesterday's kibble; the boys gave her too much again. There's a rattle-clack as she shifts the glass decanter from the dish rack to the warming plate. "A lot's changed since we last talked. Ry's moved on."

A momentary pause. "You two split up? Really. And here I thought you'd be the couple to prove all the statistics wrong." He exhales. "I suppose you're going to blame me for that, too."

"Nah. Long time coming. No big shock." She doesn't know how many scoops of grounds she's put in, but she starts it perking anyway just for background noise other than her nails ticking the countertop and her heartbeat thrumming in her ears. Through the broad open doorframe to the living room, she notices the crest of Dad's gray head over the back of the recliner, slumped to the side.

"How're the boys taking it?"

Her fingers stop. She waits.

There's a smile in Anders's voice as he leisurely draws back from the tender spot; he always has to get close enough to warm them with his breath. "Must take a lot to break up high school sweet-hearts, together some-odd years."

"Nope. Takes a little bit. Year after year. Stream wearing away the rock, all that." She's got to keep a steady hand, work him like a locked wheel. "Where you living these days, bubba?"

"What fun would it be if I told you?"

"Want to hear my guess? You got a new job somewhere, had to relocate. Some kind of big life change like that."

"I've been keeping busy, yes." There's a brief absence from the speaker, as if he's making breakfast preparations, too. "You Connollys were never far from my thoughts, though. In fact . . . I was just pondering your names. You three girls."

Shaw shuts her eyes for a second, swallowing the first slosh of acid up her throat.

"I mean—there's no flow at all. Did your parents even begin to comprehend the task at hand? You, Shawnee, firstborn, were given the trailer trash name. That tacky touch of cultural appropriation. And the littlest one may as well have had 'Madison' stamped on her ass on her way down a factory conveyor belt. It was the number-two most popular name in the country for baby girls that year. I checked." Pauses. "But then we circle back to Thea."

Steel creeps up Shaw's spine. She forces herself to the act of pulling down mugs from the cupboard. "You want to talk about Thea, okay. Talk."

"Normally I dislike bastardized spellings—Theodora is the generally accepted version of the name—but in the case of your sister . . . somehow, the inconsistency just fit. Theadora. Old-fashioned. Sweet."

"And she was neither one. Go figure."

"Like I said. Inconsistencies. Appealing, in certain people."

She stops again, bracing her hands against the counter while rocking back on her heels, a deep lioness stretch under the weight of it all, the burden of him, and her voice becomes guttural: "It'd be so easy for you." She shakes her head. "You need to feel like you got all the power, fine, you got it. Just name a place. A landmark. Something. I'll find her. You can go disappear. I don't give a shit anymore."

"Does your employer know that you say these things? Hardly becoming to one involved however peripherally in the criminal justice system"—Anders speaks right over her as she tries to cut in—"and anyway we both know what an utter falsehood it is. You could never let me go. It's not in you. Other people might talk about needing a burial, some sense of closure. But not you. Truthfully, Shaw? I don't believe you care about honoring Thea. It's never been about that. It's about grinding my bones to make your bread. Isn't it?" Waits. "Answer."

Her words emerge dry, exhausted, her eyes held shut: "What'd you kill her for, you prick?"

Silence. "You can be so uncouth sometimes."

He ends the call.

Shaw wakes the old man first, nudging his shoulder—"Dad, it's morning"—while she gathers the quilt away from his legs and pushes the recliner footrest down into the locked position.

"Hmm? Oh." His hearing aids lay right where she thought they would, side table to his left, removed while he watched TV with captions on late into the night. "Thought I was dead for a minute there, didn't ya?"

"Dead men don't fart, so I've been told."

He laughs, wincing in the process of easing himself up. "Always were a rude girl."

"Heard that once or twice, too." Shaw drops the folded quilt over the chair arm. "I'll get the boys—"

"No, no, I'll do it." He starts stiffly toward the stairs, creases crisscrossing the back of his heavy sweater and cords, worn since yesterday. "What do you pay me for, anyway?"

She snorts. "Microwaved meals and a mattress too hard to sleep on—that passes for a salary these days?"

"Well . . . got to earn my keep." He takes the stairs with difficulty, even more so than when he first moved in four months ago, grasping the railing like a lifeline between ships. Time's catching up with him, no denying it; he'd been in his early thirties when Shaw was born. Maybe she ought to get one of those stairway elevator seats they've got for old folks. Forget it—keeping the boys off it would be impossible, and convincing Dad to park his ass there would be even worse. Inching along like an invalid with his hands limp in his lap while Beau and Casey thunder up and down, basketballs dribbling down the steps? Stupid. "Was that your work on the phone?" Dad's voice carries down. "Heard you talking."

Shaw keeps her eyes on the frost-stippled morning coming into full light outside the front windows. "Yeah." Can't face telling him, but there's no other way; bad news will out, like blood. "No, I'm lying to you. It was him again. Shit."

Dad stops halfway up but doesn't turn. "That Anders guy?" Her silence is answer enough. "Thought he was gone."

"So did I. Poked his little gopher head back up this morning, though. Yippee. Knew this was going to be a banner day."

The old man's standing there, grappling, his hand now a claw on the banister. "Call Steve York."

"It's at the top of my list, believe me."

Dad climbs a couple more steps, and then his call bounces off the upstairs landing: "You boys are *late*—hup, one, two, three, four, move your asses or you'll be walking to school." He forces a goblin's grin on his way back down as they hear feet thudding the floor above. "Always did the trick with you girls, too."

She smiles crookedly, shakes her head, getting cereal boxes out of the pantry as her phone goes off again.

With breath held, she leans over the counter, checking the screen. Jesus, it really is work this time. Shaw answers, netting some bowls from the shelf: "I'll be out the door in, like, twenty minutes. Can you put whatever it is on ice till then?"

A guttural *chuff* from Lydia Gauthier; it takes Shaw a second to realize the girl is laughing.

"Okay, what? Use your words."

"It's just—you saying that. I mean . . . considering." In the put-out silence, Shaw can almost see Gauthier burrowing down into her emotional shell, all pink-cheeked defensiveness. "They need us on a suspicious death in Houghton. Jewel thought it might be quicker for you to meet me there." A light bulb flickers. "Want me to text you the address?"

"Now that's using the old walnut. See ya." Shaw rings off, tosses the phone, dumps her armload in the center of the kitchen table. No time for a shower, piss up a rope. No chance to rinse free of the used, prying fingers feeling, the residue left behind by any conversation with Anders. No opportunity to steal five goddamn seconds without an audience to confront the building darkness, the pressure behind her eyes—a black sandstorm, that's how she thinks of him, billowing, abrasive, rushing in to scour every crack and fissure, clot her lungs. She can't breathe at the thought of starting up right where they left off: him, fucking her life and mind over. So. She won't breathe.

Beau rounds the kitchen doorway first, sleeping in boxer shorts and a T-shirt now like he's grown, tall and rail-thin for his age at fifteen, but he's still got the bright, eager look she associates with his toddler years. Blue eyes, straw-straight brown hair which lays flat on his brow, every inch his father. "Mom, you eating with us?"

Her heart hurts at anyone being that excited to crunch Frosted Mini Wheats across from her. "Can't, sweets. Gotta go, go, go."

Beau gives an over-the-top groan, but he's already after the food, used to her leaving ways. "Anything cool this time?"

"Death's never cool, bud. It's just—an end." It's not the first time she's chided them on this, being insensitive, flippant, typical kids, but it's the first time within Dad's earshot, and with Thea on her mind, Shaw's feeling stiff, humorless.

She checks Dad's reaction, but he acts like he hasn't heard, instead washing down his medication. Beau's gaze is on the middle distance as he shakes out cereal, and Shaw kisses the top of his head as she passes, pressing close to the precious organic electrical processes inside which can stop, just stop, at any time; she can never forget that.

Casey, ten years old, comes into the room: he's stockier, a head shorter than his brother, and still little enough to wear print jammies without shame, thank God. Walking like he's half asleep, Casey catches Shaw around the waist for a quick connection without words before she jogs upstairs for a cabbie's shower, hearing Dad say, "What'd she do to this coffee?" before sloshing it down the sink.

Upstairs, Shaw takes a minute to call Stephen York, getting his voicemail, no surprise there. He's a state police detective with a caseload that won't quit, and nothing sets Thea apart from the rest of his dead other than the fact that she's probably the coldest, passed down by a series of predecessors since 2007. Steve doesn't use the word cold, though. Thea is unsolved. As-yet unknown. A rabbit hole into a free fall for any investigator, anybody who delves too deep.

Shaw speaks: "Steve, this is Shaw Connolly, Thea's big sister. Long time, no talk. I wanted you to know that I got another call from Anders Jansen this morning." She takes a breath; it's awkward, what with her going against Steve's advice last year after she went through the pain in the ass of changing her number and then Anders found it anyway. That's when she decided, fuck it, she's not pursuing charges. Bring on the calls; maybe he'll make a mistake and give her back her sister. "He's full of the same old sunshine and lollipops. I'd love a chat, but . . . you may not want to try me until tomorrow. My hands are going to be pretty full."

Beneath the wind-buffeted crime scene canopy tent, the man lies on his stomach, head turned to face east toward Route 2, which tumbles through Bennet County in the reckless loops of a wounded snake. The deceased—one Bernard Cloyd, 67, according to the license found in his wallet, along with credit cards and thirty-one dollars cash—landed half on the ice of Round Pond, half on the snowy crust, his right arm upraised, bent beside his head as if his last act was to try to catch himself before the world grayed out.

The blow to his head had torn a piece of scalp from the bone like leather from a tattered baseball, and his brimmed ski cap, marked by an evidence technician with a yellow number-three Versa-Cone, lies some seven feet away, thrown when whatever it was came down across the back of his skull with extreme prejudice.

Shaw sees the cap from where she stands, picturing its initial coast across the ice, catching a bit of breeze now and then until it spun to the center of the pond while the rest of the world stood still out here, save the treetops, their transitory swaying reflected in the deceased's open eyes.

Shaw pops the trunk door of her Yukon Denali, which sits parked behind two sheriff's department SUVs, and gets into her gear: the white Tyvek coveralls she zips into and tugs the hood to her hair-line, the nylon shoe covers, the filter mask she hangs around her neck by the strap until it's necessary.

Her fingerprinting field kit is secured against the back of the third row with bungee cords, and she frees it before crossing the snow toward whom she knows to be Gauthier, yet another masked, shape-less clean suit, but notably shorter than the boys' club, standing on the periphery of the activity, her raspberry-colored muck boots glowing through the spunbonded coverall material like the legs of an Alaskan King Crab.

"Where've you been so far?" They're the first words out of Shaw's mouth once she's under the tape.

The young woman's kit rests by her feet. "Jewel said to wait for you."

Shaw gives a terse sigh. "No foolin'. Who's team leader? Dun-leavy? Didn't he put his two cents in?" Shaw rubbernecks among the white-suited CSIs, recognizes the build of the scene manager—top heavy, long-legged—and gets the distinct impression that the guy's dodging her gaze while crouching over an area of snow with a couple other techs. "Shunted you off on your own, huh." Shaw feels the girl's stare keenly, those dark brown cocker spaniel eyes; Gauthier rarely seems to blink, all part of her earnest-to-a-fault awkwardness. Shaw can't decide if it's a side effect of being a noob or, God help them all, just how Lydia Gauthier is. "So, nothing's been done on our end. We need to get rolling. Have you run into Padraig McKenzie at all? He'll be lead detective on this, more than likely, unless or until the staties take over. He's from the sheriff's office." Gauthier's gaze flicks away, then back. "You know who he is? A Scot on the wrong side of the pond? Sticks out like bagpipes in a barbershop quartet?"

Shaw waits a microsecond for an answer, then swivels, heading down the safe path through the clearing that's already been decreed free of evidence, approaching the flapping tent, another tech on hands and knees nearby, no doubt hunting for any fibers that haven't already been scattered to Oz. "Right, okay. Walk with me, talk with me. There's two of us, so no need to be on each other's heels. Bisect the scene and work our way out toward the tree line and then down to the roadside." She checks the mottled, frozen snow under her boot. *Tsks.* "Tracks guys are going to be shittin' themselves. Look at this mess. Must've had every Arctic Cat and dog walker in the county out here at some point." Shaw glances at Gauthier. "This being—what, your third crime scene?"

"Second." She pauses. "First homicide."

"Unexplained death. Don't call it 'homicide' until the ME has signed off. This is Land of Make-Believe time. Pretend like a very large bird could've swooped down on Mr. Cloyd to steal his hat until we're told otherwise. Got it? Practice. Discretion. Don't even use the word 'suspicious.' You don't want a witness or reporter hearing you shoot your mouth off before we know what went on." Shaw's gaze lands on a woman with a shock-blanched face leaning heavily on a pair of skis driven into the crust just beyond the tape, where she speaks with a uniform. "A scene like this doesn't have much of an onlooker problem, but if you practice, discretion becomes second nature. Helps keep you out of trouble in the long run."

"Okay. Got it." Gauthier stumbles on the crust, then falls into step with Shaw. "And I won't be on your heels. I just . . . need to not mess this up. You know?"

Shaw glances at her, makes a quick appraisal of the girl's tense face, then nods, her attention pulled away by a two-note bird's whistle from within the tent.

McKenzie crouches beside the body, mask on, photographing an object in Cloyd's right hand with his phone. "No murder weapon yet," McKenzie says to Shaw without preamble; they've been working together on and off for two years, and they fall in together as easily as if it's been twenty. "But here's one for your lot, eventually." He indicates a gray plastic handle still squeezed in the man's left hand.

Shaw hunkers down for a better look. "Dog leash?"

"With his hand trapped under his body like that, nobody saw it right away." McKenzie rests on his heels. "Looks like he got hit, fell forward, and Fifi must've eventually worked herself loose. The tape retracted back under the body."

"Where's the collar?" She catches his mild look. "Just saying, if the dog wriggled itself free, the collar would still be attached to the bolt snap." Shaw leans in. "And the leash is a good inch wide."

"Okay. Meaning?"

"Well—that's for a big dog. More Fido than Fifi. These suckers can handle up to 150 pounds." At his raised brows: "German shepherd at home."

"Got to get you one of those Dog Mom bumper stickers. All right, noted. I sent a couple uniforms out to search the woods, anyway, and Animal Control is on its way."

"Guess they'll find out if Fido was chipped. Best way to identify him, her. I think it's inhumane myself, but then, so's chopping their balls off, and we don't mind that, do we." *Contradictions*—Anders's blunt, dry fingers forcing the word between her lips, holding her jaw shut till she swallows—and Shaw straightens abruptly, jerking her head back toward Gauthier.

"This is Gauthier, new addition to Latent Prints. Gauthier, McKenzie. He works Major Crimes in Bennet County. If you've got a question, you can always go to him, just in case I'm swept away in a flash flood or something."

"Saddle me with that, will you?" McKenzie sends a half smirk Gauthier's way, that smile like it hurts, the distinctive fan of creases at his eyes that sets him apart from every other eyes-and-forehead at a scene, at least for Shaw. Gauthier shifts her feet, saying nothing, her gaze drawn inexorably to the back of Cloyd's head, that window of bloody skull, the fluttering of the scalp flap. At least the girl hasn't puked; no sign of even coming close. "Welcome." McKenzie looks back to his work. "It's not always like this. Sometimes it's worse."

"Buh-dum-dum. Here all week, folks," Shaw says. "If he didn't say it with that badass brogue, it'd be downright obnoxious, wouldn't it? Okay. We're off."

"Hey"—McKenzie stops her—"see you at Tommy Daly's send-off?"

"Oh, ugh, that's today? Sorry, not ugh. Yeah, sure thing. Patel's, I'm guessing?" She doesn't wait for McKenzie's nod, instead giving a come-hither gesture to Gauthier, who paces away with her as Shaw surveys the rest of the scene.

Frozen pond. Small, dilapidated wooden bench on the far side for ice skaters to sit and fiddle with their laces, probably painted once but now peeled to gray. "Desolate, isn't it? Okay, so we do the bench, but unfinished wood that's been weathered in the elements like this is a toughie, rarely holds a print. Then there's this shack— what is this?"

Shaw leads the way to the lean-to standing some fifteen feet back from the pond's edge, built from plywood, the door hanging slightly ajar. "We want pictures of this—our own pics for Latent, never mind what the other techs have done. And get the position of the door." Gauthier goes for her phone as Shaw kneels and opens her kit, getting out her go-to brush with big soft fiberglass bristles and a jar of basic black powder. She unscrews the lid. "Again, porous wood, so who knows what we'll get, but obviously we want to dust all around this funny little latch they've jiggered here and this whole area along the edge where a person might touch when coming or going. Seriously, who built this and why? Shelter for the kids, I guess? What's the point?"

"Maybe it's an ice fishing shack." Gauthier stops mid-tap on her screen when Shaw looks back. "You can get plans free online. My stepdad made one."

"What in God's name could anybody expect to catch in a puddle that size?"

"Maybe that's why they dumped it here."

Shaw smiles impulsively and pats the snow. "Pull up some tundra." She waits until Gauthier is squatting beside her before she spins the tip of the brush against the inside of the powder jar lid, getting a light coating. "Make me happy and tell me the number-one rule of thumb when you work in prints, pun intended."

Gauthier hesitates, no doubt rapidly scanning a mental inventory of textbook terms, class lectures at UMass Lowell, where she got her barely dry forensics degree. "Label everything. Initial. Always get your partner to sign off."

"Well, yes. Those things. But that's not what I wanted." Shaw gives the brush a finishing spin, then continues the twirling motion all over the latch and the surface around it. "Less is more. Use it like Marie Antoinette's powder puff and you'll bury half the lighter prints you'll never even know were there, ones clinging on by aminos, not sebaceous."

Shaw peers close to the wood, searching for friction ridges, the swirls and whorls and arches that form the topography of the human fingerprint. "Yeah, the shack is crap, doesn't hold a print. This clouding here? Doesn't even qualify as a smudge." Shaw opens the door wider, peers around before stepping into the shadowy space barely big enough to accommodate the two of them. Gauthier follows.

There's another bench, this one built into the back wall, as well as a scattering of dead leaves and trash on the ground and a single window in the far wall with smeared, grime-caked glass. "Add a composting toilet and a stack of *Reader's Digest*s and you'd have yourself one hell of a room with a view." Shaw crouches, peering under the bench. "Is your stepdad's ice shack set up like this?"

"I don't know." Gauthier's still not looking at Shaw when she tries to connect again; eye contact is becoming a kind of game. "I wouldn't set foot in it."

Shaw waits for more but gets nothing. "Fair enough." She sees what she was looking for, gives a "*Ha*," as she straightens. "We're in business. Structure's unfinished, but the bench is polyurethane treated. Plus, I see empties, glass, aluminum. Something to bring back to the lab with the leash, anyway. This is going to be a thin one. Better hope the uniforms turn up the weapon out in the woods or we'll all be flying by the seat of our collective pants, if that makes any sense."

Gauthier goes out and retrieves her kit, then opens it on the floor beneath the window, ready to start on the casing, sash, and glazing. "Won't we probably just be lifting a bunch of unknowns from whoever came in here to drink that Mountain Dew two years ago?"

"Doesn't matter. We work in likelihoods when we can. Other times, we canvass. Leave motivations to the psychologists. If there's a chance that there's one print that could set off bells in AFIT, our job is to make damn sure we don't miss it." Shaw gets out her mini Maglite, shining it on the dusty but reflective coating on the wood, where it sets off telltale patterns, human oils deposited by fingers. Shaw goes for the clear lifting tape, letting loose the first two bars of "Whistle While You Work."

They dust: the entire bench, doorframe, bag the empties and two cigarette butts and a crumpled candy wrapper for a closer look at the lab.

They photograph and lift: partials and fulls captured in black powder on carefully smoothed strips of tape, the tape then applied to index cards, exact location of discovery written in Shaw's cramped dashing hand and Gauthier's soft, rounded letters, snapped away inside plastic file boxes for the ride in totes to the evidence-receiving area.

Packing it in three hours later, Shaw leads the way down the slope, kit in hand, then tugs her mask down to call to McKenzie, "Any word on the dog?"

He shakes his head. "Nothing yet."

"Huh. Well, maybe it's homeward bound and will turn up in Mr. Cloyd's front yard later, looking for Snausages." Her phone pings, text received; she checks it as she walks, wondering if it could be Stephen York touching base today after all.

Jewel, the boss: *See me when you have time thx.*

i.e., Unless this case is the Unabomber meets the Lindbergh baby, make time.

Shaw sends back a thumbs-up and tucks the phone away, working her jaw as she reaches the roadside. She glances over at a powder blue VW Beetle hatchback parked two spots behind her Beast, the smaller vehicle visible now that one of the deputy's SUVs is gone. "Yours?" Shaw watches Gauthier's nod, then says, "I shouldn't have said that earlier." Gauthier stops. "When I said, 'make me happy.' Not your job or your worry. So don't take that shit from me, all right?"

"Okay. I won't." The girl takes a slow sidestep, sensing they're not done.

"Just curious—what did Jewel say to you about me this morning?"

Gauthier continues walking, pushing her coverall hood back, smoothing a hand over her hair, which is dark brown and woven into a halo braid. "She said you'd look after me." She goes to her car without a backward glance.

Shaw watches a moment, shakes her head, then stares off hard at the tree line and the middle distance.

2

"You jazzed to use the fuming chamber again?"

Shaw glances up at Gauthier as they unpack objects from the Round Pond scene onto a work surface at Bennet County Forensic Solutions, the private crime lab contracted by four sheriff's departments from neighboring counties for evidence processing, not to mention mailings from the outlying areas.

Gauthier stops a moment, evidence bag in hand, having shed her coveralls for a lab coat, fresh nitrile gloves, and safety glasses. "Um—yes?"

"Feeling comfortable with it? You helped Tran with the stuff from the restaurant fire, didn't you?" Shaw watches Gauthier nod. "But Tran was halfway out the door on a two-week vacay and his brain was already sipping Mai Tais on a beach somewhere, am I right? Look, you take half, I take half. Team effort."

There's a moment's quiet as they cross to the CyanoSafe against the far wall. "What's in a Mai Tai?" Gauthier says.

"Not sure. Beachy, you know. Half gallon of rum." Shaw gestures back with her elbow. "Hey, you're young. You're supposed to be the one teaching me about drinking in the modern age."

Gauthier's quiet, watching Shaw open the chamber's glass door to get access to the hanging racks, both of them fitting the plastic clips onto the cans and leash as best they can to suspend them inside. "I don't, actually. Drink, I mean."

"Oh." Shaw sets the glass bottle on the floor of the case. "Probably for the best. Just skip that whole scene. Pressure to get wasted, not knowing what you've done or who you've done it with. Stupid, all of it. Not like twenty years down the line you'll find yourself saying, 'if only I'd puked in my bestie's rose bushes more often.'" She gingerly pulls her fingers back. "Want to do the honors with the test strip?"

Gauthier grabs a latent card from the box on the nearest counter, removes her gloves long enough to swipe her thumb down the side of her nose, gathering enough sebaceous oils to leave a print to develop along with the evidentiary items. "I can do the cyanoacrylate." She sounds eager, probably wanting to prove she can do something on her own.

"Go nuts." As Gauthier squeezes the superglue cartridge into the heating tray, Shaw locks onto Jewel watching them through the horizontal glass pane set into the far wall. Jewel with her posture and poise, standing utterly still, her arms crossed with fingers propped up, always on pointe, as in the final stage of some precise and elegant dance. "You should've seen the chamber they had rigged when I started here," Shaw says absently, looking back at Jewel, who still hasn't changed expression, "before we got the Safe. Before Jewel took over. Basically, an aquarium with a hot plate. You vent one of those setups wrong, before you know it, your family's bickering over whether you would've preferred your economy casket in steel or pine."

Shaw's phone buzzes in her pocket. New text. Guess who. Releasing a tense breath, she starts the timer. "Twenty-five minutes should do it." She hits the *process* button. "Keep an eye on everything through the door. You see those white ridges starting to appear on the test, pull everything, or the prints will get fogged over by the glue." One glance at the glass shows a parting glimpse of Jewel as the woman heads to her office. "Okay. I've been summoned. If I'm not back in fifteen, you can have my poop emoji stress ball."

Shaw raps twice on the doorframe of Jewel's office, waiting as the woman finishes reading something on her laptop screen, lengthy seconds passing without acknowledgment before Jewel suddenly draws air through her nose and sits back, turning her clear amber gaze upon Shaw, and says, "How's it going?" in her low, honeyed voice.

"Good, good." Shaw hesitates, leaning in the doorway, experiencing a moment of vertigo as she returns the woman's stare. "Oh, the homicide. Yeah, good. No murder weapon yet, but they hadn't finished the search of the woods around the scene when we wrapped up. Wasn't a lot to bring back here, honestly. Pretty barren. But Gauthier's got what there is cooking in the chamber now."

Jewel's been tidying her desk during all this, a simple matter of putting a pen back into the organizer and reversing a file folder sitting on the blotter to face out instead of in. "How're you finding her? Gauthier?"

"Good, good." Cringe: Shaw's in danger of becoming one of those plastic bobbing-head birds that drinks water from a cup. "She seems solid, no problems." Shaw hesitates. "Young."

"Isn't she just." Jewel gives a lift of her arched brows, which could mean anything at all, and *Why'd you tell her I'd watch out for her; why the hell'd you have to go and say that* presses hard against Shaw's tightly sealed lips. "Take a seat. There's something I wanted to show you."

Shaw sits in the steel-framed chair across from her boss of slightly more than one year, Jewel St. Bonaparte, in many ways still a mystery to her. They always seem to be at odd angles to each other, Jewel possessed of a seamless professional polish, wearing her short Afro hennaed to a reddish tint at the ends, a slim front-knotted headwrap every day, black stretch blazers and skinny slacks with ballet flats on a body as limber and toned as a gymnast's, her whole physicality about Spartan simplicity, ease of movement. Jewel ran the lab with an efficiency and a cost effectiveness unheard of in Shaw's time here. Shaw, meanwhile, generally felt like a train wreck slamming through a hot mess, barely holding together through a space-age innovation of caffeine, baling wire, and those little yellow Swiss rolls filled with strawberry and cream.

"I came across this and wondered if you knew about it." Jewel flips the file folder open and slides it to Shaw. "The state crime lab is hiring." She watches as Shaw leans forward to look over the cover page. "It's supervisory. You'd have a unit of five techs working under you."

Shaw says nothing, some internal timer guesstimating how long politeness demands she scan the blur of words before she can sit back. "Right. Thanks." Quick tight smile, pure PR, hands gripping the chair arms in preparation to stand. "Appreciate the heads-up."

Jewel observes Shaw's death grip, then leans against the edge of the desk with a wry twist of her mouth as her fingers thread. "Take the printout. It's for you."

Shaw gives an awkward gust of half laughter and palms the folder. "Will do." But Jewel's gaze pins her.

"Tell me. If I let you out of here now, how long will it take that to find its way into the trash can?"

"Well . . . Come on. I'd recycle, of course." Shaw sits back and pushes her hand through her hair, Jewel's *really?* expression draining whatever tense humor they'd shared down to a completely oxygen-free environment.

The silence is broken only by the faint static disruption of humming electronics: printer, landline, fax, fluorescent tubes overhead. "You'll have been here nine years in April," Jewel says. "Our most senior employee."

"Minus Rolf." Shaw watches question lines rise on the boss's forehead. "Custodial. Been here for twelve. You haven't talked to him? Oh, he's a riot." Shaw crosses, recrosses her legs. "Into model shipbuilding, apparently."

Jewel's inflection is tolerant, neutral. "I'm sure that you realize you've hit a ceiling professionally."

"Maybe I've got my eye on the big chair." Shaw lifts her chin at Jewel's seat. "Just riding your coattails until you leave us for the next presidential race."

Jewel smiles, no teeth revealed; oxygen returns. "Harlan Gormley told me he expected you to put in for this position when he announced his retirement, but you never did. You probably would've gotten it." Jewel repositions herself, allowing Shaw absorbance time. "Can you share with me why you didn't apply?"

Shaw shrugs. "My boys need as much time as I can give them. It wasn't right for me." Shaw doesn't bother to explain how she didn't have the energy for more supervising than she was already doing at home, rushing back to the house from the lab to relieve Ryan so he could head out to his shop and catch up on work until nine, ten o'clock at night while she made supper, gave homework help, broke up wrestling matches, bossed the boys into showers, ran in circles catching up on household chores until the boys finally surrendered to sleep. The boss can't possibly have kids; not a sign of them in this office. Not one framed photo or crayon drawing in the place. No rumors of anything but an ex in Jewel's past, that's it, and who knows how much truth there is to that. Shaw imagines home for the childless as silence, a single glass of wine, a treadmill, white furniture, carefully orchestrated emptiness. There but for the grace of God.

Jewel clears her throat. "I do realize that there's some tragic family history tying you to this area."

Shaw exercises stillness, unsure what the other woman knows, where she heard it. Perhaps from Harlan Gormley himself. How long has Jewel had it turning over in her head every time she looks at Shaw, a stamp, a brand: *tragic?* Nearly a lifetime of dealing with this shit. "That's right." There's nothing like this sense of exposure, Shaw sitting here half naked with her obscene bits hanging out. Another reminder that she'll never fully outgrow the skin of that grieving, shamefaced eighteen-year-old, so morning sick with Beau but too scared to even stand up from Mom and Dad's couch to ask the sheriff and his deputy if she could go lie down, have a break from the questions, because Mom said that she couldn't let on, not in front of the cops—*we don't want them thinking things, hon, not now*—not when it had taken three months to get them to see Thea as anything but a runaway. Shaw remembers focusing on Sheriff Brixton's knees in brown uniform trousers, two mountainous humps dominating her lowered gaze.

Your sister had a lot of boyfriends, didn't she? He'd waited, setting her up. *Shawnee? Are you with us?*

Now, Shaw mentally removes herself, focusing on the potted snake plant in the corner, nearly three feet high, possibly plastic.

"It must be closing in on twenty years at this point," Jewel says. A fleck of criticism detectable in that, maybe, if sifted for. A pause. "That's got to be hard."

"It is. Very."

It's a standoff, both surveying the other, seeing if either will get clumsy in their separate roles, maybe apologize, and then pry, or get weepy and overshare. Jewel seems to give up on the latter happening. "I won't pretend I know exactly how it feels to live with something like that. But . . . since it would be impossible for you to work your sister's case in any way, even if new evidence were to come to light, you must know that you need to leave the investigation to those not personally involved anyway. I don't see how it benefits you—or your family—to stay stationary forever." A pause. "I'm saying, it would be handled."

Shaw gazes back for a beat, her phone like a superheated ceramic tile in her pocket, grafting to her thigh, loaded with stored audio files labeled *Anders Jansen*. Then she brushes her temple as she says, "There's a difference between knowing"—Shaw taps briefly over her heart—"and knowing, isn't there. Besides, the boys are settled here, have school and everything."

"I hear they have schools in Augusta." Jewel takes in Shaw's closed body language, then places her hand on the folder, maintaining eye contact. "I hope, for your sake, you'll look into this position. The pay is considerably more than what you're making now, and I'd guarantee you my full endorsement." Jewel leans forward, looking up from beneath her brows. "You've got almost a decade of experience on Tran and Lydia." It takes Shaw a split-second to recognize Gauthier's first name. "You should have something to show for it."

Shaw stands, sliding the folder from beneath Jewel's fingertips and tucking it under her arm.

"The next election's two year's off, by the way." Jewel doesn't say it until Shaw's nearly out the door, and when Shaw looks back at the other woman, she's already working on her laptop. "The big chair's not opening up anytime soon."

Through the magnifier, Shaw sees valleys of flowing ridges forming whorls and double loops, landscapes she's traveled by sight so many times she knows them instinctively, like recognizing an aerial view of a territory where she's spent much of her life. The prints have been scanned into the system—biometric software does a lot now—but she still falls back on experience and instinct, always will.

With one of her gray eyes close to the loupe, Shaw uses the ridge counter to mark the core of the print, then hunts minutiae, positioning of the pores along the ridge paths, microscopic strand of beads that serve to identify, exclude.

"Hello, gorgeous," she says softly, sensing a twitch of Gauthier's shoulders without looking away from the magnifier. "Don't worry. I'm not talking to you." Shaw sits back. "Ba-da-bing. I knew it. Didn't I say?" She slides over, making way. "Mind taking a look?"

Gauthier stands from her computer, where an ultra-magnified partial left index from the soda can dominates the screen, leaning down to peer into the loupe glass. "Okay, you're looking at a very partial right thumb, but you knew that"—speaking over Gauthier's "I know that"—"from the dog leash. Now, Mr. Cloyd's prints"— Shaw expands the same image of the scanned print on the laptop screen beside her—"are right where you'd expect to find them— palm arched over the handle, partial digits all around the tape trigger area and scattered everywhere else, too. His, and only his. You'd have to be looking with your eyes closed to miss our gentleman's itty-bitty peacock's eye on his thumb—so crazy rare, it's a neon sign."

Shaw pops the right thumb up on center screen again. "Except this one. Which just so happened to come from near the steel clip at the end of the leash."

"Where somebody would have to grip to unfasten the clip from the dog's collar," Gauthier says.

"If I say 'Bingo,' will you slap me? Might be worth it." Shaw gives her pen a machine gun rat-a-tat-tat against the tabletop. "And my understanding is that our victim lives alone. Of course, none of this means Mr. Cloyd doesn't have a lover, friend, dog walker, neighbor kid who takes Fido out for a piddle once in a while, but it sure as hell seems strange that the only trace I'm seeing of this person so far is right here. And the dog's gone missing."

Gauthier leans back against the counter with her arms folded and her thick dark brows knitted. "You really think somebody beat that man's head in so they could steal his dog?"

"Can't really see it. Maybe if he was out flaunting some pedigree pup worth four thousand bucks or something but, even then, you'd have to know the breeding world, be able to spot the show-quality standards, all that. Still, it'll be someone he knows. Nine times out of ten. And a retired fella like that, creature of habit? I'll bet he walked that route every day, rain or shine, and everybody who lives on his road knew it. Could be his dog was leaving deposits on a neighbor's lawn and they figured—hey, tit for tat, Grandpa." Shaw looks back at Gauthier's incredulous sound. "People. No act too horrible, and usually for the stupidest of reasons." Shaw refocuses on the screen, allowing a moment's silence. "You will get used to it. What you had to look at earlier. It'll never become as nice as a hot bath and a smutty book, but . . . you find a way." Shaw clicks back over to the unidentified print. "I promise you, kiddo."

As Shaw pushes through the wooden revolving doors into Patel's Spirits, she lets her eyes shut for the briefest moment, her ash-blond flyaways fluttering around her ears in the blast of forced heat coming from the vent above the entryway, the restaurant a respite from the wind and the flat blind draining light of the late winter afternoon.

Smoothly lacquered shadows and warm yellow wall sconces abound, paired with the entwined scents of top-shelf booze, wood polish, and musky incense. There's a masculine grip to the place, a broad and steadying palm that cups your skull, directing you to a cushioned leather booth where the lights are low, and nobody looks askance at you quietly having one too many.

Patel's, situated off the highway in something of a roadhouse locale, is the enclave chosen by local law enforcement as a class joint for gatherings, send-offs, a better glass of courage before facing whatever waits at home, preferable to the downtown riverfront pubs where they'd have to rub elbows with half the assholes and addicts they haul in on domestics over the weekends.

Shaw glimpses proprietor Sunni Patel behind the bar, having a quiet word with a few of the waitstaff. He's dressed in a black silk French-cuff shirt. Sunni's not tall, not fat or thin, instead possessing a reassuring proportionalism from his shoulders to his thick middle in his fine threads, a riveting gaze, a taut, controlled sort of vigilance ensuring that the ambiance in his place isn't broken by the drunk or gauche, aware of how much consistent business is brought into his place by the crowd of police now populating the tables and booths for Tommy Daly's retirement party. Detectives, some forensics, an administrative assistant or three.

Shaw and Sunni know each other by sight—she's not sure if he knows her name—and they exchange a nod as he finishes with the waitstaff and heads swiftly back toward the party, monitoring, generating a bit of the old give-and-take if conversation lags in any corner, even fetching the select drink for a patron himself while keeping his finger to the pulse of the room.

Shaw could go over, be catered to—work's buying all the drinks, no reason why not—but she veers instead, approaching the bar, making eye contact with the bartender while peripherally realizing that she knows the man with the shaggy brown hair and the wash-worn Hawaiian shirt, choosing to lean, not sit, to her left, his legs crossed at the ankle, one oxford propped up on its toe. "Cabernet sauvignon, please, lots of ice," Shaw says to the bartender, who's dressed in a crisp, high-necked white blouse, black cravat with gold tack: Patel's dress code.

"Certainly. Bar or table this evening?"

"Think I'll park it next to the bird of paradise, thanks." Shaw chooses a stool and takes a sidelong look at Padraig McKenzie, who's smiling into his glass in that pained-tender way, working down a swallow of whiskey.

"Good Christ, you came." His voice tinged with rustiness from the liquor.

"Said I would, didn't I. I'm surprised to see you."

"Oh, I'm not really here. Just a figment of the imagination. I'm grabbing one drink to Tommy, then it's right back at it. I finished up a ten-hour, so I took myself off duty for a bit." He takes another sip. "The ME's got a backlog. It's looking like another forty-eight hours or more before she can get to our fellow."

"What about the—?" She sticks her fingers up alongside her temple and crooks them, making dog ears; he shakes his head. Shaw sits back, giving his shirt a once-over. "Pineapples, hibiscus, palm trees. Got everything on there but the luau, don't you." She leans her elbows on the bar. "Never looked at you the same since I figured out what you wore under your coveralls. Freaking Magnum."

"What can I tell you. Some people have a personality. I have shirts." Another sip. He glances around. "Where's the magician's apprentice?"

Shaw focuses on receiving her stemless glass, not wanting to examine the memory: Gauthier, gathering her things into her messenger bag at quitting time earlier, Shaw nearly inviting the girl along before swallowing the words for good and deliberately not watching her go. "My duties don't extend to babysitting." Shitty thing to say. Jesus.

He nods slowly, no obvious judgment, then looks at her glass. "You and your ice."

"Yep." A flutter through her—*he's noticed what you drink*—a risky giddiness long dormant throughout fifteen years of marriage, and she tamps it down as she does most things, trying to fit a lid on it.

"Are you heading over there?" McKenzie's face is no stranger to sun and wind, an interesting network of lines across his brow, though he can't be much older than her, late forties at most, plus a few days' growth of beard come in, threads of salt and pepper worked generously through his somewhat mad hair. "Join the party?"

"Nah."

Quiet chuckle. "Why not?"

"Because. I'll put my foot in it one way or the other." Shaw glances over as he laughs again. "God's honest truth. I got a knack for pissing people off, you've heard me. I don't know when to shut up." Her smile is gone. "I suppose I could get it labeled social anxiety if I were willing to flush away a few hundred a week to have a therapist stare at me from a cushy chair. I just—get all het up and can't breathe and you never know what's going to come out of my mouth. Because I'm panicking. Detective Braun over there? He hates my guts because he thought I was undercutting him at a crime scene two years ago. I was just thinking out loud. Didn't crank the shutoff valve in time."

McKenzie watches her. "Well. I'd never have guessed. Any of it."

"Thanks. Decent of you. So, what's your excuse for not networking like a madman?"

"Ach, I'm a Scot." He finishes off the glass. "People expect me to be morose."

"Not in that shirt."

"But I have a proper morose jumper I wear around the office, and that's what they associate me with. Nobody notices a bloke's collar unless they're selling neckties."

Shaw snorts, sips, checks her phone. "I should be moving on anyway. I want to get home to my boys."

"Better make your presence known over there first. I shook the man's hand, at least."

Shaw swivels the stool, calls, with her drink held up, "Tommy!" Half the heads in the room turn, including the intended. "Congrats. Job well done." Tommy smiles distractedly, squinting to try to place her as he lifts his beer; Shaw sips, then slides her glass across the bar. "Off I go." She tosses a few bills down. "Make sure she sees that—need all the tips you can get in this kind of work. Take care of yourself."

"Yeah. You, too." He keeps his gaze down until he's heard the door spin, then watches through the front glass panes as she steps off the front curb, a small wiry woman in a burgundy moto jacket, jeans, and combat boots, wind whipping at her as she jogs across the lot to her big black tank as the streetlights come on.

Shaw drives through dusk deepening to night, radio on at a hum, hearing nothing, unable to recall a single song that played while her head and heart are about to collide at home, where everything meets.

Her phone lights up in the dash mount—it's Stephen York—and she taps the screen, focusing on breathing because it can never just be easy between her and the detective, not with so much at stake. "Steve. Love that response time."

"I would've gotten back sooner, but it sounded like you expected to be in the field most of the day?"

"No, no, you're good. Anyway, you know I'll just keep playing phone tag until I get ahold of you."

"Hey, I admire that. Persistence is a great thing. It can make all the difference." *In a case like this*, is the echo they both hear. They both know what happens to victims without family or friends to advocate for them, to stay on top of the lead investigators and remind everyone that the deceased was a real person who deserved better than what they got. Shaw gets a sense that he's moving papers around on his desk, multitasking times ten, probably not even bound for home for another hour yet. You don't make it that high up in the staties without a unique combo of strong PR skills and a brain like a Swiss watch, not to mention being able to stomach some of the worst shit humanity doles out without turning into a shuddering substance-abusing mess à la Brando in the final third of *Apocalypse Now*. "So, your message said that you received another call from Mr. Jansen."

"Yeah. He popped up again this morning after about nine, ten months of nothing."

"Did he explain why the long silence?"

"He never explains. It's all game playing. He's right back to trying to convince me that he knows all about my family—my sisters, my husband, our boys. He's either been watching for a very long time, or he's great at cyberstalking and confabulates the rest." On the other end, Stephen remains quiet, his patient skepticism triggering an equal and opposite agitation in Shaw. "I know you think it's a crock."

"When I interviewed Anders last year, he certainly implied that it was. Full denial, even when I played back one of your recordings of his calls. He claimed it wasn't him, wasn't his voice, even said that his cell phone must've been cloned. He obviously enjoyed trying to lead me in circles. And my attempts at proving any past connection between him and your family turned up nothing. So, yes, I think he's a fraud with an obsession. I was willing to put a pause on making formal charges when you first asked, but then when he dropped out of sight I'd hoped the problem had resolved itself. This is a unique situation, and I acknowledge that you're no stranger to crime or the criminal justice system. But I think you need to decide whether it's worth sacrificing your peace of mind to find answers that Mr. Jansen most likely doesn't have."

Shaw focuses on the dark stretch of Rural Route 15, wishing they could have this conversation anywhere but on this black slalom of cracked asphalt and skeletal winter trees. "My dad's dealt with these crazies before. People have called him all hours claiming they know where Thea is, that she was hacked up and distributed between drainage ditches across the state or left tied up in some basement somewhere to starve. But Dad toughs it out and reports every single lead to you guys, because there's nothing he won't do to get justice for his kid." Not so different from when she'd finally decided to answer the third call from the same unfamiliar number that had been popping up on her recents list for a week without leaving a voicemail. She'd expected a telemarketer or robocall. Instead, she'd heard a man's voice, no one she knew, say, *Is this Shawnee Connolly?* in a way that flash froze her, her first thought being *the boys oh my God* even though they were safe downstairs, banging away on game controllers, sending reassuring white noise up the stairs. *The Shawnee Connolly who used to live at 134 Pressman Street in Rishworth, Maine?* So smug; he obviously already knew. Anders hadn't given her his name, so that had taken some digging. Worth it to throw it in his face later.

"I know how much your father has sacrificed. But he puts his phone number on the missing posters and all over the Finding Thea page. He's allowing access. That doesn't mean you have to."

She presses her lips together for a second. "What if this guy killed my sister, and we lose him?"

"Right now, there's absolutely no evidence to say that he did. If he gives you a lead, something we can move on, then you know I'll look into it, but that's a big if. You said yourself, your family has been through this before. The cranks, the false confessions. Don't buy in." Stephen's voice has a measured gentleness that could almost break her if she were in the habit of bending. "We're walking a very fine line with this. I've given you my best advice, but I can't force you to take it. It's your choice whether you're willing to speak with him again. I know you keep a log and record the calls. That's enough to file for the harassment order whenever you feel ready. Or say the word and I'll bring him in tomorrow." Stephen waits. "Shaw? Are you sure this is what you want?"

"No. Do I sound like a person who knows what she's doing? Look, Steve, I hear you, okay? I'm going to think it over. I'm turning in to my driveway now. I better let you go." She's staring at nothing but lonely road, still a good thirty minutes from home. "I'll send you the audio file of the call. Talk soon."

Finally, Shaw arrives at the farmhouse, set back from the road down a stretch of gravel, the sign for Ryan's custom automotive design business still mounted above the two-story garage, the blue reflective letters bouncing her headlights back at her as she pulls in. Shaw digs out her house keys—even with Dad's sedan parked outside, everybody knows her rules: lock up all the doors before dark, whether she's home or not.

A scrabbling sound, and Aphrodite, the shepherd, surfaces somewhere along the steps where she likes to den and pile her toys and wait for Shaw; a black hellhound with eyes the same absence-of-light shade as her coat.

"What're you doing out here—you want to freeze your tail off? Come on—" Shaw clicks her tongue, and the big dog rounds the railing and goes up the steps past her as Shaw opens the door to light and TV babble and the smell of something scorched, calling, "Letting the dogsicle in now, guys, don't trouble yourselves."

"She wouldn't move. I called her about fifty times," says Beau, who's leaning into the fridge, and Shaw spider-walks her fingertips up his vertebrae as she comes into the kitchen. He jerks, grunts, "Ahh," swatting back at her hand without turning.

"What am I smelling?" she says.

"The stove. Better not use it." He turns, a package of sandwich cheese and a jar of olives in his hands, outsize puppy paws, signs of the man he'll grow into. "Can you tell Gramps not to make supper anymore?"

"*Shhh.* Don't say stuff like that."

"He can't hear me." Matter-of-factly. "Seriously, I don't think we should've eaten that. Like, it was pink in the middle. Casey's probably got worms now."

"Where is Case?" She surveys the general destruction of the countertops and cutting board.

"Sleeping on Gramps."

"Asleep—what is it, seven o'clock? He get his homework done? Why am I asking you—" Shaw releases a pent-up breath. "Okay, Gramps sacrificed a goat on the countertop. Anything else I missed?"

Beau folds a slice of cheese into his mouth, eventually says around it, "I made two three-pointers."

"Oh, *shit.*" She cringes, bangs her fists against her thighs. "'Scuse my language. I am so sorry, bud. Probably something I should've known about, huh?"

"Probably."

"Leave the game schedule out and I'll put reminders in my phone. I'll be right there on the bleachers next time, promise."

Beau snorts laughter. "You hate it so much."

"No, I don't!" She can't help laughing with him. "It's just not my game, all right? But I like it because you like it."

A moment's comfortable silence as she forages for supper. Beau says, "Dad came over."

She stops. "He did? When?"

"Like, an hour ago."

"Why?"

He lifts one shoulder. "Getting some more stuff out of the shop."

"He ask where I was?" A nod. "And what'd you tell him?"

"I don't know. Gramps told him whatever your text said."

"That I was stopping for a drink." Shaw rests her head against the pantry shelf. "Fine. No problem."

She goes into the living room to see Casey with the faint sound of Aphrodite's nails ticking the floor behind her as the dog crosses to her bed in the corner, where she sits upright, surveying the room, alert but calm now that her human's home.

Casey is curled up on his side on the couch, the top of his head pressed hard into the side of the old man's thigh, Dad fully engaged in some '70s sitcom, a bag of chips crumpled to the floor below them. Casey's cheek is soft, the pore-less satin of child's skin as she gives him a kiss, then wedges herself into the space against his stomach, watching color and motion flash across the TV, savoring the minutes before she needs to shake him awake just to tell him it's time to go to bed.

"Everything copasetic?" the old man says. Meaning Anders, making sure she hadn't gotten another call.

"Peachy. Watch your show."

Later, Shaw lies in her own bed, wearing Ryan's old white T-shirt again, one arm wrapped across her middle, the darkness feeling too large for the space, the mattress too wide for only her. She wishes one of the boys might wake up spooked and come in with her, though they're both getting too old for that now. She doesn't think she'll ever be too old.

Shaw closes her eyes, where Thea waits tonight, dragged up again after being almost completely tucked away for months now, only slipping a hand, a painted toe, into Shaw's consciousness here and there most days, nothing Shaw can't handle.

But tonight, Shaw sees all of her, Thea, seventeen, leaving again, walking backward with the running colors of memory around her like an impressionist's blur, only her slim, grinning face with the sprinkling of freckles, her long hair swinging loose, narrow torso in the hot pink tank top beneath the unzipped hoodie, borrowed from some boy, or maybe stolen—*I'll be home in, like, an hour, okay?* That raspy, distinctive voice. *Don't tell.*

Then, Shaw hears her own voice, reciting her lines, the last words engraved on her soul from the final day she saw her sister: *They're going to kill you. You know that.*

But Shaw's thoughts are vague, defeated: *Don't go, Thee. Don't go there.*

Thea's laughing, mocking, always so much cooler, holding up two fingers in a V: *Peace out.* Spinning in a lash of hair, legging it, her edges bleeding into unreality.

Nobody says that anymore. Just so you know.

A sound wrenches Shaw back from sleep, three shrill notes from inside her nightstand, jolting her, her nerves sizzling because it's her ringtone. She opens the drawer and holds the phone up just in time to see the caller ID, white letters against black: *Anders Jansen.*

The call ends. He couldn't have let it ring more than twice. Sick fuck.

It's nearly midnight. Shaw opens her Recents, staring at the list of incoming and outgoing calls, experiencing a nauseating moment of inertia, her gaze seeming to plummet into the call icons, green and red. For the first time, she actually entertains calling Anders back, forcing herself to this new farthest point of no return, because you never know, he might slip up. Might say something he doesn't even realize he's said, and then she'll have him. She's checked the national sex offender registry and he's not on there, but she did come up with a photo of a local man with the same name and an article from about four years back. It was a roundup of new hires in the state university system for the upcoming fall semester. He'd been brought on board to fill an adjunct teaching position in the philosophy department. Polo shirt, wire-frame glasses. A barely-there smile that could be interpreted as self-consciousness in front of the camera or a self-contented smirk, depending on your perspective.

Making a rough sound in her throat, Shaw slams the phone away in the drawer. She sits up for a long time, hugging the extra pillow, staring at the darkness, at that retinal burn of Thea, little sister.

Peace out.

3

"Can we go see Mads this weekend?" Casey tears the tough edges off his Eggo as Shaw, seated across from him, stops with her mug to her lips, and then gradually lowers it, tracking Dad's movements through the living room doorway. He's in there straightening up after another night in the chair: folding the quilt, pushing in the footrest.

"Well, I don't know. Beau's probably got a game, plus Gramps is going to need help with the posters. That's Saturday. You know what a big job that is." She watches Casey's gaze fall to his plate again. "What's got you thinking about Mads?"

"Nothing."

"Yeah? She didn't post something that made you worry?" Their family social media connections are as snarled as anybody's—worse, if you include the page Dad runs dedicated to Thea's memory, reposting anniversary news reports and family photos, hoping for tips but mostly collecting voyeurs and true-crime nuts. Too many relatives with too much access, heads rammed up each other's backsides, accustomed to knowing everybody's status right down to the second. Mads is hardheaded, responsible, but still a twentysomething; maybe she shared something a little too adult-ish for a ten-year-old.

"Nope. I just miss her." Casey says it matter-of-factly, wiping his sticky hands on the edge of the table as Shaw hisses and air-swats, at which point he finally looks at her. "Are you going to Rishworth again?"

Shaw can't seem to get rid of that pause, her hesitation before discussing what she does out there, a few weekends a year, always around Thea's birthday, but also at the change of seasons, when rains or spring thaw might've caused shifting soil and washouts. "That's the plan." It's partly why she bought Aphrodite two years ago from the retired K9 adoption service: because of her previous life as a cadaver dog, having been exposed by her handler to cadaverine and putrescine, chemicals produced by decomposing bodies, before graduating to real decaying flesh, until Aphrodite's two hundred million scent receptors were able to hone in on those odors amid untold other distractions in any setting. Okay, it was mostly why; but now, Shaw's used to the old soul of the animal, the way she trails her around this place like a conscience, always shadowing the boys whenever they go outside to toss a football or start a blaze in the firepit, keeping a watchful eye.

"You're not going to sleep out there, are you?"

"Too cold for that right now, cutie." She tries a smile but he's not having any of it, watching her, his features painted broadly with the Connolly brush. At times, it's uncomfortable, like looking at herself: his eyes deep set and a shade too close, little nose, a mouth that's nothing unless it's grinning, which Casey's usually is, even with all the upheaval lately and Ryan getting his own place, but not today. Not really for the past week.

Shaw catches Beau's coat as the boys are going out to meet the bus, saying quietly, "What's up with Case?," her youngest already halfway down the front steps.

Beau's on his phone, not bothering to look up—"I dunno, acting weird"—and she releases him, not sure what she expected to hear. She watches the boys cross the yard, Beau working up to a sprint to pass his little brother, kicking the bottom of Casey's backpack hard enough to almost send Casey sprawling, and Casey yells, taking off after him toward the foot of the driveway.

Dad's got his coffee, sipping while he watches them out the window. "When's Beau getting his license?"

"He got his permit in the fall, but he has to have it for six months before he can request a test date."

"Well, the kid's got to practice, put his hours in. He doesn't want to be riding the bus when he's an upperclassman. No bigger shame than that, as I recall."

"Are you volunteering to do the ride along? White-knuckled on the armrest, pushing your brake foot through the floor? Anyway, it's not like it used to be. He won't be out cruising with his friends until he's eighteen, not even to school. State law."

"Christ. Kind of defeats the purpose, don't it. How's a kid supposed to get a job, get himself and his buddies to ball practice and back? What was wrong with the way things were? They're taking away all their independence."

"I guess the people whose job it is to clean up the messes got tired of scraping kids off the pavement on Saturday nights or cutting their bodies out of wrecks—don't you remember Melanie Pooler and Jason Devine, junior year? What a fucking nightmare. All day in a school full of crying kids."

The words rattle out of her like candy from a theater box, skittering, scattering, and she straightens up only to catch the strain in the old man's face, eyes gone glassy, staring but not seeing the boys at the end of the drive, their staggered heights, backpacks dangling from their right shoulders as local school district fashion dictates. "Sorry. I didn't. . . ." Shaw's trapped in regretful silence, the old man still looking out the window.

Kids and death. *Stupid.* He doesn't need reminding. Definitely not of the community grief fest surrounding the death of two popular honor students, athletes, killed in a collision with a tree, blamed on speed and driver inexperience, compared to the strange quiet, the uncertainty, of Thea, a girl who Never Applied Herself, one of the kinder descriptions in circulation around the town of Rishworth at the time. Slut. Druggie. Probably just a runaway, took off with some guy, looking for more excitement than small-town Maine could provide. But runaways usually call or come back, don't they—what was it the deputy said when Mom and Dad tried to make a missing person report the morning after Thea disappeared, *When she's hungry, she'll come home?* The initial giddy whispers at school fading to dull perplexity, the not-knowing drawing out, becoming an infinite stretch of night road traveled soundlessly only by a remaining few, bobbing high beams revealing nothing but a broken yellow line.

Shaw scoops up a dirty shirt dropped on the floor during the boys' usual rapid stripping of pj's and fighting on of hoodies and jeans, folding it pointlessly over her arm. "I'm thinking about going to see Thea's friends again," she says abruptly; not exactly an olive branch, but what the hell. "See if they'll talk with me."

"Brandy and James?" Dad shrugs a little. "Good luck to ya. You know how it goes. They'll talk, but they won't say nothing. Wastes of space, both of them. I haven't bothered in probably four years now. And you want to watch your step with James. He ain't what I'd call stable these days."

"I know. I just thought it could be worth touching base one more time. With the anniversary coming up in a few years and everything. Maybe find out if Anders's name means anything to them." She shifts her weight. "Do you really want to take Beau for driving practice?"

"Why not. I got the time. You and Ry are busy with work and things. Give me something to do other than being crappy at vacuuming the rug."

"Mmm. Take it slow out there. Last I knew, your vision wasn't what it was."

"I do okay."

Shaw leaves it alone for now; she's salted enough wounds for one morning. She goes upstairs to brush her teeth and hair—for what good it does with this mop—and hears the groaning hydraulics of the school bus come and go before heading back downstairs to leave for the lab. She finds Dad with the TV switched over to some morning news show for company as he folds baskets of laundry, a task she never once saw him do while Mom was alive. Funny attempts, resulting in random creases running down the front of shirts and across pantlegs, the boys cracking up at seeing socks rolled military-style, top drawers full of nesting balls.

"I'll see ya," she says to him as she opens the front door.

"Not if I see you first, jelly bean," but his gaze is on the windows again as he folds a pair of Jockey shorts into thirds, watching the place where the boys had been, as if their outlines might waver there like a highway mirage, whatever the equivalent might be when the pavement is cold. Aphrodite, for her part, has retired to the old man's feet, chin on paws, shifting allegiances until Shaw is home again.

Shaw's phone comes to life in the dash mount before she's even crossed the Axtel line. *Anders Jansen* on the caller ID. She stares hard for a second, then taps the end call button. She places her hands back on the wheel, ten and two.

She weighs the silence, seconds passing. He calls again.

She lets it ring twice, then hangs up on him; the dismissive ease of it, like flicking away a persistent insect, is even more insulting than banging an old-school receiver down on someone, and when she picks up on his third try, she doesn't speak, choosing to wait instead.

"What're you doing?" His voice, coiled tolerance.

"Not much. Just seeing what it feels like to be the fucker instead of the fuck-ee, for once."

"How're you finding it so far?"

"Pretty fun. My favorite part is that little shocked silence between hang-ups. Imagining your face like a slapped ass." Her heart rate revs higher, higher, suddenly uncertain of her ability to hold this conversation and keep the car on the road. "Guess this is what it feels like to be you all the time."

"Well. At the very least, I'm glad to hear that we're equally pre-occupied with each other."

"Nah. I'm just sick of your *el mysterioso* bullshit. Can't say I missed you while you were gone, you know? Almost felt like getting my life back."

Anders gives a soft cough of laughter. "I hate to be the bearer of more bad news, but I am your life now."

She yanks the wheel and coasts onto the dirt shoulder, the passenger side tires thudding over dirty snow as the car, which has been steadily losing speed anyway, comes to an abrupt stop in a frozen tire rut. "What's that mean? Layman's terms. Keep it simple for me."

"You're going to have to start investing a lot more in this."

She gives a strangled laugh and squeezes her eyes shut. "You got no idea—no fucking clue—how much I've given up for your shit." She chokes off, her fingers flexed into claws.

"You're referencing your failed marriage now? Jesus, Shaw. I knew you'd find a way to drop that in my lap. Let's be truthful, though, just for a moment. What we have here—our dynamic—sort of leaves a man like Ryan behind, doesn't it?"

She sustains the blow quietly. She never discusses Ryan or the boys with Anders, no matter how badly he wants to, but this time, she says distantly, "You don't even know him."

"No, I do. A real man's man. Works with his hands. What I'm saying is there isn't much comparison between whatever sweaty hormonal rutting went on between you two back in the day in— what, the back seat of his daddy's Ford, that's the convention, isn't it? And true commitment. I'm sorry that being a walking cliché has ended in a sense of hollowness and failure for you as you approach midlife, but those are the risks we take when we strive for mediocrity." He draws a breath. "I wonder what Thea would've done with all the years you've been allowed. More, obviously. She struck me as someone who could be anything, given the right upbringing." A faint click of tongue in cheek. "Sixteen more years lavished on you. Extravagant, really. Profligate."

Shaw lifts her head, refocusing her gaze on the overgrown pasture pocked with frozen snow, a few blades of straw jutting out, bent sideways beneath the pressure of crusted ice. "Who allowed it? You?" She waits. "You God now, Anders?"

"If I am, then the Connollys must be my flock. I'm not sure whether to laugh or cry."

"Just so we're clear, you're saying that you could've snuffed me out at any point? The Lord giveth, and the Lord taketh away, that it?"

"Well, saying that would be skating dangerously close to an actionable threat, wouldn't it. But you're surprising me with this display of D-grade Sunday school education. Did Ma and Pa Connolly really load you three angels into the minivan every Sabbath, doing their parental duty to raise good—what, Irish Catholics, I'm guessing? I'm picturing it. Little white patent leather shoes, dresses with lace collars. Gloves, even. Would it be exceeding the boundaries of our relationship if I confessed to being aroused?"

Shaw barks laughter. "What, a scumbag baby raper like you? Color me flabbergasted." She rakes her fingers through her hair. "Our mom and dad pushed us through the doors in potato sacks, then sat out the service at the corner bar, is that what you want to hear?"

A moment's considering silence. "You mentioned rape. Is that something you want to talk about?"

"No."

"You brought it up. Is there something you want to ask me?"

She's petrified, in the truest sense, a dry, cured husk, a scarecrow propped behind the wheel. She gets cornered by it some nights when insomnia hits, or when a particular case came up at work or in the news or even a scene in a movie, some woman treated like a flesh chew toy by another human being, punctured, throttled, torn. But the truth could be here for the taking, the app recording his every word. "Is that what it was all about for you? Why you got hung up on us? Like a fetish thing, pretty maids in a row or whatever? I mean, how'd it happen, Anders? Why won't you just tell me about your big eureka moment?"

"How do these things ever happen in a small town. Everyone's paths are bound to cross eventually. Only one gas station, one little mom-and-pop grocery store that the high school kids walked to after classes. Surely you remember shoplifting at Croft's? The titillation spiked with guilt, knowing you'd gotten away with it and would again? Just a candy bar here, a pack of gum there. Not really hurting anyone, is it, and they mark up all that stuff, anyway."

She doesn't blink for so long that the view through the windshield develops a liquid focus. He couldn't know. Who could care enough to share the memory, just two or three of them crowded together, faces close and breath mingled, a blurred recollection of the colorful wrappers and somebody with an inner pocket in their windbreaker, making it easy? "Croft's? That's where you first saw her?" She waits. "Or where you took her from?" No answer. "Then how come our paths never crossed back then? I never saw you."

"If you and I had passed each other once or twice when you were eighteen, complete strangers to each other, you'd remember? I'm sure you've pulled whatever little strings your job entitles you to and found out that I did indeed live in the area at the time of Thea's disappearance. Right next door in Shropshire"—her own voice a hoarsened echo of his—"Balsam Circle Apartments, B2."

"For eleven months." He takes over again. "Personally, I know that there was more than proximity at play in my collision with Thea. Call it the hand of God, if that helps you."

"No. Fuck that. God doesn't groom girls for guys like you. I'll never believe that. No one's path is supposed to end there. You're— freak decapitations, little kids getting cancer, a general perversion of nature. All that comes from somewhere with a more southern exposure, know what I mean?"

"Listen to you sermonize. Lost in your myopic little moral con- struct, stumbling around, bumping into dead ends. The word 'rape' is shocking to you, yet repeated petty theft, daily premeditated acts of larceny committed against a member of your own community gets a pass? I can't decide whether to be depressed that someone with your mental limitations is being trusted as even a small cog in the machine of criminal investigation or find your unquestioning hypocrisy almost dismally—cute."

"Oh, I'm all about dismal-cute. Little cartoon rain cloud float- ing over my head as we speak. Now, if you could please stop dicking around and give me something real—dates, places, *any* proof that you actually did this—"

"Is that what's bothering you? That Thea and I were strangers to each other? I know it's uncommon . . . young men tend to be the victims of stranger killings far more frequently than women.

Women are killed by those they love. All that matters is I saw her and—I knew. She did this spin"—and in the pause Shaw can almost see his forefinger do a spiral in the air, and she sees it, Thee's move, dancing backward, limbs loose, part sensual being, part loping puppy, the age when your body feels so good, excess energy creating something like euphoria—"and she looked right back at me. She knew, too. Even if those boys around her didn't. I was her journey's end." Pause. "Did you know that you can strangle someone to death in under two minutes? Which is simultaneously a blink and an eternity. Especially if it's a small someone. Young, slender. Neck like a limber branch once you've stripped the bark down to the greenwood. It's possible to feel the crushing of the larynx beneath your thumbs, thanks to all those nerve endings in our fingertips. It's an experience like none other, I can tell you."

She leans until the side of her head rests against the glass, her chin to her chest, her voice hoarse. "Don't call me anymore."

"Now, Shaw."

It wrenches out of her: "Lose my number, Anders."

"You don't mean this."

"Look, you didn't do anything, you don't *know* anything. You won't prove your story because you can't. You're just another sick-in-the-head rat-assed little pedo in love with a picture of a missing kid you found online, you're *pathetic*—and frankly, at this point I don't know what's keeping me from heaving my breakfast all down my front at the sound of your voice, so do me a favor and piss off back to wherever the hell you disappeared to and stay there. Better yet, get some help. Be the one aspiring sex offender who takes the friggin' wheel and deals with their problem before they really do hurt somebody."

She breathes hard in the long silence, throat muscles sprung and sore, eyes strained in their sockets.

A rustle. "Sorry. Were you speaking?"

"Have a shitty life, Anders."

"Remember what you learned in Sunday school. Ecclesiastes." He says it with a slight dismissive drawl, as if something else in the room has drawn his attention: a stubborn sticky spot on the countertop, a drawer left ajar. "There is a time to search, and a time to stop looking. At what point do you stop waiting up, Shaw? When are you going to stop living in that beat-up old chair by the window, the seat with the good view of the street, thinking 'She'll be home any minute now'?" His bland tone continues, even as her mouth falls open, her eyes stinging with fresh, shocked tears. "In your role as mama bear, you failed. You always will."

Shaw ends the call, starts the ignition, rolling before she realizes that she's vomiting. She has time to open the door, jam the brake, and hope the puke hits the frozen ground instead of the vinyl.

Not much comes up, it's more a dry heave, and she tries to catch her breath, wiping her sweaty face with a leftover paper napkin from the console. She counts to a beat of five.

She picks up her phone again, composing a new text to Mads—
Call me asap ok

Deletes.

Hope everything's ok with you. Casey really misses

Deletes. Tense exhale.

Shaw sends a farting cat gif and slams into drive.

4

"Okay, I'm six minutes late. Could be worse, never claimed to be a role model." The bottom of Shaw's purse smacks her desktop as she turns on Gauthier. Their desks are situated within spitting distance, Gauthier diagonal to Shaw with a view of the rest of the small Latent Print office, wedged into the back left corner of the BCFS building. The only windows in the outer office are a row of low rectangular, reinforced panes shielded in blinds along the far wall, making them mostly dependent on the overhead fluorescents—not to leave out Gauthier's white gooseneck lamp, which looks like she originally bought it for her dorm room.

Gauthier's gazing past Shaw with a constipated expression, and Shaw glances back. "What?"

A face pops up into hers on the opposite side of the cubicle walls and Shaw lets out a small cry, dropping back onto her heels, shock quickly morphing into, "Heyyy!" once she recognizes Tran. "He's back."

"What kind of welcome is that?" He hangs his arms over the top of the wall, a roll of white fabric in one hand. "You looked like you were ready to soil yourself."

"Who says I didn't? I just—wasn't expecting an adorable cherub to appear in a puff of pink glitter right in my personal space like that, okay?" She gives her chest a double tap with her fist, making sure the heart's still going, before wheeling on Gauthier, pointing a finger. "You were complicit in this." Gauthier's eyes dart down to her laptop, and she hunkers forward. "Okay, I see how it is. Filing you under 'not to be trusted.' 'Unreliable Judas Turncoat, Benedict Arnold, etcetera.'"

"Pretty sure 'Benedict Arnold' and 'turncoat' are redundant," Tran says.

A knitting of the girl's brows. "How could I stop him?"

"She's right. I was like an animal." Tran comes around the cubicle, all five foot four of him, shiny black hair pulled back into a comma of a ponytail, argyle cardigan pushed up to his elbows. "I'm surprised you couldn't smell me back there." He rubs his eyes, dragging his fingers down his face as he sighs. "Pretty sure I'm oozing coconut rum from *allll* my pores."

"Still?" Shaw glances at Gauthier, whose face is now hidden behind her screen. "Told you. Mai Tais." Shaw grabs the T-shirt as Tran slings the roll over her shoulder. "Pour moi?" She unrolls it to see a screen print of a tropical locale with a coconut bra across the breasts beneath the slogan WHAT'S UP, BEACHES? Shaw bursts out laughing, draping it over herself. "Nice. Understated."

"It was between that and the toilet-shaped ashtrays, but you don't smoke, so . . ."

"Is Oliver as bad off as you are, Mr. Drunkypants?"

"No, he's off booze, mostly. Trying to lose ten pounds, as always. Why, I don't know. Not like I care about six-pack abs or anything." Tran stops at Gauthier's desk and takes a rectangular magnet out of his pocket. "Don't worry, I didn't forget you."

First, blatant shock blanks Gauthier's face. Then a dense rosacea-like blush spreads in patches as she takes it, tucking it down beside her keyboard. "You didn't need to."

"No big. I figured, everybody's got a fridge, right?" He heads off toward his own desk, flashing a quick pouty-lipped sad face over at Shaw, who gives nothing back, looking to Gauthier instead to ask,

"McKenzie call yet?"

"Mm-hmm. Twice."

A soft clearing of the throat, and Jewel's between them, leaning back against Shaw's desk and folding her arms. "Before you get started, I'd like to check in with everyone about where we are right now, case-wise. Tran, you and Lydia finished the artifacts from the Serendipity Café fire in Dover-Foxcroft before you left, correct?"

"That's right."

"I got word early this morning that there was another one, same MO, this time right on the county line in Mayfield."

Tran pulls a face. "Where?"

"Exactly. The population's around three hundred, but it's within the jurisdiction of the Harmon County Sheriff's Department, so it's ours. The fire's looking almost certainly like our arsonist, but there wasn't much left this time. It was an abandoned building that used to house a shopfront on the street level and apartments upstairs, and it burned very hot. They're dependent on a volunteer fire department out there. By the time the Milo trucks showed up to assist, it was mostly too late, but they're sending over a few evidentiary items, not privy to exactly what."

"If it's an accelerant container, and it's the same guy, they be tripping. This is fire number three, and he hasn't slipped yet." Tran rubs his brow. "Unless he forgot his gloves this time . . . ?"

"Shaw"—Jewel looks down to see Shaw with the T-shirt still spread over herself, smoothing a wrinkle—"the Cloyd case?"

"Coming along. Still no murder weapon, but Gauthier and I isolated what could be a partial of the doer's thumb on the leash clip, no matches on AFIT. Going to run it against some of what we lifted from the periphery of the scene. McKenzie's called, so maybe there's something new on his end, I don't know."

"And you're feeling confident with your presentation for the Peters-Montez trials? Anything I can do to assist?"

"Confidence coming out my ears. I'll run back over my notes and slides today, but I should be golden."

"And that is why you're the Court Lady," Tran says with a slight spin his chair, casting his words over to Gauthier. "The last time I took the stand? I was literally shaking"—he holds his planed hand out and wobbles it—"like this. Totally phobic."

"What makes her the Court Lady?" Gauthier says, a little reluctantly, like maybe she's being set up.

"Because she's *mean*. She's a pit bull up there. Attorneys are used to people being intimidated by them, not the other way around. She's unraveling the whole judicial system. The DA taps her for expert testimony all the time."

Shaw folds the shirt and twists in her chair to place it on her organizer tray. "It helps that I'm old, and I've done it many, many times." She's highly aware of Jewel's non-comment.

Jewel looks to Tran. "I want to be your second pair of eyes on the arson evidence, so if you're the one who signs for it, I'd appreciate it if you'd come get me. Thanks, everyone."

Once Jewel's returned to her office, Tran gives a musical whistle, double clicks the ACE-V manager software icon on his computer desktop. "Mmm. High-profile case, suddenly she's all up in my grill."

"Come on, now, be fair." Shaw's light and detached as she dials McKenzie's mobile. "She's the boss. It's her ass on the line if we screw up. Can't blame her for wanting to put her stamp on the findings."

"You know, you used to be cool."

Shaw's smiling as she turns away from the room when McKenzie picks up. She greets him: "We got our weapon?"

"No, the search turned up nothing. Looks like the killer took it with them. But I knew you'd be thinking about the dog, so I wanted to touch base. Still no sign of him, but we found the name of Cloyd's vet and got in touch, and we notified all the emergency vets and shelters in the county to be on the lookout for a three-year-old, one-hundred-and-forty-pound male Anatolian shepherd. You were on the money about the size."

"Anatolian? I'll have to google that."

"He's chipped, but since these things don't have GPS, it doesn't do us a bit of good with the search unless somebody else finds Grieco and turns him in."

"Grieco? As in Richard?"

"Alas, that's a question only Mr. Cloyd could answer."

"You've seen this before? A killer taking a dog?"

"Not personally, but I've read about a few cases."

"And chances are?"

"It's dead and dumped somewhere. The killer didn't fancy having a set of canines sunk in him when he went for Cloyd. Could've pepper-sprayed or Tasered Grieco first, disabled him somehow, God knows. The body might turn up eventually, but it's easier to hide the corpse of an animal. Since there's no missing person associated with him, no next of kin wanting their pet back—"

"Nobody's going to pull out all the stops tracking him down. Gotcha."

Silence settles between them. "Made it home in one piece last night, I take it."

Inside, Shaw softens a bit, flashing on their brief closeness yesterday evening, side by side at the bar. "Nope. Coming to you live from a ditch. Yourself?"

"I got there. It felt too quiet." There's a pause in which he might say anything—she's not even sure what she'd like to hear, but now she's feeling as flushed as Gauthier, a mortified heat, kid stuff, ridiculous. A grown woman whose been through births, deaths, seen more of society's brutality than most, nursing a crush and dying to know what was happening in his head right now. "Well." He waits. "Guess we'll be talking."

"If you play your cards right. *Ciao bello.*" Shaw rings off so fast that she may have cut off her last word. *What are you doing? Just what do you think you're doing?*

Everyone can smell the smoke as the flaps of the plastic evidence tote are opened in the lab, even the articles sealed in the coated aluminum cans required for artifacts recovered from fire scenes. Jewel's in with them, lab coat and safety glasses in place, lifting out the cans inside the tote while Tran cuts the evidence tape holding the lids. Shaw and Gauthier work at the computer terminals, continuing with yesterday's Round Pond prints.

"Shaw?" Gauthier's voice is so low Shaw doesn't hear until the girl says it again. "I've got another match."

Shaw glides over from her workstation on her wheeled office chair, catching herself against the table edge with one hand.

"The points are the same, the positioning of the pores. I know the thumb from the leash clip is a partial, but so far, I think it's a match." Gauthier's gaze flicks from Jewel's back to the monitor again.

Shaw leans in toward the screen, looking at the circled, highlighted points on the magnified print. "What did we pull this from?"

"The bench inside the shack."

"You're shitting me. The pressurized wood."

"If we could watch the profanity, please." Jewel doesn't turn; neither does Shaw; it's not the first time it's come up.

"I vote that we institute a swear jar," Tran says. "You know, wrap some construction paper around a mayo jar, fifty cents for every—" He stops amid the unwelcoming silence, shrugs as he returns to his work. "Worked when my mẹ did it."

"Okay, get on those other prints," Shaw says to Gauthier. "If we're lucky, you might be able to match more digits or even end up with a full set. You figure, if the person's sitting like this on the bench, hands about—three, four feet apart, basically the width of their thighs"—she demonstrates the posture in her chair, knees together, fingers curled under the edge of the stuffed cushion—"gripping, they could leave a good imprint, including one of the thenar region on the topside, provided they've got enough oils on their skin at that moment. Seems like our doer went in and sat there, waiting for Mr. Cloyd to come along on his morning walk. Wanted to hide, stay out of the cold, both, who knows."

Jewel pauses behind Gauthier's chair. "It sounds like you may have a near complete set to hand over to the sheriff's department. Well done, Lydia."

"Actually, Shaw's the one who suggested we dust there."

"Ah." A pause. "That's one thing to take away from this case. Don't be completely ruled by likelihood. Shaw's found some impressive stuff by taking the time to consider broader scenarios and motivations. More prints in court can mean the difference between a case that sticks and one that slides through the cracks." Jewel pats the back of Gauthier's chair as she turns to head off. "Stick with Shaw."

Gauthier nods a little, then starts as Shaw whacks her arm once Jewel has moved away.

"What'd you say that for?" Shaw hisses.

"It's true—"

"So what? The boss hands out a compliment, you snarf it up like a chocolate croissant and thank you, ma'am, may I have another."

"I don't like croissants. They're too dry."

"Whatever you *like*, then—the point is, Jewel doesn't go around sprinkling gold stars for the hell of it. She's tough and strict and she doesn't have time to be hovering over us, so if she tells you 'nice job,' don't deflect it. Say thanks and move on." Shaw huffs. "How're you going to get fast-tracked at this rate?"

"Who says I'm looking to be?"

"You're young, bright, in a clueless sort of way. This lab doesn't need to be the end of the line for you. Put your hours in here, impress the boss, in a few years you'll have your pick of promotions. Anywhere in the country you want to go."

Gauthier's quiet a minute, forefinger hesitating over the touch pad. "You've spent your whole career here?"

"That's different. I'm different." The words land bluntly, and Shaw tries to soften them. "Some choices, you don't make for yourself, do you? You make them because somebody's got to mind the shop." She's said too much—the girl can't possibly care—and Shaw pushes away on four plastic wheels again. "Now earn your gold stars by finding more of our doer's prints."

Later, at home, Shaw works out in the gym on the renovated second floor of the garage. Lots of blond wood paneling, two skylights to starry blackness in the slanted ceiling.

Dressed in a racerback tank and black leggings, she rows toward the flickering flat-screen on the wall, shedding layers of shoulder and neck tension—from work, fixing supper, homework arguments, and ultimatums. It all sloughs off within the first ten minutes of rowing and then she's sleeked down to her core, the hot and thrumming drive that's always there, propelling her. Back in the moment of this morning's phone call, locked into the memory of Anders's words.

She's on the rowing machine for twenty minutes, does twelve back squat reps, thirty reps with the fifteen-pound dumbbells, then faces off with the Everlast heavy bag, putting herself through her self-defense paces again and again. She's trained for years, first in classes, now alone, practicing hammer strikes—ideal in a parking lot or street attack, with your car keys gripped inside your fist as a blade—and palm-heel strikes at the level marked on the bag with a strip of duct tape, right around five nine from the ground, the height of the average male.

Did you know that you can strangle someone to death in under two minutes? She releases a grunt of exertion on impact, picturing Anders, what his real-life size and gait might be, how accurate that four-year-old faculty photo is that she found online: his mild eyes, contented, smug in his knowledge. He doesn't have the decency to look like a monster. They almost never do.

Through Shaw's mind, Thea's running, leaving her behind. Her sister's limbs churn through transitory blackness like ink clouding water, rippling fabric and hair, Shaw's imagination stopping short of conjuring her face, the face of the doomed. *So slow, Shaw.* Each footfall a sonic boom contained in a bubble, concussive, nauseating impact, tremoring through Shaw's inner world with every thud of Thea's Adidas. *Get the lead out of your ass.*

"Coming. Jesus," Shaw says under her breath, not aware of speaking aloud as she stays stabilized, keeping a strong core and legs, leading with her dominant hand, the right side of her body carrying the force into the mass of the heavy bag. A grunt of exertion, half a curse on contact—*drive his head back, stop him—jawline, chin, nose, eyes, temple, make it count*—then she follows with a set of ten alternative elbow strikes, pivoting at the hips to swing her elbow back at an attacker coming from behind. *You failed. You always will.*

She's on to groin kicks when a rap on the doorframe breaks through her focus. She spins with her hands still up, breathless, sweat rolling down from her hairline, adrenaline cranked, locking eyes with Ryan for a full three seconds before her brain processes familiarity and she drops her fists a few inches. "Hey."

"Hi." He doesn't come in, instead standing in the threshold, hands in his jeans pockets, his usual lean and rangy self, the familiar acne scars along his jawline and slight cleft in his chin, but he's hollow-eyed in a way that's new to their separation, like he doesn't sleep. Grave blue eyes, clear, vulnerable, belied by his slow, gruff manner, his brooding periods, which he'd always emerged from on his own until the day she realized that they'd been existing within one for about two years and that this fog of dissatisfaction seemed to be a byproduct of being around her. "Just wanted you to know that I'm here."

He's already about to duck out again. She takes a step, hesitates; she forgot to grab a towel, but the slightly funky one left from the last time she was able to sneak out here, three days ago, is slung over the barbell rack, so she swipes her brow and neck with it. Not anticipating a snuggle, anyway. "I meant to tell you that Walt Sullivan stopped by last week, looking for you." She indulges in a quick once-over of Ryan again, searching for signs of change, maybe, indications that he's getting on with things without them. "He's buying new Transit vans for the business, wants you to do the graphics."

"You're just telling me this now?"

"Well, I gave him one of your cards. He's as capable of getting in touch as I am." She's prickling from his tone, remembering when they never did this, never sniped at each other over stupid mistakes or pet peeves. It wasn't who they were, either of them. They'd been together since they were kids, for Christ's sake, their identities entwined like alders grown together around the same stump, going from awed, terrified teen parents into adults with kids like everyone else, aging out of the scarlet letters on their chests, knowing each other's responses so well that it wasn't hard to avoid a misstep or even necessary for that much to be said. Now, he doesn't try to avoid anything, seems to plant those size elevens into the soft spots on purpose. He's mad at her, mad about everything, the whole last seventeen years, and could she blame him? Most days, yeah. She could.

Now, Ryan nods, briskly scrubs the back of his neck with his hand a second, facing the staircase before glancing back with, "Figured you probably already knew I was downstairs. I saw Casey firing off a text the second I came through the door."

"Oh, yeah?" She goes to her phone, taps to see *Dad's here* waiting for her from Case. That kid gets an extra scoop of rocky road. Still nothing from Mads, not even a ha-ha reaction to her stupid GIF. "Well. He's our worrier."

"Yeah." A pause, awkwardness hardening between them, becoming unkind. Ryan says brusquely: "Okay. Heading down."

She watches him go, her phone still in her hand, sweat beads traveling the length of her back. After a split second of strained indecision, she goes after him, skipping the last step to land on the concrete floor, slowing to a stop not far from Ryan's baby, the 1979 Ford F250 Lariat Camper Special, which he'd restored over a couple years' time and wintered in here even though it ate up a good portion of his workspace. Ryan glances back at her from one of the workbenches, examining her warily.

Anders is on the tip of her tongue, but she chickens out for a second and gestures with her phone. "You're taking your tools?"

"Yup."

"So—you've found a place?"

He's quiet a moment, going back to packing. "Lee and I are going in together on a bid for a place in Stanton. Used to be an import salesroom, has two garage bays out back." He pauses, then adds almost reluctantly, "Might start selling some ourselves. Select stuff, priced for collectors."

Shaw's silent, absorbing, feeling yet another tie-down snap, one of the final ropes binding Ryan to them. She flashes on a very real image of him sliding away from her across gray ice, dull and un-reflective as the surface of Round Pond, his hands outstretched, reaching the vanishing point. Her legs are trembling, feeling that chasm yawning open in the pit of her core. He's doing it to her, too: disappearing. "When will you know?"

"Not sure. When I know, you'll know. Good enough?"

"He started calling again."

Ryan stops. He looks back over his shoulder at her, his expression hard, his eyes catching the flat gleam of the overhead fluorescents.

"I don't know why—it's only been going on a couple days"—he's already turning his back, and she crosses to him, making a con-certed effort not to ramble—"but I pushed him this time, really pushed him. Told him to fuck off and never call me again. I figured if I piss him off enough, he might slip up and give me something the cops can work with. Right?"

Ryan's packing again, more roughly, dropping things into the bottom of the box.

"Listen." She taps the recording app, finding the file made from this morning's call with Anders, upping the volume. Ryan jerks away. "Just ten seconds—"

"I don't—Jesus—" His curse dies in a burst on his lips as Shaw thrusts the phone at him, watching Ryan's face as Anders's voice spills out into the workshop with the tarps and vinyl and design books full of business logo templates, racing stripes, flames, tribal patterns, any sort of image you might imagine across the side of your Mustang or company car.

"What're you doing?"

"Not much. Just seeing what it feels like to be the fucker instead of the fuck-ee."

"I kept hanging up on him," Shaw puts in, jittery, maybe wanting him to be pleased with her, *See how Mommy toyed with the psycho?* Nothing in Ryan's expression changes when Anders references him, instead staring at an invisible spot in the air, refusing to make eye contact as she and Anders's voices go back and forth.

"*Sorry, were you speaking?*" She cuts off the call, tossing the phone to the bench surface.

Ryan's gaze is riveted to the floor, one hand propped on his hip as he leans against the bench.

She tosses up her hands. "But Croft's? Come on." He turns, packing again. "That was just between us kids. Nobody went around advertising that they were lifting stuff from there—how could he know?" She pauses. "I really think he could be the guy."

"Jesus Christ, Shaw, he was *fishing.*" Ryan's intensity sets her back a step, his head turned in her direction without meeting her eyes, his expression ashen, tight. "And you bit. Again." He grabs his box and moves past her.

She's speechless for a moment—they've pummeled each other into a corner so many times over this—but she still can't quite process him turning away from her, and she follows. "Hey, it's not *nothing*—I've got him on tape, bragging about what it's like to strangle somebody in the same breath that he's talking about Thea—"

"Great. What I want to know is when are you going to stop picking up the phone." He shoves the box under his arm as he pulls down an orbital polisher, roughly looping the cord to stuff in with the rest.

"I changed my number, didn't I?" Her voice, bouncing off the rafters—why does she always have to get loud first?—"If he calls again, that's it, I'm not answering, and I'll get a protection order—"

"Bullshit, you will. He calls, you jump. You can't even help yourself—"

"Oh, thanks a lot. It's not my fault that this asshole chose me."

"Nope, it isn't. But it's your fault that he keeps coming back for more."

She yanks both ends of the towel draped over her neck, dragging down on her trapezius muscles, placing hard emphasis on each word. "I talked to him at first because I had to know if he was for real." Her voice grows thin in the middle, like a strand of putty stretched too long. "It could happen."

Ryan finally turns to her, eyes faintly damp and snapping. "This guy knows what you're after, and he's going to keep dangling it in front of you as long as he wants, because the second you decide to take the blinders off and see that he's just a fucked-up attention whore, the game's over."

Shaw shakes her head through it all. "It's not that simple—"

"Remember Daniel Belasco? Or that nut down in Providence? All cranks. Swearing up and down that they did Thea until it turned out they were jacking off at the expense of the cops and the Maine taxpayer and us. Putting you, and me, and the boys through it again, and again, for nothing—and I can't—" He breaks off, swallows. "I bet he—Anders"—his expression like the name's acidic— "planned this little break he took. You know, while we were busy falling apart? I bet he sat back and let you keep twisting that knife in all by yourself." He stops about five feet back from her. "On one point, this one point, you're anybody's fool. What'd we get, a year, before Thea happened? Where it was just us, happy, without this thing hanging over us all the time? When it comes to Thea, you and your whole family are out of your fucking minds, and nothing I say makes a bit of difference. Why do you think—" He breaks off, then jerks his thumb, speaking at a rough hush. "And mind if I ask what were you thinking, moving your dad in? You never even ran it by me."

Shaw balks, genuinely surprised. "Well—he's getting older. He shouldn't be living alone anymore, and I needed the help. Why? What's it matter? You and Dad always got along—"

"Oh, yeah, Eddie's one hell of a nice guy, minus the drinking problem and the meds he's on to keep from completely losing it—"

"That was years ago!"

"Not the pills. That's right now."

"Oh, well, shit, nobody's perfect, huh, Ry?" Shaw shouts. "Except you, of course. How could I forget with you reminding me every chance you get."

He stares back at her, pale, grim, his free hand jammed into his coat pocket. "You're drowning the boys in it, Shaw. Training up the next generation to live their lives for Thea. I know you're planning another trip to Beggar's Meadow." He sees that he's caught her off guard. "Nobody had to tell me. The fourteenth is Thea's birthday. You wouldn't miss an excuse like that to go back to Rishworth."

In her mind's eye, she sees the boulders of Beggar's Meadow, dropped hither and nigh, some child's game played by giants, then abandoned to gather moss in cool, shadowed crevices. "I can't stop looking," she says faintly, hoarsely.

"You can't keep starting off every new year saying 'Maybe this'll be the one when we find her. I got a good feeling.' Because it never happens. You've already given the boys a front-row seat to watch you fall apart, just like your mom—"

"I *never* fall apart!" The words rip out of her. "Don't you fucking say that!"

Silence settles between them, their gazes locked, Shaw's chest heaving, the whole scene devolving into the kind of thing overheard through thin apartment walls, white-trash reality-TV ugliness, cursing and posturing.

Then Ryan jerks his shoulders, his anger cooled and hardened over in an instant; she envies him for that. "I'll come back for the rest of this stuff later."

"So long as I'm not here, right?" She follows him to the door determinedly, stopping on the threshold, about to fire a parting shot into the cold night air when motion catches her eye.

She looks over at the house to see Casey standing in the living room window, backlit by warm yellow lamplight, watching them.

Ryan pauses, following her gaze. He raises a hand to his youngest.

Casey returns it, but it's Shaw he's watching, his rounded face solemn. The fight goes out of her so completely that her muscles feel wasted, and her clenched fists relax.

In that moment, the old man comes up behind Casey, guiding him back by the shoulder and letting the drapes fall over the glass again, veiling the sight of Ryan's pickup backing down the driveway and gone.

5

An hour later, Shaw passes down the upstairs hallway, a basket of folded laundry in her arms to spare Dad a trip, pausing to knock once, hard, on Beau's closed door. "No phones after supper."

A rustle from inside. "I wasn't."

"Blue light makes you depressed. And gives you cancer."

He grunts something unintelligible. Shaw moves on, drops the towels off in the bathroom, then stands at the threshold of Casey's room, assuming he's asleep; he lays in bed facing the wall, the small lamp on the nightstand left burning.

He shifts, then, and she comes in quietly, setting the laundry basket on the portion of the bureau not covered in kid detritus, looking down at him, plaid comforter up to his waist, his arms resting loosely across his middle, gazing back up at her.

"How's it going, dude?" She speaks quietly as she sits on the side of the bed, and her hand finds his knee.

A shrug. He continues to look at her, eyes somehow limitless, at least to his mother; she's often had some half-formed notion of being able to see to the edge of the universe, or more aptly inner space, in the eyes of your child. The entirety of your life, reflecting back at you. If she were a poet, she'd write it down.

"Want the extra quilt? You cold?" Just something to say; she rubs his forearm, feeling the fine blond hair there.

"I don't need it." He's quiet another moment. "Mom?"

"Yeah?"

"Is it okay . . . I mean, do I have to go on Saturday?"

She doesn't move, at first thinking he means Beau's basketball game, her mind doing a quick race—"You mean, putting up the posters?" She sees him nod. Did he hear Ryan earlier, somehow get the gist of what they were arguing about? There's no way, not with them battling it out in the garage and Casey inside the house. "We always go with Gramps."

"I know."

She sits back, not finding words immediately. "Well—why don't you want to go this time?"

Casey gradually increases pressure against his middle, the number eighty-seven on the old Gronkowski Patriots jersey he wears, which used to be Beau's, peeled down to the backing in places. "I want to help Gramps, but I just don't want to do the poster thing."

"Why, though?"

She's confounded as she watches the process of his anxiety welling to the surface, tears appearing at the inner corners of his eyes, his expression screwing up against the loss of control. There's a long pause before he speaks. "The girl's face in the picture scares me."

Her lips part, disbelieving, but she doesn't have any words ready. "You mean Aunt Thea?"

He nods; a tear escapes, slips away over his cheek in half an instant, even before he wipes at it. "Maybe"—his voice hoarse—"I could go with Mads. She never puts up the posters anyway. Maybe I could do whatever she's doing until you guys are done."

"Yeah." Her voice decides before she does, putting an end to the kid's struggle before another second drags on, and she nods vigorously, trying to keep her own voice steady. "Yeah, that might work. I'll call her, okay?" She leans down and plants a kiss in the center of his forehead, holding for a moment before pulling back to look into those eyes again. "Sleep well, lovebug." She watches him cringe and flop over onto his side, smiling a little. "I know, I know, you hate that name. Night night. Want the lamp off?"

"No, thanks."

Shaw pats his rump and heads down the hall to her bedroom, sitting on the mattress and calling Mads. Shaw stares at the full-length mirror across from her, tilted back a few degrees on its stand to give a disorienting view of the wall and ceiling.

After three rings, Mads picks up. "What's up?" She sounds rushed, a touch impatient.

"Oh. I figured I'd get your voicemail."

"Nope. All me."

Why's it got to be like this are the first words on Shaw's lips. She pictures her baby sister, twenty-four years old now, her long, floppy ponytail and side-swept bangs in need of a trim, soft, round face, and generously curved body, always dressed in a hoodie or a long sweater and jeans because she's too damn smart to flash her goods around for approval. Madison, who will always be that sweet baby in the white-and-pink-heart-patterned sleeper Shaw so vividly remembers holding when she was ten and Thea was nearly nine—or at least Shaw thinks it's the actual moment and not merely the photo that Mom had blown up and framed to keep on the mantel, the one of all three of them sitting together on the couch in the old house. Big grins, scrunched noses, two guileless little kids with a happy accident sister home from the hospital. "What're you up to?" Shaw tries to keep it light.

"I'm leaving the library."

"On Friday night?"

"I've got to study sometime, and the apartment's out pretty much always. Brooklyn's got friends over tonight. They're playing some drinking game themed around that elves and wizards show they watch, whatever it's called. The one that's all about sex."

"Well, what can you expect from a girl named after a borough. As roommates go, it could be a lot worse. She could be eating your leftovers and going all *Single White Female* on you—dated reference, I know, I don't expect you to get it." Shaw hesitates. "Find a good parking spot?"

Shaw can almost feel Mads's eyes flick heavenward. "Nooo, and yes, I've got my personal alarm on my key chain and my phone at the ready. Anything else, or just calling to hover from a distance?"

"Actually, I had a request." It's a departure for them both—the give-and-take doesn't move this way—but Shaw presses on through Mads's surprised silence. "Casey asked if you might be willing to hang out with him while Dad and I put the posters up tomorrow. Like, maybe pick him up around nine-thirty or so? I'd foot the bill for lunch out or the jump park, both, whatever."

"Oh." The posters are a sore subject. Mads stepped away from the ritual years back, refusing to give Shaw an explanation beyond a quiet 'When's it going to be enough for you?' at which point Shaw finally slammed into the realization that she'd better button her lip before she lost the only sister she had left. But Beau and Casey are the upshot of everything in this family; Mads's tone warms. "Yeah, I can do that. I'm on at the bookstore tomorrow, but not until two. Is everything okay with Case?"

"Yeah, fine, he . . . needs a break, I guess." Shaw exhales, her muscles loosening. "Thanks. Really. He's been asking about you lately, so."

"Aw, really? Sweet little nugget." Mads pauses; then, more formally, "And how are you?"

"Wondered if you'd get around to that." She forces a laugh over Mads's sigh. "I'm messing with you. I'm okay. But you, missy— you'll earn this Master's degree without studying your brains out on the universal kick-back-and-relax night, you know. Why don't you go to a coffee shop or something with your hipster friends?"

Mads laughs shortly. "I think you need to look up the definition of hipster. And I'm not huge on coffee."

"Well, you drink those foam-covered things all the time, don't you? 'Ooh, so foamy.' Bet I could slip you some motor oil with froth on top and you'd never know the difference." Warming up to the subject, Shaw crosses her legs. "If you want something with a head of foam, give me a Guinness any day."

"Okay, Dad."

"What . . . ?"

"You sound just like him." Clunk of a car door opening, then shutting. "All right. I'm locked in while I start the engine, not standing outside the car fumbling for my keys with my back to the parking lot, and I'm pretty sure that I put on clean underwear this morning. Did I check all the boxes?"

"I guess so. Drive safe." Anders glides like a film across Shaw's vision, amorphous. "Listen. You remember the guy who was calling me? The one who got my number God knows where?"

Mads is silent.

"He's started up with the calls again. I wanted to let you know. There's nothing you can do, but I thought I should give you a heads-up. The police know. We're monitoring it."

Finally, Mads draws a breath on the other end. "Okay." Her tone is flat, numbed. There's only so much fear a person can sustain on the part of another, Shaw supposes, before they start to shut down. It's not that her sister doesn't like her. Almost certainly not that.

"Call me if anything— Just call me. Okay?" Then the practiced, sacred punctuation: "I love you."

"Yes. Love you. Goodbye." Firmly, Mads ends the call.

Shaw rests the phone against her jiggling knee for a second, staring at it, then says under her breath, "Thinks I'm insane," before tossing it away into the covers.

Shaw finds herself online late that night, another bout of anxiety insomnia forcing her into a state of hyperawareness, leaning over her phone as she sits cross-legged on her bed, looking up current contact info for Thea's old high school friends.

Shaw has kept tabs on James Moore and Brandy Pike via social media over the years. They were the two main people in Thea's social circle at the time she disappeared. Also, the last known people to see her alive.

James has only one account, sporadically used, but Brandy is on pretty much every platform, reposting cosmetic giveaways and memes with poor grammar, sharing plunging neckline selfies, her brittle expression revealing little but what Shaw already knew about the woman, who appeared to be very much the same person Shaw remembered from high school: a low-ranking mean girl, a hanger-on with the druggie crowd. Not the right friend for Thea, who was never a golden girl herself, but still gave off a lot of light. Thea's vibrance could've been sharpened by the wrong person, turned harmful. It was something Shaw had worried about right up to the moment that it no longer mattered because her sister was gone.

Why Brandy had chosen Thea was uncertain. Brandy already had a best friend or two just like her, girls with too much mascara and not enough wit or cred to be effective bullies, instead brushed off by most people like hornets half drunk on malice and summer poisons. Thea had a reputation at school for carelessness, attitude; perhaps that was enough to draw Brandy's attention. And Thea was running with James. In that fringe crowd, largely regarded as losers by the student body but still granted some grudging respect for their open disregard for grades and authority, James was a king with a Napoleon complex.

Shaw goes to James's profile and sees that he hasn't posted for nearly five months, the last one a blurry selfie with partial beard growth, sunglasses, and a flannel jacket, holding up a beer, a knotty pine wall behind him like you'd see in a hunting camp. She DMs him. *Hi James—this is Shaw Connolly. Is there a chance you'd be willing to meet, talk about old times? Let me know.*

Keeping it casual, acting like they're friends playing catchup, like they don't both know it's only ever about Thea, the girl shadow that stretches long over all their lives, James no exception. All eyes were on him for Thea's disappearance at the time. The boyfriend did it, foregone conclusion. First the sheriff's office, dragging him out of class, treatment bordering on harassment, Brixton probably thinking they could scare the truth out of him. Then the state cops, when they took over the case, bringing James in for questioning repeatedly, rehashing the timeline of that April day, getting nowhere. Most people believe that James did it, that sheer dumb luck is to blame for the girl's body never being found, her remains maybe swept away in a current, eroded by elements and time, the killer himself probably amazed by his own good fortune. Shaw has never known what to believe, other than her gut conviction that he's lying about the events of that last day with Thea. Why, she doesn't know, and she sure as hell can't prove it. Maybe Anders will turn out to be a blade sharp enough to pierce the group silence around Thea's case. This is how a person disappears without a trace. There are traces—plenty of them—but hidden in the palms of people who aren't willing to show their hand.

Shaw hesitates, then searches Mercer Brixton, arriving at his glossy PR site, extolling the virtues of the conservative politician-cum-family-man soon to reclaim the governor's office in November and rescue the state from the overspending and taxation that has supposedly plagued it since he ran the show five years ago. An oh-so-transparent list of campaign contributors. The site is saturated with studio photos of him with his wife of thirty years, Patricia, good honey-blond dye job, a well-preserved sixty without looking overly artificial, as well as them with their grown children and grandkids, the whole lot dressed in coordinated denim and a variety of rich autumnal-hued sweaters and scarves, smiling away.

Brixton himself is about twenty pounds heavier than she remembers him, thick through the gut and jowls now, but the sight of his face takes her back, how he seemed to fill her whole range of vision in his brown and tan sheriff uniform, jacked, obviously lifting then. His humor, the hardness beneath it, like biting into a candy bar and finding you've left the wrapper on. And how he'd looked at her that July day when he'd unexpectedly stopped by the house, hoping to check in with Mom and Dad about the absolute nothing which was happening with the case. Instead, he'd caught Shaw half in, half out of the front doorway, her small, early second trimester belly tented over by one of the maternity shirts Mom had picked up at Goodwill.

Shaw had stopped, ensnared, a half second from hurrying into the house to her room before he could get a good look at her. She'd been caught tightly in the grips of Mom's fears, which Mom had made no bones about the morning after Shaw and Ryan had sat at the kitchen table with her parents and broke the news about the baby to a stunned and silent room.

Mom hadn't said it cruelly, but Shaw still heard her mother's words as she stood back-to at the stove, scrambling eggs for the family that she wouldn't eat herself. Mom did little more than pick at food after Thea disappeared, her every small biological function put on hold, in stasis, waiting for news to break, until her clock ran down completely, flaws in the cells, multiplying, spreading—*I just don't want people thinking things about Thea because of this. We're working hard enough to get them looking for her—your father's out there killing himself every day—and people see a girl in your situation in a certain light. You got to know that. I love you, hon, I'm not putting you down, but . . . I don't want them thinking that if one of you girls was in trouble, that means Thea must be, too.*

How Brixton had watched Shaw from the open window of his cruiser in that moment, removing his aviators, not smiling, exactly, though the glint of a silver filling became visible as his lips parted. It was a look of something fitting into place, an assumption being confirmed about her, and one not without satisfaction, either.

She'd made herself stare back at him for an inner count of five, then gone inside, screen door banging behind her, letting him find his own way in.

The chime of James's response wakes her from shallow layers of sleep, and Shaw sits straight up in a way that makes her head swim, thinking it must be Anders, though it's a direct message alert, not her ringtone.

Hey sup I'm still at my moms place. Stop by whenever. I'm usually here

The same stream-of-consciousness message style that she remembers, weird punctuation, the fruits of an early 2000s Rishworth District High School education. Either that or he's wasted.

She sends back a thumbs-up, checks the time. 12:48 a.m. At least she's not the only one with an unquiet mind.

6

"I don't need to go." The next morning, Beau stands by the front door in his black-and-white warm-up suit over his uniform, big sports bag slung over his shoulder, stretching the wrist coil key chain out over his fingers. "You know? I can text Coach. It's not a huge deal to miss a game if you've got a family thing—"

"No, you darn well will not," the old man calls from the kitchen, looking out the doorway while vigorously drying a casserole dish. "Shaw, talk sense to him."

Shaw sits on the couch, flipping through a catalog she's not really seeing. Casey is gaming beside her, dressed and ready for Mads's arrival within the next half hour or so. "Nobody wants you to miss your game. We'll be fine." She gives him a half smile. "We've done it enough times before, right?"

"Yeah, but . . . it's just you and Gramps this year. I don't—"

"You're one of two freshmen picked for varsity," Dad says. "That means something." The old man disappears, clunks the dish away on a cabinet shelf, and comes back out, reaching for his coat. "You got to prove to your coach that he was right to put his faith in you, or he might bust your butt back to JV. Your mother and I should be able to make it to the last half of the second game. Now, saddle up, buddy boy. I'm riding shotgun."

Beau still looks at Shaw. "Kick the crap out of Bearcreek," she tells him. "I always hated that team when I played softball. Think they're such hot shit because they've got a pool."

This seems to appease him, and he heads out the door with Dad, the old man's hand on Beau's back serving as support for both as they go down the steps. Shaw's seen Dad from afar when he didn't know he had an audience, jimmying his glasses up and down between thumb and forefinger, trying to find some magical balance between the bifocal line while he clutches the railing, an elderly person's fear of falling new to him over the past year or so.

Mads's little Civic pulls in as Dad and Beau are about get into Dad's sedan, and Casey scrambles up, snags his coat, and is almost out the door before he remembers to call, "'Bye!" back to his mom.

"Have fun." Shaw goes to the doorway, sliding her hands into the pockets of her fleece sweatshirt as she watches Mads get out, her long hair pulled back and held fast by a knit pompom hat pulled down to her brows, her arms held dutifully out in front like a baby doll's for Dad's incoming hug, nodding at his "You get prettier every time I see you" as he pecks her cheek.

"Sure, Dad. So do you." She points over the roof at Beau standing on the driver's side. "And you get taller every time. Is he really going to let you drive?"

"Yep."

"Oh my God." She grins at Casey, who she's shared a sympatico with since his birth, babysitting him sometimes when she was still in high school, the two of them bonding over their love of reading and art. "You ready?"

"Yeah. Can we get Frappuccinos again?"

Mads sees Shaw's grin from the doorway and hides a rueful smile as she opens the driver's side. "Sounds good." Mads waves a sardonic 'bye-'bye hand at Shaw, who returns it, her smile gradually fading as Mads backs her Civic onto the road, reverses directions, and takes off toward Dover-Foxcroft, where the closest downtown shops are located. Axtel doesn't have a real downtown, only a tiny town office with a flagpole beside a country store where you can gas up, buy a forty of Olde English 800, and tag your deer all in one stop.

Silence presses down on Shaw, the weight of the household, the inestimable ceaseless noise of dust motes falling, settling.

She looks at the empty road for a time, then goes inside and locks the door behind her, turning to find Aphrodite sitting upright in Dad's chair, facing her. The dog's panting, watching, seeming to know what Shaw's all about before her human even takes a step.

It'll take Dad about fifty minutes to get to the high school and back.

Good time to pack for tomorrow.

Whenever Shaw is home alone, the dog is glue, always present on the periphery of whatever room Shaw's in. Observing, often resting with her head on her paws, her eyes tracking her human's movements back and forth. Maybe it's some sort of residual separation anxiety: the dog's former handler was a woman, as well, forced to give up Aphrodite due to advanced MS, no longer physically able to cover rough terrain as the boots on the ground needed during a search for a missing person, with her highly trained shepherd snuffling the soil ahead. Apparently, no one in the woman's inner circle was willing to take the dog in, which eventually landed Aphrodite in the hands of the retired K9 adoption service. Shaw finds it hard to believe that a family would hand over a loved one's animal like that—but then, Aphrodite is no typical fuzzball. In her five years as a cadaver dog, she found untold corpses in various stages of decomposition, hit on blood trails and years-old burial sites; all of that might carry icky connotations for some.

Now, Aphrodite watches from the doorway as Shaw packs light, only what she'll need in case of inclement weather: slicker, rain pants and waterproof gloves, extra socks and ski cap. Plus, a mini Maglite, first aid kit, and a personal alarm like the one she's gifted to everyone in her immediate family, a black plastic key chain that, when you yank the pin free, emits a 130-decibel alarm and a strobe light.

Shaw glances up at Aphrodite. "You know you're going for the big walk tomorrow, huh." The dog shifts, giving a small wriggle of her shoulders. "At least somebody's excited."

Shaw goes to her closet. The small safe is on the floor in the back corner, and she kneels on the carpet to enter the combination, the boys' birth years, plus her own.

Inside waits a Taser and replacement cartridges, an extra full-size can of pepper spray—she keeps a 3.4 ounce in her purse always, along with an expandable steel baton—and the tactical bag of survival knives.

And the gun. A SIG Sauer P365 pistol—small, easy to handle, or so the dickhead gun seller had told her, good for when dainty feminine hands want to employ deadly force, but it had all gone in one ear and out the other for Shaw, who didn't really give a shit as long as it worked, her stomach a hard, dead mound while she stood there applying for her background check, doing the thing she'd swore she'd never do. Keep a gun around her kids? No fucking way. So what if they didn't know it was here, didn't know the safe combination? She'd bought it shortly after Ryan left and before Dad moved in, on her lunch break because there is literally no other opportunity when she doesn't need to account for her time to one person or another. She did some deer hunting with Dad as a teen, knows the basics of how to handle a rifle, if not a pistol like this. Before the gun, she couldn't sleep, couldn't shake the clinging dread, the downright biblical malignance she felt coming from this guy on the phone, even if Ryan didn't believe.

What Ryan doesn't seem to get is that it doesn't matter if he believes that Anders is the guy who took Thea, not in this moment—not as much as it matters what Anders is capable of right now, making his fantasy real, appearing outside their kitchen window or on the front step, maybe breaking in at night. No matter how much it offended all of Shaw's feminist sensibilities, having an obvious male presence around the place, like a pickup truck parked in the driveway at night, deterred these guys a lot of the time. Instead, her male presence is shacking up in a dinky little apartment on Gagnon Road like this shit is all in her head. She still hasn't found time or the nerve to get to a range and practice.

Even now, Shaw doesn't want to touch the pistol. She looks at it, the slide lock in place, sure as hell not loaded, the box of hollow-point cartridges nestled beside. But she steals a moment to indulge in the power, allows herself a wallow, a vivid mental reel playing before her: the gun in her grip, ready for him. A man's silhouette, lunging. She draws, and then he's down, a pulp of bloody, torn tissue, no face, and she's plugging him, giving vent to the base, infantile, screaming thing inside her, germinated the day she finally understood that someone had taken her sister and would most likely never pay for it. What were the chances a creature like that could ever be sated? Exhausted, maybe. Yes. Finally put to sleep, at least for a while.

Slowly, Shaw takes the Taser and knives and closes the safe, giving the dial a final spin.

In an hour's time, it's just her and Dad in the Denali, driving up to Aroostook County, the largest, most rural region in the state and known simply to locals as "the County," to reach downtown Rishworth, where Shaw grew up. It's roughly forty minutes from Axtel by car, and Shaw parks at the curb in front of the business-solutions shop Dad's gone to for Thea's posters over the past six years, after the original printer, whom the old man became friends with and who ultimately ended up refusing to take a single dime for the job, retired from business.

Dad comes out a short time later, grappling with a young clerk who obviously intends to be of help, neither willing to surrender the box of two hundred ledger-size Day-Glo MISSING posters until it's in the back seat. "Here." Dad digs out his old misshapen wallet, stuffing a bill into the guy's unyielding palm. "Don't tell the boss or he'll take a cut."

"Sir, I'm not supposed—"

"Happy New Year."

Dad gets in, settles himself as Shaw pulls out of the lot. "Five bucks doesn't get people as excited as it used to," he says.

"Bet his boss will really be missing that two-fifty." They smile a little, and the old man reaches over, giving her shoulder a squeeze and a shake, leaving his hand there a moment as they drive to their traditional starting point, the opposite Rishworth town line, where the news van from WABQ-6 should be waiting.

The van turns out to be a station wagon, the call numbers stenciled on the door with a foxtail swish beneath the Q—Ryan could do better—and Dad goes over to greet the reporter who climbs out, a man in his early twenties wearing a Gore-Tex puffer coat with a fur-trimmed hood more appropriate to subzero climates than a forty-three-degree day without wind. Another annual thing for the old man is contacting all the local news stations to carry the story, trying to get Thea into the public eye as often as possible, but these cub reporters who turn up—when they turn up—grow younger, more rushed, less interested with every passing year. Less able to identify with the girl in the photo, so dated-looking that the idea of putting themselves into her shoes—those white Adidas low-tops from the description—and walking around in them seems impossible. And if she's out there alive somewhere after all, by this point she'd be . . . well, old.

"Fella's name is either Ashley or Astley, pick your poison," Dad says upon his return. "He'll trail us a ways. I told him how you feel about being filmed."

Shaw waves to the reporter, now affixing a video camera on a tripod, eventually gesturing distractedly back at her. "He's getting those shiny shoes all wet."

"I also warned him what an ill-tempered cuss you are, so I don't think you need to worry about ending up on the nightly news."

"Wedged between a town council meeting and a story about who pulled the biggest togue out of the ice on Moosehead last week—"

"Keep your voice down, you damned snob. They run the story, there's a chance of getting picked up by their affiliates, and then maybe those jokers down at channels 2 and 8 will sit up and take notice."

"We doing this?" Astley calls, squinting around the camera.

Shaw and Dad each have staple guns and get to it, putting a poster up on every telephone pole, the photo and text identical to the year before, Astley filming, standing as close to the ditch as he seems to dare in his office attire to capture Dad's grim profile as he bangs another poster home, confronting drivers with his girl's face as they pass.

Missing. Theadora Catherine Connolly—*you down with TCC, yeah, you know me*—so old-school even then, but they used to sing it back and forth to each other, collapsing into contagious kid laughter, bubbling up pure and effortless as spring water. Last seen, April 6, 2007. DOB 1/14/1990. Height, weight, blond hair and blue eyes, three piercings in each earlobe, small birthmark on the back of her neck partially visible below her hairline. Last seen wearing white sneakers, jeans, and a pink tank top beneath a white oversize Abercrombie & Fitch hoodie.

Her photo, expanded to a black-and-white eight-by-ten, is placed central above the reward money for information—it's been stuck around eight thousand for a few years now, occasional dollars and cents trickling in from Dad's crowdfunding page—and the phone number of the state police, local sheriff's office, and Dad himself. Dad had settled on this candid shot, one of the six or seven photos of Thea in public circulation, a cropped headshot from a church benefit barbeque taken the summer before her disappearance. Her long hair hangs over her shoulders, pushed behind her ears, revealing a silver cuff earring dangling a delicate chain to a stud in her lobe, her smile smirky, tolerant, another lame sister lineup to make the 'rents happy so she could get back to her chips and Mountain Dew.

In the full photo, Shaw sits beside her, arms folded on the picnic table, head leaned down to look at the camera, squinting against the sun in her eyes, always the one who tended to keep things inside, particularly that she and her boyfriend of more than a year, Ryan Labrecque, had started having sex in the back seat of his Tercel right around that time, often after his evening shift at the café downtown, where they both worked, she as a waitress, he as a dishwasher. An exhilarating, overwhelming, terrifying time, knowing what could happen, that they rarely managed to get a condom on, keeping a secret of such magnitude for the first time ever in her uneventful life, even from her sister-BFF Thea.

But Thea had liked to tease, *You guys are totally doing it, you know you are. Admit it, not like I'm gonna judge*—but Shaw never would. Just got embarrassed and shut down. Thea probably hadn't suspected Shaw was pregnant in those weeks before her disappearance—at that point the symptoms were so minor, amplified only in Shaw's awareness: a curious tender swelling of her midsection and breasts, a cloudy haze over the world like she was never fully awake. Shaw had *known* in a way she'd never been certain of anything, proof that it wasn't as simple as the health class breakdown, sperm meets egg. It was soul-level primal knowledge that she was no longer alone in this, that she was joined by the tiny consciousness that had announced itself as male from the moment she saw the two pink lines on the pee stick she used one week to the day after Thea's disappearance, her shaking legs dropping her onto the edge of the tub so hard that she was afraid someone else in their hushed, grieving house might've heard. No way of knowing that this was simply Beau, joining their world. The joy, the wonder, wouldn't come until later, until Shaw felt Beau's independent movements inside her, and she decided once and for all that no one would rob her of this.

Astley films about fifteen minutes of Dad hanging posters. Shaw had watched the stories on the news most years, Dad shown from this same angle, the faded seat of his Dockers or Dickies workpants—Shaw could almost hear Thea say, *Hey, my dad's butt is famous,* and cackle—the blue L. L. Bean squall jacket he'd worn proudly every winter for nearly ten years, bald spot at the back of his head on full display. Astley then interviewed him briefly, same questions, which Dad fielded with the serious but not grim matter-of-factness he'd developed over time. A public face, if you will, damn near laughable on a bigmouthed, one-too-many Connolly, but necessity is a mother, so here was the old man standing at parade rest, raising his voice over the occasional rush of passing cars.

"All we want is to bring Thea home. That's it. I'm not looking to ruin anybody's life. There's already been too much of that. The police can do whatever they need to do, but we just want to bring her home to her family"—here the slightest hitch, the script not totally detached from emotion—"bury her next to her mom, and finally get some closure on this."

Astley nods, scrolling down the Notes app on his phone. "So, what would you ask anyone who had information about Thea's whereabouts or the events of that night to do? How should they pass that along?"

"The numbers are on all the posters, which we hang from Rishworth to Palmerton. And the info's online at the state police's missing person's site, too. They can always stay anonymous, if they want, I don't need no names." He doesn't mention that they'll need a name for the tipster to collect the reward check; let that come after some legit information, anything at all other than the time-wasting, often bizarre tales that roll in from people living literally all over the world. Some are simply mistaken, others well-meaning lunatics. A few are genuinely malicious, looking to accuse someone they have a grudge against. One time, Thea had been spotted in Montreal, another time in a resort town in Cozumel. Georgia, Washington, California, Virginia—Dad had traveled to all these places himself over the last two decades to follow up on leads, always met with brick walls, mistaken identities, or base, uncomplicated lies. No such girl, no such incident, no trail to put the police on to. Vapor.

"Do you think there's any chance that Thea could be alive?" Astley's eyes flick up for the first time in genuine curiosity.

Shaw releases a disgusted gust of breath. "Christ, here we go—"

Dad makes a *zip it* motion at her with one hand, not looking away from the camera. "No. Absolutely none. We had Thea declared legally dead ten years ago for a good reason. She had nothing to run away from. She was only going out with friends for a couple hours, didn't even have her purse on her. She never would've stayed away this long without getting in touch. No. I've known my daughter was dead for a long time. Long time."

7

Shaw arrives at the base of Aronson Road on the outer edges of Rishworth by eight a.m. the next day, with traces of watercolor sunrise streaking through a pondering gray sky.

It's necessary to hike in this time of year. The road is mud most seasons, traversable only by foot, jacked-up four-by-fours, and ATVs; in January, its deep ruts become pockets of ice, and some sections are entirely lost beneath drifts during snowier winters.

Shaw is geared up in a neck warmer and long insulated jacket, both in the shade of dark rose she tends toward. She parks the Beast, walks around to the back, and pops the trunk, letting Aphrodite leap down from the tailgate, eager to begin the search.

Shaw shoulders her pack—too heavy, overdid it for a day's hike—then heads off at a brisk pace to keep up with Aphrodite, who's already some thirty feet ahead, hustling, air-scenting, her muscular tail waving like a bludgeon, following the center ruts. She lives for this, hunting that distinctive bouquet of human death. Part extensive training, part instinct.

The morning is utterly still. Shaw's hand goes to her coat pocket, pressing against the shape of the Taser. In her opposite pocket, she carries a serrated folding knife.

A few frozen footprints here and there, nothing fresh. A snowmobile track passes across the road to the woods on the other side, but otherwise, there's not much indication that Aronson Road still holds the rep it once did, as the gateway to an isolated drinking spot for local high schoolers and a sprinkling of twentysomething townies, feeding off the kids like remora clinging to sharks, using whatever mystique an over-twenty-one ID and a ready supply of weed afforded them back before marijuana could be purchased legit in strip malls everywhere.

Aphrodite sticks to the road; with her training, she won't be distracted by the scent of scat or a squirrel in the trees. "Aph, where's the napoo?" It's Aphrodite's command to seek a death scent, specifically long-buried remains; the term is common among cadaver dog trainers, a slang relic from WWI, meaning, essentially, dead.

Shaw watches her run, still air-scenting, hoping the dog's nose might drop to trailing one of these times. It's possible: human-remains detection dogs have discovered bodies buried for decades, even centuries, sometimes as deep as twenty feet underground. Thea was meant to have come this way that night. Shaw's gut says maybe her sister made it, even if the other people at the party claim they never saw her. She's not sure how Anders ties in to all that. It was locals here that night, people they knew, and from what little Shaw's been able to dig up about Anders online, he would've been older than them by about six years, an academic, not running in circles with teens and small-time drug dealers. It didn't figure, any of it.

There's open overgrown pastureland to the left, and Shaw gazes out at it, linking the view with the memory of one of the few times she came up here with Thea, triggered by the scent of cold air and dried pine needles in her nose: Thea had talked her into walking up to the turnaround after school one day with some other kids, wanting to share Shaw with her new crowd of friends since hooking up with James. Shaw was no angel, but she was never a pothead or a partier, either. Too blunt and awkward for the social aspect, even while well-lubricated.

Ghosts of the sisters rise like ground mist, following in Shaw's blind spot, but some part of her can hear them speak, words she couldn't possibly remember in such detail all these years later. Maybe it's partly fiction, but maybe more being back here, retracing her own footsteps—

Thea, testing the waters with Shaw. *What? Say something.*

Okay. Why do you hang out with losers now?

I don't. Bitch. With a slow grin, all a big joke with Thea, life itself, attached to almost no one, rolling with life's changes with an alacrity akin to callousness, not unfeeling but mostly uncaring; yet, above all else, Shaw's opinion mattered. Thea gathered her hair out of her hoodie collar with one hand and tossed it back, saying lightly, *James isn't a loser.*

You talking about me? Huh? James came up hard behind Thea, putting his arm across her shoulders in a mock choke hold, tipping her back off her feet. *Huh?* Followed by Thea's delighted laughter as Shaw looked away at the woods, at anything at all.

When Shaw and Aphrodite reach the top of the gradual slope, the road ends in the overgrown turnaround, the general area where the firepit and two fallen log benches used to be, now lost in brush and overgrowth. Aphrodite does a quick loop through it anyway, sweeping the area as if she's found something of interest, though not a hit—if she scents on death, she's trained to sit immediately and wait for her handler.

Maybe someone else who remembers this place has been through that brush recently. Why else would anyone wade into those brambles? Could be they have been searching for artifacts, much like her, proof those teens once existed. A rusted pop-top, maybe, a Bud bottle, label long since worn away.

Aphrodite emerges a few feet to Shaw's right, panting lightly, her eyes black and bright.

"Find the Napoo, girl. Where is she?" Shaw watches the dog return to work immediately, leading the way to the left, where a trail used to be, following the downward slope into Beggar's Meadow, called that by everyone in town although there were no stories about this place ever being a potter's field. The soil is too rocky to be used that way, the valley covered in huge granite boulders dredged up by an ancient glacier centuries ago, all manner of shapes and sizes. Most of the ground is covered in lowbush shrubs and red sticks of dogwood, rigid soldiers among the dried brown remains of ragweed and goldenrod, particularly in the place off the turnaround where Shaw always enters, letting Aphrodite continue to lead.

They cover the area, which is treacherous right now, with hidden ice and caps of snow on some of the rocks that have dripped frozen trails down the sides of the boulders she touches to regain balance as she follows the dog.

They'll kill you. You know that. Meaning Mom and Dad. Shaw hears her own words so clearly from the last day she saw Thea, the two of them splitting off from each other when they were supposed to walk home together. They'd been out prowling the boring side streets after school with a couple of friends. It was a cold, dead New

England April, not a damn thing to do but school, work, TV. But James and his friends were braving the Meadow tonight, toughing out the cold, planning to drink away the chill.

Thea still had about two more weeks left of being grounded for the last time she came home with alcohol on her breath. Now, Shaw sees Thea's lips move with the hated, ingrained last words—*I'll be home in, like, an hour, okay? Don't tell*—lifting a hand at her in farewell, loping after the two other friends: Brandy, of course, they had become joined at the hip, and a girl named Deanne Kolbe, whom Shaw had barely known. Shaw had been first to turn away, a little disgusted but mostly amused by Thea, little sister dropping her ass into the fire again, oh, well—

After about thirty minutes, sleet starts to fall. Shaw and Aphrodite take shelter under a plateau of rock, Shaw crouching below the over-hang, chewing on a protein bar. "Want some?" she says to the dog, who doesn't even look over. "Yeah, can't blame you. Here. Brought you the good stuff."

Shaw opens two collapsible pet bowls, pouring high-protein working dog food into one from a ziplock bag, then water from her own bottle into the next. Aphrodite crunches, drinks, rests, watching the trees while Shaw strokes the animal's side.

The peace lasts maybe ten minutes. Aphrodite starts, then, remains crouched for a moment, her ears perked, tail stiff. Slow straightening of her legs into a full standing position, watching the woods to their left. Aphrodite doesn't bark, instead readjusting herself in the tight space, her head low, neck extended, peering at something Shaw still can't see.

"What?" Shaw reaches out, touching the dog's withers, feels her rigidity. "Aph, what?"

Aphrodite takes a few steps out into the sleet, which is now changing over to snow, but Shaw pulls her back by the collar—the dog resists, and Shaw reaches into her bag for the leash—

The dog leaps. It's so sudden that Shaw is dragged forward off-balance, no choice but to let go of the collar or plummet down to the rock ledge nearly twelve feet below. "Hey—!" Shaw makes a disbelieving, indignant noise as she watches Aphrodite land with a scrabble on the granite and start off deeper into the defile. "What're you doing?" She whistles thinly, curses at the dog's lack of interest, then bends to deal with Aphrodite's leftovers before she loses her altogether.

Whimsical snowflakes swirl and skitter. Shaw's not sure if they've ever traveled exactly this route before; it's rough going, not the way she would've chosen, right down the middle of the gorge where a small stream has frozen. Shaw's boots punch holes in the thin spots in the ice, and for a time, she can't move fast enough to close the distance between them, the dog plowing ahead, sometimes trailing a scent with her nose to the ground, single-minded and with zero interest in her adoptive mom.

They reach an embankment, which the dog scales in a volley of bounds and lunges, while Shaw gasps and digs her hands into the snow to climb. "Aph! No!"

Shaw's alpha tone finally gets through, and Aphrodite reappears above, gazing down at her. "Do you freakin' mind?" Shaw reaches the top, bending to catch her breath. "Some highly trained professional you are. I bet a free mutt from the shelter wouldn't have ditched me like that." She roughly scratches the dog's head before Aphrodite slips from her touch and starts hustling again. "Are you for real with this?" Frustration surrenders to uncertainty; she follows the dog.

Time passes; Shaw doesn't keep track when she's out here, her one indulgence, not being beholden to the world for six hours or so, but now, fifteen minutes melt into an hour or vice versa, no concept of where they are other than deeper in the trees, the canopy of enmeshed branches spreading overhead, reaching a place where the slash in the earth shows signs of narrowing, petering out.

Aphrodite clambers onto a pile of boulders, nosing vigorously around the gap between two rocks before she sits, tongue dangling, specks of white foam visible along her gums, signs of her thirst and exertion. This is her signal. She thinks she's found something.

They've never had a hit. Not once. Shaw stands rigidly with her fists at hip level, confronting the space beyond the dog.

"Okay. You done good, girl." Shaw digs in her coat pocket for a treat, handing it off to Aphrodite as she steps up to her level on the rock, not breathing as she stares down at the snow hardened into the gap, about four feet across at the extremity, nothing there but a few dead oak leaves sticking out of the crust.

Aphrodite whines faintly, shifting in her spot, agitated.

Shaw leans forward, exploring the space, dread turning to exasperation mingled with relief—false alarm, obviously; dogs make mistakes just like anybody, right—and she squats down to check the narrow space beneath the largest boulder, which is canted up against the others.

A small, rusted ring lies among the drift of oak leaves. A piece of metal, not worth glancing at twice along a roadside or in a parking lot, but out here? She reaches in and plucks it out of the shadowed space, holding it up, examining it in the daylight.

A simple band with an empty square setting, mostly consumed by rust except for a shiny metallic patch still visible on the topmost section, neither gold nor silver at this point. The bottom has corroded all the way through, leaving a gap.

Shaw closes it in her palm, then leans forward on one knee, getting her face as close to the space beneath the rock as she can, wishing for the flashlights in her kit. The dog whines again, and Shaw shushes her, making out faint outlines of more leaves, crumbled chunks of rock, and something like a small branch, a more complex shape than the rest, with tendrils reaching out.

Something in that form and nuance makes her lean there, her brow pressed to the rock, finally fumbling her phone out of her pack to turn on the flashlight app and get a closer look.

It's a hand. Skeletal, attached to nothing, all flesh and sinew gone, the bones stained a teak brown.

Reaction sends a burning rush of air into her lungs. Shaw jerks back with a guttural sound, losing her balance and sprawling clumsily, catching herself on hands and knees while Aphrodite jumps clear. In an instant, Shaw's scrambling to her feet, shuddering from shock as she backs away from the makeshift cairn out here in the woods in the middle of all this nothing, finding she somehow still clutches her phone and the rusted ring in either hand.

Her legs fold, and she drops heavily to the ground, doing nothing but breathing for an interminable time, gaze leveled on the rocks and what she knows lies beneath. The hellhound paces circles around her, occasionally nudging the side of Shaw's head to make sure her human is still among the living. "Thee," Shaw whispers. "Jesus."

Ultimately, Shaw lifts her phone. She makes two calls: one to 911, the other to the landline at the house. The old man answers.

"Shaw?"

Shaw is pulled from a deep inner hall of echoes by a voice she recognizes. She sits on a boulder at the trailhead, her right arm looped around the dog for so long that her shoulder's gone numb.

It's Stephen York. The state police detective is a tall man with a slightly beaked nose who keeps his head cleanly shaved, most likely as an alternative to letting his balding pattern grow in. He's always in plain clothes, but the sheriff's deputy who put in the call obviously told him that he'd be wanting his hiking boots for this one: Stephen's dressed in jeans, an insulated fleece jacket, and a ski cap. The sight of him without a suit and tie only adds to the surreal effect of seeing the world through the lens of shock.

"Shaw." Stephen's gaze is frank and steady. "I'm surprised you're still here. You must be freezing."

She shrugs and shakes her head as Aphrodite shifts beside her. "I can't leave her again. My dad would want me to stay."

"Does he know about this?"

"I called him. He wanted to come, but—" Emotion swallows her words, tries to drag her under, but she presses her lips together and waits it out until she can speak again, glancing back at the sloping trail where she's watched deputies and field techs come and go, lugging equipment to secure the scene in the woods. "He's home with my boys and I don't want them here. Neither of us does."

Stephen studies Aphrodite for a moment, not automatically reaching out to pet her like most people do. "I didn't know that you owned a human remains recovery dog."

"She isn't official anymore. I mean, I'm not trained to be her handler. She's family—" More emotion, turning her vision to water, and she swipes her eyes hard, almost angrily, sniffing. "I have to stay until they carry her out."

"That's not possible. You know how long it could be." Stephen takes one hand from his coat pocket and scratches Aphrodite around the right ear, which she leans into. "The Office of the Chief Medical Examiner is going to assume jurisdiction over the remains. There's a good chance that a forensic anthropologist will be brought in. It's going to be a process, and it's not going to be quick." He's quiet for a moment, working his fingers down to Aphrodite's withers. "You've done all you can. Now let us do our job. You know I'll be in touch."

Shaw wipes harder as tears slip down her cheeks, searching in her pockets fruitlessly for a tissue.

"Your dog feels cold." Stephen steps back. "Go home, Shaw. Be with your kids. We'll take care of things here."

She nods, sliding down from the rock, patting her thigh to bring Aphrodite to heel. "Wait—I found a ring in the rocks. I think it rusted off her finger. I gave it to the first deputy on the scene"— presses her fist to her brow—"I wasn't thinking, and I forgot to read his name tag. Make sure it got bagged, okay?"

"I'll double-check. Drive safe." He makes his way down the steep path to meet the deputy waiting to lead him through the wilderness.

She calls Dad to let him know that she's on her way, barely seeing the missed call notifications on her locked screen as she bangs in her passcode, needing so badly to hear her boys' voices and make sure home is still where she left it. The old man's voice is thick with tears, shaky: "Take it slow. We're not going anywhere."

When Shaw arrives, daylight has shrunken to a tangerine brush-stroke above the silhouetted treetops, and it's a race to the door, racing the coming night with Aphrodite at her heels, understanding none of it and excited for any excuse to run.

The boys come to meet her with a hesitance completely foreign to all of them, their faces pale and reluctant in a look she knows well: it's the innate human fear of confronting someone who's grieving, the dread that their pain will have changed them into someone unrecognizable, or that their suffering will be more than you can handle. She's worn it herself, and had it directed her way more than a few times.

Beau starts to speak, but she pulls both boys close, kissing their heads, hugging them tightly as Dad comes into the entryway and joins them, the four creating a broken circle with Aphrodite pushing her head at their legs to try to get into the center.

"Oh, thank God," is all Shaw can say.

8

Shaw stands at the stove, cooking supper, having put two days between herself and the discovery of the bones. Beau is visible through the living room doorway, draped across the couch with his phone, Casey is sitting on the carpet in front of the TV with a controller in his hand, making empathetic ducking and dodging movements along with his avatar and giving occasional soft yelps.

Dad comes into the kitchen and pulls a can of lime seltzer water out of the fridge, the brand he's drank daily for thirty-some-odd years, and which Shaw now keeps stocked. "I'm going to head out for a bit after we eat," she says in a low voice, stirring the minced onions, garlic, and green peppers sautéing in the skillet, the base for marinara sauce. "James is willing to have a chat with me, so I said I'd swing by. That was last week. I'd better hustle before the offer expires."

Dad looks at her without moving, then pops the top. "Think that's smart?"

She bites down on a snappish answer. She's been off on compassionate leave the last two days, and it's been an intense forty-eight hours of crying, never straying farther from the family than a potty break, and forcing herself not to call Stephen York every ten minutes to ask why in hell he doesn't have answers yet. In short, the walls are closing in. "Finding what I did might finally give me some leverage with him."

"Finding your sister." The old man's tone is gruff. "Might as well say it, hon."

She works her mouth, scraping the bottom of the pan.

He scoffs. "Well, I know. I know in my gut, and just as soon as they match up them dental records—"

"*Shhh.*" Shaw jerks her head toward the boys; she's been trying to shield them from the more gruesome aspects of what's going on, not easy when she and Dad have been rejoicing over any tidbit of news from the front, like the fact that a skull was found among the remains. "I don't want to go through it again. I'll be on York's ass as much as possible, but I'm back at work tomorrow and I won't have as much time. I won't let up, okay? Remember, this isn't my field. I've got no idea how long a positive ID might take."

"Christ, they know we're waiting." He shakes his head. "Look, it's colder than a brass toilet seat out there, and I don't think you ought to be going by yourself."

"I'd never go empty-handed." She fills a pot with water for spaghetti. "And it's James. Not like we don't know him."

Dad gives a grunt of disgust, waiting to see if that's really all she's going to say. "Sure, we know him. And I know that he ain't been right for a long time, and I don't think he ever will be. I've talked to him a lot more recently than you have. Guy's a mess."

"One side effect of spending a lifetime accused of a crime you claim you didn't commit." She starts cranking the lids off the cans of crushed tomatoes. "I'll never understand why he didn't just move out of state, leave it all behind him."

"'Cause the fella can barely get out of his own way, that's why. Got a different job every time you turn around, getting into fistfights with people, ending up in the police blotter. He's not like you remember, Shaw, I'm tellin' you. When's the last time you saw him? Five, six years ago?"

She finally glances over, setting her spoon down. "Do you really think James did it? Because I've never gotten that from you."

Dad is quiet a moment. "I don't know that it was him. I don't know that it wasn't. I've never liked believing that a Rishworth boy, a kid you girls grew up with, could do something to hurt Thea and not even feel bad enough about it to tell us what happened, do right by us and your sister. But finding her bones where you did changes things. That's pretty damn close to where that party was happening that night, the one he swore up and down she never made it to. And he never acted right after she went missing. I know for a fact that the staties are still looking at him hard. They made that statement to the news a bunch of times that there are people close to the case who aren't telling everything they know, which is why the case has gone unsolved so long. Who do you think they were talking about?" He shakes his head slowly, steadily, gaze focused inward. "Never got out there looking for her like he should've. A friend—boyfriend— who didn't have nothing to hide would've been out there with the rest of us, beating the bushes. Okay, he was upset—I could see that— but he never seemed shocked enough, like he should've. Showing up drunk to your mother's memorial didn't do him any favors, either."

"God. I haven't thought about that in a while." Shaw exhales, remembering James, only twenty at the time, dressed in a baggy dark blazer maybe taken from his father's closet over jeans and Timberlands, a polo shirt come half untucked, trying to get into Mom's wake. He must've heard that cancer had won, or maybe read Mom's obit in the paper; maybe he'd honestly wanted to pay his respects—with a side of proving how innocent he was.

Not sure who he was trying to reach inside the reception room— maybe her, maybe Ryan, though they had never been friends with

James; Thea's disappearance had simply forced them together, a disparate cast of characters. All she remembers is hearing a fracas, turning from the row of chairs where she sat to see James through the doorway opening onto the foyer. He was grappling with Dad, the funeral director attempting to hush the whole thing without getting elbowed in the face in the process. The next moment, James was propelled into view out the partly shaded front windows, barely catching his balance on the last step, staggering backward, his face flushed and rent with grief. He'd shouted back at the men, then, something unintelligible, a rough expulsion of frustration as the mourners inside turned to watch his unsteady progress toward the parking lot. He'd backed his truck out and drove off like that, stinking drunk, and nobody even called the cops. Too much grief in their family for too long, everyone exhausted, their give-a-shits broke, as the old man would say, and no one was sure about James and Thea, not one bit. Guess he got home all right.

James's mother used to live in a double-wide trailer on the old county road that ran past a few moose marshes, and since he didn't specify otherwise in his DM, Shaw assumes that Mrs. Moore lives there still. It's a road as popular with bored teens in jacked-up trucks now as it was when they were growing up, and Shaw detects stripes of burnt rubber on the pavement in her headlight glow as she keeps a close watch out the windshield. It's been a long time since she's been down this way. But she dropped Thea off and picked her up at James's place a handful of times back then, and she feels fairly confident that she'll recognize the clearing with the trailer centered on it and the short gravel driveway leading up to a small garage.

It's total recall as soon as the beams hit the wooden sunflowers staked in the garden by the roadside ditch in front of the property, lawn ornaments standing about two feet high; it's here, a right turn where the road gently curves left, nothing to distinguish the driveway but those wooden flowers, now nearly stripped of paint by time and the elements.

Shaw turns in, ignoring the stomach-turning sensation of—what, nostalgia? Nothing so rosy as that. *Recall* might be the best term, a mental force-feeding of sensation and recollection as if her car had pushed through some invisible membrane delivering her back to a time when they were all kids, and Thea was still around, and Mads was little, and James and the rest of them might've grown up to be just about anything, if they'd cared to try. When Shaw's own life as she knew it was poised on the edge of being blown to pieces, becoming something unimaginable to her, unrecognizable: motherhood. Then, having Beau; the regathering of the pieces, putting life back together in a way that was equally unrecognizable, but so obviously right. Being mother to this boy was right. Every piece in its proper place but Thea.

Hard to say from the look of the trailer if anything approaching rightness has ever been found by its residents. The trailer, once white, is now darkened and mossy, particularly the roof, which has an almost furred appearance in the glow coming from the outdoor light over the front steps, like a lady's mink coat hurled up to the shingles and left sprawling. The garage is also fully lit, beaming through the fogged windows in the bay door.

By all appearances, James's mother is home. There's a flashing TV screen visible in the space between the front window curtains and a dusty Kia Sorento sagging on low tires near the steps. Shaw pauses a moment before shutting the driver's side door behind her, half expecting a woman's face to the appear at the window, though Shaw honestly can't remember Mrs. Moore very clearly; just an impression of an overworked, slack-faced woman who didn't seem particularly pleased by the sight of Thea running out the door of the trailer and climbing into the passenger seat beside Shaw moments after Mrs. Moore had arrived home from work, dead on her feet. The position of James's girlfriend had a high turnover rate, James being something of a high school serial monogamist, meaning relationships lasted a couple months before self-destructing.

Now, Shaw is struck by a childlike moment of indecision, wondering if she has some obligation to ask James's mother for permission to speak with him. Depends on where James is, if he even remembers that he gave Shaw an open invitation to stop by literally whenever.

Shaw starts for the trailer, then stops at the metallic rattling of the garage bay door being lifted.

A man is backlit, one arm still raised, clinging to the inner door handle. Shaw instinctively raises her hand to shade her eyes against the light, though the short stature and the fact that, as far as she knows, no other man has lived here since James's father walked out on the family indicates that it must be him. "James, it's Shaw."

He's silent a beat. "Oh. Yeah. Hey." His voice has become reedy, husky, full of smoke. He takes a few backward steps into the garage, where she can see an old black Indian Motorcycle leaning on its kickstand, taking up most of the limited space. "You don't want to go in there." He heaves a hand toward the trailer. "She's probably sleeping. Come on."

Shaw goes to the concrete threshold of the garage floor, not eager to edge into one of the narrow aisles on either side of the motorcycle, backed by miscellaneous storage. Multiple toolboxes and wrench sets lay open on the floor, along with cans of grease and fluid, rags.

"Turns her show on, then two minutes in, bam." James wipes his hands now as he returns to the motorcycle, not looking right at her, dressed in a faded black Carhartt coat, the tail of a flannel shirt hanging below, baggy-ass jeans bunched up at the top of heavy engineer boots, much like the ones she remembers him wearing to Mom's wake.

"My dad does the same thing," Shaw says. "How else are they going to be up shuffling around the house at three thirty in the morning if they don't get that nap in?" James snuffs wheezing laughter, working his way around the hood, giving her a profile to study at last. His skin still bears a trace of deep summer tan, his jaw rough with stubble, still blond, but with a sprinkling of gray in his sideburns, which gives her a bit of a gut check, considering he's a year younger than she is. He always seemed to be vain about his hair, and still wears it in that pseudo-DA style. "Nah," she continues. "I think it's just their clock running down, you know? Messes with their systems. Comes to us all, they say." He doesn't respond, and she senses that she's misspoken, somehow hit a nerve. Finally, she lifts her pocketed hands toward the motorcycle. "Where'd you find this?"

"Got it from a guy who was going to scrap it. I said I'd take it off his hands." James tosses the rag and hunkers down near a molded plastic lawn chair smudged with greasy handprints. "What d'you think?"

"Honestly? I think it's a thing of fucking beauty, though you'd be hard-pressed to show me something with a motor in it that I didn't have a healthy respect for except maybe a Geo Tracker or something. What year is it?"

"'Seventy-six."

"Easy rider, man." The chrome was speckled with rust, the chain half eaten away. "You know a lot about fixing these?"

Another laugh. "No. Going by what I can find online, mostly. Taking parts off, cleaning them with steel wool, putting them back on." He's fiddling with something on the undercarriage now. "What made you want to talk to me?" It's hard to hear him.

Shooting the shit about the motorcycle had been easy; she'd been talking cars with Ryan ever since they were kids, plus picking up a thing or two in his shop, and she felt honest calling herself an amateur gearhead. Here comes the tough part: "I want to talk with you about Thea."

He tinkers for a moment before speaking. "Because of the bones they found. I saw it on the news."

She nods, not wanting to share that she was the one who made the discovery. Maybe it could even prove to be something of an ace in the hole. "They belong to a woman. I know that much."

He drops his hand holding the wrench a few inches, squatting there. "I hope to hell they're hers. Then we can all be put out of our fucking misery." He straightens up, shifting his shoulders back as he faces her for the first time, bloodshot eyes in a visage she knows, yet made unfamiliar all the same by the passage of time. His brow wrinkles are the deepest, visible even when he wears no expression, like now. "What good's talking going to do now?"

"Maybe none. But I was hoping for a refresher on what you remember from that day. And the night." She lifts her shoulder. "Maybe you and I can put something new together."

He exhales roughly, turns and tosses the wrench down with a clatter into the closest toolbox. He turns back on another big intake of breath, smoothing his hands hard along the sides of his head as if psyching himself up for a boxing match, and she waits motion-less, already having a pretty good idea how sensitive to judgment he is, how quick to lose his temper. "I'm only doing this because it's you, just so's you know. Anybody else asks me to talk about it, I tell 'em: *Fuck. Off.*" He shoves the planes of his hands in two lines. "I got reporters calling here sometimes, bugging my mom, trying to get me to talk about it. Like they can break me or something and get this big story nobody else could."

"I know. I'm sorry. It's all bullshit." His gaze is skinned back, reminiscent of livestock spun into a state—she'd better toe the line between sympathetic and condescending. He's still sharp enough to tell the difference. Shaw hesitates, bringing out her phone. "That said—mind if I record?"

James stares at it in her hand; he's already slightly breathless, chest rising and falling. "What're you going to do with it?"

"Just keep it for my own use. That's all. My desk's half full of stuff on Thea. I'm not planning to share this with anybody, sure as hell not the press. We've been handed the fuzzy end of the lollipop by them plenty of times, too."

Maybe it's her stupid turn of phrase, but he seems to decide to let the recording pass, looking away. "You want to pull up a seat?" He indicates a second battered lawn chair against the wall.

She shifts the junk out of the seat to the floor and drags the chair over, the plastic feet bucking across the porous concrete, where she settles across from him.

He sets his elbow on the armrest, digging at his cuticle, gazing at the square of darkness beyond the doorway. Behind them, a small space heater hums, the warm air stirring the ends of Shaw's hair. "I seen Thea at school that morning like always." He uses the tired monotone of memorization, walking through those same dusty corridors of thought, lined with battered metal lockers, the bobbing flow of the backs of heads and backpacks. "We said 'bye at homeroom because we didn't have any of the same classes that day. I took woodshop and gym, stupid shit like that, just jacked off with my buddies till the bell rang. But me and her were already planning on hanging out that night, meeting up with some people at the turnaround. Few drinks, few laughs, whatever."

Silence forms, and Shaw balances her phone on her thigh, leaning back into the curve of the chair, folding her arms as she studies him. "Was she planning on you picking her up at our house?"

"No . . . no, we didn't really work it out. She just said she'd be there. But then we got together later in the day downtown. She'd been walking around with Deanne whatshername and Brandy after school."

"Where'd you meet up?"

"You already know this shit."

"Humor me. For the tape."

He exhales. "House of Pizza. They were already there when we showed up. Me and Chuck D. and Matt."

"What were the girls doing when you got there?"

"Hanging around the arcade games in the corner. I remember Brandy saying they didn't have any money so they couldn't get anything to eat, so Chuck D. and I pitched in for a couple pizzas and some sodas to share around." Fleeting warmth passes across his features. "Used to do that a lot."

"I remember." Her own friends had done it, too, once they were sixteen or so and had a little income from after-school jobs; it was one of those hubs the teenagers gravitated to at the time. Work was never anything that had interested Thea, hence her never having any money of her own, and Shaw remembered her and Mom going ten rounds about it. Shaw had only been to the House of Pizza once after graduation, and she'd walked right back out again, nauseous with sensory input, Then and Now colliding head-on with the rich scent of melted cheese and cardboard and hot grease. It hadn't been exactly the same, of course: Donkey Kong and the Aerosmith pinball machine had been removed to make room for more coolers, less candy, the tables replaced with nicer booths and the walls painted a different color with different crap lobbed up there for decoration.

"Then we left. Deanne went home and Chuck D. and Matt went and did their own thing while I drove around with Thea and Brandy until it got dark out. Don't ask me what we talked about or what we did 'cause I don't remember. It was a regular night until everything went to shit the next morning."

"The thing I really want to hear about is your fight with Thea. That doesn't sound regular to me. What did you fight about?"

"Nothing, really. Stupid little stuff."

"But it was bad enough that she made you pull over so she could get out of the truck."

He nods once, his stare glazed.

"See, that's what I don't get." Shaw hunkers over, leaning on her thighs. "Me, I find that no matter how many years I'm alive, the good stuff goes all hazy, but the bad stuff tends to stick, you know? I can't forget no matter how hard I try. I bet if you put yourself back in that moment, you might even remember some of the words she said. The ones that hurt."

"She didn't hurt me. I never said that." He sits back, mouth working, looking to the corner as he bites down on his thumbnail. "I don't care what's online, I never said a bad word about Thea. She was cute. We had a good time together. She liked it as much as I did."

"Liked what?"

"Just—being together, messing around, whatever. Not saying she would've been my girlfriend forever or even until graduation, but . . . yeah, she liked me. We would've made up if we'd had the chance."

"You're still not telling me what was said."

"You sure you're not a fucking reporter? 'Cause you sure as shit sound like one."

Shaw shakes her head, her pulse speeding up a tick, but she keeps her expression in check. "I'm only asking what you remember. Not trying to stick it to you."

It's a long moment before he speaks next. "Okay, she was mad because I told her to slow down. We had some rum and Coke in a thermos I'd been sipping on. And some beer behind the seat. I'd stocked up for the get-together that night. She drank a lot of the

Captains fast and it wasn't even seven o'clock yet. She was going to be partied out way before we even met up with everybody."

"Was that strange for her to drink so much when you guys hung out?" Another shrug. "Where'd you get the booze?"

"Stole a little from my mom. Got the rest from a guy I knew."

"Who?"

He stares obtusely back. "Just a guy in town."

"Any special reason you don't want to share the name of this guy?"

"I'm not—I don't give a rat's ass." Roughly: "Cops know all about it, and who the hell cares at this point, anyway. I'm not trashing somebody behind their back, spreading shit around. I been on the receiving end of that enough times to know how bad it sucks. And I been of age for a couple decades now, in case you haven't noticed. We all have."

"All the more reason why it couldn't hurt to tell me his name now. He must've been older if he was buying booze." She waits but James isn't budging, so she tries a different tactic: "Was this the only older guy who used to hook you up with stuff? Or who used to hang around you and your friends sometime? Might've known Thea?" James's brows draw together, incredulous, sizing her up. "Even if he only met her one time? Anybody at all you can remember who might stand out. Maybe just—while you were filling up your tank one time or in a store or a movie theater. Anybody weird."

He hangs a look, leaning sideways in his chair, and she can feel it like ozone before a lightning strike, things getting charged. Guys like him have nothing but a short length of stiff spine; he wouldn't back down from a fight with a gang of ten Hells Angels swinging chains and pipes—his ego couldn't afford it. He sure wasn't going to take guff from her. "I didn't know about no perverts scamming my girlfriend, no. Like I would've stood there with my thumb up my ass while that was going down."

"Have you ever heard the name Anders Jansen?"

He snorts. "That's a name?"

"Okay. You told Thea to slow down before she got too drunk, and she didn't like that. What else did you fight about?"

"Nothing. She didn't like anybody telling her what to do. You gotta remember that. She wasn't even supposed to be out at all. She was grounded."

"Well, you're telling me that my sister refused to ride with you any farther and threw your plans for the evening out the window. Sounds like she must've been pretty pissed."

"She was *wasted*. You don't always think straight when you're drinking. Maybe that's news to you."

Shaw continues to stare. "Where did you let her out?"

"Everybody knows—on School Street, where the old schools are. And the playground with the ball field."

"Did she say where she was going?"

"No, she just walked off. We figured she was going home."

"Walked off where? Uphill? Downhill? Direction matters, considering our house is on Pressman Street. That's southwest from the top of School Street."

"Downhill, okay? Brandy called out the window after Thee, but she never turned around." He stares straight ahead for a second, like he's seeing it.

"I got to tell you, I have a hard time with the fact that Brandy stayed with you and let her best friend walk off alone, drunk, and upset. That doesn't sound like best friend behavior to me."

"Sounds like Brandy, though, don't it? She put the party first, always. I was her ride."

"Was Brandy who you and Thea really argued about?" Shaw crosses her arms. "Just a pet theory of mine. Thought I'd try it out on you."

"You mean was I porking her?"

"Revolting choice of words, but I'll bite."

James's smirk is lopsided. "Sorry. Maybe I couldn't do no better than her these days, but back then I sure could. No way was I gonna tap that. Brandy was okay to have around, but she was a fucking disaster area. Drama queen. Not all her fault. Her family was nuts." He sees that Shaw's expression is unmoved. "I'd promised her a ride up to the turnaround, so I took her there like I said I would. She went off with somebody else, friends, whoever. Everybody always asks who, but I don't fucking know who. Anyway, I drank way the hell too much, don't remember driving home. But I know, that whole night at the party, I was figuring on calling Thea in the morning, thinking she'd be cooled down by then. Instead, I wake up to my mom shaking me, telling me Eddie Connolly's on the phone, looking for Thea because she never came home last night. I guess everybody was thinking that we were shacked up together." He works his thumb over a plucked fray in his jeans near the knee, worn to white strings. "Sometimes . . . I wonder if maybe, when I was driving my drunk ass home that night, I passed her somewhere, and I didn't even know. When I think of her like that, she's like half a girl. Shadow girl. I dunno."

Shaw continues staring at him, immobilized by the sight of a tear appearing at the inner corner of his eye, welling there, growing fat. He doesn't seem aware.

"Thea and I would've made up if we could've. I know that for sure." It's his refrain, said with a sort of desperate insistence, as if this made all the difference for people to understand as the tear streaked down his unflinching face. "It would've been okay. Things got out of hand. And I never got 'em back. I mean, it all went to pieces that one night when I wasn't paying attention. That make sense?"

"Oh, yeah. I get it. I feel the same."

"I mean, nobody was watching. None of us. Not me, not you,

not your folks or the teachers or the cops. Every single one of us had our eyes closed or something and she just—went."

"You mean somebody took her."

"I don't know. More like she just left the earth. Leastways, that's what I used to think. But now . . . there's these bones. You really think it's her?"

"It seems like there's a good chance."

More tears now, steadily, his expression crumpling. "Why'd you come here tonight? Huh? To make me feel like shit all over again? 'Cause I don't need help with that." He's trembling. "I got nothing. No job. No wife and kids. My mom's all I got. When I fuck up bad enough and got nowhere to go, I come back here, and she takes me in. I don't know why in hell she does. Sometimes I wish she'd slam the door in my face, let me hit bottom and bust to pieces. Because as long as she holds on, I got to keep holding on, and I don't want to anymore. I'm so fucking tired. Everybody thinks I killed a little seventeen-year-old girl and they all hate me for it."

"You been drinking tonight, James?"

His look is scathing. "Nah, only one beer, officer, I swear. I seem fucking drunk to you?"

It's like dousing a stubborn little bonfire with him, forever smoldering. "I've got to ask. I can't walk off and leave you if . . ." It seems better not to finish, but she isn't done, her head slightly bowed over her phone. "Still waiting for the name of the person who supplied your booze back then."

A pause, then more wheezing laughter bursts out of him, rubbing one hand down his face, raking the stubble. "Christ, like a dog with a bone, huh?"

"I gotta be. Right? I'm Thea's big sister. If I don't keep asking questions, who will?"

"Well, I don't need no babysitter. Get on home."

"James."

"I don't have to talk if I don't feel like it." When she doesn't move right away, he adds quietly, hoarsely, "I said fuck off."

With tears still coming, he crouches back to work on the floor, leaving her sitting there a few feet away, not sure if she screwed this up or if it was screwed from the beginning. Finally, she stands, stops the recording, and returns to her car.

She's starting the engine when she sees the face at the trailer window, almost as she'd imagined it. A furtive, fearful movement, the woman maybe wondering what pain is coming down on their family this time, what kind of unsavory character might be visiting her son after dark without even the decency to announce their presence at the front door, pay her a courtesy. In the years since they last met, Mrs. Moore's hair has turned pure white.

9

Her phone goes off twice on the drive home. Anders. She doesn't answer.

As she pulls into her driveway, the phone trills again, startling her. She shuts her eyes for a long moment before starting the recording app and tapping the green phone icon.

"I've been calling. For days." Anders's silence is weighty. "I take it you've been busy."

"Very." She glances at her own eyes in the LED-lit rearview mirror: they're looking old, sunken, and she slaps the mirror to the side.

"So much so that you couldn't answer a ringing phone?"

"Come on, you know what a busy minor cog I am. Can't be dropping my work for every psycho wanting a convo, can I? I'd never get anything done."

"Next time I call, I expect you to answer."

Shaw laughs sharply. "Yeah? Expect to be disappointed. Some of us have responsibilities other than being a boil on the ass of society." The exhaustion of the past days, both emotional and physical, settles upon her like layers of sand. "I've said everything I had to say to you, so let's call it a day, all right? No more calls, no harm, no foul. I won't even get the po-po on you, because I'd be the one who ended up doing most of the paperwork."

"Don't you want to talk about our shared experience in Beggar's Meadow? It was quite a day for you. I only wish I could've seen it through to the end."

"What?" She shakes her head, making a sound of disgust. "Okay, you read some article online about the bones. Good for you, up on your current events."

"I'm telling you that I was there. I came close enough to read the brand name on your Nalgene water bottle. I saw you sitting there, crouching under that rock, eating. You looked like a child."

"Don't try to snow me, okay? I'm not a fucking idiot."

"Oh, my, we *are* in need of a nap. You'd like proof, I take it?" Sighs. "Well, I did leave you a little something. Go on. Check your car."

Shaw makes a rough, dismissive sound.

"Oh, of course you will. You're too inquisitive a creature to resist. Go look at your vehicle. Or are you in it now?" A satisfied pause. "Then that should make it easy."

She jerks around, surveying the driveway and snowy yard illuminated by the motion-sensor lights on the house and garage.

Anders speaks: "I promise that I'm not lying in wait with a sniper rifle or whatever scenario is churning around in that feverish little brain of yours."

Shaw takes the phone out of the dash mount, squeezes it to her ear with her shoulder, and reaches into her purse to find her can of pepper spray. Then she shoves the car door open and walks around the SUV, still scanning the yard and the dark road. "Okay. There's nothing."

"Well, I didn't want just anyone to see it. Under the rear bumper. Passenger side."

Trap. Her mind is screaming it, as if he could've planted a pipe bomb, or some grotesque jack-in-the-box-style horror to pop out and induce cardiac arrest. Part of her is still convinced that he's jerking her strings, but he's right: her need to know is more powerful than any of the noise. She ducks down, eyes struggling to adjust to the shadow, finally turning on her flashlight app and holding it up to illuminate the winter-grimed tailgate.

A small black box with a yellow logo is stuck to the undercarriage. And beside it, a little face looks back. Two vertical smears for eyes, an O for a mouth.

She jerks back as if scalded, breath steaming out of her, whirling again with her pepper spray straight-armed ahead of her, ready for him, almost seeing a shadow running toward her, but there's no one. The property looks as deserted as before.

She runs for the house, locking the door behind her and moving the lace panel to peer out the glass pane at the night. Casey calls something from the direction of the kitchen, but she doesn't turn. Instead, her hand lifts the phone to her ear without consent.

Anders is laughing, a quiet huffing of breath, mostly held inside. "Are you there?"

"Present."

"I thought maybe I'd lost you. There was nothing but a lot of cringing and fleeing sounds." He clears his throat. "What do you think? I'm not much of a portrait artist, but I'll bet that my little doodle was crudely accurate to your expression when you saw it. What was it you said last time? 'My face like a slapped ass'?"

"What is that black thing you put on my car?"

"A gift. A tool. It's been on there for some time. It's also a reminder that your actions count, Shaw. It's important that you understand that I can reach out and touch you—anyone in your life—whenever I choose. You'll need to become responsive. Respectful. Cordial, even."

Aphrodite rubs against Shaw's leg, wanting attention, but Shaw can't take her eyes off the darkness, afraid she'll miss a movement, some sign of life. "Jeez, wish I knew all you wanted was a friend, Anders. You need to internalize that lesson about catching more flies with honey than vinegar. And you strike me as a guy who'd really enjoy having a lot of dead flies around." She continues with forced casualness, "So, how'd you do it? In the woods. I never once saw you, hiking in or out, never heard a vehicle. Though my vicious attack dog did raise her hackles at one point."

"Mm. She is something of a deterrent. I followed you most of the way, from a distance. It's not the first time. I'm always curious to see what you might find."

"You knew what was out there?" Her voice drops a few octaves.

Momentary quiet. "Here's the issue. You pegged me wrong. When we last spoke. The terms you used—I didn't care for them." His conversational tone has cooled again. "You underestimated me. I couldn't have you seeing me as another one of the untalented misfits you spend your days cleaning up after."

"Yeah? What makes you so different?"

"Impulse control. Malice aforethought is everything. Without the ability to plan, a sense of timing, what separates us from, say, the African baboons you hear about, rushing out of the jungle to attack a tourist's genitals?"

She pinches the bridge of her nose, using pressure points to fight a sick headache. "I don't think you and I are watching the same nature shows. And the kind of planning you're talking about is the difference between fifteen years and life, cupcake. Speaking of which, did you remember to wear gloves when you drew that little Hallmark card for me?" He doesn't answer; she lowers her hand.

"You do understand what I do for a living, right?" Silence. "Anders?"

Only he isn't there anymore.

"Shawnee, you better damn well wait—somebody from the sheriff's office is gonna be here soon enough—" The old man curses under his breath, standing with the boys and the dog in the doorway, their breath steaming in the cold as they watch Shaw jog down the front steps, flipping her hood up over her head.

"It's not going to hurt anything for me to take a look. It's my car. As soon as the deputy gets here, he can have it all."

"What're you going to do?" Beau calls, jamming his hands into his pockets in frustration as his mother holds up a *one sec* forefinger before climbing into the way back of the car, opening her kit, and taking out the mini Maglite.

She kneels, shining the beam on the drawing and the area surrounding it. Moments later, the boys' footsteps approach, followed by Aphrodite. "What're you guys doing out here?"

"I want to see." Casey crouches beside her, his winter coat hanging open over his hoodie and flannel pajama pants.

"Well, that's nice, but until I know what this thing is, you need to back off." She pushes at the dog's nose. "All three of you. Go on, scoot."

Once they've fallen back as far as the steps, with Beau holding the dog's collar, Shaw shines her light on the face again: there's at least one patent she can pick out, almost certainly an index, molded against the steel surface in dirt at the top of the first downward eye dash. Who knows what a dusting of white powder might bring out—magnetic powder is a possibility, but if the Beast's original owner sprang for the undercoating, the wax spray could pose an issue. She can't take the prints herself—the deputy would recognize the dusting powder left behind in an instant, and that's straying into serious conflict-of-interest territory—but she takes photos of the patents before turning to the box.

The box itself is roughly three-and-a-half inches long, with the words STATUS printed on the case, along with the logo she'd noticed, which incorporates a location arrow icon. A GPS tracker.

"Shaw? What's happening?" Dad's voice is raised, tense.

"It's okay." She reaches up and pulls the box off, then rests heavily back on her haunches, not giving a shit about the snow soaking through her pant legs, her expression lined with incredulity as she turns the box over, pockets it, and heads inside with her family until the deputy arrives.

She sits on the couch, phone in hand, debating calling Ryan. He's one of the few who will fully grasp the implication of what's going on, but she also knows the shitstorm she'll bring down on herself, ranging from *This is your own fault* to *Happy now? You let this go on too long and now look*—she can hear exactly how he'll say it, and she isn't spoiling for another fight, not now. But. There is McKenzie. It's then that she makes up her mind to text him, holding her breath as she types:

Any chance we could meet at Patel's tomorrow? She hits the send arrow, panics, realizing how it reads. Immediately adds: *Looking for some pro advice.*

McKenzie's response is almost immediate: *Can it keep till Thursday? I'm off then.*

Shaw swallows dryly, her thumb hovering. *I've got court Thursday a.m. Try for lunch, noonish?*

I'm there.

The next morning, Shaw's called first thing to a scene in a sketchy subdivision in Devane, maybe twenty buildings clustered around a wide rectangular green, back lots studded with plastic playhouses and charcoal grills and snowed-over bikes, a suspended animation stillness laying over everything.

It's too cold for many residents to emerge, only a few coming out of the nearest houses, lighting cigarettes, watching the uniforms and CSIs come and go, waiting for a stretcher, wondering if there's a corpse or just another OD getting a blast of naloxone up the nose.

Shaw keeps an eye out the apartment windows for Gauthier's powder-blue bubble pulling up to the curb across the street, Gauthier needing to go the long way around because uniforms had blocked off traffic from Union Street with sawhorses, officers in HiVis orange jackets protecting the perimeter, pacing to keep warm while a line of others conduct an outdoor grid search, combing every inch of the walkway and the green behind the building for evidence.

Shaw meets Gauthier at the tape, lifting it for her. "Welcome to the monkey house. Well, maybe not monkeys, but the tenants obviously keep some sort of mammals and aren't too fussy about the use of litter boxes. We'll be burning our coveralls when we're done with this one, gore notwithstanding." Gauthier's gaze levels on the partially ajar door of unit 201. "Not to worry. Corpses aren't in residence anymore. ME's people took them away a few minutes ago."

Gauthier gives a nod, pulling on her shoe covers and mask, adjusting the hood over her hair. "Jewel said that it was drug related?"

"Mm, magic eight ball's leaning toward most likely, judging by the paraphernalia inside. Deal gone wrong, suspect already in custody although there may be a second shooter or accessory, not clear yet. Uniform pulled the one guy out of a dispensary on Main Street, and he hadn't bothered to change clothes, either, by the looks of it, so that's a win." Shaw stands back, giving the door a push inward. "After you, m'dear. Follow the yellow-marked road."

The entrance opens onto the kitchen, clear plastic stepping plates placed around a blood trail across the linoleum, large splatters and small droplets leading to a doorway on the right, yellow evidence markers dropped here and there to note shotgun shells scattered around. Every countertop is covered with crap, towers of dirty dishes and take-out containers and evidence that someone has been shooting up at the table in the corner: foil, needles, baggies, Bic lighter.

"You'll want to keep your mask on, and not just for contamination reasons. I pulled mine down for a second when I got here—this place's signature scent is eau du crusty ragu with base notes of hamster cage." Shaw follows Gauthier like kids on stepping stones toward the hallway, unconsciously trailing the path of the killer, a confrontation which began in the kitchen and escalated to the victims fleeing gunshots down the hallway, one breaking for the back door in the living room while the other was funneled into the master bedroom, a dead end in every sense.

Shaw taps Gauthier's shoulder as they reach the first bedroom. "This room will be your project." Again, the space is crammed with junk, possibly left untouched since the tenants moved in, the common scenario of migrating from one eviction to the next in state rent-controlled housing where they can make a side income dealing while collecting welfare and EBT benefits. "You know the drill. Focus on the doors, open surfaces if you can find any, windows."

Gauthier surveys the pile. "Where will you be?"

"In the master bedroom."

"Is that where it happened?"

"One of them, yeah."

"Can I help you?" Gauthier finally meets her eyes, some defiance there.

"Do the work in here first. Then, pop your head in and I'll let you know what's left to do. Sound fair?"

Later, Shaw peers at Gauthier around the ajar master bedroom door as the younger woman comes down the hall. "Perfect timing. I've decided that I'm taking it." Shaw gestures to the door. "The whole thing. I've photographed and lifted what I can, but I think it would be valuable to chemically treat this at the lab and see what we can bring out, especially if there's a question of a second doer. A little irregular, Jewel may not love the idea, but that falls under the heading of tough titty. I'm here, she's not." Shaw bumps her toe against a small tool kit lying on the floor. "We should bring the hardware, too, but it's easiest to pull the pins out of the hinges and take the door off first."

Gauthier comes into the bedroom and sees the mess on Shaw's side. Darkened, drying blood spatter with smeared handprints, spackled with whitish-gray brain matter in a 60-degree spray.

"Somebody tried to get out." Shaw's voice is even, almost serene; work is an escape today, anything to distract from the memory of forcing herself down to the county sheriff's office bright and early to fill out the paperwork for a temporary protection from harassment order against Anders, following the advice of the deputy who'd come to the house last night and taken her statement along with the GPS tracker Shaw had removed from the Beast. Silly, really; Shaw deals with those brown uniforms almost every day, but maybe some part of her believed that an early 2000s version of Mercer Brixton might still be sitting behind a desk in the station somewhere, badge and name tag on his chest pocket flaps catching the gleam of the fluorescents, a porch-sitting backward tilt to his posture as he waited for her shadow to flow across the pebbled glass pane in his door. *Shawnee?* Slightly coffee-stained teeth, silver bridgework. *Are you with us?*

"Serology has already been here, so now we'll get our crack at it. See?" Shaw points to visible prints in the spatter. "I'm guessing you haven't done prints in blood yet?" Gauthier's gaze has a dilated distance to it, but she blinks rapidly and shakes her head. "Then it'll be all you when it's our turn with the door. Okay, you hold, I'll pull."

Gauthier grips the door, her masked face turned sharply away from the bodily fluids while Shaw uses pliers to yank the greased metal pins out of each hinge, then whistles to a uniform coming out of the bathroom. "Hi—Who are you?"

"Mitchum. Perry." He regards Shaw with the slightly gruff wariness many of the younger male officers use with her, a woman who gives the first impression of being a few bricks short, who maybe they've heard stories about.

"Looking fit, Mitchum, and I mean that in the most platonic sense. Care to help us wrap this to go?"

He and Gauthier hold either end of the door while Shaw wraps plastic sheeting around it from top to bottom and seals it with evidence tape. "Evidence van, if you please." Shaw watches as Mitchum carries the door down the hallway with some difficulty. "Okay, the whole living room has yet to be touched, and that's the largest square footage in this place, also high traffic area for the victims and their associates, also where the second shooting happened, so we'll take that on together. Heads up that lead detective is Van Sickle. She's the only other woman here besides us, so you can't miss her. My advice is keep your head down. They call her Old Ironsides, and this is coming from Old Iron Underoos, so you know she's tough. She's had to be. Now, let's skedaddle."

Shaw gives a nod to Van Sickle as they pass near the threshold to the open-plan kitchen and living room. The detective is a tall woman with a formidable sloping bosom who returns the gesture distractedly while dressing down another officer for God knows what.

Shaw and Gauthier split the room, Shaw working around the left side, dusting the small TV on a stand covered in empties, bagging what looks worthwhile as Gauthier kneels beside the glass coffee table, using her brush and black powder on the few open surface areas where prints might be lifted. The floor in front of the back door is all blood, smears on the carpet, splatters on the wall.

Shaw straightens, turning toward Gauthier. "How's it go—" She stops mid-question at an unpleasant smooshing sensation beneath her heel, then checks daintily. "Shit." She holds her foot out for Gauthier to see. "Told you I smelled mammals."

"I stepped in some a couple minutes ago." Gauthier tears a strip of tape, then drops into a scooch to examine the closest pile of pellets. "Looks like rabbit poop."

Shaw frowns, turns back to applying fresh powder to her brush and then stops, fist on her hip. "You seen any other sign of rabbits in here? Cages or anything?"

When Gauthier shakes her head, Shaw lets herself out the back door, walking down the short flight of concrete steps to the dirt dooryard behind the unit, nothing to see but a wooden wire dowel turned on its end to serve as a table in the warmer months, pocked with cigarette burns and forgotten Solo cups. Shaw sees more pellets scattered around, some frozen and dried, others fresh. She picks her way along the side of the building until she notices a section of plastic skirting yanked off the track around the foundation and shoved unevenly back, revealing a black, open space beneath the subfloor and the ground.

She squats, pushing the skirting flap farther back. A length of chicken wire has been fastened to the inner side. Shaw hesitates, then applies pressure on it until it comes free and falls to the dirt.

She has one second to register a brown projectile hurtling out at her head, and she gasps, plunging to the ground as rabbits rush out from beneath the building, black, brown, white, starved and dung-coated and crazed with freedom, their little paws pummeling over her, nails scratching across her coveralls as they pelt away onto the frozen green between the units.

Shaw yells, scrambling on all fours, someone finally grabbing her arms and helping her get to her feet as rabbits bounce off both of their legs, tumbling pell-mell and heading toward the parking lot instead.

By now, a couple uniforms have rounded the building, drawn by the cries. As Shaw straightens, she finds Gauthier holding her steady while two of the younger uniforms attempt to round up the rabbits, slipping and sliding on patches of ice. One officer's feet go right out from under him and he ends up on his ass while at least six or seven onlookers laugh from behind the tape, phones held up, taking video.

10

"I counted at least fifteen of the fuzzballs. Animal Control's going to have a hell of a time digging them out of that development. Be like playing Whac-A-Mole." Shaw bites into her sandwich, ravenous, as she and Gauthier take a quick fifteen in the basement break room of the lab before getting to work on the prints from the scene, both having thrown out their coveralls and shoe covers in the biohazard disposal bin. "All those buildings are the same, modulars, so that won't be the only one that was dropped on support legs. Plenty of new places to burrow. I'd feel bad for the little carrot heads if that first one hadn't scratched me with his nails." Shaw digs another chip out of the bag, considering it, the scrape beneath the Band-Aid on her cheek still throbbing. "There isn't enough Neosporin in the world."

Gauthier smiles, holding the sushi wrap she's barely picked at. "I can't believe they didn't freeze to death under there."

"I guess they had the run of the inside of the apartment often enough to keep them alive. Looks like the owners were tossing food scraps under the house. I'd be surprised if they didn't have a few rats in the menagerie, too." She watches Gauthier place her sandwich down. "Damn. You'd think I'd stuck you with a croissant."

"No. Sorry. It's good. And thanks for . . ." She gestures with her wrap, awkwardness over Shaw insisting upon buying them both lunch on the drive back to the lab.

"Hey, least I could do. You rushed right into the fray there. Not everybody would've done that. No woman left behind, huh?" Shaw waits. "So, what's the matter? Still thinking about the scene?"

Gauthier nods. "The handprints on the inside of that door." She presses her own hands between her knees for a second. "Do you know if it was a man or a woman?"

"It was the woman. The man died in the living room." Shaw's careful to keep her voice modulated, not giving in to what lies on the other side of the evidence: the human factor. That's how a scene works its way inside, becomes something that haunts you. "Yeah. It's grim. But, hon, wait till you work one of these in the heat of summertime, when the body has been marinating awhile? The masks help. You can try a dab of Vicks under the nose, too, no shame in using that. Tran does, though he's mostly on benchwork now. And whatever lemon-scented shampoo and bodywash you can find will be good to have. Citrus takes the stink right out of your hair the way nothing else can."

Gauthier nods, taking a sip of iced tea. "Were you sick?" She sees Shaw's confusion. "The last couple days. Jewel just told us that you were off."

Shaw takes a breath. "Family stuff, you know. I needed to be around." Shaw had given Jewel the rundown of the weekend's events over the phone on Monday; she'd never doubted that it would be kept confidential from the rest of the staff.

"Oh. It's nice that they wanted you there with them." When Shaw raises her brows: "I still live with my mom. And my stepdad. They don't like me."

Instead of admonishments, there's silence, Shaw crunching as she looks back fixedly at Gauthier. "That's a shame." She crumples the bag. "Can't be easy. Families are weird, mutated animals, though. Every last one of them."

Shaw finds her own mom's image waiting for her in her mind's eye—Mom in that familiar blue roll-neck sweater she wore for years, in the way she made most things last, knew how to stretch a hundred and twenty bucks into a week's groceries for a family of five, reusing containers and duct-taping ripped sneakers and obsessing over the thermostat setting, all habits learned from a lifetime of scrimp and save, many things that Shaw now does herself. Mom, gazing back at her with that expression on her face that even now Shaw knew she hadn't imagined, wasn't simply survivor's guilt. The look Mom never seemed to be able to erase after Thea went missing and Shaw's pregnancy happened, not even when Shaw announced that she was going back to school to become a real adult with a job that mattered and everything. It was a look of vague, exhausted distraction, like, *what do you want from me*, or *what am I going to do with you, Shawnee.*

"I'm saving up, though." Now, Gauthier nods to herself, her focus obviously elsewhere, much like Shaw's. "I have this job now. I'm going to get my own place, somewhere closer to the lab." She bites her bottom lip methodically. "They can have their life, and I can have mine."

"Sounds like you've got a plan. That's a good thing."

Gauthier nods quickly, before Shaw's even finished speaking. "Yes. I do. I always do."

Their held gazes are broken by Shaw's ringtone, and she grabs the phone, fully expecting it to be Anders, ready to tear into her over being served his copy of the protection order. Instead, she sees Stephen York's name on the screen.

"Excuse me, kiddo. Need to take this one."

Shaw goes out into the hallway, filling her lungs completely and closing her eyes as she picks up. "Steve. Hi."

"I hope I'm not catching you at a bad time, but I know you've been waiting for an update on the ME's progress with the remains. Also, I received a call from Sheriff Duhamel of the Rishworth office this morning. He mentioned that you'd asked that I be notified about the protection order you've taken out against Mr. Jansen. I'm glad that you've gone ahead with it."

"So am I. Did he tell you about the tracker that son of a bitch put under my car? Eighteen-month battery life with real-time updates as to every move my vehicle makes. We're talking over a year of this."

"He told me. And also that Mr. Jansen claims to have followed you through the woods on Sunday."

"I know he did. I have zero doubt. What have you got on Thea?"

Stephen hesitates. "The medical examiner is still investigating the remains, and they've brought in a forensic anthropologist like I expected. Cause and manner of death are still undetermined, and it could be challenging to get a definitive answer with nothing but partial skeletal remains. There are plans to contract a forensic odontologist to examine the teeth in hope of learning more, but the preliminary examination of the vertebrae which compose the sacrum, and the state of the cranial sutures suggest this woman was somewhere in the range of twenty-three to thirty years of age. All the experts involved agree that these bones couldn't have been out there for more than three years. Likely much less."

Shaw takes it like a body blow, bending forward, expression creased, lips pressed tightly together in pain. She doesn't speak or breathe for a full four seconds, finally rocking her head back against the wall hard to enough to create a thump that Gauthier probably heard on the other side. "*Shit.*"

"I'm sorry, Shaw. I know how much was riding on this."

Her voice escapes thinly. "You're sure it couldn't still be her? Maybe the bones were . . . preserved, somehow? Protected from the elements in that space under the boulder or . . ." The silence on the other end is tolerant but final, and she cuts herself off, kicking her heel back against the drywall for another resounding thump. "I can't believe this. Who the hell *is* it, then? Who else would be out there?"

"We're going to try our best to find out. But so far everything indicates that it's not Thea."

"My dad was already planning the memorial, you know. Nothing but the best. I tried to tell him to be cautious, but—" She swipes at her eyes, fighting to keep her voice from breaking. "What about the ring? Did that turn out to be anything?"

"It could help further down the line, if we're able to locate next of kin who could identify personal effects. But it looks like cheap department store fare, mass produced, not the kind of thing that would've had a jeweler's mark even if a significant portion of the band wasn't rusted away."

After a moment, Shaw laughs softly, shaking her head. "You know, I've always believed that I might find Thea out there. That . . . something went down at that stupid party at the turnaround, an accident, an overdose, who knows, and maybe her friends hid her out there in the Meadow so they wouldn't go to prison. I guess my instincts weren't completely off, but it wasn't Thea calling me, it was . . ." She shrugs her shoulders, her vision softening with tears. "You need to talk to Anders about this. I think he knew those bones were there. I don't think he was bullshitting me about that."

"I certainly intend to speak with him, yes, and my understanding is that the deputies delivering the protection order today will be having a sit-down with him at the station. In the meantime, as I'm sure you know, if he calls or contacts you or your family in any way, get in touch with the sheriff's office immediately. He'll be arrested." Stephen pauses. "Are you going to be okay?"

"No. Yes. I'm still standing, if that's what you mean."

"Well, I'd like to stop by your place and have a talk with you and your family in person about everything that's happened, if that'd be all right. Maybe Friday?"

She clears her throat. "That would mean a lot to Dad. And me. Okay. I need to call him and my sister. They shouldn't have to wait any longer to hear this."

By the time Shaw comes up to the outer office of the lab, she's washed her face, twisted her hair back with a covered elastic, and stashed her phone mercifully away, still hearing the bottomless quiet on the other end of the line after she broke the news to the old man that their search wasn't over. Mads's phone had gone straight to voicemail, letting Shaw off the hook momentarily. Small favors.

She finds Gauthier already seated at her desk. The young woman straightens up, peering over her laptop. "Jewel said that the door's ours. She double-checked with Serology and they've already taken their samples. They're bringing it up to us on the elevator now."

"Okay," Shaw says. "Time to get wacky."

They pull on scrubs, lab coats, gloves, goggles, and particular masks. The door lays on a table in the small room in the back of the lab area, and Shaw takes a pair of shears to the plastic sheeting and evidence tape, carefully unwrapping and piling it on a nearby counter space. She's determined to force her thoughts to the task at hand, exist in this moment only, preventing grief and disappointment from crushing her until she's in a setting where she can execute a complete and graceless collapse. Dad's voice over the phone had sounded so colorless, so weak. Another sucker punch delivered. Thanks a mill, cruel fate.

"Okay, so clearly we've got patents here." Shaw waves her hands at the visible prints in the blood. "And my guess is that most on the lower half of the door will belong to the female victim, but we've got the knob to think about, and this chipped edge here. I already photographed everything visible at the scene with my phone, but since we're about to dose this baby with chemicals and probably end up washing some of them off in the process, let's get some higher quality shots first. Can't have too much for court."

Shaw adjusts one of the lab cameras on a tripod, angling it for ideal lighting. "Jewel says both victims and the suspect in custody are already in the system, thanks to priors, so we've got all the exclusionary prints we can handle. Grab a few rulers. We'll get these out to Tran and Jewel ASAP. Let's get this mother's joy in so deep he'll wish he had gills." She zooms in so that the first print, roughly three inches above the doorknob, fills the frame, then takes a metal ruler from Gauthier. "Take a peek through the viewfinder. You want the print, centered, with the ruler beside it like that, demonstrating size. That's it. I'll take a couple, then it's your turn."

When the patents have been photographed, Shaw moves the camera aside. "Okay, let's see what we get elsewhere on the door. I mean, this laminate surface is filthy and beat to hell—there could be latents along this edge where you'd grab the door to pull it open without using the knob that we're not able to see right now. Let's mist some amido black solution around and then bust out the alternate light source."

They gather a plastic tub, distilled water, a container of citric acid, and combine them, then set the tub on a mixing device until the citric acid is dissolved, setting it aside to be used as a rinse solution. Next, the developer solution—1,000 ml of the citric acid rinse, two grams of the amido blue-black, then two mL of Kodak Photo-Flo 600. Again on the stirring device.

"Now, when the amido stains the hemoglobin protein, it's going to destroy the integrity of the DNA." Shaw measures some into an empty spray bottle. "Which is why we're last to get the door in this case. We can muck the whole thing up for our purposes without hamstringing Serology too badly, though we're keeping them in the loop, natch. Chances are, this is the female victim's blood and hers alone, so we're not likely to be blowing away any profile that the lab doesn't already have."

Gauthier's gaze is steady behind the lenses of her glasses. "But there's a chance we could be."

"You bet. It's not perfect. Sometimes, you got to roll the dice. I pulled that gem right out of the manual." Shaw holds the spray bottle out to Gauthier. "Your time to shine."

Gauthier aims it evenly along the edge of the door, around the knob, down to the bottom edge. "Is that good?"

"Golden. Now we let it develop." Shaw looks at the wall clock, letting the minute hand travel one complete circuit. "Okay. Let's rinse, see what we've got."

They apply the citric acid stock, drying it as deftly as they can, drops still sliding off the edge and splashing onto the plastic sheeting laid out on the floor.

They both don their orange contrast glasses, the personal alternate light source flashlights from their field kits at the ready. "Dim the house lights for me, okay?" Shaw says.

Once Gauthier had switched off the overheads, she joins Shaw, both working their way along opposite sides of the door, playing the LED UV beams over the surface with painstaking slowness.

Minutes tick by. Inky-looking latent prints made in blood have developed in the chemical reaction, blood spatter reacting just as vividly, speckling the door, and becoming a mostly undefined blotch in the blood-heavy area, but Shaw's working the upper edge.

"Okay. Look at these." Shaw keeps her eyes on three now-visible prints as Gauthier comes over. "They're incredibly light." Shaw straightens, right hand up, fingers splayed. "Right index, middle, and ring, little smudge here where the pinkie didn't make much contact when he pulled the door open to leave after the victim was shot?"

Gauthier nods, leaning close to the prints, holding her flashlight beam a few inches above. "I don't see the central pocket loop on the index. The suspect in custody has one on his right."

"Very good. They don't make an immediate visual match for me, either. One possible scenario is that this accomplice either killed the woman or was in the room at the time it happened, then shoved her aside so he could get back out the door to the hallway, getting his hands bloody in the process. She was still lying with her head and shoulders resting back against the door when I arrived, so it makes sense that she would've been blocking the way when the killer or killers tried to leave the room. Again, it's not a perfect process. The DNA profile has most likely been ruined by the chemicals, making it impossible to prove that this blood belonged to the victim, so the defense will argue that it could've belonged to someone else and the prints were left prior to the crime, especially if they can establish a prior relationship between the victim and the accused. Oh, well. We have our job and they have theirs. If a little justice shakes out in the end, it's the best you can hope for." Shaw steps back. "Let's get pics and send them to Tran to upload. With any luck, he'll have some good news for us by the time we've cleaned up our mess here."

When they emerge nearly an hour later, Tran glances back from his terminal and says, "Ding, ding, ding."

Shaw heads over. "We have a winner?" She looks at his monitor, where he has the results of the AFIT search pulled up. "Herman Wilhelm Straker, 28. No stranger to the law. And, look, he's a Gemini. Why am I not surprised?"

Tran clears his throat, twiddling the mouse. "So, you two. I heard things got kind of *hare-y* out there today?"

Shaw folds her arms, leaning back against the table edge. "You might say." Narrows her eyes as his shoulders begin shaking violently. "In fact, you might say that I was 'hopping mad,' right? You little brat?" He finally bursts out laughing. "How'd you hear so fast?"

"Oh, I received video footage from some bunny."

"You're shitting me." She leans on the back of Tran's chair as Tran pulls out his phone and plays a twenty-two-second clip showing the backyard of the crime scene taken maybe thirty seconds after Shaw opened the skirting panel; the shooter's phone was shaky, but you could still catch sight of Shaw in her crime scene gear, staggering to her feet with Gauthier while the uniforms grabbed at the ricocheting rabbits. "Jesus. Is this online?"

"No, *no*, relax—and no sender name for you." He shuts his screen off as Shaw tries to appropriate the phone.

"So, you're saying that was taken by one of ours—"

"Nunya. I keep telling you, honey, I've got connections, I've got sources. Something about me inspires trust, you know? People flock to me."

"Yeah, well, I ever find out which one of those little piss squirts took that instead of helping while I was getting mauled by Flopsy, I'll flocking string them up by their utility belt from the station flagpole. I don't need that winding up on the nightly news—stupid human videos have a way of getting leaked for the entertainment of the public, you know."

Tran cackles. "Wait, I've got it: 'Local CSI Exposes Underground Cottontail Trafficking Ring, Footage at Eleven.' Nope. Not sexy enough. I'll keep mulling." He spins partway in his chair to face them, looking somewhat rumpled from the early morning call to the arson scene. "But I've got to warn you, if this video exists, there are others. And not taken by our people, either." He spins back, miming a tiny explosion with his fingers. "Out of my capable hands."

"It wasn't her fault." Gauthier's pinking up again. "She knew there were pets, and she didn't want them to be left without food somewhere. Somebody had to find them."

Tran's brow arches. "Damn, Shaw, you've got her trained already." He lowers his hand at Gauthier. "Down, girl, no offense meant. I know Shaw's the S-H-I-T. Ya'll know I'm keeping my quarters." He's already swiveling back to work, tossing to Gauthier, "Peace offering, 'kay? I've got some nonfat nondairy peppermint-gingerbread-flavored creamer in the staff room. It's all you."

Gauthier's still staring intensely back; Shaw nudges her with her shoulder. "Be honored. He usually marks the level with a Sharpie, I've seen him. Okay. Onward." Shaw gives her a nudge with a bit more *oomph*. "Come on. Step lively. Miles to go before we sleep."

11

"Did you do this?"

The next morning, Shaw holds up her black blazer for Dad to see; she'd found it hanging, ironed, from the knob of her closet door last night after she'd seen the boys off to bed and turned in, staring at the dark, watching her worries swell into unconquerable giants as her exhausted mind grew increasingly irrational, imagining the moment when Anders opened the door to a uniform and realized that she'd violated his terms and turned him in. It's sickening and exhilarating at once, perhaps the sensation of power landing back in her hands, or maybe more the sense of things finally being broken beyond repair, nothing she can do to piece them back together.

Now, with the boys having hopped the bus, Shaw has showered and applied makeup, something she only does for court: dashes of eyeliner, dabs of coverup on the odd age spot and blemish, lips colored in with a conversative dark pink liner and blotted dry, just enough to bring out her features for those listening from the jury box.

Dad doesn't look over from reading the local free paper that comes in the mail each week, mostly news of the local scout troop's do-gooding and town council decisions. "Took two seconds."

"I'm stunned."

"You don't think I know when my daughter's giving testimony in a big case? I might be half deaf, but I do listen when you talk, you know."

"I mean, I'm stunned that you know we own an iron. And how to use it without burning a hole big enough to play horse-shoes through." She flips the blazer around on the hanger, double-checking. "This jacket's wool, you know. Not the easiest to deal with."

"Ahh." He waves her off with a rough gesture. "Even I know you can't dress like a slob in court."

"Does that mean the thong and pasties are out? DA Prito's gonna be devastated."

Dad laughs and chokes on coffee, slapping away drops that leak onto the tabletop. "Don't talk like that in front of your father. What's the matter with you?" The moment of levity extinguishes quickly; this is a house of mourning, in a way—mourning the loss of Thea all over again, the potential for something approaching peace—but the family is used to forcing one foot in front of the other. Shaw's eventual phone conversation with Mads yesterday had been short, stiff, Mads's responses clipped and unemotive, somehow worse than if her littlest sister had broken down into hysterics. Whatever Mads feels about Thea's disappearance, it's buried too deeply for Shaw to excavate in a phone call.

Aphrodite walks up to the old man and rests her chin on his thigh, her liquid black gaze fixed on him.

"Wanna go out?" The old man gets up and opens the back kitchen door, letting the dog slip down the steps and around the corner of the house. "Wants a pee and a sniff around the back forty."

"You're a dog whisperer now, huh."

"Hey, we pass the day together pretty well, Aph and me. We got an understanding. I keep her dish full and operate the doorknobs, she keeps me company until Casey gets home." He tops off his mug, growing quiet again.

Thea enters the room in the stillness, the way she does when conversation lags between Dad and Shaw, settling into an empty chair at the table, shaking her hair back, and sitting with her skinny arms folded, feet kicked out and crossed at the ankle in the posture that used to drive Mom crazy, like Thea was trying to trip everybody walking past. Shaw's fine hairs tickle along her forearms and the back of her neck. In her mind's eye, her sister's gaze is fixed, unblinking, first on the old man, then on Shaw. As in, *I should be here. I should be in on this. Did you seriously forget about me for a minute?*

"I'm not going to ask," Dad says, but in a trailing kind of way; not even he can erase the faint, defeated interrogative. "I don't s'pose York said anything about searching for Thea near where you found this other woman. If there's one, there could be others, couldn't there?"

"He didn't say. But you'll have a chance to ask him tomorrow." Shaw tucks the blazer under one arm, deliberately angling herself away from where the memory of Thea roils, like air churning from a kettle spout. "I've wondered about having another big search, bringing in volunteers again, but . . . I don't have the time to organize all that right now." She shrugs. "If the cops don't beat us to it, maybe we can save up, talk about it more in the summer. Not a clue who owns that land out there now, if we'll need special permission or something."

"Well, I got my social security. And the rent coming in from the people living in our house." He always referred to the Hendrickses that way, not resentfully, but like they had chewed their way in through the foundation of the old family home instead of by signing a lease. Beneath the mildness of his tone, Shaw knows, lies bone-deep exhaustion from the hemorrhaging of money he doesn't have in the name of this search. Shaw had hoped to take the pressure off when she'd suggested their current arrangement, convincing him to turn 134 Pressman Street over to a property management company, so somebody else could play landlord to the young Hendricks family while Dad simply collected his profits via direct deposit every month.

"Forget it," Shaw says to him. "That cash is yours. Let me worry about that end of it, okay?" She swallows the option she's only dared suggest to his face once: selling the Rishworth house, finally letting it drift from their family like a dory with a loose towline. She and Mads have talked about the possibility plenty. Who knows . . . maybe it would drag some of the past along with it, shrink it to a dot, then gone. Glory hallelujah.

What if she comes back, had been Dad's answer to her question of selling that day, his words listless. *I know she's not coming back, but what if she did. And nobody who answered the door could tell her how to find us.*

And the fact that his argument had made sense to Shaw might've been the hardest thing to accept. Hadn't a similar rationale been at the heart of her decision to keep her maiden name when she and Ryan married? Remaining a Connolly had felt more important than becoming a Labrecque, in case, someday, a mythical adult Thea, long-lost but with stories to tell, tried to look her up. Mad as shithouse rats, all of them, when it came to Thea. What had Ryan called Shaw—*anybody's fool?*

Shaw goes to dress, knowing that Thea's presence will dissolve and dissipate once she and Dad are apart, the bond broken.

She catches a glimpse of Aphrodite out the front window, in the driveway bouncing back and forth around the rear of her car, excited by something. She still smells Anders. What else could it be?

Shaw opens the front door and leans out, hissing, "Hey!" The dog takes a couple steps around the tailgate, looking at her. "Come on." She makes forced kissy sounds, beckoning. "Come on, girl. Come inside. Want treats?" Aphrodite vanishes behind the Beast again. "Get away from there! *Psst!*" Shaw is nauseous at the thought of his scent hanging around the place, his presence at least as tangible as the ghost of Thea.

At last, the dog comes, tail held high, allowing her attention to be drawn by the promise of chicken jerky. When Shaw leaves for the Bennet County courthouse, she glances at the back of the car and finds dog urine, not quite dried, splashed all down the tailgate and rear tire onto the frozen dirt.

Eight jury members in the box this time, five men, three women, no sound in the courtroom but the hum of the forced air system as Shaw clicks over to the next slide in her voir dire presentation. She's already taken a sip of water and needs another, but she won't do it; it connotes nervousness, uncertainty. She's neither one, simply punchy from exhaustion, but neither she nor the prosecution can afford that, definitely not during the first phase of her expert testimony, when she essentially needs to impress upon eight angry personages that she's qualified to do her job.

"When you touch an object, the sweat, grease, and residue from lotions or cosmetics that coat your unique friction ridges, or the high point in our fingerprints, are transferred to the surface of that object," Shaw goes on. "As we speak, I'm essentially "stamping" the sweat and grease covering my own friction ridges onto the touch pad of this laptop. But unlike when we use a rubber stamp on paper, which deposits a visible imprint in ink, our fingerprints are often invisible. An invisible fingerprint is also called a latent fingerprint, *latent* being Latin for 'hidden.'"

God. Water, please. Her throat is crawling. She grabs a sip, taking a moment to compose herself, hoping to give the impression of a gathering pause rather than one that feels more like she's staked on a dune in the Sahara.

The Bennet County district attorney, Romy Prito, maintains her standing position behind the prosecutor's table, hands clasped behind her back. Standing six-two in heels, the sort of height that, in a woman, draws tiresome assumptions from strangers about having a God-given jump shot and an empty dance card, Prito's courtroom style is mostly stationary, using her stature to her advantage. She rarely refers to her notes; she and Shaw have been through this waltz enough times over the past three years since Prito's promotion from ADA after her mentor, Nick Luen, took a position with the Commonwealth of Virginia. Today, Prito wears a gray tweed skirt suit, her tightly curling black hair held back with a claw clip, the mole near the right corner of her mouth as dark as her penciled brows. "Ms. Connolly, can you explain the process you went through to make the fingerprint found on the document in question visible to the naked eye?"

Shaw nods, turning back to the screen. "In order to compare latent fingerprints with known fingerprints, we need to make the invisible visible. We've all seen fingerprint brushes and powders used by crime scene investigators on TV." Click—new photo of CSI in full field gear, leaning close to a tabletop with a fiberglass brush. "We also use various chemicals to make prints visible. The chemicals we use vary depending on the type of surface being treated. In the case of Mr. Montez's prints"—Shaw doesn't give him a look, the hulking attitudinal elephant in the room, his thick muscular neck strapped into a maroon tie with a subtle figure, paired with a sedate navy-blue suit, no doubt handpicked by his defense attorney; judging by what Shaw's heard from Prito about Juno Montez, he's about as subtle as a junkyard car crusher—"I employed ninhydrin.

The object in question was a piece of paper found at the scene, on the floor of the bank manager's office. Paper is porous, therefore absorbent. Sweat is about ninety-nine percent water, and the rest are products excreted from the body, like salts and amino acids. When you touch a piece of paper, it absorbs your fingerprint, and keeps it there. Ninhydrin turns purple when it meets amino acids. In the case of the evidentiary document, when I applied the ninhydrin to the paper, this print emerged"—she clicks a new slide into place, a photo of the crumpled receipt before treatment, the next of the purple-stained thumbprint visible on the upper-right corner— "along with a partial index, shown here."

"Thank you." Prito finally sits and confers inaudibly with her assistant, who then sets up a court chart with an enlarged photo of the same thumbprint, red circles marking each minutia, beside Montez's on-file inked thumbprint. Prito gestures to the photo on the stand. "Do you recognize People's Exhibit Eleven?"

"Yes, that's a copy of the photograph I took of the thumbprint after I processed it on the receipt, enlarged for detail, beside Mr. Montez's inked thumbprint for comparison."

"And did you perform a fingerprint comparison?"

"I did, with the record fingerprints belonging to the suspect, Juno Montez." Shaw still doesn't grant him a look.

"How were Mr. Montez's fingerprints recorded?"

"In ink, on a ten-print card. He was in the AFIT system, which—"

"Objection." Stawarski, Montez's court-appointed attorney, a young man of no more than twenty-six, shoots to his feet, his face a portrait of strained sincerity, his light brown hair blown straight back as if in a gale. "Witness has no qualifications to bring Mr. Montez's past criminal record into this testimony."

"Ms. Connolly is merely stating where she sourced your client's fingerprints," Prito says, glancing at the judge. "As a fingerprint examiner with nearly ten years of experience, she's more than qualified to comment upon the AFIT database. She isn't offering up an expert opinion on your client's lengthy criminal record."

"The objection is sustained." Judge Feingold remains unflappable, a heavyset, gray-haired magistrate in his late sixties with startlingly black bushy brows, who has presided over three other trials where Shaw's testimony has been subpoenaed. "And I'll thank you not to slip in commentary of your own, Counselor."

"Certainly, Your Honor." Prito takes a breath, the rest of her body language so sedate that it no doubt achieves her goal: communicating to the jury the frustrating incompetence of the defense. "Ms. Connolly, to get back on track, can you please tell us how you performed this comparison of fingerprints?"

"Yes, when I first examine a fingerprint, I use the ACE-V methodology, which stands for analysis, comparison, evaluation, and verification. I then evaluate whether the fingerprints are from the same source, first by pattern type, then the line of flow, followed by the points of identification and positioning. I like to use the traditional loupe—or magnifier—method initially, but most of these determinations are now finalized by computer software. Our lab utilizes Thayer Parent ACE-V Manager, which is how I prepared this chart I brought with me today for the purposes of demonstrating the points which identified this print as belonging to Juno Montez."

"Can you walk us through?"

"Of course." Shaw angles herself to point out twelve dots circled in red, concluding with, "Given the correspondence of the twelve points of minutiae, including the presence of the central pocket loop whorl characterized by the ridge, which makes a complete circle here with two deltas, found in only about two percent of the population, I concluded that fingerprint is consistent with the right thumbprint of the suspect."

"And given the education you've just given us on the uniqueness of each specific fingerprint, and the fact that our fingerprints do

not change over time, what are the chances of it belonging to anyone other than Juno Montez?"

Shaw looks over at him at last. "Absolutely none." She watches
the working of his mouth. He's one of the haters, the ones who sit
and stew during the trial, personally resenting every person who
takes the stand for the prosecution, regarding the world with a ven-
detta that doubles as a justification for every law they've ever broken, every person they've ever hurt.

"Thank you, Ms. Connolly. That's all I have for the moment."
Prito drops her gaze, making way for cross examination.

Shaw grabs another sip of water, crossing her legs on the opposite knee as the young counselor, name of Stawarski, shuffles some
papers before getting to his feet. "Ms. Connolly," and the words
are already coming fast, employing the method of rapid questioning Shaw's run into before, a common tactic used to disconcert a
witness, "you mentioned that exhibit one, upon which you found
fingerprint 1001, was a receipt, isn't that right?"

Shaw mentally counts to three before speaking, giving the kid
her blasé face; she's been bullied and bluffed by better, and certainly longer in the tooth. "Yes."

"Where did that receipt originate from, can you tell us that?"

"Walmart."

"Do you recall the date stamped on the receipt?"

"Objection, Your Honor." Prito's sorting papers, swiping across
her phone screen. "The witness isn't tasked with giving expert testimony on any evidence other than the fingerprints she processed."

"Sustained. Stick to the subject at hand, Mr. Stawarski."

The lawyer takes a breath. "The date on the receipt is not September twelfth, which was the date of the robbery, wasn't it, Ms.
Connolly?"

"I don't remember the date on the receipt."

"Well, I'm happy to refresh your memory." Stawarski goes for the receipt, inside a sealed plastic bag, and walks right up to the witness stand; Judge Feingold shifts, his feathers clearly ruffled at somebody entering the well of his court without permission. "Please read the date and time for the benefit of the jury?"

Prito is now looking at them, her brow creased. "Objection, relevance?"

"I'll establish relevance shortly, if given the chance."

Judge Feingold shifts in his chair, then exhales loudly through his nose. "All right, I'll allow. Keep it brief."

Shaw leans forward, finding the automatic stamp. "It says September ninth, 3:14 P.M."

"September ninth. Mr. Montez remembers purchasing these items at Walmart that day very clearly, as well as stuffing the receipt into his pocket with the intention of throwing it away later. After that, his memory fails him, as it would most of us, I think, when it comes to something as mundane as the disposal of a grocery store receipt." Stawarski paces with frantic energy. "So, this little piece of paper, which was found on the floor of the manager's office in the Cross National Bank on Merchant Avenue, could've been dropped there at any time during the duration of those four days between the time of the purchase and the robbery, couldn't it?"

"Objection, drawing conclusions for the witness."

"Overruled. Witness will answer."

Shaw sets her jaw a moment. "It's possible. If you're asking for my opinion on the likelihood of that, I have a different answer for you."

Stawarski ignores that. "Mr. Montez lives only two streets over from the Cross National Bank. Were you aware of that?"

"No."

"Therefore, it's fair to say that he may have had reason to enter the bank for legitimate reasons at any point over the course of those four days?"

"I doubt they'd invite him back into the manager's office, don't you?"

Stawarski's reaction is almost comic, hand to his chest, hamming it up. "Well, a slip of paper doesn't weigh much. They've certainly been known to travel, haven't they? Particularly across the slick surface of a tiled floor, pushed by a breeze let in by the opening and closing of the entrance doors, even the passage of customer's feet as they come and go? Who's to say that, after this dropped from Mr. Montez's pocket on a completely benign visit to the bank, it ended up in the manager's office, by misadventure, if you will?"

Shaw tilts her head, gathering control. "I suppose anything's possible if you're not concerned with the question of likelihood. Anything except the idea that this fingerprint we're looking at could belong to anyone other than the suspect. Beyond that, there's nothing more I can tell you about Mr. Montez's adventures in, out, or around that bank from the ninth through the twelfth of September."

A stillness, Shaw's big fat foot landing in it. She feels the tension in her shoulders and neck, the tightness of her face, unable to stop her gaze from going to Prito, who gives nothing away, but isn't stepping in either, indicating to Shaw that she's the one who's out of line and Prito isn't about to make herself look any worse by association. The jury stirs, their body language suggesting a shift in the balance of power at the stand.

Stawarski looks at her, his high, pale brow shiny in the overhead light, tie slightly canted. "Let's talk about stress levels." He paces over toward the jury box, drawing their gaze. "You were working several other cases at the time, weren't you?"

"Yes."

"And how many employees does Bennet County Forensic Solutions have?"

"I believe it's around fifty, but I don't have anything to do with staffing. That may not be exact."

"How about within your department? Can you be exact about that?"

She looks flatly at him. "There are four of us."

"Handling about how many cases total, in, say, one month?"

"It varies. Roughly twenty to thirty, I'd say."

Prito speaks: "Your Honor, I don't see the relevancy of this line of questioning when all the witness is—"

"I'm trying to establish the average workload at the lab, and how it affects the stress levels of the witness and her coworkers. I'll be brief." Waits until the judge gives a wave of his heavy hand, looking on at the young attorney with an abstracted interest. "Ms. Connolly, some common effects of workplace stress are irritability," a significant pause, glancing her way, "insomnia, and difficulty focusing on tasks. Often, we make mistakes we wouldn't have made otherwise. Are you familiar with these symptoms?"

"You mean personally? Of course. I have a full-time job and a family. Stress is a constant."

"So, you're admitting that mistakes can be made, even in a highly specialized field such as yours, even by an expert with as many years on the job as you?"

Prito starts to speak, but Shaw leans in to the microphone. "Mistakes happen in all lines of work, sir. And that's exactly the purpose of the verification stage of the ACE-V method I told you about earlier. If you look closely at the paperwork I supplied during discovery, you'll see that my findings were verified by an experienced colleague, Jewel St. Bonaparte, who is in fact department director, with seven years of experience in the field of forensics, including the processing and evaluating of latent fingerprints. So, again, if you'd care to base this conversation in reality, the chances of two senior level latent print examiners misidentifying one fingerprint as belonging to the same suspect would be something in the ballpark of you or I strolling out of this building and being hammered into the ground by a meteor." Her voice is aggressive, raspy. "Though not being an astronomer, of course I can't offer expert testimony as to the exact percentages."

12

Patel's is unusually hushed today, only a few tables taken, and Shaw claims a place among them nearest the bar. When a member of the waitstaff doesn't appear immediately, she moves to a barstool, leaning on her elbows, her arms folded close to her chest.

Sunni stands close by with a clipboard in his hand. He sets it down as he notices Shaw and approaches. "What can I get for you?" His cologne is redolent with bergamot and peppery notes, awakening an impulse in Shaw to close her eyes and inhale, which she shrewdly denies, along with a desire to feel the patina of his satin shirt between thumb and forefinger, the shade of which might best be described as blood orange, his cuff links black obsidian circles.

She almost orders seltzer with lime. Fuck it; it's been a day, and it ain't over yet. "Vodka and cranberry. A double." Sunni gives a nod, reaches for a tumbler, but Shaw stops him with "Could you plop in one of those little umbrellas, please?" He glances back. "I'll pay extra?"

He mixes the drink, selects a paper umbrella from the plastic bin and opens it with care, saying, "On the house," before he hangs it off the edge of her glass and slides it over.

She nods, too worn out to dream up a quip, returning to her table to find that the waitress has come and gone, leaving menus in her wake.

Shaw sips steadily, her unfocused gaze following people passing back and forth or cars pulling into the lot outside visible through the front window, still agitated from the trial, wondering how pissed off Prito is right now. The DA will probably be in court until late afternoon, but Shaw digs out her phone and texts her *At least they didn't declare me hostile,* wishing the vodka would hurry the hell up and work its magic. Warm sense of well-being, where are you? Prito's a type-A personality all the way, always prepared, never looks the fool; but she obviously hadn't foreseen Shaw making an ass of herself up there today.

Shaw still hears the murmuring reaction to her little tirade on the stand, mixed with some laughter that spread through the gallery of the courtroom, the defendant himself cursing something under his breath, jerking his labels, straight-up machismo, followed by Feingold bringing the gavel down once—"Control your client, Mr. Stawarski. No second chances, is that clear? And Ms. Connolly, keep it less vivid, more precise, if you don't mind."

Not exactly on par with being held in contempt, but still. Shaw knows better. More precise, hell—let's face it, she'd let some sweaty glorified paralegal get under her skin, completely lost her cool, and ultimately made him—or his task of defending his client, anyway— more sympathetic to the jury. Big friggin' oops.

She's deep into her drink by the time McKenzie gets there; she'd let him know when she was on her way, but she wasn't sure where he was coming from on his day off. Home, wherever that was, or someplace else. He looks good, wearing jeans and a black all-weather parka, the sporty kind with all the bungees and grommets, an azure-patterned collar visible above the zipper. He probably smells good, too. Maybe not as good as Sunni.

He takes the seat across from her, looking at her mostly empty glass. "Sorry. I kept you waiting?"

She checks the time on her phone. "Look at that—only six minutes late. Time flies when you're drowning your sorrows. Get you one?"

"I may." He watches her take another long sip, her gaze still restless, roaming the room. "You all right?"

"I'm okay." She needs to come up with a snappy comeback to that question. "I made an ass of myself in court earlier." She gives a grudging jerk of her head. "I'm afraid that I hurt the case."

The waitress comes by, and McKenzie orders a stout, picking up a coaster and turning it in his fingers. "We've all been there. That's a defense attorney's job, to try to get you turned around. Some are better at it than others—"

"I actually knew that, you know? It's only the umpteenth time I've given testimony." She curses softly under her breath. "Shit, I'm sorry. I'm not trying to be a bitch. Just mad at myself. Everything's been going crazy all at once." Shaw works her lips over her teeth as the waitress returns with a bottle and a pint glass, waiting until the woman has left before leaning across the table toward him. "Listen, I don't want to waste your day off, so I won't take long." He starts to speak but she won't stop. "I guess what I need to know is if you're willing to talk with me off the record about something job related."

"Something internal?"

"No. Criminal. If you're not comfortable, there are other people I can go to, so don't feel obligated." A lie. She doesn't have another colleague she'd trust with this; as it is, Jewel only knows the most basic details of the Jane Doe discovery in the Rishworth woods, only the minimum of what Shaw had to tell her to request a couple personal days. It's not like Shaw and McKenzie are that close, and maybe that's part of the appeal: his lack of emotional investment in her life. "If I stick to the hypothetical, you feel like that would put us in the clear?"

He sips his beer, leans back. "I'm listening."

She takes a breath, releases it slowly, her stomach sloshing with acid, vodka and cranberry and no lunch. "Say I had somebody after me." She can't pause to check his expression, or she'll never finish. "Up until recently it was nothing but phone calls—and I've kept a digital log, date, time, all that—but now I've got reason to believe that this person followed me on at least one occasion. Probably many more."

"Did this hypothetical person approach you?"

"No. He stayed hidden." She pushes her glass away. "But he left me a note, essentially. And a GPS tracker stuck to the undercarriage of my car." She finally looks at him. "Crap. I forgot to say hypothetical that time."

McKenzie gazes back at her, his left forearm resting on the table, hand wrapped around his full glass, otherwise motionless. His eyes are brown, a deep and steady shade like the rich leather of a well-worn chair in a hushed study somewhere posh and studious where she would never find herself in a million years. "Hang hypothetical. Sounds like you've got a stalker."

She releases the last bit of air she's been holding on to. "Yeah. I guess I do."

"You've let the police know, gone through all the proper motions?"

"Yeah. I put up with the phone calls for a while. That's on me. I didn't let myself believe it would go this far. My ex thinks I'm being an idiot."

McKenzie half smiles. "That's why he's an ex."

Her smile flickers briefly. "Even with how toxic this guy sounded, I didn't . . . You got to understand . . . Look, do you know about my family?" She glances sharply at him. "My sister? I'm guessing somebody's probably told you around the watercooler." He shakes his head. "Huh. That's amazing. Okay, I'll run it down for you in thirty seconds flat. She went missing in 2007 when she was seventeen and we've never found her. A lot of assumptions and mistakes were made early on. The sheriff's office pretty much botched those first few precious days and weeks. By the time they admitted that there was probably foul play involved, everything was cold." She swallows. "You familiar with Mercer Brixton?"

"You're talking about former governor Mercer Brixton? About-to-run-again Governor Brixton?"

She nods. "Lucky us. He was sheriff of Aroostook County at the time. We lived in Rishworth, so Thea was his case. By the time it was turned over to the staties—a Detective Stephen York has it now, I've been in touch with him—she'd been missing five months."

"Christ. I'm sorry."

"Thanks. But you know how it is with cranks crawling out of the woodwork on a cold case. I wasn't even all that surprised that this particular shit was able to find my phone number somewhere. Dug it up online, probably through one of those people-searching sites I used myself to find what I could on him." She bites her lower lip, nodding. "But he felt different from the others, right from the beginning. Sincerely evil, you know? I'm not saying that I believe one hundred percent that he killed Thea. But I believe that he genuinely hates me. It comes off him like heat. I can't think of another reason for it other than . . . maybe he is the guy. He knows things about my family and details about her disappearance that I can't shrug off. Like he's been watching us for decades."

"How long has this been going on?"

"About a year and half." At this, McKenzie rubs his face with one roughened, red-knuckled hand. "On and off. He went underground for nine months or so, then got back in touch out of the blue a couple weeks ago. Since then, it's been random phone calls, any time of the day or night. I never know when it's coming. Then, on Sunday, I went on a hike to a place I associate with my sister. A place I've had reason to think she probably died. I challenged him the last time we talked, basically called him out as pathetic, dickless, told him never to call me again. He followed me there. And while I was in there . . . my dog found human skeletal remains in the woods." She holds her hand up. "It's not Thea. They've already ruled her out. The remains are too recent. But for a minute there, I thought we had her back."

"This is the Rishworth Jane Doe? That I did hear about around the watercooler. I never heard a word about your involvement."

She nods, maximizing a browser window she's left open on her phone and showing him the Amazon item page. "That's the kind of tracker he put under my car. Anybody can buy one online for sixty bucks. All-weather, real time, sends him a notification on his smartphone app whenever my vehicle moves, complete with a GPS map of my route. It can also go without a charge for almost two years. I have no idea how long it's been on there." She slides her phone back to her vantage point. "Now I'm trying to figure out what in hell to do next. I've already filed a complaint under the Protection from Harassment law."

McKenzie takes a drink. "Is he in the system?"

"Not that I know of, but I doubt any of the police involved will tell me straight up. No offense, but you guys play everything so close to the vest that victims' families are left wondering if everyone's forgotten about them, and I'd like to know who I'm dealing with here. It'd be nice to believe that if he had any really juicy priors, Steve York would've filled me in, but if the staties have access to information that's strictly need-to-know, I wouldn't put it past them to leave me in the cold." The waitress drifts by with a questioning air, and Shaw says to her, "Can I get something to soak this up?" Shaw gestures to her empty glass. "I'm not picky. Anything between a couple pieces of bread that won't bite back."

"Same for me," McKenzie says. After the young woman pulls a face and heads for the kitchen, McKenzie looks back to Shaw. "All educators in the state have to pass a background check and submit a ten-print card before they're brought on board. You could run a basic criminal history record check via the State Bureau of Information, see if he's been charged with anything since that date of hire you found, but you'll run into restrictions. If he's had records sealed or expunged, you'll never know. But you're right—if he's still employed as a teacher, he must at least make a good show of keeping his nose clean. Were you thinking maybe he was doing time during that period when he stopped calling you?" She shakes her head helplessly. "I'll run a check on him, let you know what turns up."

She looks back at him, her fist curled on the table, hardly noticing as sandwiches are plunked before them, though she instinctively eats a chip. "That's not why I asked you here." She winces. "Sounds like complete bullshit, doesn't it?"

He holds her gaze, smiling faintly. "Look. I'm in a position to help, and I'd like to. If getting some background on this guy will help you feel a little more secure, then I'm happy to dig up what I can."

"What if somebody questions why you were running a check on this guy who isn't linked to any active case?"

"The chances of that are slim to none. I'm not going to have IA getting narky over one background check. I'll get your answers for you, all right?"

Shaw takes a huge bite of her sandwich, aware that she has mayo on her face. "You're a peach, McKenzie. Without a stone. Anybody ever tell you that?"

"Not since me sainted mum." He peels back the top of his sandwich. "What am I looking at here?"

"Fancy a drive?" McKenzie asks. Shaw insisted on covering the bill, and now they're gathering their coats, ready to split off. "Clear our heads?"

"You mean mine. I'm safe to drive, don't worry."

"Just thought it might be nice. You don't have to get back right away, do you?"

"I've actually taken the whole day." Shaw gathers her hair out of her collar, stomach rolling a bit with nerves now instead of booze. "Okay. But no sexual favors, all right? I feel a headache coming on."

"Never crossed my mind."

McKenzie drives an old Ford Bronco with a spotless red and white two-tone paint job and vinyl bucket seats. "Be still my heart. Where did you find this?" Shaw pats the hood before she climbs into the passenger side. "God, this takes me back. Everybody and their uncle drove one of these when I was a little kid." She laughs. "With smiley face KC lights and jacked-up tires. The reboot SUV models got nothing on these."

He starts it up. "Most people's uncles drove them into the ground, too. It wasn't easy finding an 'eighty-six that's still inspectable. I bought this one from a woman down in New Hampshire. Always liked the look of them, so."

"A Scot ex-pat turned Mainer who's enamored with 1980s American auto design and tacky Hawaiian shirts. Talk about a mystery wrapped in an enigma wrapped in polyester covered in—" She reaches over to check his collar, her fingertip brushing his neck, soft with the slightest resistance of a fresh shave, and they both feel it, the resonance of her touch. "What are these, woody station wagons with surfboards?"

"Don't forget the little sailboats." He hangs his elbow over the back of his seat as he reverses into the parking lot. "Those struck me as a masculine touch."

"Mature, too." They smile together, looking out their separate windows. "So," Shaw says, "what's your story, morning glory? Why'd you come here, leave everything you knew behind? That's a big move."

McKenzie focuses on waiting for an opening in traffic before he pulls out. "It seemed like an adventure at the time. I used to be kind of obsessed with American culture. Just seemed like everything was happening here and nothing was happening where I was—that's Nethy Bridge, middle of nowhere—so I applied to Boston University as an international student and got in. Ended up switching majors to criminal justice. I was with the BPD for fourteen years. Relocated here looking for a slower pace, smaller scale. Guess I saw all the action that I cared to."

She examines him while his eyes are on the road. "Get back across the pond often?"

"Every five years or so. My mum's still in the house I grew up in. And I've got a brother in Plockton."

"Now let me ask you this. If I yanked open a random closet in your house, would bagpipes and a kilt with one of those hairy cod pieces fall out?"

McKenzie laughs. "You mean a sporran? No, no. I suppose I wear my Scottish pride on the inside."

Conversation reaches a natural lull. "I can't help looking for Mr. Cloyd's dog," Shaw says after a few minutes, as they drive down a back road. "Know what I mean? The odds are one in a million, but I keep hoping it might run out in front of me one of these days, hungry, looking for home."

McKenzie nods, braking at a STOP sign. "Did you want to make a pass of the crime scene?"

"Yeah, actually." She's never spent much free time with anyone else who does the job, a little unsure of what to do with the lack of resistance or shaming for always having at least half her mind on a case. When was the last time she and Ryan wanted to do or even talk about the same thing at the same time, without that sense of resentment and exasperation radiating from him, followed by her flying off the handle at the slightest sign of criticism, sick of being punished for something she didn't see how she could help. It was hard to pinpoint when they'd stopped sharing interests besides the boys and started to drift from each other; she'd been frankly blindsided that Friday morning she'd found him standing in the kitchen doorway right after Beau and Casey had gotten on the bus, looking oddly staged, his expression both tense and hardened. *We've got to talk.*

And after their argument the other night in the garage, it all seems so broken. Thea's not going anywhere; neither is Dad. Short of a frontal lobe lobotomy, neither is Shaw herself, and according to Ryan these days, she's their biggest obstacle. Jesus. They used to be buddies—shoot the shit and sink some beers together and just love the boys. This is what the burned-out end of that looks like, her own life as some flickering tearjerker film reel with a Joe Cocker tune laid over it. Fuck a duck.

Now, after a twenty-minute drive to Houghton, McKenzie pulls onto the dirt shoulder alongside Round Pond, nothing left to indicate to a passerby that the killing ever happened unless they notice the single scrap of crime scene tape clinging to a stake toward the back of the clearing nearest the woods.

They stare out the window at the scene. "Now I'm going to have to get out." Shaw looks at him. "We're good to walk around?"

"Yeah, more than good. We finished processing the scene over a week ago. There's no damage that you and I can do that the elements haven't already done." McKenzie pops his seat belt free.

They walk independently of each other around the scene, probably a strange sight from the road, like planets in opposite orbits, but neither needs company in that moment, both caught up in their own thoughts.

Shaw walks out onto the ice where Mr. Cloyd's hat was found, standing, looking down at the opaque surface that shows nothing but the faintest shading of her form blocking the thin daylight. She lifts her head, calls, "Did our guys test this area for chemical compounds like you find in pepper sprays?"

"None found. Not on the ground, the leash, or Mr. Cloyd himself."

She exhales slowly, looking at the woods. "How far a walk is the Cloyd residence, anyway? Think I can manage it in my go-to-town shoes?"

Bernard Cloyd's home is a modest saltbox-style house with cedar shingles. There's a tidy look to the entire property: fresh paint on the trim and shutters, a one-car garage with a large put-to-bed vegetable garden alongside it, and a chain-link pen for Grieco.

A plastic insulated doghouse is positioned toward the back corner of the pen, and Shaw can discern a rubber Kong toy lying near the entrance and another toy of knotted rope near the gate. There are no close neighboring houses; the road is heavily wooded except for the cleared lots the houses sat back on, only mailboxes visible at the end of dirt driveways.

Shaw checks the time on her phone: fourteen minutes from here to the pond. McKenzie, who had walked slightly behind, hands in his coat pockets, stops beside her now at the edge of the yard as she checks the time on her phone. "So, this was his daily routine with the pooch, right? Down the road, past the pond, and then back again?"

"Basically. Creature of habit, as you'd guessed. He really didn't have any close associates that we've been able to find, but his neighbors confirmed they'd see him walking his dog daily. In short, he was a quiet man, and every other unhelpful cliché in the book." He gestures toward the house. "The inside's minimalist, neat. He even kept his email account wiped down to nothing. Tech's still working on his desktop computer, trying to recover what they can."

Shaw stands with her hands on her hips, the haze of the drink mostly gone now, thanks to the sandwich and the walk. "Then it's got to be about the dog. Right?"

"How's that? He wasn't worth anything to speak of. Not particularly lovely-looking, either. There's a picture of him stuck to the fridge inside. Yes, he's a purebred, but there's no reason to think that Cloyd participated in the show world. Plus, Grieco was big. Not a creature most people would want to tangle with, especially right after they'd assaulted his owner."

"But they didn't tangle. Or at least there's no evidence of it. No blood found at the scene except Mr. Cloyd's, no sign of pepper sprays or Tasers used. Did anybody on the road ever report hearing a dog barking around that time?" She watches McKenzie shake his head. "So, Grieco knew the person." She shrugs at his skeptical look. "I mean, Occam's razor, right? Nothing stands out about this old duffer except the fact that his dog, the center of his life, is missing. If the dog doesn't have monetary or status value for anyone else, it has to be emotional."

"The man retired over six years ago. He's been divorced for nearly ten, and the ex-wife's since remarried. We haven't found anyone close enough to him to have formed a connection like that to Grieco. No kids. No friends. Sorry, but the dog is most likely dead, chucked aside as an obstacle to killing his master."

She presses her lips together, shaking her head. "Bet you fifty bucks he's alive. You find the dog, you'll find your killer. Ba-da-bing."

"Ba-da-boom. Let's head back."

"Leave the detecting to the detectives, is that what you're saying?" She steps it up a little to keep pace with him. "It's not all black powder and brushes in my line of work, you know. A keen deductive mind is a must."

"I don't doubt it."

"Aw, now you're trying to spare my feelings. Who's the dog mom here?" He glances over, trying to hold back a smile, and now she's walking faster than him. "He would've at least barked. I'm tellin' you."

Shaw misses the boys so badly it hurts and decides to surprise Beau after practice, since Casey's already off the bus and back home with Dad at this point. It'll save the old man a trip back into town.

She waits in the parking lot in the Beast rather than try to penetrate the high school's sadly necessary fortress-like security measures to catch the last few minutes of Beau and his teammates running drills and dogging it through laps. As she sits, Roma Prito's response to her earlier text finally pops up: *You're fine. Stawarski's so green he's in danger of tripping over his umbilical. Feingold just wanted to see what he can do. Montez mouthed off again, booted for the duration. We got this. See you soon to prep for the Peters trial, 2/7.*

Shaw taps the horn lightly as Beau emerges from the rear gym exit with two of his friends, her boy's joggers and hoodie visible beneath his unzipped coat, sports bag slung crossbody, his fringe of shower-damp hair plastered to his brow by his hood.

He calls 'bye to his friends and trots over to climb in with her, smelling of cold air, the deodorant she buys him, and faintly rank sneakers. "What're you doing here?" He says it amiably enough for a jock with a b-ball impaired mother; she's rarely known him to be anything but easygoing, even with teenage hormones in full bloom. As the oldest, he's the kid who remembers when they didn't have anything, were living in a tiny second-story apartment while Ryan worked in an autobody shop and Shaw rang up groceries part-time, spending evenings after Beau was asleep doing her coursework, a couple class credits at a time to earn her forensic science Bachelor's degree after it hit her, at twenty, that there wasn't any job she considered worth doing other than catching bad guys. So, Beau had been through more upheaval than Casey, who'd never known anything but the farmhouse they'd bought at foreclosure and relative financial stability and having Ryan home full-time, running the shop he'd managed to start up with a loan from his former boss at the autobody place, who'd been more like a dad to him than his real father had ever been. Maybe those early years had left Beau more resilient, more able to roll with life's little gaffs and pratfalls.

"I had the rest of the day free after court." Shaw watches him jam his bag into the back seat. "I called Mickey's Quickey and ordered a couple of pizzas to pick up on the way home." He snorts, rubbing his eyes. "What? I didn't name the place. Mickey did, whoever he may be."

As she pulls out into the street, her gaze goes to the rearview mirror, something she hasn't been able to resist since discovering the tracker; every parked or passing vehicle holds an irresistible draw, making her wonder if it could be Anders, what he drives, if that's the kind of info McKenzie will be willing to hand over to her. Behind them now is a white minivan with a silhouette of cluttered air fresheners visible through the windshield; unlikely choice.

Beau gets out his phone, scrolling quietly as they drive. "Mads says hey."

"Oh, so she'll talk to you, but not me, huh?" Shaw shifts grumpily. "Well, hey right back at her."

He doesn't speak for a moment. "Have you talked to Dad?"

She's startled, her conscience tricking her into thinking that he somehow knows about today, with McKenzie, the long goodbye in the cab of his car, the loaded pauses where they simply looked at each other. *I'm going to need his name,* McKenzie had finally said, reminding her that she still hadn't filled him in on Anders beyond "he" or "this guy." She'd written Anders's name and his old home address she'd gotten from running the online person search down on a scrap of paper and tucked it into McKenzie's coat pocket, not even wanting to take the chance of texting it, leaving any kind of digital trail that could be dug up by techs during an internal investigation, were there ever to be one, the day punctuated by her blurting "See you 'round," and practically leaping out into the Patel's parking lot to hurry to her car. "About what?"

"I dunno. Anything." He shrugs, eyes on the phone again. "After the other night, I thought one of you would . . . I dunno. Never mind."

"No, wait a minute. Don't shut me down, okay?" Shaw looks back to the road, setting her shoulders. "It got ugly the other night. He's mad at me, thinks that I screwed up our marriage by being too distant, spending time and energy on the wrong stuff. Maybe he's right. I don't know how to fix it. That's as straight as I can be with you." She stops at a red light on the way to the small shopping center where the take-out place is, and she looks at Beau before the light changes. "Pissed at me?"

"No." Now he's annoyed. "I know it's not just your fault. Dad was being a jerk, too. He spent all his time being mad at you and not talking about it. Then it was too late, and all you guys did was fight. But not about what you should've been fighting about. You know?"

"Yep. I know." She gives his knee a small shake—crazy, the size of that kneecap now, a handful, bigger than her own. "Fresh out of answers, kiddo. I'm sorry, is all."

Beau's gaze is trained on the screen. "I wish he'd come home. Especially with this guy bothering you. He should be with us." She tries to glean any sign of tears in his eyes, but supposes he's too old for that, his hide toughened by those early years, not to mention plenty of practice burying emotional responses to maintain respect from other guys. Maybe respect from her, too. Not like she's a shining example of transparency and emotional health.

Never thought to beat herself up about that one before; now she's off, and the idea leaves her mired in maternal guilt for the rest of the ride. She hands Beau her debit card as he heads into Mickey's with zero threats of recrimination for buying the place out. Let him have as many Cokes as he wants, for God's sake. Let him have the moon.

13

nders calls at first light or, technically, a little before, the window a vaguely distinguishable rectangle in the ashen dimness of Shaw's bedroom. Her reflection in the mirror is a dark unfamiliar thing, something she watches with swollen-eyed detachment as it mimics her movement, holding the phone for several rings until Shaw comes to a decision and puts it to her ear.

"I want you to know that your ass is mine now," Shaw says quietly. "No contact means no contact, bucko. Remember that little piece of paper those deputies hand-delivered to you? You were supposed to read that. It had all kinds of fun facts in it. Like how you're not supposed to come within a hundred yards of me or contact me in any way or they take away your shoelaces and put you in a little cage with a door that's very hard to open."

"Ah, but they'll have to catch me first. Isn't that the expression?"

"I'll be on the phone to the sheriff's office next." She swallows, staring ahead, her chin nearly touching her chest, the hem of the wool blanket rough beneath her jaw. "Why'd you give me your prints?"

"Did I? Well, I suppose I'm at peace with you having them. I don't want there to be any barriers left between us. Wearing a glove would've been so much less intimate, don't you think?" Anders pauses. "Have you looked me up in your system yet?"

"Nope."

"Whyever not?"

"Because I think you know that it would be unethical for me to use the lab for personal reasons, and you're hoping I'll get caught at it."

"But the temptation must be overwhelming. Here I am, handing you my past on a platter, allowing you to truly know me, and you're refusing to act. Hardly the terrier-like tenacity I've come to expect."

"Yeah, but, as Professor Jansen, your record has to be clean, doesn't it? Otherwise, you'd be working a fry-o-lator somewhere instead of getting your rocks off teaching co-eds that Plato isn't the stuff that came in the nifty little yellow canisters back in pre-school." He's quiet, and she props herself up against the headboard, adjusting the pillow. "I'm not saying I haven't done any looking into you, understand."

"Allow me a moment to savor this—are you telling me that you know where I live, Shaw?" More of that contained, vibratory laughter, ending in a sigh. "Please tell me you're wearing a trench coat and exuding an air of world-weary virtue."

"And if you think that's easy to do while lying down . . ." She tucks her free arm around herself, gazing at her shadow form in the mirror, at rest. "I've been asking around about you. Meeting up with an old acquaintance or two, seeing if they remember anything about a suspicious older man hanging around giving them smarm chills back in 2007."

"Hmm. Old acquaintances. Not many left in the area these days. Unless, of course, you mean that shell of a man who hides in the trailer with the old woman. Tinkering, day and night, to keep from ending it all."

"Did you follow me that night, too? Before I found the tracker?"

Silence. "Do you know who I found in Beggar's Meadow, Anders? It's not Thea, so who is she?" No response. "Did you put her there?"

The quiet drags on too long, but when Shaw is almost ready to hang up, he speaks: "Do you want me to tell you what Thea was wearing that night? April sixth, 2007. I'm talking about undergarments. It's not public knowledge, you know. Not part of the online Thea lore, like the white hoodie and pink tank top and jeans."

Shaw shuts her eyes. "How the hell am I going to know what kind of underwear my sister had on sixteen years ago?"

"Well, I have them right here. They're laid out on the table in front of me."

She stares at the mirror, where burgeoning daylight has finally given her features, a dull gleam on her hair. "Oh, really. Why do I think that if I FaceTimed you right now, it'd be you sitting there in a filthy undershirt under a bare bulb with jack shit on the table except maybe a bottle of Wild Turkey?"

"Your parents went cheap, not surprisingly. If she were mine, I would've bought her the finer things, but . . . as it was, cotton and synthetic lace were the best Mom and Dad could do." A pause. "I kept these, after. The rest of her clothes I did away with. Just threw them in a public trash can." He clears his throat. "The bra and underwear don't match. The bra size is a 34B, white, covered in the cheap, scratchy lace I mentioned, and one of the hooks is bent. The underwear is size four, pink, with a floral pattern and a depressing little bow that hangs there by one stitch."

"Not exactly Frederick's of Hollywood, but I guess deviants can't be choosers. And without verification, this is you beating off for an audience. 'Bye."

"I expect," he continues, "that a crime lab might be able to get something from the underwear. Traces of her. And of me. To verify, as you said. Proof of what transpired that night. I've handled them some over the years, but the things forensic science can do these days." *Tsks.* "But then I suppose I don't need to tell you."

Shaw's quiet a moment. "Are you making me an offer?"

"Well . . . I can't *give* them away. The sentimental value is price-less. We'll have to think of it as . . . more of a reward. In the end. To the victor go the spoils." At her stymied silence, he speaks closer to the receiver, slowly, with disdain: "You have to earn them."

"What 'end'? What're you talking about?"

"There's a natural timeline to all things—and I firmly believe this—a life cycle. Even for you and me. Perhaps especially us. We've hit a critical point where we must evolve or die." He breathes for a moment. "I'm choosing evolution. Time for us to grow, Shaw. Expand into new areas. I'm not going to be satisfied to watch and wait and carry on these little sparring sessions much longer, espe-cially now that you've insisted upon involving the police. When you think about it, our lives have been entwined for almost two decades. Imagine, never moving beyond the hand-holding stage in a relationship as long standing as ours."

She presses herself back against the headboard a moment, sum-moning strength. "Jesus, you must be hung like a kangaroo rat—either come out and say you're going to kill me or stop wasting my time."

"You seem preoccupied with my manhood, which leads me to believe that it captivates you." She gives a genuine laugh, which he ignores, talking right over it, "What I'm talking about is offering closure. A sense of an ending. Don't you feel better already, be-lieving that your destiny has already been mapped out for you by a higher power? Churches everywhere are relying on it. Since I know you've lapsed, consider me that power. I'll urge you into a corner and we'll see what happens. And . . . in the unlikely event that you come out on top, you'll have your proof."

"I want Thea. Give her back and we'll be square. I'll forget all about eviscerating you and hanging you from the nearest tree by your small intestines, Scout's honor." Shaw waits with her jaw clenched, the silence dragging out. "Anders?"

"I've given you everything you need to get your answers. It's not my fault that I know your own life better than you do."

"Do we have a deal or not?"

"Hmm. How much is my word worth? Impossible for you to know. We'll just have to find out."

"I have a gun. I'll use it."

"I'm sure you will." Then comes the soft sound of the disconnect.

She sits for a long moment before calling the sheriff's office, the phone resting in her lap, her boys' silent presences on either side of the bedroom walls, soft breathing, deep and undisturbed innocence. Total trust.

Again, Shaw's riveted to the rearview as she drives to work, wondering if Anders could be tailing her, wondering how quickly deputies would be dispatched to arrest him for violating the protection order. Anders may be sleeping in right now, resting his depraved little head while she has kittens all the way along her daily commute. Too bad she can't be there when he hears the knock on the door. She's the kind of tired that aches, remembered from when the boys were tiny and waking up five times a night to nurse, her eyes sore and sandy, her head too heavy for her aching neck. Ibuprofen and a coffee IV loom in her immediate future.

Her phone rings as she pulls into the lab parking lot and she snatches it up, glimpsing McKenzie's name. "Your ears must be burning. I was mentally willing you to call while telling myself I couldn't expect you to put everything else on hold in favor of my problem." She glances at the still-rising sun on the horizon. "What, you beating the early bird to the worms this morning? My God, man."

"I came in early, wanted to take advantage of the peace to check out your guy. I figured you'd like answers first thing. I know I would." He clears his throat. "I emailed you some results."

"He does have a record, then?"

"No arrests. You're right, the university wouldn't have him otherwise, and the flagship campus is his last known place of employment. He's got a more recent home address than what you found, though. Right over in Millburn."

It hits hard, the proximity. Millburn is two towns over from Axtel. "You're kidding." Her voice sounds thin, inflectionless. "Well, it shouldn't matter. He called me this morning, violated the protection order, and I turned him in."

"Glad to hear it. For what it's worth, I've got his home address for you and the make and model of the vehicle registered under his name. Gray Dodge Charger, right off the assembly line. He got it about three months ago."

"So that's it. He's clean."

"No record isn't proof of innocence. I've dug up what I can so far, but even an expedited FBI background check takes time. If he's had something expunged or sealed, it'll turn up."

"I thought expunged meant it was erased forever."

"For employers and landlords, yes. But law enforcement can still get a peek." He pauses. "I'm glad he'll be off the streets. These obsessive types tend to become dangerous when they see that they can't control you through intimidation alone."

She exhales shakily. "And I've got my boys and my dad living with me. I've been trying to keep a lid on all this Anders crap, handle it myself, but it's gone beyond that now." She pauses. "He likes to say that I can't protect them, like I didn't protect my sister."

"It wasn't your job to protect her. You were a kid yourself."

"Doesn't matter. Fairness, learning to forgive myself—none of that shit helps. Being rational has nothing to do with it, you know? Love's not rational. Thea was a piece of me, and somebody ripped her out and now I want to make him hurt like I do. Worse. I want him to die screaming. I want to throw him down a few flights of stairs, maybe use his skull as a planter. I've got an African violet that needs re-potting." She pushes the heel of her palm against the tears burning her eyes. "So, am I crazy? As bad as him? Who's even making that judgment?" McKenzie is silent, and Shaw grips her brow, her elbow propped on the windowsill. "You didn't hear any of that, copper."

"You sound like you've convinced yourself that Anders is the guy."

"I hope to hell he is. It's a lot easier than hating smoke, some idea of a monster who could take a kid from her family forever. Gives me something to focus on. And if he knows anything about that woman in the woods, I guess the cops will get to the bottom of it sooner or later."

McKenzie releases a heavy breath. "Will you be all right?"

"There's that question again. What if I say no?"

"I'll say I'm here for you. Anytime."

"I appreciate it. Really. You've already helped a lot. I'll see you." She quietly ends the call, realizing she'll be late if she doesn't hustle inside the lab.

Shaw scans her badge, takes the stairs up to Latent Prints, and heads for her desk, seeing Gauthier glance up at the same moment that Jewel moves from her open office doorway to intercept her. "Shaw. Can I see you a moment?"

Inside Jewel's office, Shaw sits in the hot seat again, setting her bag on the floor by her feet. "What's up?"

"Have you seen this?" Jewel clicks around on her laptop, then swivels the screen around so that Shaw can see the YouTube video playing.

She recognizes herself at the double-murder scene, a video taken from a distance and far shakier than the other one she'd seen, Shaw scrambling up from the ground while the dirty rabbits pelt out from the foundation, uniforms slipping around on the snow and ice, the one guy crashing onto his derriere.

Laughter escapes Shaw in a gasp, a big, hysterical burst of tension, and she slaps her hand over her mouth. Slowly, she focuses in on Jewel's unamused expression and her laughter dries to a trickle, hand lowering to her lap. "Sorry. Not funny but funny. Amiright?" Jewel's look is unwavering. "I've been known to be wrong."

"Going viral as the keystone cops isn't what I consider a good look for the district. I'm not alone in that. And it's doubly unfortunate that your mask was down at the time, so you can be identified by people in the know." Jewel pauses the video, leaving Gauthier and Shaw frozen in a desperate embrace. "I received a phone call from Harriet Van Sickle. She, at least, is taking this very seriously. She's got Tech working on tracing the person who posted this using a dummy account, with full intent of pursuing legal action against them in any way she can maneuver. And she had some questions as to why you and Lydia were outside investigating the foundation in the first place."

So much for the sisterhood of the iron maidens. "I wasn't—it was never an investigation. I'd seen signs of animals, pets, inside the house, but I hadn't been able to locate them, so I checked outside. I had no idea they were under the house. Or that there'd be five million of them. Gauthier happened to notice through the window that I was in trouble and helped me to my feet." Shaw puts her hand to her heart. "Mea culpa. Truly. Sincerest apologies." She stands.

"Next time you have a concern about endangered animals at a scene"—Jewel raises her voice a decibel above normal speaking range, making Shaw stop where she is—"mention an issue like that to a uniform. Let them handle it. We need your skills elsewhere. Clear enough?"

"Absolutely. Yes."

"Shaw." Jewel leans back in her chair to regard her.

"Yes."

"How did court go yesterday?"

"Good. Fine, bracing day in court. Prito seems confident."

Jewel studies her a second longer. "If you don't mind me saying, you look exhausted. And you seem very on edge. Have you heard anything about the identification of the remains you found?"

"Uh, yeah. It's not her—not my sister. They're a long way from an ID, is my understanding."

Jewel's expression remains unchanged, but she nods. "I'm sorry. That must be incredibly hard. I may not be HR, but my door is always open. And if you'd feel more comfortable speaking with someone from that department, I can arrange a meeting. Let me know what you need." Shaw nods once in return as Jewel straightens her posture. "I'm afraid that I'm going to have to send you back out again. There's been another fire, and Tran is tied up processing items from the last. Lydia's assisting him, but I'd appreciate it if you'd bring her along for the sake of experience. I appreciate you being clutch in her training, by the way. She seems to be coming along."

"Pleasure's all mine. And—wow. The firebug's escalating hard."

"With no pattern as to the type of building he's choosing, either, which is making it extremely difficult to predict where he'll hit next." Jewel rubs her brow with one hand, texting Shaw the location to the latest scene. "It's ranged from an apartment building to a diner after hours, nothing to link them other than they're in isolated areas and lack security."

"Whenever opportunity knocks, huh. On it." Shaw goes straight out, feeling Jewel's gaze following.

"Hi, kids." She joins Tran and Gauthier in the lab, finding them both standing by a work surface with strips of ragged-edged duct tape laid out before them.

Tran's gaze goes significantly toward the glass pane in the wall, which looks onto the outer office. "Everything all right?"

"That's what I keep trying to tell everyone."

"O-kay, sassy lassy. Last time I make an effort."

Shaw looks at Gauthier, forces a smile and a wink, meant to be reassuring, but the younger woman stares back, two lines between her brows. Then she blinks agitatedly and looks down, and Shaw realizes that Gauthier's probably already had her own visit to the principal's office this morning.

As Tran readies chemicals in a plastic tub for the mixer, Shaw stands back, checking out the various bottles on the table. "Ooh, you've got her working with crystal violet. And hey—he already knows this, but I've got dibs on that as my stripper stage name, so no stealing it—" She squeezes Gauthier's shoulder—ad-libbing, distracted by the craziness of the morning—and feels the young woman jerk under her touch, almost involuntarily, out from under Shaw's hand.

There's a stunned moment, Tran staring at them openly through his safety glasses.

"Sorry. I'm sorry." Gauthier's gaze is on the table, impossible to tell much around her air filter mask, but her eyes are wide, directed at the floor.

Shaw's already shaking her head. "No, my fault. I should keep my stupid self to myself." She shoots a quick warning look at Tran not to blurt out whatever's first on his mind and tries to move on while Gauthier continues to keep her gaze down. "Is that tape from the last arson scene? Gauthier and I are on our way out to the latest."

"Mm-hmm. He always ditches the gas can off-scene and it looks like he got desperate last time and used an old one he had lying around, patched it with this stuff. I'm hoping he was in a rush and slapped it over the crack in the can before he put on his gloves."

Gauthier finally raises her eyes to the doubled-over loop at the end of one strip, seeming to deliberately seal Shaw out of her peripheral view. "Can we try to unstick it from itself before I go?"

"Okay, but don't, like, go crazy, okay? Slow and steady or we could stretch the tape and distort the prints, if there are any." Tran calls back to Shaw as she turns, "And hands off the chamber. I've got an AR-15 cooking."

"Yum. Don't you worry, I'm basically out of here." Shaw turns to Gauthier, talking fast, pretending like the awkwardness of the girl seeming repelled by her touch never happened. "Jewel wants us on the Alburgh scene, pronto. No stiffs, just stuff, done extra crispy. You calling shotgun?"

"Do you want to ride together?"

"Why not. I've got plenty of room in my Beast. You'll be my wingwoman. Or I'll be yours. Whatever."

The Alburgh fire is about a twenty-five-minute drive northeast from the lab, an antique shop or junk shop, depending on your perspective, which used to house a locally owned department store when Shaw was growing up. Today, she can't get close: the street is closed off with sawhorses and uniforms at both ends. She and Gauthier end up parking two streets over, pulling on their coveralls and grabbing their kits for the walk.

The façade of the antique shop is gone, blackened timbers stretching up to where the second floor used to be before it collapsed during the fire, which raged most of the very early morning, fire crews blasting it with hoses from the trucks that remain along each curb, in case of a flare-up.

Shaw lifts the scene tape for Gauthier, saying offhandedly, "Brace yourself. Arson is the worst," as they duck underneath and head across the pavement, water black with ash and debris still rushing steadily in the gutter.

After checking in with the team leader, she spots McKenzie with his mask hanging down. Shaw experiences some percolating sensations she tries to put a lid on as she heads over, compelled to put up a brazen front now that she's facing him so soon after their soul-bearing conversations. She speaks a bit louder than caution permits: "You stud dick on this one?"

He turns fully, smiling in that way he has, with the sad lines. "For the moment. Fire marshall's just got here, then it'll be his show."

"And then you turn back into a regular stud, like the coach into a pumpkin, huh?"

"I've resigned myself to that inevitability."

The things they want to say to each other—Anders, the rest of it—are too much to take on right now with the volume of work to be done and Gauthier absorbing every second like all she's missing is a balcony seat and a box of Jujubes, so Shaw breezes on by McKenzie with, "Nobody at home?"

"Quite the contrary. The owner and his wife live upstairs. Smoke detectors woke them up, but they were lucky to get out the back door before it ate through the stairs."

"Boy howdy. Fire number four, correct?" Shaw says. "One of these days, a propane tank is going to blow, and we'll lose a lot more than some old birdcages and butter churns. All due respect and everything." Shaw never stops walking, heading off over the heaps of fallen blackened timbers, chunks of drywall, and other scorched hunks of detritus from the shop. She finally glances over to see Gauthier looking back at McKenzie and then pointedly at Shaw. "Do as I say, not as I do. Always remember that, kitten."

"I'll add it to my notes."

Shaw grins, Gauthier surprising her again with one of those unexpected deadpan funnies. Then Shaw stops and sniffs, glances around, watching a couple of firefighters talking with some deputies, everyone in hardhats in case of more structural collapse. "You can smell the gasoline, can't you? Even through the mask." When Gauthier doesn't answer, Shaw looks over to see the younger woman squatting to open her kit near her feet. Shaw lowers herself down to the same level. "Just jumping in? Not waiting for my kernels?"

"I appreciate your kernels. But it seems like I should be able to get started on my own by now. I mean, unless you think—"

"No, no. By all means. Keep going. Doing good."

Shaw stands, watching as a paunchy man in a fireman's helmet, anorak, and rubber boots enters the scene. Don Hale, sergeant with the Office of State Fire Marshal. "Okay. There's often not a lot for us at a scene like this, though we'll see what we can do about soot removal with Mikrosil paste back at the lab. Most of the water in a fingerprint deposit evaporates at these temperatures, and the sprinklers and hoses take their toll, but it's possible we'll find something of value. They'll be sorting through this weenie roast for days."

Shaw and Gauthier work for several hours, always careful where they set their feet, Shaw aware of Hale and McKenzie talking in the background as Hale does a walk-through and checks out burn patterns. Shaw collects a number of cards, though most likely the prints will be cleared as belonging to the owner or other employees. Any footprints left in the snow by the arsonist are now buried under rubble or trampled by firefighters and other first responders. Arson is truly the worst.

"Okay, let's head back to the lab with what we've got, start running them through the system," Shaw says to Gauthier, resisting her natural impulse to bump shoulders or do something equally chummy and unwanted. "I know Tran said the guy's religious with gloves and we haven't had any luck yet, but you never know.

Something's got to break eventually, right?" Shaw fastens the clasp on her kit lid, and she and Gauthier leave the scene together, both stopping to pull off their soot-blackened shoe covers so they don't go flying on a patch of ice along the sidewalk.

"When did this guy start setting fires?" Gauthier keeps pace with Shaw as they head down the side street toward where Shaw parked.

"Last fall, I think. Started small, no big loss, but now he's mixing it up. The news has been all over this one, and anybody could tell you that the guy's probably pouring over the reports and articles, getting that sexual contact high off the footage and photos. Typical arsonist profile, young, white, socially awkward male with low self-confidence, so getting all this attention is—wait for it—adding fuel to the fire, nyuck. He won't stop. We'll have to catch him, that's all."

At lunchbreak back at the lab, Shaw makes for the outdoors, craving total privacy, going to the picnic tables on the green in the center of the complex, ostensibly meant for lunch in the warmer months but mostly belonging to the few hard-core smokers who work at BCFS, who shuffle out thrice daily to pretend they find the eye-watering wind stimulating while they feed the nicotine monkey.

A text from McKenzie, sent about forty minutes ago: *How're you holding up?*

Her mouth is dry, stomach a little fluttery, just a fool in the rain—there were a few frozen pellets nipping down at her now: *Like a piñata at a five-year-old's bday party, how's by you?* No immediate response; busy again, no doubt.

There's also a DM from Mads: *I hate asking, but can I borrow some money? I'll pay you back with interest.*

Shaw pauses, standing halfway between the table and door,

knowing Mads would never ask if she had any other option. *Of course. How much?*

$500. This really sucks. Sorry.

Shaw pictures her baby sister with her mouth ground down, agonizing over this more out of pride than anything because of how she sees Shaw. When are they going to get out of this teenager-resenting-mom-figure stage and get on with being friends? *I'd give you the heart out of my chest if you needed it,* Shaw thinks. *Don't say sorry.*

Shaw decides to hell with it, get in there, get nosy. *Everything ok?*

A longer wait. *Things blew up with Brooklyn. She's a selfish slob, doesn't help out with anything. I've even been cleaning her stupid cat's box lately. I moved out. Some of my stuff is still there but I'm gone.*

Are you sleeping on somebody's couch?

No answer. Meaning floor.

Shaw pauses, struggling against her natural inclination to open mouth, insert foot. *I'll send you some cash online right now.* She does so, adding an extra three hundred because Mads never asks for as much as she needs regardless of what it is; she was a self-serve kid, quietly and studiously navigating the coves and inlets of her grieving household, who grew into a wry, at times scathing teen during Shaw's frequent pop-ins at the old house to help where she could, often flopping down on the end of Mads's bed for girl talk, which Mads had absolutely no use for. Let's face it: Mads got screwed out of the simple joys of childhood by being fast-forwarded to emotional middle age, while Shaw herself hit a wall in her teens, remaining as emotionally gawky as a gangling filly. Maybe she couldn't imagine maturing along with a future that Thea would never be a part of, so she'd sabotaged herself by acting like an ass all the time. If Shaw never grew up inside, then Thea could always live inside her. There. Who needs therapy.

Shaw calls Mads. Her sister's eventual response is a sigh into the speaker.

"Couldn't pretend you weren't around to hear your phone ring this time, could you?" Shaw hears Dad in her voice too late, remembers what Mads accused her of last time they talked.

"Guess not. Thanks for the loan." Mads sounds tired.

"What are big sisters for, other than disapproving of all your choices and prying into your personal affairs?" Shaw's pacing the ground, her boots crunching on the snow. "Look, do you need a place to stay?"

"No. I'm with friends."

"Who don't really have room for you, right? Let me guess. One of those typical apartment houses on College Avenue, split into as many bedrooms as the zoning codes will allow, with twenty-four-seven foot traffic passing through the living room and half the time you don't even know who it is perching on your futon arm to eat ramen at two-thirty in the morning?"

"It's not like I have a lot of choice, okay? It was very cool of them to let me stay."

"Agreed, but you're not going to get any more studying or sleeping done there than you were at Brooklyn's place, right? I know you've got the bookstore job, but you can't afford a place on your own, can you?"

"Obviously not, since I had to borrow money from you." Mads takes a breath. "I'll save up. Find somebody else looking for a roommate. People are always advertising around here." She pauses. "I almost wish Dad wasn't renting the old house. I could stay there and cope with the long commute for a while."

Shaw stops, staring off at the building. "Okay, I'm just going to say this. Don't bite my head off until I'm done talking. We'd love to have you stay at the house with us for as long as you want. We've got the space. Dad doesn't even use his bed, or Casey would love sharing half his room with you—"

"Oh, that's smart, using Case—"

"Yeah, not finished. We want you here, but there's something you've got to know." Shaw steels herself. "I've been having more problems with that guy I told you about, who was calling me. I took out a protection order against him and he violated it pretty much right away. They're taking him into custody today—I'm waiting for an update—but I didn't want to ask you to stay without telling you the whole story. Stephen York is coming over tonight around six to talk with us."

"Who?"

"Stephen. The detective on Thea's case."

"I thought it was John something."

"John something retired. Stephen took his case load." She's a little stunned that her sister doesn't remember this. "I think it might be nice if the whole family was there to show support for Thea and hear what Stephen's got to say. Sorry. You know I don't like playing the guilt card." Shaw gauges her sister's silence. "You can spend the night if you want or drive back to your friend's place after we talk with Stephen. Up to you."

Mads is quiet a moment, then says, "Okay. I'll be there," in an unreadable tone.

"Bitchin'."

"Don't say that." Shaw's doing a poor job at containing her laughter and Mads makes a frustrated half-laughing sound. "I'm coming early so you can feed me supper, and I'm not bringing anything, either. I'm broke, remember?"

"If I don't, my checking account does." With a *ha* into the speaker, Shaw crams in, "Love you, sis," before cutting Mads off, feeling the low pummel of her heartbeat, clutching the phone to the center of her chest for a moment. Then she calls Ryan.

14

That evening, Stephen arrives a few minutes early in a dusk full of light snow, wearing a black woolen topcoat that shows the flakes like a fine spray of paint. "Hi, everyone," he says easily, glancing around at their faces, not seeming surprised to find Shaw, Dad, Mads, even the dog, all standing in the entryway restlessly, as if ready to set upon him, unsure what to do with themselves in the half hour after supper before the state police detective was due to arrive.

"Here, let me take that." Dad uses gruffness to cover the fact that he's badly shaken as he hangs Stephen's coat on the rack.

Beau and Casey are upstairs with the promise of an extra hour of screen time, but the boys were uncertain about heading to their rooms, finally trooping up the steps with a couple of backward glances. She'll be answering a barrage of questions later.

"Appreciate it, Eddie." Stephen shakes Dad's hand, which seems to ground the old man some, the routine masculine normalcy of it. "I won't ask how you've been."

They share a laugh, the old man saying "Won't hear me complainin.' Come on into the living room, have a seat. Coffee?"

"Too late for me, but thanks." Stephen settles his lanky frame into the overstuffed chair with the shot springs and a real sag to the bottom, which Shaw hasn't paid much attention to until now, and rests his forearms on his jutting knees.

"We've got one more coming," Shaw says, choosing to stay on her feet, glancing out the window toward the driveway. She senses Mads watching her from where her sister has curled into the corner of the couch, dressed in a fleece tunic and joggers, Fair Isle crew socks pulled up over the cuffs to seal in warmth, one knee hugged to her chest, gone into a silent, defensive place where Shaw knows better than to try to follow.

Ryan was stony, mostly silent on the phone earlier, letting her babble, but after a pause, he'd simply said he'd try to make it. Other than walking out on Shaw, she's never known him to be a no-show, not in all the years they'd been together—but then, he never fully committed to coming, either.

Concurrent with her thought, headlights glimmer through the drapes, a vehicle slowing, turning in.

Ryan lets himself inside, stamping his boots once on the mat as he glances into the living room, where all eyes are on him. He hangs his hard-loved John Deere ball cap on the rack, but doesn't take his coat off, instead coming in to shake hands with Stephen, who stands partway. Then Ryan chooses a seat beside Mads, his face grim, his hands staying in his coat pockets, returning Shaw's gaze for a steady moment before looking to Stephen as the man begins.

"So, I'm glad to have a chance to sit down with you all and catch up. I spoke with Sheriff Duhamel not long before I left to come here." Stephen withdraws a small tablet for note-taking as Shaw finally settles into the wicker rocking chair. Aphrodite comes over and sits beside her, surveying the room. "Have you heard from or seen Anders since we spoke on the phone?"

"Well, no. Do they have him? I never heard back from anyone."

"I'm afraid that Mr. Jansen hasn't been located as of yet."

Silence. The Connollys sit, immobilized.

Stephen picks up again slowly. "My understanding is that when two deputies were dispatched to his house earlier to make the arrest, it didn't appear that Mr. Jansen had been home in a number of days, possibly not since he was issued his copy of the protection order. There was mail and newspapers piled up, snow on the steps. I checked with the university and the fact is that Jansen has been on a leave of absence for months now."

"Did they say why?"

"He sold them a story about family issues he had to attend to out of state, and they agreed to an extended leave, but lately he hasn't been responding to their emails or phone calls. They're on the verge of terminating him."

"Okay, what now?"

"A BOLO has been sent out to all the law enforcement agencies in the area. If his vehicle is spotted, he'll be pulled over and arrested. We'll also keep an eye on his house in case he does return, but my guess is that he's staying on the move to avoid arrest. When Mr. Jansen violated the order, he became a fugitive from justice, which places your case firmly under the state police's jurisdiction. I'll be spearheading the investigation from here on. The sheriff's office will remain peripherally involved."

"So, she just has to wait?" Mads says, her eyes wide and brilliant with tears as she looks between Shaw and Stephen. "What if he comes here?"

"With any luck, he'll be trying to get as far from here as possible and won't risk contacting Shaw again now that the police are heavily involved." He returns Shaw's gaze. "Install new locks, leave some lights on all the time, try not to go places alone if you can help it. Get personal alarms, make sure everyone's checking in with where they're going and when they'll be back whenever they so much as head out for a gallon of milk." He gazes back at Shaw. "I take it from your expression that you're already doing some of these things."

"Have you seen her purse?" Ryan's tone holds grudging respect. "The only things missing are a couple of hand grenades."

"It's not a bad idea to inform your boys' schools about what's going on, either. The administration and the resource officer should be on alert for anyone matching Anders's description, anyone ap-proaching the boys during drop-off and pick-up times, trying to take advantage of that chaotic window when it's easy to get on school grounds. If I were making the decision for my own kids, I'd request that someone on staff escort them from the building to the buses and vice versa." Shaw meets eyes with Ryan, the sheer mag-netism of two parents realizing that shit just got real. "If you don't already keep your phone charged and on you twenty-four-seven, start. If you're driving and think you're being followed, go to a pub-lic place, lock your vehicle doors, and call 911. Those are the rules to live by until something breaks."

"Will somebody keep an eye on the house? I mean—do drive-bys or whatever they call it?" Mads asks, grabbing for the tissue box on the coffee table.

"I'll arrange for an officer to pass by when possible, yes. And you can call me at any time with questions or concerns." Stephen clears his throat. "Shaw, I'd appreciate it if you could start at the beginning again, go ahead and run down what's happened between you and Anders since last year."

"Okay. But hold on." Shaw goes over to the base of the stairs, peering up to the top, which is hidden from the angle of the living room.

As she suspected, the boys are sitting together on the top step, Beau with his hand dangling between his bent knees, Casey wedged in between him and the wall, both of their faces somber. Casey's the only one with sufficient parental fear to flinch when she stops with her hand on the newel post. "Go to your rooms. Okay, guys?" She keeps it low-key, needing them to know that she's not angry. "I want to hear the doors shut."

They don't argue, but Beau doesn't hurry, either, looking back at her, maybe disgusted that he isn't being rated a seat down with the adults. She can tell from the direction of their footsteps that they both go into Beau's room together. Click of tongue in groove.

Shaw finishes her recap with, "I've got all the calls saved on my phone. I've sent you the files. I don't think Anders ever knew that I was recording him."

No one's making eye contact anymore except Ryan, but no safe harbor there; only a hard, opaque expression, giving her a strangely objective view of him, how rough he can look, with the tracing of scars along his jaw from that rashy, sore-looking acne he used to get, and a shadow of a beard coming in this time of night.

"What I can't figure out are those little details he drops, things that I can't figure out how he knows." Now Shaw isn't sure how to shut up. "I mean, he knew about me sitting up in the old armchair most of the night when Thea didn't come home, watching out the window for her. Mom and Dad were at a friend's anniversary party at the Elks Club that ran long—and she was only little"—gestures to Mads, who seems to recoil even more at the mention of her child self, pressing her chin hard into her knee—"so she'd been in bed for hours. I fell asleep there. That's where you guys found me when you got home." She looks to Dad, but he seems snared in the pain of the memory, his posture in the recliner with a lowered head like an invalid, a man bowing to age.

"Why did you try to deal with this yourself?" Mads's voice is sharp, and now it's obvious that she's using all her restraint not to cry. "Listening to that man's nastiness, day after day?"

"I told everyone. I told you guys what was—"

"No, you *didn't*. Not that it was this bad, you didn't."

"Well, what did you think it was like, a life-coaching session with Tony Robbins? Christ on a crutch, Madison!" It explodes out of Shaw, leaving her to do nothing but watch her sister's blanched and humiliated face.

"I knew what she was going through." Ryan clears his throat, and the focus of the family shifts.

"Why?" This is Mads at her most obtuse and incredulous, not really asking, because she's already disgusted with them all, a tear streaking down from one eye over the soft round of her cheek. "Why the hell would you let her go through that?"

"Because your sister wanted to make sure this guy was for real, that's why. We've all been through it so many times." He gives his knee a disgusted brush, rocking back against the cushion. "She hung in there to see if she could get some answers. She was trying to protect the rest of you." Ryan folds his arms and leans back, kicking one leg out straight, returning his gaze to Stephen.

There's a moment of quiet; Mads sniffs audibly and dabs her face with her sleeve. Dad's the first to speak, his question directed at Stephen: "How can we find out if he's the one who took Thea?"

"We'll continue investigating him, and I'm looking forward to the chance to speak with him once he's in custody. You know how it goes. I won't be able to share all of what we find, but I will keep you apprised as best I can while we determine if there's any real link between Anders and Thea for us to take a closer look at."

"And the Rishworth Jane Doe?" Shaw's voice is worn out, scratchy. "Where are you with that?"

"Her cause of death is still undetermined. If she was strangled, beaten, or stabbed, we may never know for sure. All I can say is that there are no obvious signs of blunt-force trauma to the skull." Stephen links his fingers, looking between Shaw and Dad. "At this point, I want to remind everyone not to jump to the conclusion that these bones have any connection to Anders Jansen. There's no proof of that."

Dad's rubbing his face, pulling his fingertips over his eyes. "Can't decide which is harder. Finding out she isn't Thea or knowing that some other family's out there going through this, not knowing if their daughter's dead or alive." He makes a thick scoffing sound. "Twenty-four hours, they told us, my wife and me." The old man's expression is slack, eyes difficult to see behind the lamplight glare on his lenses. "Minimum wait time before you can report a person missing. That wasn't even a rule hardly anybody was enforcing any-more, goddamn hayseed outfit. Sitting there telling me that my girl probably just forgot what time it was or was staying with 'a friend.' Shacking up, is what they meant. They saw a picture of a pretty teen-age girl and just figured she was a runaway or sleeping around. Got to be her fault, right? If she ain't interested in choir or fuckin' field hockey, she must be up to no good, right? Excuse my French, Steve, but goddamn it."

Stephen nods, lips pressed together, clearly used to hearing emo-tional family members vent their grievances. The words still have the power to wound Shaw, though: sleeping around, slut, whore, the very marks painted on Shaw during that long, hot, surreal summer, Thea gone and baby coming. She knew that she and her family were being whispered about, and she'd had a few friends drop off the ra-dar at that time, never to be heard from again. Shaw's own pride and defensiveness could've been a factor in that; she couldn't have been much fun to be around.

Dad starts up again, like a windup toy jerking to life: "And here we are. My little girl's spent all these years, God knows, somewhere, alone, dumped—" He chokes off and goes still; Shaw's seen it before with Dad, some internal fire door coming down. Mads stares at him, transfixed.

"I hear what you're saying, Eddie. I wish I could undo all the years you and your family have spent wondering, I truly do—"

"Ahh, shit, I know it ain't your fault. I'm not that far gone." Dad stands, more abruptly than he should, wincing as he does a stiff circuit of the room, waiting for emotion and pins-and-needles to pass, stopping by the window to lean surreptitiously against the sill.

As Stephen gathers his things to leave, Ryan goes up the stairs to the second floor, followed by the faint sound of Beau's bedroom door squeaking open, then shut.

"Any worries or questions, I want you to call," Stephen tells Shaw. "I may not get back immediately, but I will get back."

"I know. Thanks. We'll see ya." She and Aphrodite walk him to the entryway and see him off into the night, where the snow has stopped, leaving a powdered coating on the steps.

Shaw fastens the chain lock and the dead bolt, and presses the button into the knob. She exchanges a look with the dog, who remains inscrutable. "Don't ask me. I'm just the chicken jerky lady." Shaw gives Aphrodite's head a quick scratch, then finds herself lingering, smoothing her hand over the sleekness of the dog's noggin, the reliable bumps of the animal's skull.

The old man and Mads are gone when Shaw passes back through the living room with the dog trailing her, Dad not likely to have gone farther than the bathroom, Mads most likely headed up to sleep in the twin bed wedged against the study wall that the old man never uses. Without a word to Shaw, of course, completely out of touch with the concept of clearing the air, far more inclined to put her emotions in a slow cooker and simmer on low for six to eight hours; furious with Shaw, probably, feeling trapped here.

Shaw's eyelids are heavy, and she's feeling an almost drunken muscle weakness as she heads into the kitchen, where she grabs one of the old man's seltzers, wishing it was the hard variety, then turns at the sound of footsteps.

Ryan comes in, sliding his hands into his jeans pockets as he looks back at her. "Casey's in with Beau. Says he's going to use his sleeping bag. Beau's catching up on reading for school."

She sets the can down, unopened, unappetizing. "They miss you. I'd say it's harder on Beau, but then, other days, I think maybe it's harder on Case. I don't know." Her voice breaks. "Just hard."

He bites one side of his lower lip, a habit she knows well. "It's hell, being away from them. I hate it. I never—" He stops, his throat working.

"Thanks for stepping in during all that." He glances up. "You know. Not letting me take a beating for talking with Anders."

"I know how Mads is. I don't think you've done a single thing right since she was about twelve years old." They laugh a little together, Shaw wondering if he realizes that his approximation was exact to the year that Mom died.

"She listens to you, though. You're big brother meets father figure."

He takes a few steps toward the end of the counter. "The way I went off on you last time, out in the shop . . . I wish I'd kept my mouth shut. This isn't your fault. Nobody in your place could think straight. You were doing what you thought was best for everybody, trying to get some answers. Instead, I made it all about how sick I am of the Thea stuff. And of seeing you hate yourself for what happened to her."

She doesn't expect tears to overtake her, but she doesn't fight them, either, at least not much; never has a good ugly cry felt more welcome. When she attempts speech, her question tumbles out of her, clumsy and blunt: "What if we left?"

Ryan meets her eyes, guarded, scrutinizing, leaning one fist on the countertop. "What're you talking about?"

"Moved away." She gestures roughly. "Anywhere. I don't care. We've both got skills that travel. The boys could be happy anywhere, maybe. Probably. If we were together." She rocks on the balls of her feet, hears her breathing rattle softly as she looks at him, pleading for him to fill this vacuum.

His mouth has an incredulous slant. "You'd be okay with leaving your dad behind? Mads?" Shaw doesn't move; Ryan's jaw muscles flinch. "You'd leave Thea? Because there's no way you and me can work unless you're willing to let her be dead." He drives the word home with his forefinger against the laminate: "Get it through your head that she is beyond saving. Think you can do that?"

Shaw's lips part farther, her gaze never leaving him, her jaw shuddering as she draws breath. "You ought to know better than anybody . . . it's not as easy as that."

"No, but it's not impossible, either. Other people lose family and keep on living their own lives, Shaw. It doesn't have to be this— fucking—sinkhole, that pulls everybody and everything into it, you know? That's your doing, not Thea's. And not this Anders guy's, either."

Her voice emerges low and tight. "So, it's not my fault or it's all my fault? Make up your mind."

"A big part of it is, yeah. You're the family crutch. I mean, look"—he pulls his thumb back toward the living room—"now you've got them all moved in here with you. I couldn't pry myself back into this house with a crowbar. Ever think that maybe if you took a few steps back on your own, they would, too? Like, they wouldn't have any choice?" He looks at her wet eyes. "Shit." He shakes his head and steps back, flashing his raised hands. "I wasn't going to do this again. It's getting late. I'm outta here."

She clears her throat hard and shakes her hair back, her voice too loud and brassy. "Got a date?" Her face flushes, McKenzie on her mind, along with a strident dash of guilt—what if Ryan knew? Or more accurately, what if Ryan knew and didn't give a frog's fat ass?

"Yeah. First thing in the morning, with a paint roller and about ten cans of ecru." Instead of walking to the front door, Ryan goes to the stairs, having to dodge around Aphrodite, who tries to fall into step with him across the living room, then abandons the pursuit and returns to Shaw, apparently as invested in the outcome of all this as anyone. "We got the place in Stanton. The interior needs a good going-over."

The new shop. With the showroom, and the potential of selling cherry Mustangs and Corvettes. Shaw's lips part but she can't find words—like maybe, "Congrats on your new life without me"—so instead, she posts herself at the bottom of the stairs, watching as he comes down with one of their bed pillows and a bundle of blankets. "What are you doing?"

"Sleeping over the garage tonight."

"On what, the weight bench?" She lifts a brow as he holds up the bedding in his arms to show her as he passes. "We have a perfectly good couch, remember?"

"Pretty sure it's spoken for." He pulls the front door open, hesitates without looking back. "I'll stop in to say hi to the boys in the morning before I leave. G'night."

When the door has shut, Shaw goes through the triple-locking routine again, leaving the outdoor and entryway lights to burn all night. It's too black out there to tell if a vehicle might be parked on the road, if Anders could be watching the place. Part of her would almost chase Ryan down, invite him back into their bed, see if he'll still have her; but the thought of rejection—or that his presence might be passing, brought on by tragic, stressful circumstances only to have him wake up next to her in the morning to find that, nope, the thrill is well and truly kaput—is more than she can stand tonight.

Her phone is a weight in her hoodie pocket, and all she wants is to chuck it somewhere out of reach for the night—on top of the fridge, under the couch—but knows she'd be leaving herself vulnerable. Instead, she sets her usual morning alarm in the Clock app. At least Mads is here tonight rather than in towns away, another loose thread that Shaw can't quite catch hold of.

Shaw goes back into the living room to find Dad in his chair again as if by some *Bewitched*-style magic, obviously having stayed out of the way to give her and Ryan space to talk. The old man wears his ratty cardigan; the TV is flashing, and Aphrodite is now in sphinx mode on her bed. A bag of peanuts in the shell lays open on the stand at Dad's elbow. Shaw's stomach rolls at the prospect of all that cracking and crunching. "Isn't it kind of late for those?"

He opens one between his incisors, continues the act of splitting the shell between his thumbs. "I didn't know there was peanut-eating rules. Got to write those down somewhere, put 'em up where people can see them."

She rests her hand on his shoulder as she passes. "I'm going to crash."

"Ry will be coming back now." The old man's voice is steady, succinct. "With everything that's going on."

Shaw stands still, looking down at him, realizing that, with his hearing, he probably couldn't make out much of what had been said in the kitchen earlier, instead choosing to assume they'd worked everything out. "I don't think so, Dad."

He's quiet. "He has to be. You didn't give him a chance."

"Uh, yes, I did. Many chances. He's happier in that apartment of his."

"What the hell's happy got to do with anything?"

"Look, I just went through this with him. He doesn't want me anymore. That's it." After a beat, she squeezes his shoulder again in apology, a little surprised to feel the boniness beneath his layers of clothing. She remembers the muscle and healthy fat that used to round it out when she'd rest her head against him as a kid, Dad book-ended by the little girls who wanted to crawl and bounce and yank on him at the end of the day, his shirt smelling of the sulfurous process-ing chemicals from the paper mill. Always gentle, the biggest man in the world. It took her many years, teenagerhood, to realize that he was only five foot eight, built like a fireplug back then in his green Dickies work clothes, but strong, yes, all kinds of it, even though a lot of it leaned toward beer fat later on, after Thea, before AA.

"I don't mind getting my own place again. Suits me fine." He shakes his head as if he hasn't heard her. "You two don't need to worry about me taking offense to that. A married couple needs their privacy."

Shaw's head sinks, and she silently counts to ten before veer-ing the subject hard in the opposite direction. "Did we hold on to much of Thea's stuff, in the end? When you cleared out the old house?" She waits. "Clothes, jewelry, things like that?" She needs to satisfy her curiosity, most of all, kill that nagging doubt Anders planted inside her—the underwear, the bra. Maybe DNA, maybe proof, maybe nada.

"Clothes? Yeah, some. Some your mother gave away to Goodwill, you know, after time had passed. But she held on to plenty." *Just in case* goes without saying. "I've still got my storage in the shed there. The tenants know that. It's padlocked and all." He jerks his head a little to glance back at her. "Looking for anything in particular?"

"No, just thought I'd sort through it, see what we have left. Mind if I swipe your keys? I might head up tomorrow, after Beau's game."

Dad lifts his hand, drops it back to the chair arm. "Go ahead. Knock on the front door first and let them know you're around. I'm guessing that'll be okay."

Upstairs, Shaw carefully lets herself into Beau's room.

He lays stretched out, one leg protruding from beneath the comforter, Casey cocooned in his sleeping bag and quilt on the floor alongside the bed. Shaw walks quietly over, touches Beau's head, folds Casey's quilt down to his chin and finds that the hair at his temples is wet with sweat, but he doesn't wake.

Shaw gets Beau's sleeping bag out of his closet and spreads it on the floor at the foot of the bed, curling up inside. Sleep is like the ever-traveling windows of a passenger train, transient flashes streaming by her, glimmers of awareness that quickly tunnel away into full darkness.

Shaw's up early, first in the shower. She'd checked her phone before she did anything else, wondering what venom Anders might've spewed across her voicemail during the night. But there's nothing. He never called.

Huh. She rests back a little. So, crazy, not stupid, maybe. Maybe after their chat yesterday morning, he got into his car and drove like Stephen suggested, trying to get as many states as he could between him and his impending arrest warrant before the next daybreak. The thought allows her spine to soften a fraction of an inch. There's hope that maybe Ryan spent the night cuddled up to a stinky

194 o GILLIAN FRENCH

exercise mat for nothing. She'd cut his toast into heart shapes of gratitude except that she doubts he'll linger over the breakfast table with her this morn.

As Shaw makes coffee, the hellhound watches her every move until Shaw shakes kibble into the dish. There's simple satisfaction to be had in watching Aphrodite devour her breakfast, both enthusiastically and economically, the dish always cleaned down to the last morsel. Then the dog gulps water and rests back on her haunches like *What else you got?* In the living room, Dad's sleeping head is visible above the chair. Shaw's got Saturday-morning time for a rare second cup in peace before she rousts the boys.

Peace. Chortle; guffaw; what's that? Shaw's eyes close as she tastes coffee but sees Thea: hoodie, jeans, Adidas, running down School Street, so painfully slow, away from the pickup. The silhouettes of James and Brandy in the cab. Not moving. Not calling after her at all. Only watching her go in the side views.

Footsteps come down the stairs, and Shaw cracks one lid to see Mads dressed in yesterday's clothes, her face sleep swollen as she sets her overnight bag down and goes for coffee, opening the pantry to stare at the contents.

Shaw waits until her sister has tucked into a bowl of Casey's cereal before she speaks. "Go ahead and wash your laundry. If there's anything in the cupboards that you want to bring back with you, go for it. You know you're always welcome here."

"You're telling me to go?"

"No. I don't know what the right thing is. I don't have answers for you. I'm assuming you're still mad at me and want to get back to your life."

Mads takes her time swallowing. "It's just that 'here' comes with a lot of complications." Shaw nods. Mads pokes at the floating grain squares. "It's a long commute to school."

"True, true."

Mads turns her mug left, then right. "I told you I wasn't going anywhere. I'm not leaving you with all this happening. You would never do that to me." She jerks her head in the direction of the overnight bag. "I'll get the rest of my stuff today. What's left at Brooklyn's will have to wait. I don't really feel like hauling a mattress down two flights of stairs."

"And I don't feel like helping you do it." Shaw won't show her complicated flood of feelings: relief, dread, gratitude. Maybe Mads does get it, all the ways in which Shaw has tried to show her what's in her heart over the years. Shaw glances over at stirring sounds from the recliner, the fleece blanket falling to the floor. "Now look. You woke it up."

Beau's game starts at eleven, and they all go, double-checking the door locks, Shaw casting one last glance back at Aphrodite, who's watching them from the front window, paws on the sill, consistently seeming blindsided by the fact that there are places that don't welcome dogs.

The memorial gym is crowded, people bottlenecking around the lobby concessions table where they're selling popcorn, plastic-wrapped brownies, and orange drink for the senior class fund. The scene could be grainy footage of Shaw's own high school experience of going to the occasional game with friends, right down to the warbly school band accompaniment and the echo of squeaking sneakers and thumping basketballs across the gym floor.

Dad digs into his wallet for cash. Shaw pushes his hand down. "What've you got your eye on? My treat."

"I see a coffee carafe over there, high roller."

"Okay. Case, you're a popcorn man." He gives a thumbs-up, bobbing along in the crowd beside her, bumping her side every five seconds or so. "Mads? You want anything?"

"A brownie, maybe, unless they have nuts. If they do, don't bother."

Shaw waits her turn until she reaches the table where a teenage girl and a mother of one of Beau's teammates who Shaw recognizes are selling the refreshments. The woman, Krissy, is brawny, with a cloud of curly hair and a school logo sweatshirt dressed up with chunky silver jewelry and full makeup. "What can I get you?" She's forthright, friendly, making Shaw smile in return.

"A large coffee and popcorn, and a couple of those brownies, too, if they don't have nuts."

"They do have nuts. Walnuts. I made them."

"Oh. Well—throw 'em on the pile, anyway." Shaw's laughter feels strained, and she's overheated now. "How's Mathias liking the glory this season?"

The woman's gaze is unfocused, traveling over the line behind Shaw as she fills a foam cup and starts punching in figures. "Pretty well. He's one of only two ninth graders on varsity, so he's feeling good about that."

"Yeah . . . I know. I—" Shaw puts a hand to her chest. "I'm Shawnee. Beau's mom? I think we met at that benefit car wash last spring?" Of course, they did, but faking vagueness makes this all feel less lopsided.

"Ohhh. Right, okay. How are you?" Krissy's eye contact drifts away again as she accepts the cash from Shaw with a sort of dubious knowing quality, probably thinking she wears some poker face the whole time. The woman has no idea who she's dealing with. Shaw's sense of paranoia is overdeveloped to powerlifter status, and she knows when she's being talked about behind her back—and when someone's making a small game of putting her in her place. Instantly, Shaw pictures the other basketball moms watching Beau on the court, the whispered remarks: *that's the poor kid whose mom is a complete absentee,* Shaw never known to drop in on practices or cheerlead at every game or sell diluted fucking orange drink for an unjust three dollars a pop.

By the time Shaw locates the old man and Mads and Casey, it requires a wobbling mountain-goat climb up the loaded bleachers and an impolite wedging of her ass into a gap the width of a shoe-box beside Casey, then jabbing her arm over to deliver everyone's snacks. "Brownies." She thrusts them under Mads's nose, startling her. "They have nuts. Pick 'em out."

The first quarter begins, Shaw under a fog thanks to that woman. Beau isn't starting, but that's typical. Instead, he rides the pine pony next to Mathias, the general sense being that next year, they'll both get more of a chance once this year's seniors have had their moment. Shaw's gaze drifts down the stands and she meets eyes with Ryan. He's sitting about eight rows down, making good on his promise to Beau to come straight to the game after putting in a few hours painting this morning.

Ryan's really trying to catch Casey's gaze, but he gives Shaw a nod before exchanging a wave with his son.

"Can I go see Dad?" Casey says eagerly.

"Well—sure, I guess—" The words are barely out of her mouth before he clambers past her, not minding having to shove through people's bulks and trod on feet on his way to freedom. "Okay. 'Bye." She can't help it: she feels a pang. Goddamn the mean moms for making her maudlin.

15

The drive to Rishworth that afternoon provides solitude that Shaw hadn't realized she needed. The old man gave her some hassle about going alone, and usually, she dreads silence, anyway, too much time to think. But after the intense family togetherness of the past couple days, a break from the circled wagons isn't a bad thing, and Dad could use the chance to catch up with his youngest while they've got her in captivity.

After the game—67–50, the other guys—as they filed out into the parking lot, Ryan had paused beside her long enough to say, "I'll be back before dark," on his way to his pickup.

"It's a date," she couldn't resist calling after him, making heads turn; probably should've resisted that impulse. No wonder she's the leper of the basketball moms.

Now, she cruises, listens to her music, manages to pull over to check her phone only three times—nothing from the home front, and no new arson scenes to work yet, though the pyro's track record proves that the clock is ticking—and checks her rearview three thousand times for gray Dodge Chargers.

She passes a few maroon-and-white BRIXTON FOR GOVERNOR signs along the way, staked in snowbanks, and taped to vinyl siding, put up early by avid supporters. "You've got to be fucking kidding me." Shaw holds up her middle finger as she passes.

Much of the drive to the county is unremarkable stretches of woods, sometimes old pasture with fallen snow fence, a washed-out barn with blistered paint somewhere off in the distance. Rishworth was a mill town once. Textiles. Shaw remembers the sepia-tone photographs they'd been shown in school of grim-faced Gilded Age women and children in charge of massive looms and various other machinery capable of severing digits and limbs. The downtown still displays the original brick of that industrious time in the late nineteenth century. Some attempt has been made at renovating and gentrifying, certain sections of the huge mill complex converted to terraced apartments about twenty years ago, initially considered upscale, now caked with the damage and filth of decades like a used-up working girl shedding concealer and false lashes in a downpour.

The shops, too, have changed hands many times since the initial downtown makeover and several now stand empty, though there's a banner strung across the façades reading BIANCHI VENTURES RESTORATION PROJECT—COMING SOON. Only the river remains unchanged, a tributary of the Allagash, the same shades of brown and steel, the small hydroelectric dam, and a few big hunks of sod sprouting grass and alders that one could grant the title of island if feeling generous.

Are you in there? Is that where he put you? It's what Shaw thinks every time she crosses the low, rust-flecked iron bridge into town since Thea disappeared. *If he did, that means we'll probably never get a piece of you back.*

She pictures her sister's face, dappled with sunlight through coursing water, the textured many-fingered currents in the shallows rendering her as if in stained glass, sainted by youth and tragedy, lying on her back in the silt with her eyes as open and washed-out blue as they'd been every morning when she'd clambered onto Shaw's lower bunk, waking her up by holding her face about three inches back from Shaw's until her big sister finally opened her eyes a crack to find that grinning kid with crazy haystack hair sticking out everywhere from sleep.

Saints have to be virgins, genius. Beneath the water's surface, Thea's head jerks with laughter, whipping and darting, her hair now a ripple of silk behind her as she lets the current pull her, gliding below the frame of Shaw's mental picture. *Leaves me out.*

Shaw's mouth moves in a half smile, shaking her head and looking away from the water as she says aloud, "'Bye, Thee."

The old family house on Pressman Street, a dead end which lies toward the western edge of town backing onto the type of woods known colloquially as "trash woods," the scrawny stuff that grows back after a clear-cut, holds a sense of waiting that Shaw knows has nothing to do with the structure and everything to do with her and those in town who still remember.

For Shaw, the place is marked, standing out from the other houses on the street of comparable age and design, many built in the 1950s, when the mill was still supplying jobs and therefore incentive to live in the northernmost climes of a cold, rural state.

There are changes, though. A plastic child's art easel stands on the porch, along with a milk crate of outdoor toys, a pair of men's rubber boots, and a folded blanket forgotten on the swing from the fall months when the Hendrickses must've sat out together on a chilly early evening when the leaves were coming down, as Shaw and her family had done. But even from this close perspective, as Shaw parks her car in the curbside spot directly in front of the house, the place puts her in mind of the little plastic dollhouse that she and her sisters shared growing up, decorated with adhesive windows and hedges, easily split open on its hinges to be crammed with whatever toys were favorites that day. Just props. This could never be any more or less than the house of the family with the missing daughter, maybe not unless a hundred years passed, five hundred, laying them all to dust. Or maybe she needs to shit or get off the pot already. Time to say hidey ho to the Hendricks.

The driveway is empty, but she goes up the steps, slowly, her gaze focused on the wooden primitive art angel hung on the door, with a homely smiling face and corkscrew curls made of straw, clutching a star that reads WELCOME.

She knocks, ready to announce her presence before she lets herself into the shed to go through Dad's stuff, anxiety leeching stomach acid into her throat, staying several feet back from the threshold so that her eyes can't focus on the objects beyond the sidelights flanking the door.

Dad wanted to get the place spiffed up a little before he rented it, but funds only allowed for a few new fixtures and repairs, or so he'd said; Shaw knew better. Tearing off the pinstriped wallpaper in the living room or slapping new paint on the clapboards might be a jinx, as if a grown Thea might drive down this street someday, looking for home, and not recognize the place because it was yellow instead of white. Again, rationality took the slow boat to China a long time ago, for all of them. It wasn't about making sense; it was about surviving the grief, staying sane enough to keep going to work and paying bills and feeding children so they could keep surviving, too, and it didn't look pretty, not at all.

No one answers, and after her second attempt, Shaw leans close to the nearest sidelight, feeling like a creeper but with a sense of duty, like, how could she leave this place again without looking it in the eye? This was home.

A view of the front hall, the narrow central staircase. Same pinkish-tan walls, bargain paint her folks had used here and there throughout the house—salmon, that's how Mom would defend it when she and Thea would make fun, which was only setting them up for even easier rude remarks—and that nondescript watercolor of a flowering bush still hanging on the wall in the same place. Dad had mentioned that the house was being rented partially furnished, but she still hadn't expected it to look so similar. There's a different runner on the hallway floor, and she sees a hint of an unfamiliar dining set through the kitchen doorway. A small toy sits forgotten in one corner of the hallway, some sort of purple-and-green wind-up animal.

If Shaw keeps her gaze low and shifts it back maybe three feet to the left, she knows she'll see Thea standing there in her platform heels on the fifth step from the floor. Thea was asked to the prom by a senior when she was only a freshman, while Shaw herself had sat home dateless, but she'd been there to see Thea come down the stairs in her first real formal getup, a strappy sky-blue gown. Mom had been glowing, she'd been so excited, probably thinking neither of her roughneck daughters would ever do something like this—and if Thea had managed to wipe the sarcastic humor off her face for five seconds, she might've even looked the part. The boy— Donnie something, tall, skinny, nice enough—had arrived in his suit and buttonhole carnation and full-on Rockwellian blush of innocence at Thea's beauty while she mugged for Mom's camera and finally yelled, "Let's *go*!" over the tumult of everyone oohing and aahing and little Mads running her hands down the shiny fabric of big sis's gown.

Shaw turns away and jogs back down the steps, heading swiftly across the shoveled path to the garden shed in the back corner of the property, surrounded by a wooden privacy fence she remembered Dad and his best friend Pat Delgado putting up over the course of one weekend and four six-packs while she farted around on the swing set and watched the process. A thousand years ago. Or yesterday. Sweet Jesus.

She pops the padlock and lets herself inside, leaving the door hanging open so she won't take the tenants completely by surprise if they come home while she's here. Plus, the shed is dark and cobwebby and not exactly a place where she wants to dillydally.

Dad's boxes fill most of the space, a potting bench lining one wall and some cruddy, forgotten tools and watering cans left behind. Cardboard cartons and plastic totes labeled with marker across strips of duct tape: MOVIES. DISHES/POTS & PANS.

Shaw takes a guess that anything belonging to Thea would be toward the back. She shifts the mountain, having to stack most of the containers outside in the snow because there's no room to maneuver, finally reaching some old U-Haul boxes sealed and resealed with clear packing tape, marked *Thea* in Mom's cursive script, the retaping evidence of all the times they'd thought they'd put them away for good, like hiding Thea's belongings was the same as putting the entire matter to bed. More magical thinking.

Shaw steels herself as best she can and digs in, trying to keep that inevitable time-capsule feeling from taking over. The first box is mostly photo albums and yearbooks, the covers of which Shaw isn't even tempted to crack; in another, she finds an odd, intensely evocative assortment including Thea's extra pair of sneakers with skull and crossbones laces, her winter coat, a blue puffer that Shaw puts her nose to, even though it smells like nothing but the petroleum-based fabric it's made of and the faint mustiness of time.

The next box is a few favorite books and comics—Thea was never a big reader—ziplock bags of jewelry and a few knickknacks, and beneath, a sampling of her clothes. The idea is shattering, Mom's hands folding these careful creases in the jeans and T-shirts, and, yes, beneath it all, as if granting her dead daughter modesty, are a couple pairs of underwear, socks, and a gray heathered bra. Shaw isn't breathing as she unfolds the black underwear and checks the size. A four printed below the waistband, nearly washed away. She swallows, checks the bra. Size 34B.

Exhaling hard, she drops the undergarments into her lap, staring unseeingly at the scarred planks of the back wall, feeling her heartbeat.

Shaw adds two unnecessary loops on the one-hour drive out of her way to Vesper Falls, where Brandy Pike lives.

She drives through a couple little neighborhoods and back out onto I-95 in case Anders might be following. She watches the cars stream by, wondering if she's a fool, if he's officially won. She called to check in at home before she left the old house, and everything was fine. Still no word from Stephen York or the sheriff's office.

If Dad hadn't stayed in touch with Brandy, Shaw herself wouldn't have known how to track down the woman, who seems to move about every two to three years from one efficiency apartment or rent-controlled subdivision to the next, trailing her children behind her like a troop of baby elephants.

Vesper Falls is also on the Allagash, another rust-speckled, former-site-of, sporting the vestiges of both a steel mill and an iron works, now mostly defunct except for the few small contracts the iron works plugs away at. The air itself seems tinged with a metallic taste, a whiff of cinders drifting from the rail yard near the waterfront. GPS leads Shaw to a downtown apartment building off Main Street, with a tiny tenants-only parking lot and nary a free spot in sight along the curb, the parking lines mostly obscured by slush and dirty snow.

By the time Shaw walks back to the building and buzzes up, she's cold, in a funk borne of facing down the homeplace and her extreme dislike of this woman, intensified by the royal pain in the ass of trying to gain an audience with her.

"What?" An abrupt female voice over the intercom. Could be anybody, but Shaw's not in the mood to dick around with polite inquiries.

"Brandy, it's Shaw Connolly. I need to talk to you. Can I come up?"

There's a pause, a long one, and Shaw steps back, squinting up the full height of the building only to see a curtain flick shut in one of the second-story windows. Wonder who that could be.

A buzz, and Shaw seizes upon the door handle.

The stairwell holds the odor of old carpet and urine that all aged apartment buildings seem to share. Shaw hears the dead bolt being thrown open behind Brandy's door in nearly the same moment she reaches it, as if the woman has the timing down cold from the entrance to apartment 2-C and has no intention of leaving her door unlocked for even one extra minute.

Shaw knocks once and watches the door swing open under her fist, Brandy having already walked away. The woman now stands at the small kitchen island counter jutting out from the wall, fiddling with her cigarettes as Shaw comes in. "Lock it up, will you?" Brandy speaks around the wagging Virginia Slim in the corner of her mouth, sparking a pale pink Bic at the tip.

Shaw slides the bolt and turns to watch Brandy, who still hasn't acknowledged her with a direct look as she crosses into the living room and parks her butt on the glass coffee table, blowing smoke. "Long time since I've seen you." Brandy's expression is flat, her face curiously without even fine lines, as if that mask of makeup she's applied daily since middle school has shielded her from UV rays, as well as damage from smoking and drugging and drinking, although a more likely explanation might be that Brandy's never been one to get outside for vitamin D and a daily constitutional, maybe plant a few marigolds. She's more of a perennial feature in neighborhood bars and flophouse living rooms characterized by endlessly droning TVs and flotillas of pot smoke, or painting her toenails with her phone a half-inch away from her face while her kids chew on the electrical cords.

"Where are Kieran and Camdyn?" Shaw says it to be a bitch, glancing around, maybe proving that she knows Brandy's kids' names even if Brandy doesn't. The quiet is broken only by the predictable murmur of the TV. Shaw remembers the kids well, how they'd bound into the lap of any visitor, soaking up attention from literally any source, the baby shampoo smell of Kieran's curls.

"Kieran's dad got custody. A long time ago." Brandy looks around the room as she lets the smoke out. "My mom's got Camdyn staying with her now. Cam's got a kid of her own. Believe that shit? Thirteen, and she's popped out a baby." A faint sullenness is all that can be read into Brandy's attitude as she taps the extra-long cigarette over an ashtray. "I'm a fucking grandma." She snorts laughter, resting her arm across her bent knee, looking off. "I'm too cool to be a grandma."

Shaw lets that pass, nothing to be said about the fact that the woman's lost her children. The last time Shaw met with Brandy—five years ago, at least—it was in a tiny apartment in Bangor, Kieran a toddler howling from a playpen while Brandy stared back at Shaw with soaped-window eyes sunken into sleep-deprived hollows. Shaw's hands had itched to pull the boy out, but she hadn't quite dared. Brandy's home, Brandy's kid, Shaw had no claim. The other woman had carried such an air of deep melancholy about her, maybe something like postpartum depression, that it had preoccupied Shaw in the weeks that followed, nearly causing her to pick up the phone to DHHS. But she never did; again, her nerve failed her, because who wanted to be the one who tossed somebody else's family into crisis, yanking screaming kids away from their mother?

"I won't take up much of your time." Shaw barely gets the words out before Brandy's up again, wandering into the kitchen. She wears white leggings beneath an oversize black concert T-shirt with some country singer on it, printed columns of venues and dates running down the back, her curly brown hair hanging loose between her shoulder blades. "I thought maybe I could ask you a couple of things about Thea."

Brandy gives a testy exhale as she bends into the fridge. "There's nothing to say. What's the point of bringing it up over and over again?"

"Like you're not thinking about her all the time anyway." Shaw's pushing too hard—she knows it—but she doesn't look away from Brandy's irritable glance over the top of the fridge door. Like it or not, they come from the same place, made from the same basic clay, small-town peasant stock, nothing special, and they grew up knowing it. Big-girl professionalism isn't going to get Shaw anything here but an extra hour wasted on Brandy's couch, breathing her passive smoke and staring down this month's dead-eyed machismo hunk on the sexy firefighter calendar over the small flatscreen. "Some things have changed, and I need to talk to you about what you remember. I'm sure you probably heard about the bones they found in Beggar's Meadow last week."

"Bones? No." Brandy toes the fridge door shut and pops the top on her diet soda before she asks "Want something?" as she passes, her tone anti-interrogative before she plops down on the love seat. "I guess it's not Thee or I would've had the cops up my ass again about it by now." Brandy swallows a sip; that annoyed nettle between her brows never seems to completely relax. "You're one of them now, aren't you? Or something? I forget."

Shaw's debate is immorally brief. "Something like that, yeah." Let Brandy infer whatever she wants; the suggestion of a badge wields a hell of a lot more power than a factual brush and a jar of powder.

Shaw takes a few steps deeper into the living room, glancing at old, framed photos of Brandy's children, beaming, their innocence born as naturally to them as their small, sweet features, yet to be dulled by Mom's influence. "Mostly I want to know if you remember any older guys hanging around you and Thea. Anybody from the community showing an interest in either one of you back then."

Brandy narrows her eyes, then flips her gaze to the ceiling. "Lemme think. There was Mr. Lorenzo freshman year, who used to stand over me in class so he could look down my shirt whenever he got the chance. And then there was Mr. Walsh, who everybody knew was fucking at least two girls from his senior class every year. Oh, yeah, and the townie assholes who hung out in the lot by the park who'd follow us around and snap our bra straps and grab our asses, and don't forget all the randoms who used to yell shit at us out their car windows whenever us girls would walk downtown—getting all this?"

"I get it. Young girls are targets, always have been. Believe it or not, I got some of that myself growing up."

"You did?"

Shaw gazes steadily back at Brandy's smug, incredulous expression, clenching her teeth until she trusts herself to speak, inadvertently having the effect of pressuring Brandy with silence, something the woman doesn't seem to deal well with. Brandy straightens up, crossing her legs and reaching out to tap her ash again, saying, "Look, Thea and I didn't hang out all that much—"

"Oh, yes, you did. As I remember it, you moved right in and made yourself at home running her life. What she did. Who she hung out with. BFFs, right? For that six months, you guys were attached at the hip. There wasn't room for anybody else. Except maybe James."

The jealousy is rubbed raw again in a way Shaw didn't expect, like the back of her bare ankle blistering against a sneaker on a moist summer day.

"Well, if she was willing to let me do all that, then I guess she must've been looking for a change, huh?" Brandy's tone is light, laced with acid, and she takes a moment to let the words settle and corrode Shaw's skin before she goes on. "I'm not saying Thee and I didn't have some times. But we only got to be friends our junior year. It's not like I knew every single detail of her life. Somebody could've been bothering her and maybe she just didn't tell me, I dunno."

Shaw moves her head from side to side, weighing options. "Mm. Not buying it, but let's move on." She pauses. "You talked about teachers. What about subs from that time, the men? Remember anybody named Anders Jansen?"

The woman sighs loudly. "How the hell would I know? That was, like, twenty years ago."

"Try, Brandy."

"Eat me, Shawnee."

Red closes in at the edges of Shaw's vision, but she clings to the last remnants of cool long enough to try something she'd learned, both parenting and on the job: in the heat of the moment, do the opposite of what you want. Flip expectations.

So, instead of cramming her boot down Brandy's throat, Shaw walks over and sits beside the other woman, getting a slight payoff from the fact that Brandy starts a little, maybe wondering if Shaw's about to pull out her service weapon and pistol-whip her or whatever Brandy imagines to be standard police procedure.

Shaw trains her gaze on the play kitchen set pushed up against the side of the island, tucked out of the way beneath the edge of the countertop. Little plastic fruits and veggies, tiny cardboard cereal boxes; it's obvious from the neatness that it's barely used, and the vision of Brandy carefully organizing everything after a rare visit with her grandchild is enough to ease Shaw's desire to work on her backhand. "I get that you don't like me much. You don't have to. But my family's got a guy harassing us, saying that he's the one who hurt Thea. I'm trying to figure out if it's true." She's got Brandy's attention now, the woman finally grinding out the butt in the dish. "You've got your place locked up tight. Have you had any trouble with someone following you, or a stranger coming around? Getting weird phone calls?"

"The dead bolt's because of my last ex. And you never know when Cam's dad might drop by for a booty call after he's had a few. I got sick of never knowing when I might come back and find one of them waiting for me on the couch, that's all, so I got my landlord to put in new locks." A rare flicker of curiosity. "Do the cops think this guy is legit?"

"What he's done to me is legit harassment. That's all I know for sure. Look, I've already talked with James. Now I'm coming to you, looking for anything at all about that day, April sixth. Anything that stands out, that didn't seem odd at the time but makes you wonder now."

Brandy kitty-corners herself against the cushions of the love seat. "I'm not changing my story. It went like I said. I caught a ride to the turnaround with James and Thea. Those two got into it about her drinking and stuff, and then Thea made James pull over and stormed off home all mad. Then we went to the party."

"She was definitely going home?"

"I don't know. I figured that she was. And James said something like, 'whatever, let her go.' He could be a dick like that. I wanted to get to the party because I had plans to meet a guy, so I shrugged it off."

"What guy?"

"How is that your business?" Brandy keeps it up for a couple seconds, then shrugs, a little reluctant mirth bubbling to the surface. "Rolly Metzger, okay? Remember him?" A hard giggle. "Lost IQ points every time he took a leak, but he wasn't bad. Used to score off him for free. He did that for some of the girls he liked."

"Did Thea ever score off him? Or anybody else?"

Brandy studies Shaw, a knowing twist to her half smile. "Nah. She'd do shots and stuff, smoke a little, but she hadn't had a chance to get into pills or anything yet." She's obviously taking pleasure in Shaw's discomfort. "You never did any of that, did you? Never even used to have a beer with everybody. Too good to party, huh."

"God, you're perceptive. How do you think I got knocked up at eighteen, Brandy? By staying home, washing my hair every Saturday night?" Normally Shaw wouldn't talk about making Beau that way, but it's worth it to sour Brandy's rebel act a bit. "You're sure that there's no way Thea could've made it to the party later in the night? Maybe she could've caught a ride with somebody else after walking away from James's truck on School Street? My guess is that everybody was pretty drunk by the time midnight rolled around, not super observant, and that's a large, wooded area up there. Pitch dark at night. They've found one dead woman in the Meadow. Doesn't it at least seem possible to you that there could be more?"

"Like a serial killer? In the county?" Brandy stares back. "I think it makes more sense that Thea finally decided to ditch Rishworth and your mom clucking after her and grabbed a ride out with the first logging rig she saw."

"If you believe that, then you never knew her."

"Then go back and talk to James," Brandy says crisply, sipping more soda. "I'm not saying he definitely did it. But he's the only one who had a reason to want to hurt her that night that I can see." She shrugs a slim shoulder. "Maybe he caught up with Thea later and decided to slap some sense into her. Like, payback for making him look whipped, leaving him on the side of the road like that. He's a complete mess now, I heard. Could be guilt."

"But how would he have found her? You see the problem I'm having? I'm supposed to believe that James, drunk off his ass, somehow hunted Thea down after the party? Not one single person from the community has ever come forward to say that they saw Thea walking home that evening, or that they saw the three of you parked on School Street in his truck at all. That's a heavily popu-lated neighborhood. The old ladies in those houses have big eyes and ears." Brandy looks back. "So, for me, the only verifiable part of the timeline is up to the moment that my sister and I turned away from each other on the sidewalk after school, around three P.M. When she walked off with you."

"What're you saying? That James and I did something to her?"

"Did you?"

"Fuck *you*, no, we didn't. Thea got drunk too fast and James got mad. That's it. And if you don't believe that, you can go ahead and get right the hell out of my house."

"Thought you'd say something like that." Shaw gets to her feet. "Thanks for the hospitality."

Brandy stands, following her. "You didn't own Thea, you know." When Shaw turns back, Brandy wears a look of sallow triumph, her hands in fists at her sides, the ropey physique of a woman whose body runs on little more than a daily loop-de-loop of stimulants and downers. "You still can't get over the fact that she had more fun with me than you. Little Miss Straight-Edge, Stick-Up-the-Ass, always thinking you were so much better than the rest of us."

"Anybody ever tell you that you're a fucking moron, Brandy?" Shaw's face lights up. "I just knew it. You be sure and lock up be-hind me, okay? Stay safe now."

Brandy's answer is a profanity, and she kicks the door shut hard enough to make a loose bulb flicker in the overhead light fixture as Shaw takes herself on home.

16

"I'm not having Officer-Freakin'-Smiley walk me to the bus." Beau's having a rare surly Monday morning after a bad night of sleep once his little brother climbed into bed with him, not to mention his mom tossing and turning on the floor below again. "I'm not six. Like I'm going to walk off with some weird guy because he says he's got candy."

"Do you think he'll do that?" Casey looks between the two of them as he pulls on his coat, but Shaw and Beau are wrapped up in each other as they prepare to head out to her car for the drive to school. "Like, come up and try to talk to us?"

"You call him Officer Smiley?" Shaw shoulders her purse and searches in the pockets for her keys. "Because he's so nice?" she asked hopefully.

"No, because he's a cranky ass. He's ready to draw down if somebody laughs too loud or drops a pen."

"A high school resource officer with a hair trigger. The guy wouldn't last five minutes. Chances are, he's sick of you and the rest of the little darlings riding him and wants to establish his territory. Face it, Smiley's the thin blue line between you guys and a spree killer, it gives me great pain to say. Anyway, you're not meeting the bus anymore. Gramps will pick you guys up from school from now on, until things—Ow, Case, that's my heel." She notices a tissue-wrapped bundle she'd forgotten beneath her wallet since Saturday, and glances toward the kitchen, where Mads stands at the table, checking her backpack to make sure she's got everything she needs for today's classes.

"Do you really think that's going to happen?" She looks back at the tenseness in Casey's face, now, pinched with exhaustion, as he fumbles on his own backpack. "That guy's going to try to take us?"

"No. I don't," Shaw says. "Really. I think he's going to back off now that the cops are involved. He knows they're watching for him." Although she's going to have to be the one to call Stephen, it seems, since she's still heard bupkes from state or local law enforcement. She leans in close enough to touch noses and holds Casey's gaze until he smiles and looks down. "Let me talk to Mads for one second and then we're gone, okay?"

Mads looks up as Shaw comes in and says, "Listen. When I stopped by the old house, I went through some stuff, brought some boxes back. They'll be safer stored here than in that old shed." Shaw holds out the object, found conscientiously folded into a sheet of pink tissue paper among a small scattering of keepsakes in a shoebox. "I thought you might like to have that."

Mads sets her pen down, carefully opening the parcel to find a suncatcher Thea painted from a craft kit that had hung in the sisters' bedroom window for much of their childhood, the colors now faded to a mere suggestion.

Mads's expression freezes for a moment, and then she lowers the plastic sun to the tabletop. Shaw adds, "Thee made that," watching her, thinking maybe she doesn't remember.

Mads doesn't speak right away, and when she does, her voice is low, hoarse. "I thought you meant something of Mom's."

Shaw's surprise is honest, leaving her blindsided. "Oh. Sorry—I—"

"It's fine." Mads folds the paper back over the sun and yanks the zipper closed on her backpack. "It's nice. Thanks." She sweeps her bag off the table. "I'm late."

Shaw watches her go, feeling stunned, grabbed by the collar and yanked around in a one-eighty to see things from a completely different angle than how she went into this, the considerate big sister doing a nice thing, now wondering why in hell it never occurred to her to bring something of Mom's, too. What that says about her, about everything.

As she and the boys leave the house, the timing coincides with Ryan emerging from the side door of the shop.

"Dad," Casey says impulsively—a more mature variation of the ecstatic little boy duet which used to greet Ryan at the door any time he came home from as quick a journey as a run to the post office—and Beau lopes over with him. Ryan claps shoulders, pulls them into an embrace, his eyes sunken, jaw darkened with full-on beard action, clearly having spent a wretched night of sleep up there surrounded by the dark humps of the exercise equipment and the skylight beaming down a relentless shaft of winter moonlight.

Ryan ruffles Beau's hair. "Hey, bud. Looking out for your mom?"

"Like she'd let me." Beau pins his dad with his gaze. "Are you home now?"

The implication is obvious, and Shaw and Ryan look at each other, seeing beyond the discomfort for a moment to the toll this tug-of-war is taking, the weight of the resentment they're both carrying now, the easy blame. "Leave Grizzly Adams alone," Shaw finally says curtly. "He's been up half the night."

"I'm sticking close right now to help keep an eye on things, okay, guys?" Ryan says. "I've got to get back to my place, hop in the shower, get to work."

My place hits home painfully. Beau stares back at him, while Casey acquiesces with a quiet, "Okay."

"Are you having supper with us?" Beau says.

Again, Ryan and Shaw make helpless eye contact. "We'll see," Ryan says. "I might not be back by then. There's a lot that needs doing in this new shop of mine. I'll have to get you guys over there soon, check the place out. But if I'm not home in time to eat, you know I'll be over the garage all night if you need me."

Beau looks like he has a few opinions about the arrangement, but Shaw ushers them on with, "Come on, say 'bye, guys, we're going to be late." As she goes, she notices a movement at the living room window, and then Aphrodite sticks her nose through the drapes, paws up on the windowsill, not quite as canny as the old man, who had the sense to book it before Shaw caught him watching.

They part ways in their respective vehicles, Shaw noticing how Beau jams his backpack down between his high-tops, then turns to his window, unspeaking.

Shaw releases a breath, then starts the engine, checking her rearview, imagining a quick, no-fuss, no-mess scenario where Anders is standing at the end of the driveway and all she has to do is back over him going a good thirty miles per.

Shaw's walking through the front doors of the lab when a text pops up. She braces herself as she pauses in the breezeway, wondering how long it'll be like this, *What if it's him* the first thought in her mind.

It's from McKenzie: *Thanks for pointing me in the right direction.*

That's it. But the typing dots are flowing, and a moment later, a photo pops up of a dog: massive head, fawn-colored coat with a brown mask and ears, a man's fingers visible, looped loosely into his collar.

She blinks, types, *Grieco?*

Thumbs-up.

!!! Where? Is he ok?

Seems to be. He's been to a vet to get checked out. Second message: *Can I thank you with dinner sometime, tell you all about it?* Third message: *Also planning on talking with a friend of a friend about our professor.*

She stares, her heart rate picking up—when she didn't hear from McKenzie, she'd assumed Anders's FBI background check had come back clean—but she doesn't want to hesitate too long, make it awkward. *Sounds good, but it's hard right now. Things are kind of on lockdown at home.*

No doubt. Play dinner by ear?

That works. Dying to know about Grieco. And just plain dying. Her first impulse says pink sparkle heart emoji—then she balks—but she's got it on tap because she sends them to people all the time, so she shoots him one anyway, and it's off, no grabbing it back.

She exes out fast before she can second-guess, color high in her face, Ryan on her mind, but paling behind *I have a date, an almost sometime date, oh my God what the hell is happening.*

"Where oh where has my little Tran gone?" Shaw drops her coat and purse at her desk, glancing over at Gauthier as Jewel emerges from the lab area behind them.

"Another fire." Gauthier glances back at Jewel. "He was gone before I came in."

"He never came in at all." Jewel pauses near their desks, leaning one slim forearm along the low cubicle wall, her cream-colored peasant tunic setting off the changeable bluish hazel of her eyes. "Typical timing for our arsonist, the middle of the night. The fire burned for at least an hour before someone noticed it and called it in. This time, the woods caught, so my understanding is that emergency services have been out at Lake Heron since around one A.M. I got the call around four, and Tran's been out there ever since."

"Lake Heron?" Shaw sits back. "Don't tell me one of those rich outtastaters's summer houses got torched this time?"

"I was told it was the public beach area. Some outbuildings and restrooms, a playground—"

"Oh, no, really? Everybody used to go there." At their blank looks, Shaw clicks a pen distractedly with one hand. "I mean, it wasn't all that close to where we lived, but even we used to go swimming there a couple times a summer. It was tradition to carve your initials into the big tree with the rope swing."

"Well, if nothing else, we may be a step closer to catching the person doing this. Tran and Lydia did manage to isolate one partial print on the edge of the duct tape. He may remember to wear gloves to the scenes, but not—"

"When he was tearing off strips of tape from that roll before the fire even happened, got it. Nice work." Shaw sticks her palm up, but Gauthier's looked back to her screen. "Hey." Straining further. "Leaving me hanging here."

Jewel watches. "Lydia. Have mercy."

Surprised and flustered, Gauthier delivers the high five, but it's a reminder of the barrier between boss and staff, never quite on level ground, and Jewel seems to sense it, too, straightening up to move on. "Anyway. Hopefully this could mean there's an end in sight."

Once Jewel is in her office, Shaw turns a little in her chair, lost in thought, picturing the dark brown, stained wooden buildings of the Lake Heron shore, the shack with all the old Maine license plates nailed to it where you paid your seven-dollar fee to get in, the little bridge spanning a stream between the dirt parking area and the shore, barreling across it with an armful of towels, flip-flops slapping the planks.

On impulse, she digs her phone out and texts Tran: *Do you have all the arson locations saved in your Maps app, my pretty?*

Tran doesn't respond until lunch, when Shaw convinces Gauthier to come with her for goodies: "I'm thinking convenience-store fare? Coke, Funyuns, piece of pizza on one of those turnstiles, if we're lucky?"

"That actually sounds . . . nice."

They head about ten minutes down the road to a mom-and-pop, then eat for a while in the Beast, heat on, radio playing, Shaw dropping her chip bag to her lap when Tran's text comes in, or rather a series of them, GPS locations sent individually, followed by a raised-eyebrow, skeptical-face emoji. Explanations later. Right now, Shaw wants to see something.

"Okay, look at this." She holds her phone up to Gauthier, showing her a multi-location route in her Maps app. "This is what our arsonist's trail looks like, when you line each fire up chronologically." A blue line crawls along a green state map, displaying five pulsating circles marking each address. "Anything strike you?"

Gauthier swallows her bite of salad, studying the screen. "I don't know . . . it looks all over the place. If they have anything in common, I don't see it."

"I don't, either, but the trail is leading roughly north, isn't it? Or northwest-ish, with some zigzagging." Shaw shakes her head, setting her phone down. "I wonder if it could be that he's choosing locations along his commute, some route that he travels as part of his work. Or maybe even driving to college and back or visiting family? Generally, arsonists aren't given a lot of credit for intelligence or social skills, but at the same time you often find them living lives of quiet minimum-wage desperation like the rest of us, so . . . He's got to live and work somewhere. Maybe these locations are convenient to him in some way, easy marks." She eats another chip, mulling. "It's a hell of a thing, trashing that side of Heron, though. It's the only part of the lake where just plain folks are allowed to cool off. The rest of it is rarified air for the über-rich."

A Madonna throwback comes on the radio, and Shaw cranks the dial. "Ooh, yes—quick—strike a pose." Voguing an invisible box around her face, Shaw looking over at Gauthier's baffled look, gaze following her frantic movements. "Vogue. Vo—?"

Gauthier shakes her head slowly.

Shaw blows out a breath, settling back, staring out her window at the faded open flag flapping in the breeze. "Jesus. You remind me of my little sister. Now, that girl has no use for me, either. I try to be on my best behavior, at my most charming, and—*pffft*. Nothing."

Taken aback, Gauthier's hands lower to her lap. "I have use for you."

Shaw laughs. "Well, that's kind." Shaw sighs and props her head on her fist, watching occasional traffic. "I don't know. Sorry to vent. You mind? Because I'm not done."

In answer, Gauthier angles toward Shaw and takes a sip of coffee.

"My sister's living with me right now, and . . . I don't think we'll ever recover from the shit that's gone down over the years. I don't like being like that—negative, you know, but sometimes, you've got to face facts. I ended up playing a part in her life that she never wanted me to. I was filling in for somebody else who wasn't there anymore." Shaw gives a short, dazed cackle. "And completely bitching it up, apparently." Shaw glances over. "Okay, are you like, 'Oh my God, get me out of this car before the crazy woman tells me her whole life story' right now?"

"No. I like listening." Gauthier fiddles with the closure on her cup lid.

"You better watch it with that sweet talk. No putting this genie back in the bottle."

"I mean it. You make me feel like I belong. Here, in all of this. I'm not stupid. I know that training the new person sucks, and you'd probably be a lot happier working on your own." Gauthier eats a cucumber slice with that careful chewing, takes her time in speaking. "You know what I said about my mom. And my stepdad."

Shaw nods, sobering some, watching the girl.

"They don't get me. They think I'm weird. It didn't used to be so bad between my mom and me, but then she met Jack, and he really changed her. He doesn't like how I am."

"What's that mean?"

"He's pretty much convinced Mom that I'm defective." Gauthier takes a breath. "All I want is to be able to afford my own place so I can get out of there." She clears her throat and digs out a Wet-Nap from the canister in the center console. "I'm on the autism spectrum. And I have OCD. That—complicates things, sometimes." She focuses on folding the used nap. "Mostly for me. But it's embarrassing for them, I guess."

"You're autistic?" Shaw leans back. "Get the hell out."

"I wouldn't make it up."

"But—you don't act like . . . I mean . . ."

"I know. 'High functioning,' is what they call it. I hate that. Makes me feel . . ."

"Like they're calling you impaired?" Shaw readjusts her position again. "So, what's that like?" Gauthier gives her an uncertain look. "Really. I'm asking, not giving you shit. I'd like to know."

"Well, it's not exactly the same for any one person. That's why there's such a big range of diagnoses out there. When I was first diagnosed, they called it Asperger's, but doctors don't differentiate between the two anymore." She looks out the window as a pickup tears by, loose exhaust rattling. "For me, looking people in the eye is hard. And being social, you know. Making conversation. It used to be a lot harder when I was younger—like, in school, especially. But Mom got me into therapy, and it helped a lot. Touch aversion is part of it. That's what the other day was about." She presses her lips together for a moment. "I've worked hard at that—really hard—but I was so focused on what Tran was teaching me, and Jewel was mad at me, and I wasn't expecting you—"

"It's okay. Really, I'm an idiot. I was just messing around."

"But I want you to know that I didn't pull away because I don't like you. Or don't have use for you." She bears down on each word. "Basically, the therapist couldn't 'fix' me. You know? Not like Mom wanted. I am who I am."

"It's got to be tough, though. Her telegraphing her disapproval all the time."

"That's what it is. Exactly. Neither of them will come right out and tell me that they wish I'd snap out of it and be normal and love parties and social stuff and go get myself a boyfriend and whatever else they want for me. It's . . . always there at home, pushing down on me. I go to work, I come back, and then I pretty much hide in my room until the next morning. I let them have the living room to watch what they want and have friends over to eat dinner and drink wine or whatever."

Shaw rests back in her seat for a moment. "You could look at it this way—and remember, I'm seeing things from an approaching middle-age view here—but chances are, if you didn't have this stuff to overcome, you probably wouldn't have worked as hard as you did to reach this point. I mean, most kids your age are either still in college or working some crappy dead-end job. You're already on track professionally and making way better money than most. Your mom and stepdad should be talking you up every chance they get at their little wine soirees. I would be."

Gauthier nods. "I guess they don't get why I want to do this job. It seems—morbid, or traumatizing, to them."

"You told them about the dead folks?"

"Mom asked. I didn't say too much because she's already scared by the whole thing."

"Mm. How are you feeling about it at this point?"

Gauthier pauses. "I've had some bad dreams. I keep seeing some of it. The blood on the door, especially."

"That's normal. You'll never get totally hardened to it, kiddo. You shouldn't. That would be like saying what happened to the victims didn't matter, when they're the whole reason we got into this gig to begin with."

"Why did you get into it? Really."

Shaw inhales through her nose. "I wanted to stop the bad guys. But I knew I didn't want to be a cop because I didn't want my kid to be scared every day that he might lose me. My sister was young, too, just starting high school at the time. Our mom had passed away at that point. And our other sister. Nothing but respect for the officers who put their lives on the line, but I couldn't live with that. So, I chose prints instead. You show up after the crime's happened and bust your ass to prove to these guys that they can't get away with it. They can't just—take."

Both women are quiet. "Wish I could explain it to my mom like that," Gauthier says.

"Go ahead and steal my lines, if you think it'll help." Shaw hesitates, then reaches for her handbag. "And I found something that helps me a little, after the really bad cases. Don't laugh, though."

Gauthier smiles a little, her brows going up.

Shaw digs into her bag and produces a miniature diecast car. It's a yellow souped-up VW Beetle with chipped flames painted on the side and rocket boosters in the back. Gauthier turns it over in her hand, reading from the undercarriage, "'Gassup'?"

Shaw takes it back. "My oldest's favorite from when he was little, and then his brother played with it after Beau outgrew that kind of thing. They think I packed all their Hot Wheels away for posterity, but I kept this guy out. I bring him with me everywhere. When I'm feeling really shitty—like, wondering what the hell is wrong with the human race and why I thought I wanted to do this kind of thing in the first place—I get him out. Just squeeze him, think about my kiddos. It keeps me going. Helps me walk through the door of a scene when I don't know what's waiting inside."

Shaw pops him back into the inner zippered pocket. "Just saying. Find yourself a focal point. If it's not family, choose something else that makes you happy. Keep a Pinterest page with pics of the most beautiful apartments you can find, something like that. Try to stay focused on the good stuff, because that's what you represent when you go to those dark places. You're a force for good, no matter how small you feel." Shaw shakes herself. "It's a process. You'll get there." She checks the time and starts the engine, then she hesitates, not looking at Gauthier this time. "And I'll keep it to myself, what you told me. I'm guessing that's what you want."

Gauthier shrugs, looking out her window. "I don't mind people knowing. It's a piece of me. I've never had much luck trying to hide it."

17

Suppertime: the boys bicker as they set the table, Dad shakes more kibble into the bowl while Aphrodite hops back and forth impatiently, and Mads dumps cooked veggies into a serving bowl. Shaw tries to box step her way around everyone to reach the fridge.

The dog fed, Dad straightens with difficulty and leans toward the window above the sink to look wistfully at the fading daylight. "Ahh. It was a bluebird day."

"What does that even mean?" Mads sets the bowl on the table and goes back to get the rice pilaf; she and Shaw are stiff with each other after what happened with the suncatcher, and Shaw doesn't offer to help. Mads insisted upon cooking tonight, so Shaw's more than happy to stay out of the way. "I hear people say that and I have no idea."

"It's a day that's as blue as a bird. You heard the man." Shaw grabs a drink for herself and milk for the boys, then parks herself at the table, nudging Beau's elbow. "When's your next game?"

"Thursday." Beau gives her side-eye. "You coming?"

"Yeah, hell yeah. We all are. Well—I don't know about Mads this time." A misstep—Shaw has to remember not to plan things for Mads; she hates that.

Mads pauses after she sets the big tray of cornmeal chicken down in the middle of everything, looking at Shaw. "Did you get ahold of anyone today? Like, the sheriff, or that state cop?"

"I texted with Stephen a little, but there's nothing new on Anders. You've got to keep in mind that Stephen's going to be doing his own thing at his own pace while working five other active cases at once. As for the sheriff's office, no news is good news, as far as I can see. I can call them to check in." She looks at her family. "None of you guys have noticed anything weird, right? No cars parked in strange places, nobody hanging around the school lot who doesn't belong there?"

Beau shakes his head. "And I was looking, too. Somebody needs to kick the crap out of that guy."

"Absolutely, but it's not you, buddy boy. Not even with five or six of your friends to help, so drop it. This is a severely screwed-up individual, okay? You don't take chances with somebody like that. When you think you've got them cornered, they'll stoop to a level you don't expect, okay? You leave it to the cops." Says the woman with a gun in her safe.

Outside, tires crunch over the driveway. Casey's up like a shot. "That's Dad." He shoves his chair back from the table and heads for the living room.

"Hey, Case." Shaw drops her first forkful back to her plate uneaten, about to follow, but the old man beats her to it, trailing Casey to the entryway, where Shaw can hear him hollering out the open door, "'Course there's plenty, come on in here—no, no, I bet you ain't had a decent bite in weeks. Your chair's right here waiting for you and I'm not hearing no ifs, ands, or buts. . . ."

Shaw covers her face with both hands, her shoulders shaking with silent, helpless laughter as Ryan is pulled into the room, his expression a marriage between hostility and resignation as he takes the empty chair, Casey thumping his dad's shoulders a couple times to nail him in place before bouncing back into his own seat.

Shaw drags her fingers down to cover her mouth for a moment, holding Ryan's gaze, then slaps on a salesman's smile and extends the serving bowl. "Baby peas?"

The call comes early, Shaw pawing invisible cobwebs from her face as she rolls over, squinting at the digital clock—a little past five—before taking her phone out of the nightstand drawer. Jewel.

"Sorry to wake you. You probably have an inkling as to why I'm calling."

Shaw clears her throat. "Firebug's being naughty again, right?"

"This is the first time he's hit two days in a row, and this time there's a fatality. It's ugly, looking deliberate. Tran's knocked out from working the scene yesterday, and he's got a lot to process. I was hoping you might be willing to pinch-hit."

"Sure, yeah. Want me to pick up my wandering lamb along the way?"

"She's already heading to the scene, and it's a trek, almost into the county. I should warn you, it's a Catholic church. I'm not sure if or how that might affect you personally, but I wanted to at least let you know what you were walking into."

Shaw sits up, blankets pooling around her waist. "What church?"

"Saint Anthony's in Dighton." Jewel pauses, listening to Shaw's utter silence. "Do you know it?"

Shaw's caught, shock tightening like a cuff around her neck, making her lower the phone, distantly aware of Jewel's questioning voice, tinny, an insect pinging off a jar.

Shaw tells no one about Saint Anthony's. The house is still sleeping, and everyone's used to her having to leave at all hours for work—a note to Dad about Ryan needing to drive the boys to school will suffice—and then she's in the Beast, unshowered, barely remembering to drag on some jeans and a sweatshirt before heading for the county line.

Time peels back seamlessly, delivering her to the small town of Dighton over the span of a breath, it feels like, a blink, all the roaring intensity within her own head, denial battling with nauseating understanding.

She finds one of the quiet side streets near the church and parks there, able to gear up without so much as thinking, jogging down the sidewalk with her kit banging her thigh, driven by a panicked need to see for herself, to witness.

Beyond the day-glow sawhorses and crime scene tape lies the modest parish church, Shaw holding her ID out to any face she sees turning her way as she advances on the building she knows well, though she hasn't set foot inside since Mom's funeral service.

The fire collapsed the steeple; the Latin cross, which had perched atop, now lies in a heap of blackened rubble roughly in the vicinity of the nave, where she walked, and Thea, and Mads, dressed in white, brides of Christ, confirmation at seven years old, right here.

The fire looks to have originated in the parish house, the auxiliary building used as the priest's living quarters when Shaw was growing up, and by the looks of the activity coming and going through the scorched doorway, still is. Or was. Jewel said fatality.

Shaw sways slightly where she stands, ruled by a sense of detachment, her limbs weighted and separate from her core. A small tech is coming toward her, those raspberry-colored boots showing through her coveralls revealing her identity from a distance. Shaw says, "I went here, this was my church," before Gauthier even closes the space between them.

"Are you serious?"

"Heart attack." The dazed, disgusted humor of her tone covers the fact that Shaw feels lightheaded, close to vomiting. "Since I was a baby. This was my dad's family church—he grew up one town over. That's why we made the drive here on Sundays instead of the churches closer to the house. It was special"—her voice breaks, awful, sucking her breath in and holding it at the threat of breaking down here in front of everyone—"it meant a lot to him that we went here."

Gauthier pulls her mask down, fingers working against her palms. "Do you think you should—I don't know, go home, or—?"

"Is McKenzie here?"

"I haven't seen him. There's another detective—"

Shaw curses, stepping back. "This isn't Bennet, it's Piscataquis—different first responders—*Shit*." Her phone's going off. Jewel, the boss she left hanging on an empty line earlier. Shaw turns away from Gauthier, putting the phone to her ear. "Jewel. Sorry about before. Listen—I know who did this."

"Pardon me?"

"This fire." Shaw can't stop snapping, her tone splintery, looking back at the building, every small detail springing to the forefront: the broad front steps, the stained-glass windows along the eastern side, the hand-painted sign directing parishioners to park in the rear. "This was my church growing up, my family went here for years. Christenings, weddings, the whole enchilada. I think it's the man who's been calling me, Anders Jansen."

Jewel is quiet. "Did he confess to you?"

"No, but the cops don't know where he is right now, and—

Christ, this is *coincidence?* He burned my church down. I don't know, maybe he burned them all down, all the buildings, all the fires." Shaw claps a hand to her face, squeezing her eyes shut. "He kept talking about religion, giving me shit, but I never thought . . ."

"Okay, Shaw? I need you to find the team leader and tell them that you're going to have to step away from this right now."

"I can't—"

"Oh, yes, you can. If you handle even one evidentiary item at this scene, you could very well blow away any case the state ever makes. Against Jansen or anyone else. You are as personally in-volved as it gets, and you need to leave. I will get on the phone to the Piscataquis Sheriff's Office and relate what you've told me, and I'm sure they'll be in touch as soon as possible."

Shaw's breath is tearing out of her as she looks between the church and the street and Gauthier. "Right. I know you're right. I'm gone." She rings off, turns to Gauthier. "Sorry, kid. I'm kicking you out of the nest way too soon. Happy landings."

Gauthier hesitates, then follows. "I'll walk you back."

Shaw sniffs, shaking herself. "Think I'm going to need smelling salts?"

"No. But I don't think you should have to be alone right now, either."

Shaw falls quiet, and after a second, nods her thanks.

Gauthier stays by her side as they follow the winter sidewalk back to Shaw's car, no conversation, Shaw deep inside herself, trying to grab down locations, dates, facts that she doesn't have the stability to piece together right now, never knowing when a flash of memory will blindside her: filing in and out of Saint Anthony's countless times with the rest of the parishioners, a child's perspective, her parents two large, warm, secure presences moving in front of her;

standing beside Thea to sing at countless Christmas Eve masses; seeing the priest wet Mads's smooth little head with holy water at her christening, how she hadn't made a sound, fascinated by the sensation of trickling warmth.

"Did he kill the priest?" Shaw's voice is low, barely emerging from her tight jaw.

Gauthier nods. "I'm sorry. No one was spreading any theories around yet that I heard."

Shaw's stomach plummets. "Was it Father Joseph? Did anyone say his name?"

Gauthier doesn't answer right away, and Shaw follows her gaze over toward someone standing on the raw, scoured-looking knoll between houses to their left about twenty feet away. He says, "Shaw."

Recognition isn't immediate. First, she's held in place by his look, not so much the familiarity of it as the intensity, pinned by the unexpectedness of encountering someone who knows her on this unfamiliar street. She starts to speak, then the images, visual and mental, overlap. There's frisson. She knows him.

Anders, in real life, is quite tall, well over six feet, emphasized by how thin and long-legged he is beneath that tan overcoat he wears unbuttoned over a looped, layered gray scarf, white fisherman's sweater, and jeans. His hair is dirty blond—the photo Shaw found online was black-and-white, so she wasn't sure—wire-framed glasses resting on an aristocratic nose, a well-defined chin, skin somewhat sallow, his expression creased into hard lines of mirth.

"You've kept me waiting," he says, and hearing that voice, here, in the cold clear air, is enough to jumpstart Shaw's nervous system, making her jerk back even before he starts coming down the slope toward them. "Standing in the cold isn't my favorite pastime, I admit."

"Shit." She shoves Gauthier's shoulder, trying to get her moving. "Go, get in the car. Right now!"

Gauthier allows herself to be urged forward, glancing back at

Anders, who has reached the sidewalk and is smiling at them, still coming. Shaw yanks down the zipper on her coveralls to reach the pocket where she stashed her keys, clicking the unlock button on the fob as the taillights blink manically.

"Where do you think you're going?" Anders's voice carries, and the panic is like a siren inside her, light and sound, hustling Gauthier to the passenger side and pushing her in, ignoring the younger woman's attempt to speak, Shaw running around the front bumper only to see him some ten feet away now, walking with his hands in his coat pockets. "We need to talk, Shaw."

She feels the oblong shape of the personal alarm on her key chain, never looks, just yanks the pin.

The alarm deafens the world; Shaw's tested it before but this time she leaves it dangling, pin clenched in the opposite fist, cringing from the sound and flashing strobe light, not taking time to check his response, only hoping it drove him back.

She swings herself inside the cab, stabbing down the master lock button and cranking the engine. She lurches forward within inches of the car parked in front—blocked in—and then she reverses, glancing over to see him standing there at the curb, watching her maneuver with a faintly quizzical, amused look, still wincing slightly from the alarm.

Shaw's dropped the pin and doesn't know it until Gauthier manages to jam it back into place, and there's only the radio and Gauthier saying in a voice made distant by the ringing in Shaw's ears, "Who was that? *Shaw?*"

Shaw stomps the gas without looking, some miracle allowing the Beast to skim past the bumper of the car in front and peel off down the street.

Shaw drives right through the stop sign at the end, cutting somebody off, at least one horn honking behind them along with the squeal of their tires. She can't breathe, keeps waiting with an endless plummeting sensation for her lungs to unlock and air to return, but it keeps stretching on, the ringing in her ears swelling, swelling, Gauthier's voice buried, Shaw only aware of the girl's mouth moving, her hand gesturing back toward where they came from.

Shaw's vision darkens and shrinks at the edges like a film burn—she needs to pull over, needs to stop this car—but Anders could be following and how far is far enough, where would be safe—

Then comes the sensation of the car slowing, her own foot on the brake, her hands turning the wheel, but Gauthier's are there, too, helping guide the Beast out of the flow of traffic, Shaw aware of very little until they're stopped with the engine off, at which point Shaw chokes out, "Oh my God," and scrubs her face with her hands, dragging down on her skin until it hurts, still waiting for her lungs to work. "Don't unlock the doors, keep them locked. Keep them locked."

Shaw stays that way, bowed over the wheel, face covered, fighting for breath, distantly aware that Gauthier's on the phone: "—don't know what to do, wasn't sure whether to . . . Okay. Yes. I didn't know who else to call."

By the time the ambulance pulls up beside them and shuts off the lights and siren—the Beast is in a bank parking lot, it turns out, smack in the middle of two spots—Shaw has mostly emerged from her tunnel, little left from the episode but jumping muscles around her left eye and a pounding headache. Her jaw held tight, Shaw steps out to meet the EMTs, feeling shamefaced and ridiculous. The techs have her sit in the ambulance while they take her pulse, count her respirations, check her pupils with a penlight, and quiz her about her symptoms. Gauthier stands outside, hugging herself, glancing over as a sheriff's office squad car pulls up and a female officer climbs out, her right hand resting on her duty belt as she approaches them, stopping to speak quietly with Gauthier.

"It sounds like you had a panic attack," the older EMT with the graying moustache finally says, folding up the flap on the blood pressure cuff. "Inability to catch your breath, those intense fight-or-flight feelings, tunnel vision. This is the first time something like this has happened to you?"

"Yeah, I've never . . . I'm not somebody who loses it."

"Well, we can take you to the ER, have a doctor take a look?"

"No, no, I'm fine, never better. Sorry to waste your time. If it were up to me, you wouldn't have been called. I'm not sure who's footing the bill for this, but I hope it's not me. No offense."

"None taken. Have somebody drive you home, and follow up with an appointment with your PCP as soon as you can, all right?"

Shaw climbs down from the ambulance to face the deputy and Gauthier, both watching her like she might either shatter or start spasming violently, attempting not to look humiliated when that's pretty much the definition of this moment. It's the first time Shaw's ever had people treat her like she's made of porcelain, and it's not a welcome sensation.

"Lydia here tells me you two are crime scene techs, working the scene at the church fire?" Shaw nods, and the officer continues, "I understand that you had an encounter with a man on Wingate Avenue."

"Yeah, I originally brought charges with the Piscataquis County Sheriff's Office, but the state police are the ones who issued the BOLO. This guy's name is Anders Jansen. I've got a temporary protection order out against him until my restraining order gets pushed through. I guess he must've followed me here today." Shaw swears. "He must've been watching my house. I've got to call Dad." She reaches for her phone. "Anders knew where I'd parked, and he was waiting for me in somebody's yard when I came back. He started following us down the street. Gauthier happened to be walking with me and got pulled along for the ride."

Once the officer has taken their statements, they're free to go; Shaw is determined to drive herself, though she can't blame Gauthier for accepting a lift in the cruiser back to Wingate Avenue to retrieve her own car rather than taking another jolly spin on Mr. Toad's Wild Ride.

Shaw and Gauthier look at each other for a moment before they go their separate ways, and then Gauthier says abruptly, "I called Jewel. In the car. I'm sorry. I didn't know what else to do. She's the one who called 911, I didn't . . ." Gauthier trails off, shaking her head.

Ah. Shaw takes a moment to speak. "It's okay. You did the right thing." True or not, in Shaw's experience, it's all any of us really wants to hear.

Shaw heads to the lab, her kit in the back seat, where she'd apparently thrown it upon diving into the SUV earlier, her ears still ringing from the combined decibels of the personal alarm and the phone conversation with Mads in the bank parking lot right before Shaw left to come here. "He came after you?" Her sister's voice sounded tearful over the speaker, still processing the news about Saint Anthony's before Shaw tacked this on. "Oh my God, are you *okay?*"

"He confronted me, yeah, but I'm fine. I got the hell out of there." Shaw drew a breath, so conscious of getting enough oxygen now; she can't think of anything quite so stupid, her own body depriving itself of air. "The cops have what they need now. His ass is as good as arrested at this point. And then, maybe, we'll get some real answers out of him. Why the church? I just don't . . ." Shaw pauses, gathering control. "I'm going to call the sheriff's office, see if they can have somebody swing by the house and check on you guys, so don't freak out if you see a cruiser pull up. And do me a favor and don't tell the boys until I get home, okay? It'll just scare them."

Now, Shaw turns in her seat to survey the lab parking lot before getting out, searching for gray Chargers or anything else even slightly out of place. Had his car been parked in the line of vehicles along the curb on Wingate Avenue, and she'd walked right past it without noticing, too busy running her mouth at Gauthier to be on her guard? It proves how impossible it is to be a hundred percent aware all the time. Which is why one carries pepper spray. Shaw tucks her can into her coat pocket and heads inside, turning around to walk backward a couple times to scan the lot and the road.

Their little cube of desks is deserted, Tran coming in late after pushing it so hard at yesterday's fire, and Gauthier still flying solo at today's scene. Shaw makes it as far as her desk before she becomes aware of Jewel standing a few feet away, staring at her. When Shaw glances over, the boss's face is blanched, disbelieving. "You came in?"

Shaw stands awkwardly, still gripping the plastic handle of her kit. "I thought I could still get in a day's work."

Jewel blinks, holding still for a moment, and then she sweeps the wheeled chair from Tran's desk and parks it beside Shaw's. "Have a talk with me."

Shaw sits woodenly at her desk, where Jewel regards her in a way most unlike her, as if she isn't certain of her next move; usually she seems to follow some internal Pac-Man maze from dot to dot to dot, task-oriented from the moment she opens her eyes in the morning. "You should have gone straight home after everything that's happened. I can't believe that wasn't your first instinct."

Shaw crosses her legs. "I'd rather stay busy. What good is sitting around worrying going to do."

Jewel watches her, her brow lined incredulously. "I need to know what happened on the street today, and what you know about these fires. And I'd appreciate it if you didn't hold anything back this time."

Shaw's temp has spiked up, sweat beginning in her pits and beneath her bra line. "I don't know anything about the fires that I haven't come right out and told you. And you know that man's been harassing me. You know about my sister. I've kept everybody one hundred percent informed. Don't make it sound like I've acted unethically because that's crap." Jewel continues to watch, unmoved. "This guy violated the order I had out against him. The cops are searching Dighton and the surrounding area for him now."

"So, this is who approached you and Lydia on the sidewalk." Jewel sits back. "You should've told me that things had reached this point."

"How am I supposed to know what he's going to do next? I'm accountable for this lunatic now? And I guess I'm not totally clear on what's considered my personal business and what I need to report to you—"

"When another staff member is pulled into a dangerous situation, that's over the line. Okay? Lydia was caught in the middle today with no idea what was going on. If that man had had a gun or a knife, we might not be lucky enough to be sitting here having this uncomfortable conversation." Jewel's tone is blistering. "When your work and professional demeanor is being affected, that's when you come to me. I did suggest that you take more time off after you discovered the Jane Doe, and you were extremely dismissive. Now you show back up at work after discovering your childhood church has been burned to the ground and you've nearly been assaulted or abducted or worse."

"Because I'm *fine.* Hey, I didn't go out looking for all of this—I tried to do the right thing, I went to the cops, took out a protection order. So, now I'm supposed to stay home and hide under the covers? Excuse me, but that's complete bullshit, and the fires"—Shaw shakes her head frantically—"I had no idea it was him, how could I—none of those other locations mean anything special to me—Lake Heron could've been a coincidence—"

"I'm not implying that it's your fault that you're being stalked or that Jansen may be the arsonist. I'm saying you should have dealt with the problem differently, mainly by fully looping me in right from the beginning. I'm not sure if this is indicative of a personal issue between us or your resentment of authority in general, but as your supervisor, I can take steps to make sure you take the time to care for yourself mentally and physically until the authorities have dealt with this problem. I understand that you had a panic attack behind the wheel." Jewel watches Shaw give a burst of frustrated, scornful laughter and look away, her arms folded. "It's also clear that this man knows where you work and was hoping to lure you to the scene today to force an encounter. Maybe that's what the fires have been about all along, trying to draw you out."

Shaw stares fixedly at her for a second. "You think that's why he escalated? Because Tran was working the scenes instead?"

"It seems to me the bigger and more frequent the fires, the more likely we were to have all hands on deck, correct?"

"Jesus Christ." Shaw's stomach does a slow turn, and she wonders if she can make it to the nearest wastebasket in time if necessary.

"You have to understand that I can't allow the lab or the other employees here to be compromised or threatened again in any way," Jewel says. "And I am seriously concerned about your judgment right now. Until Jansen is arrested or something major changes, I'm placing you back on compassionate leave."

"I'm laid off because of this asshole?"

"Watch your language around me. And you did hear me say

'compassionate,' didn't you? So, no, not laid off. On leave with pay until the problem has been dealt with."

"You cannot take this job away from me."

"We're talking about a temporary solution, Shaw. I'm sure you'd rather be home with your family right now, anyway."

"What do you know about family?" Jewel stops, lifting her gaze. "You can't know what it's like to be scared for your kids' lives, or your own. Not knowing if somebody might take you away from them forever. What kind of hell that is. And I'm living it, right now."

Jewel's quiet, sliding the pen back into the desk organizer, then she says, in a modulated, careful tone, "I had a son." She returns Shaw's stare. "He lived for three and a half minutes after birth. But I still think of myself as a parent. I think I have some sense of the level of distress you're feeling." Jewel's slender throat works, a slight fluttering there. "The helplessness."

The regret is absolutely crushing, bad enough that Shaw simply squeezes her eyes shut and rides the wave, tilting her head forward, saying, "Fuck," softly, in awe of how badly she's screwed up this time.

"It's all right. Stop cursing. It's like working on the set of a George Carlin HBO special."

Shaw puts her head in her hands, squeezing the sides of her skull. "No, really—I am an asshole. I am so sorry."

"Again, it's fine. You didn't know. No one knew because I didn't want to talk about it. Simple as that." Jewel smooths the front of her blazer, dry-eyed, but not as she was before, not quite, or perhaps that's only in Shaw's perception: her edges seem softened a little, a distance to her gaze. "I hope you'll take me at my word that compassionate leave is a good thing, and you need to take advantage of it. Think of it as time to regroup. When you're ready"—Jewel waits until Shaw finally locks eyes with her again—"the job will be here waiting for you."

Shaw's voice is rough, sandpapered with tears. "You sure that's what you want?"

Jewel's look is steady, and she takes a moment before answering. "I didn't pair Lydia with you simply because you're the most senior employee, you know."

Shaw runs her fingers through her hair, sniffs, swipes at her eyes. "You didn't?"

"You haven't figured it out by now?" Jewel's expression changes by half a degree, a quirk at the corner of her mouth. "You're a nurturer. Albeit a foul-mouthed one, but a nurturer all the same. And Lydia needs that. It's the only way she'll grow."

Then, impossibly, they're laughing together, Shaw's shoulders shaking hard enough for the vibrations to travel down to her toes. Jewel holds out a tissue. "We couldn't get by without you."

It's early evening when Anders calls, shortly after the supper table has been cleared, catching Shaw in a superfluous nook of the house, the passageway outside the small, cramped laundry room. Dad, last she saw, was in the living room, the tube off, sitting in the lamplight with a book in his lap, lost in thought. She'd lingered in the doorway long enough to see him reach up and rub his eyes, tears shed in private over the loss of Saint Anthony's. Their priest, Father Joseph, was due for retirement but had stayed on; to Dad's knowledge, Saint Anthony's was still his parish. There is every chance that he was the victim who had been trapped in the parish house.

Shaw looks at Anders's name on the screen for maybe a second, then taps on her recording app, waiting.

"You know, I saw someone very much like you on the street today," he begins conversationally. "So much so that I called out to her, but she kept right on walking. I must've been mistaken. It's amazing how many gone-to-seed white trash bottle blondes one encounters on the average day."

"Maybe you scared her off with your poncy-as-fuck scarf and sweater combo. You burned my church down, you piece of shit."

"Oh, so now it's your church again. To my knowledge, you haven't been to mass in over a decade, haven't raised your sons with any sense of faith. Well, as always, the burden of proof lies with you. Though I will say that the flames crackling behind the stained glass in the dusk gave off a light that was almost transcendent. Tell me, what will you miss most about Saint Anthony's? Those long, dark, gleaming pews where you must've spent so many hours, or perhaps the enigmatic Madonna near the entryway, arms outstretched?"

She slams her fist into the doorframe, focusing on the pain radiating from knuckles to her wrist, taking a moment to steady her voice. "Why set the fires? Why take the risk just to draw me out?" Silence. "Why kill the priest? Nobody else had to die but him?"

"That was merely a bonus."

She swallows tightly, shaking her head. "The other locations were completely random? You're done now?" Again, he won't answer. She goes down the dim hallway past the kitchen, catching Beau's attention from the sink where he and Casey are washing dishes. In the living room, she touches Dad's knee—he's sitting with his eyes closed, head resting back—and she does a hectic mime of pointing to her phone, then making a phone shape with her free hand; Dad heaves to his feet, going for the kitchen landline to call the sheriff's office. "Let's see. You're calling me right now on a phone that's registered to you, so they'll be able to track the pings off the towers in the area to narrow down your location. I'm sure that you're still driving around in the car that's registered to you. Every law enforcement agency in New England has been flagged about those plates. And by the looks of it, you're no John Dillinger. Life on the run can be tough on the sensitive, intellectual, poetry-spouting type."

"You're really enjoying yourself. You didn't seem quite so smug when we met on the street earlier. In fact, forgive the vulgarity, but you looked like a woman with a river of piss running down her leg. Then you had your fun with that little key chain toy. I'll be expecting it next time."

Shaw feels the boys' eyes on her, and she turns back to the hallway, struggling to keep her voice down. "No next time. I'm hanging up on your sorry ass, but feel free to write down all your threats in iambic pentameter while you're in the supermax, okay?"

"I'm surprised at you, Shaw. I can't seem to get over it." His voice is up, a veneer of normalcy on the surface, but something shaky, barely controlled beneath. "I understand that you suffer from poor impulse control, but bringing in the police? We had so many conversations about the consequences of that. And now look. Saint Anthony's is gone. Father Joseph burned. All laid at your feet."

"Fuck you. This is *not* on me."

"It is on you!" His shout comes out of nowhere, and Shaw jolts. "There's action and consequence. Because of your actions, a man is dead. You are so inexcusably *blind,* Shaw. I have led you by the nose this entire time, and still you refuse to see. You betrayed my confidence, which shows how little you care about those around you." He pauses for breath. "Who was your young friend? Today, on the street?"

Shaw sees Dad coming down the hall, holding his phone out to her. "The cops have all they need on you now. I don't have to talk to you anymore." Shaw hangs up, then takes Dad's phone from him. "This is Shaw."

It's the same deputy she dealt with when she made her original complaint. "Your father tells me you had a phone call from Mr. Jansen?"

"Yeah, I just hung up on him. And, honestly, I'd feel a lot better if you guys could send somebody out here to keep an eye on our place tonight. He's pissed and dangerous and I'm afraid he might try something."

"Did he threaten you?"

"Always. Every time I talk to him. I've got my whole family under one roof right now, and he knows it. I understand the manpower thing, but if you could spare somebody, we'd really appreciate it. He came right up to me today, and I don't—" She hits an emotional wall, pressing her lips together.

"Somebody's on their way to your place right now, should be there within fifteen minutes. The warrant for accessing Mr. Jansen's phone records is in the works now, but the state police may be able to track him anyway if his smartphone has the location services switched on. I'll be calling Detective York, your state police contact, after we hang up to discuss next steps."

The night passes, somehow, Shaw waking intermittently to prowl the house, leaving her nest on the floor in Beau's room, where Casey sleeps squished together with him in the twin bed, his big bro good enough not to put up more than a grumble when Casey came bolting in around eleven o'clock and burrowed under the blankets.

Shaw looks out random windows at the blackness of the old pasturage around the house—there could be a Mack truck parked out there right now and who could tell—and checks that the deputy's SUV is still parked in the driveway, which it is. The officer may well be fast asleep, but at least the vehicle is there to serve as a deterrent. She checks the locks on the doors and the sleeping old man in his chair; tonight, Dad's got one of their aluminum baseball bats leaned against the recliner. Then Shaw goes back up the stairs to lay in the sleeping bag for fifteen minutes or so before giving up and going through it all again.

Aphrodite gets up from her bed every time Shaw comes downstairs and walks after her, black-on-black eyebrows lifting as her human paces, checking out windows, finding no peace.

Shaw's sitting at the table when everyone comes down at the usual time the next morning. For Shaw, there's no work to get ready for, no reason to keep one eye on her phone, instead watching through the hazy aquarium filter of exhaustion as her family goes through the motions, subdued, Mads engrossed in her phone, everyone aware that Shaw has been put on leave and wise enough not to mention it.

Dad's been awake with her for a while, not saying much, scratching the dog's head, looking out the windows. It's a sense of being under glass, the house like a thin lid placed upon them, easily lifted to reveal them squirming defenselessly through the rooms like ants. "Think it'd be all right to bring that fella a cup of coffee?" Dad asks, leaning forward to look out the front living room window where they can see the SUV, or possibly a different one, some changing of the guard happening while Shaw was catching forty winks.

"Couldn't hurt to knock on the window and ask, I guess."

Dad fills a travel mug and takes it out, Shaw watching the boys crunch for a few seconds before saying, "Okay, I'm thinking about keeping you home from school."

Both look up, Casey's expression clearing, Beau's eyes widening. "How long?" he says.

"I don't know. Until they catch this guy?"

"That could be forever—we've got the away game at Chamberlain today—"

"I don't mind not going," Casey says.

"Shut up, that's because you don't have playoffs coming up—"

"*Don't say shut up!* Jesus Christ!" Shaw settles back and exhales unsteadily. "Mommy's operating on about three hours of sleep right now, sugar dumplings, so don't push it, okay? Beau, if you want to go to school that bad, fine. Have at it. It was just a thought. Casey, your call." She hesitates, forces herself to continue. "But starting tonight I'm sending you both to stay with your dad at his apartment until things are safe here again."

No immediate objections. The boys are uncertain, both watching her, maybe trying to guess how she wants them to react, what will hurt her feelings. Okay, yes, her feelings are hurt. Missing a chance to ride the bench against Chamberlain had elicited a bigger response.

"I'm going to catch Dad before he heads to work and talk it over. It sucks—I don't want to do it, and you know my heart'll be breaking, being here without you guys." Tears come with a wrenching sense of grief, and as she stares at the tabletop in a half-assed attempt to keep them from noticing, Casey comes over and hangs his sturdy arms around her neck. "But I don't know what's going to happen next, and— Come on, you guys will have a blast with Dad. Hang out in his new shop, order pizza, watch NESN." It hits her that she's reeling off the list of things that used to be the norm in their household when Ryan was around, and she presses her fist to her lips for a second. She misses him being more than some insubstantial concept standing nighttime guard over the shop. She misses what used to be life.

Mads puts down her phone and pulls up the seat beside her, not reaching for her, not quite, instead placing her entwined hands down on the tabletop, and Shaw wonders if it might actually kill her sister to hold her hand for a second, give her a squeeze. If roles were reversed, Shaw would be hugging Mads so hard right now, she wouldn't have any stuffing left.

"But . . . like I said, that could take forever." Beau folds his arms on the tabletop. "Why doesn't Dad just move back in? I mean, for real."

"Because. It's not the same." Two pairs of blue eyes focus on her, refusing to let her off the hook. "That would mean something. Between Dad and me, him moving back in. Get it? I can't ask him, and he wouldn't want to give you guys the wrong idea."

"But that's so stupid," Beau says. "This our house. We should all be here."

"Couldn't agree more." The old man's back inside, pulling off his coat, his cheeks ruddy, somewhat cheered by his success in foisting the coffee off on the deputy. "Snowin' out."

Shaw narrows her eyes at him, but having something to bristle at helps brush off some of the self-pity. "Look"—she speaks to the boys—"I know Dad will be super excited to have you guys, so I'm going to talk it over with him and that's how it's going to be."

Casey's face is close to hers, his breath moving her flyaways. "What if they can't catch him, though? What if it does take forever?"

"I won't let it."

"How?"

"Never mind. Finish up your breakfast, then get dressed and brush your teeth. Unless you want me to see if Dad will let you hang out with him at work today?"

Casey hesitates, shakes his head. "It's okay. If Beau's going to school, I guess I will."

Once Casey's pounding up the steps after Beau, Shaw puts on her coat and crosses to the shop with a dorky sort of wave to the deputy, who she can't see through the tinted windshield, anyway.

It doesn't take long. Ryan's dressed, already got one foot out the door, and he says yes immediately, both of them taking lots of too-long pauses where the need to say something of significance is undeniable but neither of them is wise or brave enough to do it. "I like this," she finally says, indicating his beard growth by stroking her own chin.

He cocks his head in the sardonic gesture Beau imitates all the time. "You called me Grizzly Adams."

"That's a bad thing? The man wrestled bears."

"No, he didn't." But it tricks a smile out of him.

Shaw returns to the kitchen table, content to sink into a tired haze again as Mads prepares to leave for class, rifling through her backpack. "Should I check in with that cop? Do they need to know if one of us leaves?"

"You should say something, yeah." Shaw watches her sister over the rim of her mug for a moment. "I'm sorry for being stupid about the suncatcher." Mads's head dips lower, her sheaf of bangs hiding her eyes. "If I'd known, I would've given you something of Mom's instead. I'm happy to go through the boxes again—"

"But you didn't know. That's the whole thing." Mads pauses. "I'm not trying to be mean or ungrateful. I know that you were just being nice." Mads straightens, pulling the zipper shut on the bag. "Do you know that most days I can't even really remember Thea?"

Shaw stares. "Well, you were eight. It's probably the trauma of it all, making things hazy."

"No. I see those pictures of Thea online, and that's all I have in my memory, too. A handful of the same images of a girl I didn't know. I know she had blond hair and a bunch of piercings in her ears because all the articles and news reports say so. But I don't feel her inside of me. Not the way you guys do. I don't miss her every day like I miss Mom."

Shaw inclines her head and can't believe the stinging water-works are back, twice in one morning—"Mads."

"I mean, Thea wasn't home very much, and when she was, I'm sure I was the annoying little sister who wouldn't stay out of her way or keep her hands off her stuff. You guys had the Irish twins thing going on, but I wasn't a part of that, how could I be? There were so many years between us."

"She was your big sister, too. She loved you. I don't get where this is coming from."

"Well—look at what's happening right now—look at our lives. Everything always comes back to Thea. That's why I stopped helping with the posters. I guess . . . some stupid part of me actually believed maybe you and Dad would stop doing it, too. And maybe we could start living for ourselves instead of some memory of a seventeen-year-old who never even had a chance to grow into somebody interesting, and some depressing old step-by-step story about the last time we saw her alive. I mean, do you even really remember that day? Or just remember the telling. See what I mean?" Mads lifts her gaze to Shaw's stricken expression. "And, yeah, maybe if we'd had the chance to grow up together, Thea and I would be friends now, but as it is, I don't even have any good things to look back on. She's like this floating blind spot that's moving all the time, passing over everything, and . . ." Mads releases a short breath. "I wish I could get my childhood back, I guess. I mean—I'm defined by somebody who I don't even remember. How unfair is that."

Shaw shakes her head slowly. "I don't believe it. I can't believe that you've forgotten how crazy she was about you—I'm sure that if you sit down and—"

"No, Shaw. *You're* the one who's crazy about me. I was your little baby doll growing up, not Thea's. I think I'd remember having two stand-in moms back then. You were the one I went to whenever I had a question or needed help or wanted to play. *You* always made the time. So, stop giving away the credit." Mads shoulders her bag then, reaching back to pull her ponytail free of the strap. "Maybe you're the one who should sit down and look at the Thea you think you remember. See if you can even separate her from yourself at this point." She heads for the doorway. "Sorry. I didn't want to hurt you. I have to go."

Shaw stands partway, words caught on her lips, *What do you mean by "go" first and foremost, go as in never come back, as in I can't live here with you anymore?* Shaw manages, "Tell the deputy when you'll be back." Choked, a little shrill, answered only by the closing of the front door.

18

Once the boys are squared away at school, Shaw comes home, where the house already seems too quiet, the usual weekday lull amplified by the fact that the boys won't be sleeping here tonight, that the ensuing hours will be horribly empty without them. No work. Nothing to do but let the dread eat her alive.

Dad, meanwhile, is sweeping around the kitchen chairs, watching her pass by and go upstairs; he stops to lean on the broom but says nothing.

Shaw's phone rings, and she's surprised to see Gauthier's name on the screen, feeling a flicker of hope, like maybe Jewel changed her mind and the lab really can't get through one morning without her. "What's up?"

A moment of cramped indecision on the other end. "I feel like I got you fired."

"She didn't fire me. Is that what people are saying?"

"No. No one's saying anything. At least not to me." An agitated hesitation. "It's my fault. I shouldn't have called Jewel from the parking lot. I never should've brought her into it."

Shaw sighs, leaning against the hallway wall. "Look, you acted responsibly, okay? She's the boss, you had to tell her what happened. Jewel had good reason to boot me onto leave, whether I love the idea or not." Shaw listens to the girl's processing silence. "I command you to stop beating yourself up and get on with carpe diem-ing, okay? Cheer up. Eat some Swiss rolls. The kind from the vending machine that I like, with the red junk in the center. In honor of my memory."

"That really makes it sound like you won't be back."

"I'm *kidding*. I will be back. I'll be dragging you all over crime scenes, making tasteless remarks, and dancing to music older than your grandmother again before you know it, I promise." Shaw pauses. "Take care of yourself, kiddo. Be seeing you."

Shaw goes into each boy's room and packs overnight bags with enough to last them four days or so, extra underwear and socks, those thick flannel pajama sets given as Christmas gifts which the boys never wear because they're way too hot, but who knows what the temperature is like in Ryan's new apartment—probably warmer than here, central heating instead of a roaring, oil-guzzling old boiler that wakes everybody up when it kicks on—

Then she yanks the bag to the side, hurls the pajamas down, throws the bag against the wall with a rough grunt, where it flops limply to the floor. Shaw spins and drops onto the edge of the mattress with her face in her hands.

She indulges her rage and pain for maybe ten seconds, then scrubs her face, inhales deeply, and pulls her phone from her hoodie pocket to type in M-C-K into the texting app, making his name pop up in the address line. Shaw types: *Hi—are you free at all today?*

She's cleaned up her tantrum mess by the time he answers: *I can be. Are you taking me up on that lunch?*

Name the place. Her heart's doing sixty in a thirty-five.

A pause. *The Sicilian in Dover-Foxcroft? Do you mind eating around one-ish?*

I'm there.

She arrives at the restaurant early, a remodeled Victorian with tall angular windows and a fancy stone fountain out front which implies disapproval of pennies and wishes. Shaw sits in her car, dressed in a soft, rose-colored boatneck sweater she usually saves for court dates and her best jeans, basically trying to regain her equilibrium, recognizing this dangerous mood in herself, a flame licking around a fuse, but fuck it, why not set a few things off.

McKenzie shows up a few minutes late like last time, raising a hand as he recognizes her vehicle. She climbs out to meet him.

Immediately, the atmosphere is different, charged, and she can't remember being this butterflies-in-the-stomach nervous, like a kid going to the senior prom. Absurd, really: she never went to her own prom because she had a baby belly out to here and Ryan hated formal stuff, anyway—and now she tries to remind herself of the current state of things to sober up. But a three-martini lunch was what she had in mind from the beginning, wasn't it, that and a little gazing at McKenzie's weathered, worldly face.

"Hey, sweet cheeks." She links arms with him immediately, glad when he's surprised but rolls with it, settling in beside her like it's comfortable, like they fit. "Glad we could make this work."

"I'm glad you texted. I'd hoped the dog case might be enough to lure you in."

"You don't need bait." It's a relief to wear a mask, be flippant and funny and order a great big drink she could backstroke in. She waits until the waiter has left before she leans forward. "Okay, spill about Grieco—it's killing me. He's not locked up in some pound somewhere, is he? Because I've got room at my place, and I'm already putting myself in the poor house buying dog chow, so—"

"No, he's moved in with Mr. Cloyd's only relative that we were able to locate. A second cousin, lives in Rhode Island." McKenzie leans forward. "Order something expensive. I owe you. You nudged me onto the right track. The killer was somebody the dog knew, true enough."

"Caviar-stuffed lobster tails soaked in absinthe it is." She glances over the menu. "Okay, so I cheated and googled the case, found an article. It was the ex-wife after all. What the hell was her beef with the old guy after all those years? They'd been split up for close to a decade, right?"

McKenzie snorts softly. "As it turns out, Grieco is the last pup from the last litter produced by the dog they owned together while they were still married. A female who went by the name of Fergie."

"As in the Duchess of York?"

"God only knows. Apparently, they used to sort of—hire her out, I'm not clear on the proper term—to people who were looking to breed their male dog, then sell these Anatolian pups for quite a bit of cash back in the day. But, as Fergie was getting on in years, they agreed to retire her after this final litter was born. All the pups were sold except for Grieco, who the ex-wife claims they kept for sentimental reasons only. When she and Cloyd separated, she kept Fergie, and Cloyd took the male pup."

"Was she looking to start up stud services or something?"

"Essentially, yes, although to hear this woman tell it, it was a crime of passion. Fergie died about a year and a half ago, leaving the lady heartbroken. All she wanted was permission to hire out Grieco's talents to start a whole new generation and maybe get her hands on a new pup for herself from this same bloodline. But Cloyd wasn't having it. Told her this dog was his, strictly a pet, and she should go buy her own. From what I saw online, we're talking upwards of two thousand a pup from a registered breeder."

Shaw rests back against her chair, snagging a breadstick out of the basket before their waiter even has a chance to set it on the tabletop, washing it down with the first swig of her margarita, and coughing out an order for five-cheese ziti and a garden salad. "So, what she's selling as unpremeditated manslaughter actually washes out to be a case of follow the money?"

"I have my suspicions about how it played out, but she's insisting it was unplanned. And there was no digital footprint to uncover, no phone records leading back to her because apparently this argument about the dog took place in two parts, both in person, first when she and Cloyd ran into each other in a grocery store parking lot about two months ago, where she broached the idea and he shot her down, then again when she trailed him to a favorite dog park in the area to have another crack at him. In their third and final confrontation, she claims she was desperate and decided to wait for him on his usual morning walk, neutral ground, to try to convince him to let her use Grieco."

"Wait—satisfy my burning curiosity. Did she go inside the little shack or not?"

He nods. "You know how freezing it was that day. She sat on the bench to get out of the wind while she waited for him to turn up. She's got no record, so her prints wouldn't have turned up when you ran them." He smiles and sips his drink as Shaw laughs, smacking her knee with her palm. "The woman uses a cane when she walks long distances. Heavy, hand-carved. When Cloyd said no for a third time, in what she considered very rude terms, then turned his back on her to walk on, she let him have it across the skull. She was surprised when he didn't get up."

"Yet she somehow found the presence of mind to slip Grieco

into the back of her car and make good her escape. Where was she keeping him all this time?"

"In the early weeks of the investigation, she hid him at some house belonging to her auntie who's been in a nursing home for years, so the place is empty. Later, when she and her current husband figured it was safe, she smuggled Grieco back to her place, moving him between the toolshed and the basement so the neighbors wouldn't catch a glimpse. They kept him muzzled. Poor lad didn't stand a chance of raising the alarm. This last time, we got a search warrant, and there he was. Waiting at the bottom of the steps, tail wagging."

Shaw's well into the margarita now. "So, what was her plan? Secret dog brothel below stairs?"

"Her online search history suggested that she and the second husband were thinking about selling up. The plan may have been to relocate, leave the crime behind them. Breed Grieco as they pleased where no one would be the wiser."

"Holy hell. That is truly twisted. She'd have to falsify AKC papers, give him a new name, the whole nine yards."

"Well, these dog moms. They're a cutthroat bunch." He smiles at her, his face losing its levity as her own expression tenses, crumbling a bit at the edges. "Sorry—did I say something?"

"No. It's not you." She pauses, swallows, says apropos of not much, "They took me off the job. For now."

His brows raise. "You're joking."

"Wish I was." She forces a smile, which probably looks ghastly. "The latest arson, the church in Dighton? I know, that one was outside your jurisdiction. But my whole family went to that parish."

McKenzie stares. "The Piscataquis office knows about this?"

"Of course. He's already a fugitive, but supposedly they'll be doubling up their efforts to find him. I stopped by the scene at Saint Anthony's. As I was leaving, Anders came up to me on the street. He just came over, expected me to stop and talk to him. He fucking did it. He set those fires and locked that priest in to burn. There's a good chance that all of the fires were just traps to try to get me within his reach." McKenzie stares. "The boss says I'm on leave until something changes."

A moment's silence. "And here I sit, prattling on, when you've got that on your mind? Holy God. Can't believe nobody put a call in to our office about this yesterday. We're supposed to be working in conjunction with those lads." He shifts, clearly wanting to do something, act, and has to settle for squeezing her hand across the table. "So sorry you had to go through it, Shaw. Sorry for your loss."

"It's okay."

"No, it bloody well is not."

"Nah, I mean I liked listening to you. I felt almost normal again. I'm sick to death of my own problems at this point." She goes to lean her elbow on the table and overshoots the edge slightly, jerking. "Oops. Sloppy drunk here." McKenzie looks simultaneously stricken while trying not to laugh. "I ordered the most fattening thing on the menu. That'll help."

"Who's the primary on Anders's case?"

"Stephen York now, the state police detective who's also handling my sister's case. He seems solid. There've been a lot of detectives since 2007, and he's been one of the more communicative with our family. Never more than a phone call away, old Steve."

"I'm going to need to touch base with him. So, they must be sitting on Anders's place at this point, waiting to pick him up?"

"That's what I was told. Only problem is, he hasn't been back in days. Basically, he's in the wind, and they're hoping to track him using his lovely little calls to me, or maybe pick him up at a speed trap somewhere." She squeezes her brow. "I don't know. Maybe they will."

Their meals arrive, McKenzie not seeming to notice as his food is set in front of him. Shaw tucks into hers, completely absorbed in cheese until she glances up, mouth full, and sees him gazing at her abstractly. "You've got five seconds before I steal your chicken. Fair warning."

"Sorry. The rusty wheels are turning. If Anders is behind the other fires, it stands to reason that it all goes back to you or your sister. Nothing rang bells with you about the other locations?"

"Not personally, no. I mean, I knew of some of them, but that comes from living in the same general part of the state my whole life. Maybe the church was the target all along, hopefully some kind of end point? I looked at the chronological path of the fires and they do lead roughly north toward Saint Anthony's. This morning I put in a call to the bishop in charge of the diocese, hoping he could tell me if Anders was ever a member of Saint Anthony's, but according to him, those records would've been stored in the church itself, and might very well have been destroyed. I'll have to wait until they've released the building back to the church and they've had a chance to sort through the wreckage. But even then . . . I mean, anyone can sit in on a Catholic mass from time to time. They're not demanding three forms of identification at the door before you're allowed to commune with your maker, know what I mean? He could've sat behind my family, watching Thea, and we'll never know."

McKenzie leans on his elbows, tenting his fingers. "I hadn't planned on bringing this up while you were digesting. But, given the circumstances, I'm sure you'd rather hear about it now." He leans on his elbows. "Anders's background check did throw up a flag. He had a juvenile record sealed in the state of New York. And I took the liberty of reaching out to some contacts of mine."

Shaw looks up. "Did you?"

"I hope you don't feel it's an intrusion. I got the sense you wanted me to back off, but I haven't been able to let go of it. Call it . . . freelancing."

Shaw makes a soft sound. "I've been doing some of that myself lately. What'd you find?"

"I called in a favor or two so I could get the details on that juvenile offense. I got a little backstory on him in the case file that you're not going to find anywhere else." He nudges his plate aside so he can fold his arms on the table before him. "Anders Jansen grew up in Finsette, in the Hudson Valley, the only son of a fairly wealthy couple with some status in the community, which was probably why things went as smoothly as they did for Anders after he was arrested at sixteen.

"Their neighborhood was your typical safe little cul-de-sac, until a fifteen-year-old girl from one street over went missing for the better part of a day. She went for a jog, didn't come home." He meets eyes with Shaw, who listens without budging. "Her mother and some neighbors went looking for her and found her in a park area nearby. Dragged into the trees, struck hard enough with something to knock her unconscious. Sexually assaulted. She survived. When she was able, she pointed the finger at our boy. They were friendly acquaintances at school. The toerag most likely followed her there from home that morning and took his chance when he saw it."

Shaw presses her lips together a second. "Did he confess?"

"Never. His family lawyer swept in, and that's basically where details get murky. Whatever bargaining went on behind closed doors resulted in Anders being charged with something like class one assault and battery, no charges for the rape, which kept him off the sex offenders registry, no doubt his lawyer's goal, given Anders's age. With the lesser charge, I'm sure it wasn't difficult for his parents to ensure that the file was sealed."

"Right. Wouldn't want something like that following him through life, warning people who they were really dealing with. And once he turned eighteen, he was free and clear. No record." Shaw pauses. "So, he stalks. Rapes. Gets rid of the victim. You could make the argument that he was perfecting his MO at that point. Jesus. The Jane Doe in the woods."

"I thought you should know about the parallels. When the MSP get a chance to talk to him about your sister's case, I suspect they'll be interested. There are six years between this assault and your sister's disappearance."

"Do you actually have the case file?"

"I have a copy at home. Would you like to hear the second part?"

"Absolutely. I didn't know there was one."

"I put in a day's surveillance on our friend. This was about a week and a half ago, before he violated the protection order." He finally takes a bite of his meal. "I decided to see what a day in the life of Anders Jansen looks like."

"McKenzie. That is frickin' awesome—what happened?"

"Not much, at first. He lives in this little modular home, non-descript, blinds pulled on all the windows. It's a tough place to sit on without being made, really, this biscuit tin of a house plunked down on a half-acre lot, but right on Route 15, so I had reason to think I could pull over behind the house a ways down the road without him necessarily noticing. He didn't leave until about one, at which point I followed him way up into the county, to Presque Isle."

McKenzie gets his phone out of his pocket and opens the camera roll. "This is where he went."

It's a photo of a North Star Health Care member hospital— they're all over the state—this one on the smaller side, the sign visible in the shot: NORTH STAR SPECIALTY HOSPITAL. The photo was taken from the vantage point of the sprawling front parking lot. Shaw fixes on the man walking toward the big glass automatic doors, rec-ognizing the height, his skinniness, the color and style of his coat.

"He was there for an appointment," McKenzie says. "I took that picture and followed him."

"You're Batman. I'm swooning."

McKenzie smiles. "Well, I was too slow. He'd already taken the elevator or stairs by the time I reached the lobby, but I chanced it that he'd leave the same way he came in. I grabbed a seat and waited. He showed after almost two hours. Afterward, he went home and didn't leave again."

Shaw hands the phone back and sits there a moment. "Might be nothing. A hernia or back problems or something."

"Nothing quite so general as that. I looked up their services and they have programs for everything from severe head injuries to weaning patients off ventilators. He could've been seeing any type of specialist in there."

She thinks of him, Anders, standing on the rise, the look of him, only six years older than her but the depth of the lines etched into his face. "I'm thinking about that long break he took from our chats. You know. 'I just called to say I loathe you.'" McKenzie nods; he's a swift and efficient eater, now taking big, deliberate bites and making little mess, clutching his napkin in his left hand for periodical dabs. "I'm thinking, what if he's sick? Maybe last year was a bad year for him, and he decided to give it up. Didn't have the strength, it wasn't fun for him anymore, whatever. Then he rallied somehow . . . went through chemo, maybe. Or found a prescription that helped with some other kind of illness."

"If he is seriously ill, that might explain why he started calling you in the first place and started setting the fires, forcing you to pay attention to him. If he has reason to think he might not be around much longer, maybe he decided that taking what he knows about your sister to the grave isn't half as much fun as lording it over you."

She nods, a hectic sort of excitement building in her. "See—this is the problem with the state cops. They may already know all these things about Anders. But I don't know what they know until they want me to know it, you know? Maybe they're already watching that hospital, hoping he'll still show up for a scheduled appointment, if he needs treatment that badly."

McKenzie folds his napkin in half and lays it on the table. "Anders probably approached you yesterday because he feels he's got nothing left to lose."

"The last few times we've talked on the phone, he's brought up evolving our relationship, reaching the end. All kinds of foreboding shit." She sits back, grazing the tines of her fork across her plate. "I really failed myself. Yesterday, on the sidewalk. I've been taking self-defense classes for years. I work out at home. I've imagined coming face-to-face with him so many times—not necessarily Anders but whoever took Thea, you know, whoever he was—and exactly how I would take him apart. Instead . . . I ran. Got out of there as fast as I could. When Anders called me later, he said I looked like I was pissing myself. And he's right. I was scared out of my mind that I was going to feel a bullet tear into me and that would be the end."

McKenzie places his hand over hers. "My understanding is that the idea behind self-defense is to escape a dangerous situation so you can get to safety."

"I just always thought—"

"That you'd kick his ass?" He watches as her smile finally appears. "You think that's what your sister would want?"

"Forget think it, I know it." Shaw laughs a little. "We always, always had each other's back. If somebody was mean to Thea, they were dead to me, no thought required." Thea's voice floats so easily to the surface; Shaw can hear it word-for-word now: *thought you were some kind of badass, what the hell happened—come on, get your fists up, badass, let's see it.*

In Shaw's mind, she's pounding Thea's opens palms, her sister's freckled, grinning face just behind, and was it all conjecture or a partial memory, slanted to suit the moment? "She would've wanted me to kill him for her."

They go outside to find a genuine snowstorm happening, both bending forward into the wind with their hoods up, Shaw following McKenzie to his Bronco, where Shaw scraps the idea of your standard thanks-bye in favor of climbing into his passenger seat, taking a moment to shove her hood back before turning to look at his somewhat startled expression.

"I also lost it on the drive," she says. "That's what I didn't mention. Gauthier was with me at the time, and when I tried to get us away from Anders, I—melted down. Couldn't breathe, couldn't function. She had to help me park. An ambulance came." She looks at him as the heater runs, McKenzie still with his hood up, some snowflakes already reduced to tremoring glass beads on the waterproof fabric, yet to break and bleed. "So that's pretty much what I meant when I said that I failed myself."

McKenzie's quiet a moment. "You set impossible standards for yourself. You should stop that." He holds her gaze. "Seems to me that you were facing down the boogeyman. Unlike most of us, yours can reach out and touch you in the daylight. I'd say a case of the shakes is understandable."

They kiss, then. No real way to discern who initiated it, simply a gradual sense from each that it's right to lean in, brush noses, then lips, then more urgently.

Watching from some far-removed place, Shaw's surprised at her own intensity, as if it's been forever since she's been touched. In a way, it has been—an emotional lifetime since there was someone in her bed, a man close enough to put her hands on, anyone other than the whispering serpentine voice on the phone. Upon coming up for air, she manages, "How far to your place?"

"Ten minutes. Sixty, when driving through Shackleton's arctic."

And she's laughing, closing her eyes, resting her forehead against his cheek.

McKenzie's place is small, an apartment in a Federal-style building now split into four residences, his on the first floor left. The two of them go through the door together like kids, her pressed to his back; the sense of time slipping away from them and the need to rush, to seize this moment before it's gone, is irresistible.

The lights are all off in the living room but one, a small lamp on the table beside the couch, and that's where they fall together, dropping their damp coats to the floor, Shaw straddling him and running her hands under his shirt, the smooth warmth of him crossed with the reassuring roughness of his chest hair and then his collarbones. She squeezes the muscles of his shoulders and leans down to kiss him, lightly biting his bottom lip and then kissing her way down his throat.

She's somehow surprised to find that his body is his own, not like Ryan's: McKenzie's has its own wiriness, and a patch of scar tissue on his lower back. As she sits up to pull her sweater over her head, he pushes the hem of her camisole up to kiss her stomach like it's some desired, sought-after plain, and it slams home: this isn't Ryan, so maybe she doesn't have to be herself. Maybe she can go against the signals her body's sending her—*slow down, stop*—and be a woman who jumps on a man and takes whatever she wants.

They're both still working off articles of clothing, Shaw's jeans coming down in stages, twisting and wriggling and dragging her heels against the worn leather softness of the couch until she can kick them off her toes. The jeans knock the lamp to the floor with a thud, and she and McKenzie laugh together, face-to-face, and return to kissing, McKenzie finding her breasts inside her bra cups, caressing there, probably hoping for a front clasp. No such luck.

Tinkling chimes and a buzz break the quiet of their fumbling—Shaw's phone going off—sending her into a graceless slide from the couch and onto the rug, where she lands on her side and crawls over to her coat in her bra and underwear.

It's Mads. Shaw claps it to her ear: "What's up?"

An uncertain pause. "Where are you? I just got back and Dad's not here."

"What do you mean?"

"I mean, he left a note saying he went to pick up Beau."

"Beau's supposed to be at the away game at Chamberlain. They don't play until three-thirty."

"I texted Beau and I guess the game was canceled because of the snow. They must've turned the bus around and headed back."

Shaw checks the window, sees a near whiteout, and curses, aware of McKenzie sitting up on the couch behind her. "Well, where's Case?"

"Dad took him with him. I was at class, there was nobody else here to stay with him. And the deputy is gone, did you know that?"

Shaw rubs her face with her free hand. "No, but it doesn't surprise me. They probably pulled him off our place because they needed him on a call and didn't have enough bodies to send a replacement. If nobody was home, he probably just left. You locked the doors?"

"Duh. And I'm literally taking Aphrodite from room to room with me."

Shaw rests back on her haunches, mind ticking over the distance from here to the high school calculated by the slick-as-goose-shit roads. "Dad should not be out driving in this—"

"You think? I've been freaking out. If he would get a phone like everybody else—"

"He's got one. It's fifteen years old and half the time he leaves it in the junk drawer. And let me guess. Casey left his on the coffee table again." Shaw breathes out at Mads's silent confirmation. "I'll try to meet up with him at the school and drive everybody home in the Beast. I'll let you know. In the meantime, do not answer the door for anybody, not a delivery guy or somebody yelling for help, no one. Got it?"

"I know." Mads hesitates. "Thanks, Shaw."

When she's hung up, Shaw turns, aware that she's crouching here barely clothed, not all that confident about her mom belly now. "Has the moment passed?" McKenzie sits on the center cushion, shirtless, pants unbuttoned, looking back with a thousand-yard stare, the hair on the right side of his head airborne with static electricity. "Looks like I kind of ground you into the couch there."

"No complaints."

She stands slowly, clutching her coat in front of her as she edges toward her jeans. "I'm sorry. That was my sister. The other one. I've got to get going. My dad's out driving in this and his vision isn't what it was. We probably shouldn't be letting him drive a pedal car down to the mailbox and back at this point, shit—" She drops the coat and hops into the jeans, fastening the button and then yanking her sweater over her head, rolling the neck down flat.

"Shaw." He's focused on her now. "Was that okay?"

"Yeah. Of course. No, no, it was great." Her fingertips remain on the sweater neck. "I think I might still be in love with my husband."

McKenzie's initial reaction is a couple blinks. "You think?"

"It's tough. He's sick of me and he's probably got a point. And I've never"—she tosses a hand in the direction of the couch, finishes a bit stiffly—"he's the only one I've ever been with."

"Really?"

"Mm-hmm. First kiss and everything. Father of my kids. Maybe that shouldn't matter to me as much as it does. If a person's dumped you, they've dumped you, right? Stick a fork in it already and move on." She zips her coat, then goes to the mat by the door to stuff her feet into her boots. She hesitates. "Am I dead to you now? No more yuks at the crime scenes?"

"I may yet come around." He sits with his elbows resting on his thighs, watching her. She realizes that the scar tissue she felt on his back exists in the front, too; it looks like a bullet wound that passed through and exited on the other side. "If you get yourself sorted—" He glances toward the entrance. "Well. Now you know the way."

Shaw doesn't move, taking in his lowered head, the bare curve of his shoulder, his hands dangling, loosely twined. "Thank you." It's nowhere near enough, but for now, it'll have to do. She goes out into the snow.

The roads are already packed under a good two inches that the plows can't stay on top of. It's coming down steadily, fat, ragged flakes; Shaw keeps her wipers on high, the fun-fun-fun of waiting to see if the sliding cars at the end of each intersecting street will be able to brake in time to avoid T-boning her almost enough to keep her mind off what had happened between her and McKenzie. There's no going back now, no rewinding to when they were coworkers with maybe a little extra spice, but somehow, she can't decide if she's made a mistake. Part of her would still love to go back and climb on top of him. Maybe she'll always want to climb on top of him. Could prove awkward.

Her progress is slow, and what passes for daylight in a storm has blued by Nordic shades until, by the time she passes the HAVERHILL JUNCTION town sign—Axtel kids are bussed to the district school system here—everything is cast with the stage light of an arctic cave. People with front-wheel drive are traveling at practically negative speeds, the occasional jacked-up pickup with a plow roaring around them in a display of tractional superiority, and Shaw's muscles are granite, never daring to completely remove her foot from the brake. It's taken her almost an hour to close the distance between McKenzie's place and the school.

The high school building is locked up for the day, all after-school activities called off due to the weather, the teachers bundling up their grading and bringing it home with them. Shaw pulls around the building to the side parking lot by the gym doors where the sports team busses pick up and let off, crunching to a stop over enough snow to suggest that the plows haven't been here in at least an hour, probably prioritizing other areas because it's post-dismissal.

Dad's sedan isn't among the five other cars in this lot, only one of which she recognizes, although Beau often gets rides home with friends—but he would've texted her or Mads to say so. She parks, engine idling, and turns off the driving silencer setting on her phone to text Mads: *Are they home?*

A twenty-second wait. *No—Dad's not there yet???*

No, and the bus hasn't come. Shaw exhales, bites her bottom lip a moment. *I'll text Beau for an ETA and start driving toward home. Maybe I'll spot them.*

Shaw messages Beau but doesn't expect to hear anything back soon; service is iffy on bus trips and sometimes things don't come through until the team is within range of the school Wi-Fi network. She pulls back out onto the road, driving into what's become a tunnel of white, only the occasional car trundling down the oncoming lane going maybe twenty miles per.

Shaw leaves Main Street, one eye on her phone for a message from Beau in case she needs to turn around and go back, hoping every single crawling vehicle will be Dad's. It never is.

She's almost halfway home when she finally sees a snow-dusted sedan sitting on the shoulder on the opposite side, a hunched, huddled look to it like a pet left outside to fend for itself. It's the old man's.

Not realizing how frightened she was until now, her heart sinks down to reside in her chest again as she navigates an extreme slow-motion U-ey and stops behind them, seeing the silhouette of Casey's head through the rearview as he cranes back to watch her walk up to the driver's side window.

Dad powers down. The flesh of his face looks papery, his expression slack, his eyes like she's never seen them. "I had to pull over," he says. "Thought I'd wait for it to let up a little."

"Turn your hazards on and climb in with me." Shaw scuffs her palm over Casey's pom-pom hat as he gets out of the car, hugging him to her side, and he leans into her as they walk to the Beast, uncharacteristically quiet, his look directed inward, maybe trying to reconcile this experience when the grown-up didn't know how to fix everything.

"I don't think I should leave it. Might get sideswiped." But the old man is talking to himself, doing as he's told, locking the sedan behind him as he goes.

They don't speak much, returning to the high school parking lot, where they weather the worst of the storm, the SUV shaking, battered by the wind. Shaw runs the engine now and then, when it starts to get too cold in the cab, alternately checks her phone for texts from Beau or Mads and squints at the next to nothing she can see beyond the houses across the street, where everything devolves to white.

At last, big, wide-set headlights coast down the hill, and it must be—the bus. Able to breathe again, Shaw watches it pull in, sees other parents' cars, who have trickled in over the past half hour, starting up, high beams flashing in signal as the players start filing out of the open folding doors, pulling up their hoods, searching for their rides in the gloom.

Beau comes to the passenger side and sees Gramps looking back at him, so he swings into the back seat with a thump of gear and a cloud of cold air. "Man, the roads are terrible. The bus driver almost put us in the ditch near Janesville. Everybody's stuff went flying."

"Get my text?" Shaw's voice is terse as Beau fastens his seat belt.

"Which one?" He grabs his phone. "Oh. Yeah, like right now."

"It's okay." No one else contributes anything, Dad still staring out the window, Casey, exhausted, sitting with his head leaning against the glass. Beau obviously notices the strained atmosphere and settles in to thumbing on his phone now that service is back, occasionally watching an orange town plow roar past, pushing a cascade of snow. They pass Dad's car, its wheels now half-buried, the windshield masked in white, hazards blinking like frosted amber eyes.

At a certain point, after they've left downtown, passing the last-chance service station and diner, Shaw notices the car behind them for the first time, the way you do in a snowstorm in the dark when you reach a stretch without streetlights. Low halogen headlights, and moving at a good clip for this weather, probably somebody with studded tires and all-wheel drive who wants to make a show of passing everyone because they can.

"Jesus, bub," Shaw says, checking the rearview as the headlights grow. "He's going to have a helluva time driving up my tailpipe, but more power to him."

Dad snorts faintly, his first sign of life since she picked him up, and Shaw hears the acceleration of the car as it passes them on the left, picking up their headlight glow as it slows some eight yards in front of them. Gray paint job. And she's thinking of Anders, how could she not, as the car's brake lights go on, flickering, steady, flickering, the driver pumping, avoiding a skid.

And now the gray car is slowing more. Shaw clenches her jaw, pumps her own brakes, trying to hold steady, knowing there's every chance she'll lose traction but there's nothing to do, nowhere to go on a rural route except off the road or into the back of the guy in front of you.

She manages to crawl to ten miles per hour, ending up within five feet of the other car's bumper. It's a Charger. "Dad," she says, pitching her voice low, hoping the boys won't notice right away over the noise of the radio, "grab my phone." He glances over at her, unfocused, dragged out of his thoughts. "Call 911, tell them who you are and where we are, and that your daughter's got a protection order out against a guy who's tailing us right now."

Dad straightens, leaning forward. "That's him? You're sure?"

"Yeah. Go ahead, call them." She's struggling not to lose it because they're close enough to kiss license plates now, barely able to make out Anders's silhouette and the shape of his rearview mirror in her headlight glow.

Dad calls, stammering out, "My name's Eddie Connolly, and I'm driving with my family on Route 15 just outside Axtel—we need some help here—" The boys look up in the back seat, and Shaw says sharply, "It's okay, guys"—"We've got a fella following us, harassing us on the road. He's been stalking my daughter and I think he's planning on hurting somebody—"

There's a roar of acceleration, and as they watch, the Charger picks up speed, making space between them, cutting two runners through the fresh snow as he pulls farther ahead, fifteen yards, twenty.

"Hold up—I'm not sure what he's doing now. I know it's storming but send anybody you got in the area. I got my two grandsons in the back seat and the roads are slicker'n hell—"

"There he goes," Shaw says quietly, watching as the Charger's taillights disappear around the curve in the road ahead.

"He's leaving?" Beau leans forward as far as his seat belt will allow, jarring her back into reality, where her kids are trapped in this moment right along with her.

"I don't know, hon, I don't know—Sit back, okay?" Shaw's attention stays on the road, craning her neck as if that will somehow allow her to see farther than the curve and visibility deems possible.

When they come out upon the stretch of highway ahead, no taillights. Only two oncoming cars quite a distance away.

Dad, who has been alternately answering questions and holding, says into the receiver, "I don't know, he went tearing up the road and out of sight. You still want us to pull in somewhere or . . . ?" He presses the phone to his chest for a second to tell Shaw, "She's saying we should keep driving until we can pull into the first public space or business parking lot we see, wait for help."

"Public space? I take it she's never been on this road before." The roadsides are black, occasional squares of light shining through the snow to denote a house set back among the trees.

"Keep it slow and steady and we'll get there." A murmur of speech from the phone and the old man puts it back to his ear. "Yup, still here."

They reach the lowest point of the slope, where the road becomes a straightaway for three-quarters of a mile, passing where the steeply inclined Brinks Farm Lane joins with Route 15 on the left. There, lights flare in her mirrors, making her glance back. "Is it him?"

Dad and both boys look over the seats, but the rear window is light blasted. Dad's back with the 911 operator, "He's behind us again, I'm pretty sure—"

The engine roar of the Charger reverberates inside their cab; now he's riding directly on their ass. Shaw curses, hears Casey's thin noise of fear as he crouches down, and she's raging, all at once, inflamed, the sonofabitch making her kids think they're going to die.

No choice but to go faster, ease that accelerator down, down, all the while trying to intuit the next bend in the road, how long before they'll need to make a curve that even this all-wheel drive won't be able to manage at speeds higher than thirty, not in this slop—she hunts for any place with lights on now, anywhere she could maybe pull in at this speed and be able to stop in time—

The Charger rides their bumper, edging to the left suddenly, maybe sliding, maybe attempting another pass, and he flashes his high beams a couple times—*hi, still here*—then floats into the on-coming lane, driving neck-and-neck with them.

"Mom!" Beau, scared, a little kid again, all of six.

"It's okay!" She's yelling, glancing over at Anders, able to see nothing but the faint shadow indicative of him at the wheel—can't just ride here, waiting for him to bash into them, or collide with another car head-on—

Ahead, an outdoor light appears. Most likely the American Legion Hall; almost never anybody there, but it's a parking lot. She cuts the wheel to the right too soon, rumbling onto the snowbank, their cries mingling as the passenger side wheels slope down into the ditch—if they go in, they'll roll, or end up nose down, the weight of the car crushing the front end and them with it—

Shaw's grip is iron on the wheel, jerking vibrations shooting all the way up through her shoulders, but she won't release, the whole while carrying one thought of pure, detached clarity: *I've killed us.*

There's a moment where it can go either way. Then the tires hit a patch with more traction, maybe some plow dirt frozen into the bank, enough to make the car start obeying the steering system again, and she curves it back onto the pavement for maybe twenty seconds before they make the Legion Hall lot, going way too fast, Shaw having no choice but to let the Beast hurtle into the side lot, braking, fishtailing, Casey yelling out again, junk from the dash tumbling down. Finally, they ram straight into what looks like, for that millisecond in the headlights before they hit, a sheer wall of snow.

Ragged crunch. The impact yanks all the seat belts taut against their bodies, forcing the air from everyone. They've stopped.

After a stunned moment, Shaw lifts her head, coughing. "Everybody okay?" out of her mouth before her eyes open.

She jerks around to look at the boys, finds them staring back at her, faces pallid in the scant light, tears streaking down Casey's cheeks. "Yeah? You're not hurt?"

As they shake their heads, Shaw sees headlights through the rear windshield.

The Charger idles on the roadside; he must've pulled over and reversed back up the shoulder. Now, he's rolling forward slowly, and she waits, seeing if he's going to turn in, keep coming for them. She reaches over, hits the master lock button, hears the thud of the doors securing.

But the Charger keeps on going, picking up speed, pulling back into the lane and disappearing past the next snowbank and down the hill. And the only sound is Dad, back on with 911, saying, "Yeah, we've gone off the road at the Axtel Legion Hall, he chased us—everybody's okay, but I'm not sure he's really gone. Is somebody coming to help us, or should we start trying to flag down a goddamn sleigh for a lift home?"

19

They don't get home until nearly nine, no choice but to wait until help arrives in the form of a state trooper who was attending an accident six miles away.

By that time, Shaw had backed out of the eight-foot-tall frozen bank where plows had been pushing the Legion Hall lot snow all winter, relieved to find that the Beast was running loud but running. Some crushing incurred to the front end, the bumper hanging partially off the frame, the right headlight broken and dark, but still capable of idling. Shaw steered it to face the road in case Anders came back, the 911 operator staying on speaker with them until the trooper arrived.

The trooper took statements, offered to follow them home to make sure they got there in one piece and stayed until a member of the sheriff's office arrived to take over, waiting inside his cruiser while the Connollys headed into the house.

Now, they come through the front door, exhausted, eyes hollow, Mads waiting for them in the entryway with Aphrodite at her heels. "Thank God—are you guys sure you're okay?"

Beau heaves his sports bag and backpack, both thumping the wall and dropping heavily. "*Fucking* asshole—"

"Knock it off," Shaw says harshly.

"Why, you say it all the time—"

"Well, you don't hear me saying it now, do you? Grab something to eat and go to sleep."

"I don't want anything."

"Get in the kitchen, microwave yourself some friggin' Hot Pockets, and get your butt to bed, okay? We all went through it, bud, not just you. Don't punish us for it." She watches as Beau goes furiously, tearfully, into the kitchen, feeling an almost irresistible need to hug him, apologize mewlingly, but she won't. The kid's got to learn to blow up at the right people. Speaking of which, she's got a powder keg ready for whoever shows up from the sheriff's office after leaving her sister completely alone.

Shaw reaches out and impulsively pulls Mads into a tight hug, not voicing the dread which has plagued her all the way home, the thought of finding that Anders had gotten here first. Finding a silent house, the front door hanging open, snow drifting in across a blood trail. Or possibly even worse, Mads simply gone. Never to be seen again.

Mads squeezes her back, her gaze following the old man as he walks a silent, stunned Casey into the kitchen.

Shaw goes down the hall to the laundry room, old reliable, the one place nobody in the family will follow her. She pulls her phone out and stabs a number she never thought she'd call, her heartbeat thunderous in her ears, one fist ground into her hip as the rings seem to come from far off. Three, four.

Anders answers without greeting, but she can hear him. She speaks before he can, the words tearing out of a vital, guttural place, "The next time I see you, I'll kill you. You're already dead." Then she ends the call, chest heaving, sitting down on the floor with her knees pulled up because at once she feels a need to go to ground, hold on to something that won't crumble into ice crystals and blow away. Shaw only gets up once she hears the front door open and the mingled voices of the officers coming inside, stamping boots, declining the old man's offers of coffee, tea.

"Can we go to Dad's now?" Casey asks without much hope as Shaw walks up the stairs with him. It's hours later, the trooper since moved on, the deputy assigned as protection outside in his SUV for a cold, cramped night, most likely resenting every minute after she went off on him about his predecessor being pulled off his post to go assist with damage control in the storm and no one even bothering to call Shaw to let her know.

Beau's mad at her, too, at every aspect of the situation they're trapped in. He's already gone up and slammed his bedroom door shut, making it clear there won't be any familial puppy pile happening in there tonight. Probably for the best. Let him cry out the fear without having to worry about somebody seeing him.

"It's late, and we don't want him driving in this. He'll be here in the morning to get you guys, don't worry. We've got the deputy outside. Safe as houses."

Casey rubs his eyes. "You mean, safe as somebody else's house."

"Yeah. That was kind of dumb, huh." She kisses his brow. "'Night, sweet."

Her legs feel ready to fold and drop her flat like a card table, but she makes it down the stairs, mind flickering and buzzing with residual adrenaline and apprehension, partly freed, partly horrified by her own words to Anders. How much she truly wants him dead, what she imagines as a moment of pure release and reward for her, animal satisfaction.

She finds the old man sitting heavily at the kitchen table, a small plate with a reheated portion of last night's chop suey almost untouched in front of him.

She doesn't speak, instead dragging a chair over to the fridge and standing on it to reach the built-in cupboard above, withdrawing a three-quarters-full bottle of Jameson. She sees Dad's look and lifts the Irish toward him. "Will it be too hard for you to watch me get hammered?"

They sit in the living room together, Dad in his chair, Shaw on the couch, feet propped up, a juice glass in her hand with two fingers' worth in it because apparently Ryan took the tumblers with him, or maybe they've all been broken over the years; she so rarely drinks hard stuff that she isn't sure. "He was always expecting me to become a lush." Dad glances over from the TV, looking haggard, questioning. "Oh. Ry. I was thinking about him. He never liked me to drink. Especially going out for a few after work. I always joked around that he thought I was going to hook up with Tran one of these nights, but that wasn't it. He'd always get real stiff with me, like he was pissed, then deny that he was when I asked him."

"Well. You're the kid of a drunk. He was there to see me stumbling around, didn't want the same for you. Can't blame the guy."

"You didn't stumble around." Dad doesn't move. "Well, not often." She takes another sip, taking a moment to taste it, watching him. "Are you sure this is okay? I've never drank in front of you before."

"Oh, for God's sake, if I start foaming at the mouth and try to wrestle the bottle away from you, you'll know you got something to worry about, all right?"

Shaw laughs, falls quiet, watching commercials. "You weren't so bad, you know. You kept going to work, paying the bills, made sure everybody had enough to eat and shoes on their feet. I went to school with a lot of kids whose dads couldn't pull that off, and they weren't carrying half the load you were."

"The difference between me and those guys you're talking about is that they didn't really want to be home. Me, that's all I wanted. Come home after work, turn the game on, catch up with your mom and watch you kids run around." He takes off his glasses, cleans the lenses on his sweatshirt hem. "Grab a cold one, get that nice buzz to take the edge off things. Before you know it, one turns into four, then six, and then the wife's pouring you into bed five nights out of seven. Half my paycheck was going toward keeping the fridge stocked with Bud." He jerks his head. "But then, after Thea went missing . . . couldn't face being home sometimes. That empty bunk over you, the poor kid's school picture hanging on the wall. You all looking at me like maybe I could fix it, like if I looked hard enough, I could find her. I'd go out, hang more of the goddamn posters, drive around talking to people for hours, trying to find anybody who might know anything we ain't heard before. Then I'd wind up holding down a stool at Sharky's until midnight, trying to drown it all."

"Come on. We knew you loved us. Take a compliment, for crying out loud."

"Yeah, well. I was worth a lot more to you girls and Mom after I started hitting my meetings. 'Course, you were out of the house by then, so I'm not sure how much good it did you. Mads, it did, I think." His fingers, somewhat swollen with mild arthritis, grip the armrest and tighten there. "That's what today reminded me of when I went to get Beau. Coming home loaded behind the wheel. The road sliding back and forth in front of me. Not knowing what lane I'm in." A pause. "I couldn't see."

"It was storming."

"Wasn't the storm. I should've been able to see better than that. It's been bad for a long time, but I've been pretending it's not happening. I never should've been driving Casey anywhere."

The nakedness of his tone shuts down any impulses she might've had of reassurance. "We'll get you into the doctor's."

"I already been. Remember? Macular degeneration. Nothing they can do. They said it'd keep getting worse." His lips are a tight line. "What good am I going to be around here if I can't even give the boys a ride to school, do a grocery run?"

"So, you'll be chief cook and bottle washer." Shaw takes a drink. "Beau'll love that."

Dad gives her a sidelong look and a bit of the devil glimmers in his expression again. "He's never tried my Beanie Weenie chili. Eat that on a slab of the brown bread that comes in the can, pile of Veg-All—mm-*mmm*." He shakes his head.

"See? I knew there was a reason to keep on living." They laugh, punchy, trying to keep it down in case anybody upstairs has been able to close their eyes for more than a second without seeing those headlights swelling into supernovas, consuming the cab, or feeling the gut-plunging sensation of a car in a slide—

"I'm going to see Brandy again," Shaw says finally.

He huffs softly. "Thought you said she kicked you out."

"She did. After she sat there and lied to my face again about her last day with Thea." Ironic, listening to Dad's recollections of his drinking days as the whiskey lowers its translucent golden rings down over her, until those edges he was talking about acquire a burnished gleam; it's already taking extra effort to enunciate. "God, I hate that bitch. That's one thing she's right about. I was so jealous that it was like walking around every day with a knife stuck in me. She stole my best friend and my sister and left me with nobody to talk to"—Shaw laughs haltingly—"and I really needed somebody to talk to. Ryan and me"—Shaw's so used to edging around that time when Beau was conceived, never going to feel completely comfortable bringing it up with the family, all the sexual sneaking around—"we were going through some heavy stuff, and I really could've used her. Instead, she was off with Brandy. And look where it got her."

Dad shifts in his seat. "You think Brandy's mixed up with this Anders guy somehow?"

"I can't see it. He's intellectual, arrogant . . . I doubt that he'd consider somebody like Brandy human, let alone worthy of his time. How would their paths have crossed, even back in 2007?" She finishes off her glass, directionless frustration grating against her. "I don't know. Maybe I'm not looking at this from the right perspective. I mean, I wasn't attending mass regularly by late high school. I had a part-time job, and Ryan. And I remember Thee catching hell from Mom for oversleeping and blowing off church a lot, too, so she couldn't have been going to Saint Anthony's much by 2007." Shaw takes out her phone and opens her Maps app, looking at the GPS route of the fires. "What about Merritt's Department Store? Do you remember anything significant about that place from around that time?"

"He burned the Merritt's building, huh?" The old man thinks for a while. "Your mom used to go shopping there once in a while. Maybe school clothes a couple times."

"They had a pretty big formal section, didn't they?" Dad's look is blank. "You know, dresses and tuxes."

"I don't remember—"

"Well, I do. Now." Shaw takes another sip, staring unseeingly ahead. "Mom didn't save Thea's prom dress from her freshman year, did she. I didn't see it when I looked through the box of clothes." Dad shrugs, shakes his head; Shaw curses. "Maybe I could've checked the label, somehow traced it back to the retailer. Forget it." She rests back against the cushion with her eyes closed. "I'm going to take care of this, Dad."

"It's for the cops."

"We need this to be over. We need it so bad." The statement is heavier than its parts. "I can finish it."

"How're you going to do that?" He waits until it's clear that she isn't going to answer. "Remember you got two boys counting on you."

"I never forget that."

"They're never going to stop needing you. And me. I need you."

Her words come hard. "I've been working toward this since I was eighteen. For Thea. And Mom."

The quiet between them is dense, layered. "Mom didn't expect anything from you."

"I know. That was the problem."

"I'm saying Mom didn't want you to be anything but yourself, kiddo. She was so proud of how you handled Beau, what a good mom you were." Shaw looks over, unbelieving. "I remember her saying that you were a natural."

"You're sweet. But I let her down."

"She was hurting and desperate because one of her kids was missing. When you came up pregnant, I don't think she knew what to do. But anything she might've said or done that year was out of pain over Thea. She was never ashamed of you. Never. She loved you. Loved her grandbaby."

Shaw allows a sob, just one—there's a creak on the stairs, someone coming down—before she presses the back of her hand to her lips, drawing a steadying breath through her nose.

Mads appears, dressed in a T-shirt and flannel pajama pants, her hair hanging loose around her shoulders. She takes in the tableau for a moment. "Can I join the party?"

"This is an exclusive club for those being stalked by homicidal maniacs. You may enter." Shaw makes a sweeping gesture. "I'd offer you a drink but all I have is whiskey."

Mads goes to the kitchen, comes back with some in a mason jar. "You say that like it's a problem."

Shaw and Dad look at each other. "Well, don't keep acting like it's up to me," Dad says.

"Holy crap. Drinking with my baby sister." Shaw pushes herself up to go for a refill. "Another first."

"You guys going to be like sardines over there?" Shaw says when Ryan comes for the boys first thing the next morning. She never sets her coffee mug down, trying to caffeine-away the dull, muzzy hangover from last night's drinking until one a.m. with Mads, both laughing into their hands at the sight of the old man eventually drifting off to sleep in his chair a bit at a time, jerking upright with a surprised look only to sag down into a slump again.

"No." Ryan's abrupt, then seems to check himself, glancing over at her. "The apartment's not that small. You should come see it sometime."

It's the first time he's offered. "Maybe I will."

Ryan stands squinting at her as a scudding wind blows around them, pushing dry gusts of snow across the fields on all sides. "You can't keep staying here. Not after last night."

"We've got a deputy around all the time now."

"How long are they going to be willing to do that? No way is the county paying to keep somebody sitting on this place forever."

She shakes her head once. "Anders will try something again soon. I'm not letting him take my home away from me."

"So, we wait."

Shaw feels the atrophied movement of her own smile, the expression more suited to the face of a hundred-year-old woman. "That's the name of the game."

Ryan glances away, biting the inside of his cheek, and finally says, "Everything's fucked. I don't know what the hell's even happening anymore. I wake up and still expect to be in this house."

It's gratifying, in a way, seeing Ryan unstrung for once. She lets the moment stretch out as long as she can stand it, part of her hoping he might ask her to come with them. But it can't work, not now: he'll try to be the voice of reason, run things with Anders, and Ryan simply is no match. He's a white hat, and he's too goddamn sane. Shaw doesn't suffer from that affliction. "You won't let the boys out of your sight. I got no worries about that." Ryan's look is so reminiscent of Beau when she says something of monumental obviousness that a sob crossed with a laugh hiccups out of her. "Let me kiss them."

Saying goodbye to the boys is agonizing, even worse than she'd expected as she hugs them, kisses their heads, Casey crying because he's an empath when it comes to her, Beau watching her conflictedly as she pulls back, fear and grief in their shared silence. Shaw tries to think of anything to make it better, manages, "It won't be long."

She steps away before her voice fails her completely, watching as Ryan ticks a salute off the brim of his cap and backs out.

Shaw showers and throws on clothes, then comes downstairs to pour more coffee into a travel mug and toss back a couple ibuprofen. Dad watches her as he unloads the dishwasher, knowing what she's got planned, instead choosing to say, "I think Mads is planning on hauling me with her to class today."

"Hey, I can totally see you chilling in the union, a matcha-latte-whatever in your hand. Let's see if we can hunt you down some skinny jeans."

"It'll look a lot more like an old coot snoring in a chair in the corner with everybody wondering if I'm missing from a rest home somewhere." He shrugs, digs a piece of stuck-on food off a plate. "If it makes her feel better, there's no harm in it." He pauses. "Good luck with Brandy. She's not going to be happy to see you."

"She never is."

Shaw does the now-familiar evasiveness thing on the way to Vesper Falls, unnecessary turns, parking in a lot for a few minutes to see if Anders's Charger will show itself, but no one passes by. If he's switched vehicles after last night, of course, she's screwed, but there are only so many precautions a person can take before she winds up crouching in a bunker surrounded by a year's supply of bottled water and powdered chickpeas. Anyway. Not an option.

Outside Brandy's apartment building, Shaw makes another fruitless circle of the jammed parking lot, braking at the sight of a familiar car in one of the three coveted visitor spots. A blue, road-salt-coated Kia Sorento. Shaw clicks her tongue in her cheek, heads down the street at unsafe speeds to find a spot of her own.

Shaw waits outside the building in the cold for about fifteen minutes until a woman comes up the sidewalk and slows as she nears the entrance of the apartment building.

Shaw steps right up behind her, trying to look distracted by searching for keys in her purse, flashing a relieved smile as the woman holds the door for her. "Thanks." Shaw feels like a bit of a scumbag, using one woman's trust in the safety of her own gender against her, but hey—desperate times.

Shaw goes straight up to the second floor, knocking on Brandy's door. There's faint music coming from inside; no sound of approaching footsteps. Shaw bangs harder.

A muffled voice, then, maybe. "Brandy, it's Shaw. Open up, now!" What the hell, why not let it all hang out: old resentment and petty shit and every dirty little reason why she can't stand this woman.

Finally, footsteps on the opposite side of the door. "Who buzzed you in?"

"The Blue Fairy. Open the door, I want to talk to you."

"We did that, remember? Fuck off."

Shaw sets her jaw and hammers the side of her fist against the door again. "Brandy!"

No answer. Shaw takes a few steps back, then makes a harsh sound as she kicks the center of the door. The shock zings up to her kneecap, and she staggers back, nearly falling. Galvanized by satisfaction of it, Shaw kicks it again, then beats with her fists, then lays her shoulder into it—*do like on TV, hammer the bastard down.*

It hurts like hell; Shaw's not big and the door is, her whole body vibrating in stunning, painful waves, switching sides after she bashes her shoulder hard enough to wonder if she tore something. "Open the door, Brandy!" Shaw rebalances, braces her hands against the doorframe and starts kicking the base. *"Open the goddamn door!"*

Shaw doesn't hear the rattling of the locks until she nearly falls through the gaping doorway. Brandy stands back, her eyes wide, dressed only in spandex shorts and a cropped tank top. "Jesus, shut *up* before somebody calls the cops—what do you even *want*?"

"Just a quick look in your boudoir, you mind?" Breathless, Shaw heads straight for the corridor, shoving off Brandy's clawing hands, the other woman's fingernails making brisk zipping sounds down the waterproof fabric of Shaw's coat sleeve.

"Hey, get your ass back here! You can't do that—" Brandy wrenches Shaw around by the crook of her arm. Up close, Brandy's face is a carved mask, drained of color, as flintlike as she's always seemed, like you could take chips off her and she'd spark. "You're no cop, you're just some little pissant lab tech. You got no right to come in here—"

"Now, where in the world did you get that information, Brandy?" Shaw yanks free and there's a brief shoving match there in the corridor, Brandy trying to restrain her and Shaw having none of it, a little savage, a little silly, like any physical fight, Brandy finally trying to drag Shaw back by her coat hem while Shaw mule kicks the air. At last Shaw drives her elbow into the woman's sternum, forcing her back against the wall with an audible whoosh of air—a moment's chagrin on Shaw's part, she hadn't set out for things to get so real—but she's already heading to the door on the left, the only one that's closed.

Inside, the foot of the bed is revealed first, the splashy black and hot-pink comforter rumpled back, then James, sitting on the edge of the mattress with the distracted, hangdog look of a man who's just zipped up his fly.

"James. How's it going." Shaw stands on the threshold, watching as he reluctantly lifts his gaze to hers, one of his eyes freshly blacked, the lid swollen and purple hued. She nods back toward Brandy. "So much for not being desperate enough to tap that, huh."

"Bitch, you got *no* right—" Brandy comes up behind Shaw, but Shaw jerks around and slams up close to her, holding a finger under Brandy's nose.

"Don't. Touch me again."

Brandy drops back on her heels, but slightly, breathing through flared nostrils.

Shaw swivels back, looking between the two, shrugging. "Okay.

So. You're caught. Two consenting adults. Who the hell cares, right?" Shaw takes a couple steps away, not eager to turn her back on Brandy again or to go any farther into the cramped bedroom where the smell of intimacy and the tension of what she's interrupted feels thick, heated. "Do the cops know you're fucking? Probably. Or—wait—should I say, still fucking. As in, you never stopped." With forced high spirits: "High school sweethearts? You're giving me cavities here, kids."

Brandy's expression twists, and she nearly goes for Shaw again, but James's hoarse, "Brandy, stop it. Goddamn," holds her back. He emerges into the hallway a moment later, and Shaw finds herself continuing to move back.

"I told you. I never would've hurt your sister like that." At that, Brandy snorts, flicking her gaze heavenward, and James rasps, "*Shut up*," like one would to a Pekinese that won't stop yapping; Brandy lifts her chin, staring truculently back at him.

James looks to Shaw, his face seamed with exhaustion and drink. "Me and Brandy hook up sometimes. Okay? I don't have to go around explaining it to people." He waves his hand. "She gets it."

"Gets what?"

"What it's like. Everybody looking at you like you're a killer. Or a liar, anyway. People talking about you online like you're somebody from a story, not even real. But nothing was going on between us back then. I was into Thea. That's it."

"Hmm. Still stinks like horseshit, James." Shaw swings a look at the other woman. "And here I thought that was Brandy's signature fragrance—"

"Why are you telling her anything?" Brandy's words tear out of her. "You'd throw her ass out of here if you weren't fucked up all the time—man *up* and tell her to get out of my place—"

Someone knocks on the door, followed by a muffled, "Everything okay in there?"

"*Yes! Fine!*" Brandy shouts.

James looks at her flatly, unfocused. "I'm tired, Bran." His words are slurred.

"You're not thinking right. Get rid of her and we'll talk it out, you and me."

"If you're tired, put it down," Shaw says, keeping her eyes on James, her tone low, as steady as she can. "Whatever it is you're carrying. If you're tired, just put it down."

James rubs his face, remembering his black eye too late, wincing, his words a near whisper. "I fucking can't."

The shape of it, whatever they've been hiding all these years, is front and center, almost illuminated, stage lights coming up; Shaw's so close now that she's almost crying. "It was a long time ago. I'm sure you know that the police can't touch you for much of what went on back then." She doesn't dare take her eyes off him and break that link, like facing down a dog that hasn't made up its mind whether to get ugly or not. "I don't believe you killed Thea. I never did."

"Shut up and get out of here." Brandy's vicious. The gatekeeper, of course. Shaw should've pinpointed their roles long ago.

"Sorry, Brandy. I don't think anybody's listening to you anymore." Shaw continues holding James's gaze. "Are you going to keep doing what you're told?"

James scrubs his face harder and walks to the corner of the kitchen island, leaning there. "She's Thea's sister. Let's tell her."

"Are you out of your mind—?"

"What difference does it make anymore?" James bellows, head low, looking from beneath his brows, logy, belligerent. "Huh? We're not talking to the fucking cops here. Shaw's her family. Why not tell her and let it the fuck go. What—everybody's going to hate us? They already do, they always have. Your little plan didn't work out so goddamn well, did it?"

There's a span of maybe five seconds without motion, the battle of wills between them taut as steel cable—and then James lets it fall out of him with a passive turn of his head, a quick murmur Shaw can barely make out, "We put something in her drink."

"*What?*" Shaw's starting out of her skin, glancing between them as if the words might roll out of sight if she doesn't stomp them flat. "When was this?"

A motion of his head. "Earlier. That afternoon. Before we left the House of Pizza."

"While you were sitting at the table?"

Another pause, and then he shakes his head. "We didn't leave when we said we did. After we left through the main doors, we went around back. In through the loading dock doors."

"Who's we?"

"Me, Brandy, Thea. Nobody knew we went back there except Michael. He had a desk out there." James is making eye contact with Brandy again, locked into her strained, outraged stare.

Shaw takes a few unconscious steps closer. "Who was Michael?"

"The owner. Michael Bianchi."

Maybe a flicker of recognition for Shaw, but that's all. "Why did you go back there?"

"I wanted to buy some stuff. For the party. He'd sell to you if he knew you. Alcohol and smokes out of their stock, write it off as damaged or something. But also weed. Pills. Probably harder stuff."

Brandy curses him, throws her hands up, and heads down the corridor again, leaving James and Shaw together.

Shaw goes over to him at the island. "So. Michael was selling to the high school kids. He's the guy you didn't want to tell me about."

"Yeah. He sold to lots of people. Townies, and kids from the community college. He owned a shitload of properties even back then, not just the House of Pizza, because of how much he was making on the side. He's bought up half the friggin' town of Rishworth at this point, probably." James swallows. "I used to deal a little for him at school. Just here and there. If I wanted some e and didn't have the money, he'd let me work it off."

"Okay." She's careful not to show anything, no judgment, because she wants this, needs every word so badly, terrified that he'll somehow take it back. "What happened after you guys went into the back room?"

"I paid him for what I bought. Some booze, also some pills Brandy wanted but didn't have cash for. And Michael asked me to move some more weed for him at school. Thea didn't like that. She knew I did it and all, but she was afraid Michael was gonna end up, like, owning me or something. She thought he was sketchy."

"She was right. What next?"

"Thea mouthed off a little." James's eyes are closed. "It was her attitude more than what she said. Michael thought she was being a snob, like she thought she was too good for him." He falls silent a moment, struggling, and Shaw's hands curl to fists on the countertop. "When we were leaving, Thea was first out the door—she couldn't wait to get out of there, and—Michael kind of came up beside me and slipped me a little bag with a couple green pills in it. Said my girlfriend could use one. It'd guarantee me a hookup later. Roofies. I think he was probably joking, I dunno. Then Brandy and I went out."

"You know for a fact that they were roofies?"

"Well, what else would they be?"

"Got me, James, but hell, don't stop down now—what next?"

James is picking up on her incredulous, virulent rage, and he stares into it like the headlamp of an oncoming train, fixated, no plans on dodging. "We went and drove around like I always said we did. Drinking, smoking. We'd mix stuff up in old soda bottles in case we got pulled over, you know, hide the liquor bottles under the seat. Outside of town, Thea had to take a piss and she didn't want to go on the side of the road, so I pulled into this gas station that had a port-o-potty outside—you know that place, they sell feed out of the mini barn."

"Brockton's."

"Yeah. I always thought that'd be where we'd get caught. Like, somebody'd go to the cops and say they saw us at the store, or saw Thee, or something. Never happened. Place like that doesn't get cameras until somebody robs 'em." He wipes his lips, which are already dry, chapped. "While Thea was out of the truck, Brandy started talking about the pills Michael gave me, and we were joking around, saying it'd be funny to drop one in the Smirnoff that Thea was drinking from, see her get really wasted. We weren't thinking. Just being stupid asshole kids, you know? Maybe I was kind of mad that she might've screwed things up between me and Michael by acting like a bitch, you know. I knew it wasn't cool to do that to her, but Brandy—"

"Told you it would be okay."

"Yeah. I thought a whole pill might be too much. Because Thea was pretty small and everything. So, I bit it in half, crushed it, shook it up in the bottle. When she came back, she didn't even know we'd done anything."

"And later?"

"She was . . . floating. Kind of fighting off sleep. She knew something was up, then, and started saying how weird she felt, like maybe she was sick. Brandy and I were trying not to laugh, you know, still thinking it was this awesome prank, and then Brandy—I remember her yelling, 'You got punk'd, you got punk'd," over and over."

Shaw stays still, seeing the moment in her mind's eye, teen Brandy, bone thin, brown hair lashing, shrieking laughter on the bench seat beside Thea, who can barely focus or keep her head up. "What did Thea do then?"

"Got mad. Started swearing at us, shoving. Brandy pushed her back, saying, 'don't you push me, bitch,' and then Thea hit her in the side of the head. You could tell those two were probably done. Thea was seriously pissed, not only that we did it but that it was something that Michael gave me. Like . . . it was the same thing as me letting him touch her. You know. Then she started saying that she wanted to get out, that I'd better pull over or she'd jump."

"Where was this?" Shaw watches his gaze trail downward again. "It didn't happen on School Street, did it?"

He slowly shakes his head. "It was near that tote road, you know, about ten minutes from Aronson Road. Maybe another twenty minutes and we would've made the turnaround." He watches Shaw squeeze her eyes shut for a second as it sinks in.

"It must've been almost dark. There's nothing out there."

He doesn't speak right away, and when he does, his words come slowly, obviously something often recited in his head, insisted upon, until it became gospel. "She should've walked to the party. She wasn't that messed up, and she knew the way. We'd been out there plenty of times."

"Really? Smirnoff and Rohypnol in a scrawny seventeen-year-old's body, and she wasn't that messed up?" Shaw is trembling. "Where did she go after you dropped her off?"

"I don't *know*. I laid a patch getting out of there, and I didn't look back. I was pissed. Ashamed of myself, too, I know that now." He's struggling to take a full breath, his arms spread to brace against the edge of the countertop. "We got to the party, and Brandy went her way and I went mine and I got wasted. I kept thinking Thea would show up—that she'd get to the turnaround eventually, but she never did, and after a while I figured she must've gone home instead."

"That would've been almost an hour's walk. In the dark, in the cold. It never once occurred to you"—he starts to speak but she raises her voice—"to go back and look for her?"

"I wish to hell I had. That's all I can tell you."

"It was Brandy's idea to make up the story about dropping her off in town? All that crap about Thea getting too drunk before the party?"

There are tears tracing down his cheeks, mottling in with the scruff. "We thought she must've passed out somewhere, maybe got lost in the woods. Froze to death. We knew that it was our fault if she—" He breaks off, throat working. "Brandy said we'd get blamed if anybody knew. We'd go to prison. That it'd sound better if we said we dropped her off in town, didn't say nothing about the roofies, or Michael, ever. He's connected. I heard stories. You don't want to cross him. We kept thinking that they'd find her body, and it would be over one way or another. But they never did."

Shaw nods, fighting against tears, drumming her fingertips on the countertop a few times before drawing herself up straight, inhaling deeply to keep control.

"You want me to say that I'm shit? I'm shit. Don't you think I know? I did an awful fucking thing." James's expression twists. "Other people do awful things. But they get a chance to fix it. How come I never did? How come I got to keep on paying forever?"

When the constriction in her throat lessens, Shaw steps back and manages, "Karmic hangover," before she directs herself toward the hallway, to the open bedroom doorway that gives a view of Brandy, looking coiled, spring-loaded, bent double at the edge of the bed with her chin nearly resting on her knee as she vigorously removes polish from the toenails on her left foot.

"James have any idea how long a con you've run on him?" Shaw watches as Brandy adds more remover to a fresh cotton ball, then gets to work on the last of the stubborn paint around her cuticles. "Not too bright, is he? You've always counted on that." Shaw tries to get a look at the woman's face, but her hair is hiding her features. "Well, don't worry. I can appreciate the full scope of things. You were trying to break them up back in the day, weren't you? You saw your chance to convince James to do something cruel and dangerous to Thea, bad enough to make sure that you'd drive them apart. Then maybe, just maybe, James would settle for you on the rebound. Back then, it was the only way you thought you'd have a shot with him." Shaw tilts her head, narrowing her eyes. "Did you ever want to be Thea's friend? Or was it all about getting close to James, right from the beginning?"

Brandy flips the soiled cotton ball to the carpet, then grabs a bottle of pale blue, shakes it. "Get fucked."

"Not right now, but thanks. Anyway, it worked. You've been leading him around by the balls for a couple decades, jerking him back whenever his guilty conscience started acting up. That guy in there, what's left of him? The pathetic, needy, mess? At this point, I bet you'd give anything to have him out of your life." Shaw ponders her coolly. "Instead, you got rid of my sister."

Brandy has pedicures down to a machine-like routine, rapid, uniform stripes with the brush from left to right, cuticle to tip, then on to the next toe, her words muffled, unemotive. "Nobody made her get out of the truck."

Shaw unfolds her arms, stepping back. "That's quite the bedtime story you've concocted. No wonder your kids want nothing to do with you."

Shaw leaves the doorway, aware on an instinctive level that the other woman's motion will cease as soon as Shaw steps out of sight, Brandy's arm dropping, wasted, doll-like, against her own thigh.

20

n the car, Shaw screams. She batters the steering wheel, hammers her feet against the floor, flails her fists against every surface, then begins driving her fist into the dash over and over, seeing James's face, Brandy's, Thea's, vague and doped on the side of a night road. *Shaw. You going to help me or what. Where are you. I'm scared.*

Vigorous grunts of pain and fury escape Shaw, until something finally gives inside her hand and she gags in sickening agony, slamming back against the seat, tears coursing down her face. Her emotions shut down like a tripped breaker. Self-preservation.

She sits, cradling the hand, staring at the pale downy sky without seeing anything at all.

Eventually, she tries flexing it. Hurts like hell, but it moves. Hands are sort of essential in Latent Prints. Might be nice to have the use of them both if Jewel really does allow her back through the doors of the lab after Shaw made such a colossal ass of herself the other day. *Christ.* In the middle of all this, she misses the job. It's like the need for water.

Once she's wiped her face with tissues, she gets out her phone, switches on data, and starts googling with the hand that doesn't resemble a grapefruit dropped off an interstate overpass.

Detective Stephen York answers after one ring. "Shawnee. It's good to hear from you—how are you after last night? I got a call from the sheriff's office that—"

"I want to ask you something"—she sniffs, still dabbing her running nose and tearing eyes, gaze set on the blur of Main Street moving and living all around her stationary car—"and you need to promise me that you'll give me a straight answer. Can you do that right now? I mean, I didn't catch you in the middle of something life-or-death?"

He's silent a beat. "Go ahead."

"Do you know that a man named Michael Bianchi is involved in my sister's case? Like, is his name somewhere in those secret files of yours? That he was the owner of the House of Pizza and sold liquor and drugs and God knows what else to underage kids in the Rishworth area in 2007?" Silence; she rubs the space between her brows. "Don't give me the line about it being an open investigation. Nobody knows it better. But I just had a long talk with James Moore and Brandy Pike, and now I think I know as much about this case as anybody in the world. Treat me with that much respect. Give me a simple yes or no answer."

A long pause. "I'm aware of Mr. Bianchi, yes. I know his name."

"Was his involvement something that the Rishworth Sheriff's Office knew about back in the day, before they handed Thea's investigation over to the state police? Specifically, did Sheriff Mercer Brixton know?"

More silence.

"Maybe it was more like an unspoken decision not to investigate Bianchi too hard, even though his restaurant was the last place my sister was seen by objective witnesses. What I think is that Mr. Bianchi had friends in the right places. When James brought up that man's name, something clicked for me. It's the same name on the holdings company behind some renovation that's planned for Rishworth's downtown. I read it on a banner the last time I was there. So, then I thought I'd try cross-referencing it against the list of campaign contributors on Mercer Brixton's website. Bianchi's on the list."

"What is your question, Shaw?"

"Why was that information never released to us, her family? You cannot tell me that it wasn't because Bianchi and the sheriff had a personal relationship of some kind in 2007, and that Brixton was trying to cover up for a friend of his or, more accurately, cover his own ass. His association with Michael, once the public learned that he had drug world ties, wouldn't have made Brixton look too spiffy in the eyes of the average voter."

Stephen sighs, and says with deliberate articulation, "No charges were ever brought."

"Against Brixton? Or Michael Bianchi?"

"Either. Bianchi was never a person of interest in your sister's disappearance. He was working at the House of Pizza until almost midnight, with a whole restaurant full of witnesses. But he was on our radar as an unsavory character, yes. Still is, despite his professional accolades."

"Bianchi gave Rohypnol to a seventeen-year-old boy and encouraged him to slip it to my sister the night she died. Which James did. You did nothing, said nothing, about Bianchi or Brixton's friendship with him, even though the circumstantial evidence of corruption against Brixton alone would be enough to convince pretty much any jury to give St. Frances the needle."

"I'm sorry, but I don't agree. The connection you're talking about between Bianchi and Brixton is thin at best. They may be friends, they may have a history, but you're talking about two prominent citizens rising professionally at the same time in the same area of a small state. It's only natural that their paths would cross. I have no reason to believe that Brixton didn't do a thorough investigation of Bianchi at the time." Stephen's voice is gentle. "I think you're reaching too hard for a conspiracy that isn't there. And this is the first I've heard about Rohypnol in relation to Thea's case. Did James—?"

"You do realize that Brixton is running for reelection in November? And if the chucklehead faction of this state has their way again, he'll win?"

"Shaw. Understand that even discussing this aspect of Thea's case with you is endangering our chances of eventually bringing it to court at all. It's a cold case with no body and no crime scene. Unless someone leads us to your sister's remains, the chances of convincing the attorney general's office to take it to trial is slim." He pauses. "I wish that simply loving someone entitled you to information, but unfortunately, that's not how it works in a criminal investigation. You of all people must understand how important it is to protect the chain of evidence and confidentiality."

She nods slowly, her throbbing hand sending neon flashes of pain all the way to her elbow. "Then I hope it interests you that after James and Brandy drugged some vodka that my sister was drinking that afternoon, they left her on the side of the old county road in Rishworth, south of Aronson Road. That's where she really disappeared from, not School Street. That's why no one ever saw James's pickup parked along the curb, why no one saw Thea walking through the neighborhood toward home. All that time wasted doing door to door, searching sheds and basements, in the wrong part of town. But then again, maybe you already knew that, too."

The quiet lasts so long this time that Shaw is about to hang up.

"Did James or Brandy admit to knowing what happened to Thea from that point on?" Stephen says.

"No. But I do. I think she was out there alone, vulnerable, and somebody who had been following her and waiting for their moment for a long time came along and took her." She hesitates. "Maybe following even longer than I'd thought. Years, maybe."

Stephen exhales. "I think we should talk about the possibility of setting up a safe house for you and your family until Anders has been arrested. Now, keep in mind—"

"Let me fill in the blanks. Money. Manpower." Her throat has gone dry. "I'm not willing to sit around and let you guys play God anymore. Maybe it's my turn." She swallows with difficulty.

"I don't like what I'm hearing. It sounds like you're drifting away from us. You're a professional, a mother. Remember how much you have to lose and, please, don't consider doing anything rash. We will find Anders. We will get through this. Can I meet with you? We'll talk it out—"

"I have to go now, Steve. My hand is broken." But the phone has already dropped from her ear.

Hours later, when Shaw hears Mads arrive home with the old man, she doesn't come down from her bedroom. She crouches on her knees, the closet door hanging open, the storage boxes she'd brought home from the shed at the old house dragged out onto the carpet. Aphrodite lays with her chin on her paws, her questioning gaze flicking with Shaw's every movement, whatever emotions she senses coming from her human enough to keep her vigilant from a safe distance.

Mads's footsteps climb the stairs and stop at the doorway. "What're you doing?"

Shaw remains bent over a box, her injured hand resting in her lap with an ice pack over it while she digs with her left, the glass of Jameson she'd used to wash down ibuprofen sitting on the floor nearby. "Looking for it."

"What?"

Shaw shakes her head. "Whatever we're missing." Her eyes are puffed from weeping, her cheeks sticky with salt; still, she doesn't turn, but she's talking fast, setting aside those same pathetic arti-facts from before, Thea's sneakers with skull laces, the winter coat.

"Please don't get that stuff out. Come on, let's go downstairs."

Shaw pulls the rest of the clothes from the box, shaking them out as if something microscopic but of dire importance might be hidden among the folds, then she shakes the box upside down before tossing it. Gone is the reverence—it's all useless and exists only to tantalize and then disappoint, again and again—"You know what, you're right about this junk. Why the hell are we keeping it? More to the point, why did I bring it home? Why'd I do that?" Shaw rolls onto one hip and sees Mads's still, guarded face and for some reason, Shaw wants to go for her, get her hands on her and dig her fingers into her. "Compulsive behavior. I can't stop myself, right? If there's a little broken sliver of Thea anywhere around, I stab myself with it, then I yank it out and stab it into anybody close to me—my husband, my kids. You. Maybe I just want to spread the hurt around, and that's been my problem all along."

Mads's gaze goes to the glass on the floor. "I think I'll leave you alone for a while. Okay?"

"Don't you fucking dare." Shaw's laugh issues from a strained and sore throat, with off-key braying quality. "Because I don't know what I'll do. Maybe make a bonfire of all this crap. 'Bye-'bye, Thea." She stretches out one leg to push over the remaining boxes. "Think now she'll stay gone?"

A silence. "Okay. What is wrong?"

Shaw barely even hears the question, staring at the wall where a framed photo collage of her unit of four hangs, now scattered to the wind. "I need you to think for me. Because I can't anymore." She looks back at Mads, who has moved a few steps back, her brows drawing together, already defensive. "Try to remember everything you can from that time. You were home a lot then and I wasn't."

"I told you, I don't—"

"Not *right* when Thea disappeared, not 2007. The year or two before that. There's gotta be a link between these fires. He expects me to get it, but I don't, not all the way, because I don't think I have all the information. Like those stupid math problems they used to make us do with a piece missing. What did you and Thea do when I was working after school, or out of the house? Where did Mom take you? Do you remember going to Merritt's?"

"*Where?* I don't know what you want from me—it was a long time ago, and I was a little kid, and everything was horrible, and I need you to stop pushing." Mads turns, heading for the stairs.

Shaw scrambles to her feet, off-balance but still able to grab her sister's arm before she gets away and jerk her around, eliciting a frightened, indignant, "Hey!" from Mads as they come face-to-face. "Stop backing off from it! You were seven, eight years old, not a baby, for Christ's sake—you must remember something! You're not even trying! I love you like you're my own kid and you won't even help me!"

"You're drunk, Shaw, get off—"

"No! *No!*" Shaw shakes her, then, hard as she can, hard enough to make Mads's shoulders rock and, God help her, it feels great, latching on to her yielding, accessible there-ness and just letting her have it; the old man's on his way up the stairs, calling something that Shaw ignores. "Use your fucking head! Help me! Stop acting like you're too good to miss her!"

Mads sobs, suddenly, the sound punctuating the crackling tension.

"There wasn't anything that we did! Just regular stuff—school, hanging around the house—Thea was so much older that she didn't want to play with me, just talk on the phone and be with her friends. Mom was always after her to be with us more, be responsible like you—she didn't want a job—"

"What else?" Another shake, slightly less rough. "Those summers must've been long, Mads, come on—how'd you guys pass the time?"

"What the hell is this?" Dad stops on the top riser. "Shaw, let her go—"

"Nope. Never. I'm never letting go until she *thinks*."

"There's nothing! I went to my friend's houses, day camp, swimming—Thea usually wasn't even there!"

"What camp? At the church?"

"Yeah, but that was for little kids. Thea didn't go."

"What year?"

"Every year! I don't know."

Shaw's hands drop, and she sways a little, turning to see Dad's consternated expression as he watches her walk slowly toward the bedroom. "Was Thea ever a counselor? I don't remember that, but . . . ?"

"No." Mads rubs her arms where Shaw had gripped them. "Like I said, she didn't want to work. She and Mom fought about it."

Shaw looks at the old man. "But isn't there, like, a program or a picture or something? Am I making this up?" She moves faster, back into the bedroom, where the boxes and Thea's belongings are scattered, dropping to the carpet and getting rug burn on both knees as she pushes boxes around until she finds the one with the photo albums, the deep dive into memory that she always avoids like a bad case of poison oak. Nine in all, mismatched covers and designs, generations of their family with Mom's careful handwriting labeling everything.

Shaw starts flipping through, scanning page after page, the year all wrong, black-and-white photos of centuries' dead ancestors on Dad's side. "I swear to God, there's something like that in one of these. I've seen it."

A few moments later, Dad scoops up two albums and says, "Help her," gruffly to Mads, who, after a long hesitation, takes an overstuffed book and goes to sit on the bed with it.

Time scrolls out unevenly, Shaw's perception smeared by drink and pain and an effervescent sense of urgency, the drive to search. It takes physical effort to force herself through the years, image by image, herself and Thea as toddlers, juice mustaches and remembered outfits and favorite toys and beach days and fairs and birthdays, Mom rarely featured because she was always behind the camera. For Shaw, it's like sawing through the thickness of her own thigh with a dull knife, but she won't stop, can't, driven as if this can somehow equate to chasing a drugged and abandoned Thea down that dark road, drifting further and further away from Shaw's outstretched arms. She hasn't even told Dad and Mads yet. The thought makes her ill.

They each finish a book, set it aside, no one speaking, maybe no one fully believing but Shaw, who doesn't even know exactly what she's hunting for other than a vague recollection, an impression of something's existence.

It's Mads, ultimately, who says. "Is this anything?" and holds up the cream-colored album with a pattern of little birds on it, the photo pages covered with crinkly clear plastic sleeves. "It's Saint Anthony's, anyway."

Shaw grabs the book and spins it right-side up. It's a sun-faded photo with a pinhole in the top, like it had once been tacked to a bulletin board somewhere. And perhaps it had, maybe in the church, in the basement meeting room where Sunday school and Bible readings were held, where the walls were kept cheerful and decorated. Perhaps, at the end of summer, when the bright-colored paper and sun-and-fun cutouts were being taken down in favor of fall shades and autumn leaves, someone had given it to Mom to take home, because it had her daughter in it.

It was a group of teens vaguely familiar to Shaw, kids from church, most of whom they'd grown up with even if they hadn't gone to the same school. Dressed in shorts, tank tops, dated brands and hairstyles, standing or kneeling in the grass alongside Saint Anthony's while holding up a hand-painted paper banner decorated with suns and music notes and peace signs: *A Joyful Noise: SAC Summer Youth Camp 2005.*

Thea kneels in front-row left, partially hidden behind a boy's legs, too much sun in her eyes and not looking in the direction she's supposed to. She wears a blue-and-turquoise tie-dyed T-shirt Shaw remembers, sleeves rolled to her shoulders, and frayed-hem denim shorts. The attitude in her smile is spot-on, bursting with barely withheld laughter at herself, at all of them, dweebs of the first order.

The tallest members stand behind the banner, helping hold it aloft, these obviously group leaders or counselors, somewhat older, college age, and wearing matching green T-shirts with the church logo on the chest. There are seven of them, clustered together, everyone squishing to fit inside the frame, and Shaw leans close, so much so that her nose almost touches the plastic sleeve.

She breathes out slowly. "What do you think?" She hands the album to Dad while tapping her thumb over the face of the young man two over from the right, smiling, squinting, angled a little to the side. No glasses, at least not then.

Dad looks a long time. "Could be. That other kid's big head's in the way. I don't remember this. Don't even look familiar." He peels the photo off the page and flips it over. "No names. Nothing on the back but the date."

"Let me see it again." Mads holds it, and her gaze snaps up almost immediately to Shaw's. "I think it is. Holy shit."

There's a long interval where Shaw feels the frantic energy drain from her, going from resting on her heels to her ankles turning so that she sits directly on the carpet, her hands at her sides. The old man and her sister stare at her, waiting.

"There's something I've got to tell you guys. James finally broke. I know what they did to Thea that night."

The final call Shaw makes comes much later, the house a hollow network of tunnels with the boys gone, both settled in at Ryan's place when she called them earlier, her voice a phony blast of sunshine as tears worked down her cheeks, swallowing more ibuprofen with more Jameson and icing her swollen, gnarled hand at the kitchen table, the photo of the 2005 summer youth camp within easy reach. She didn't think she'd be able to fool Ryan—he's sharp, and more than wise to her bullshit—but she managed it, maybe because she didn't have to fake relief when the boys' voices chimed in together on the speaker. They were safe. Ryan would give his life for them. She's never questioned it.

Now, Mads and the old man are below, keeping each other close in grief as the night deepens around them, a new deputy's vehicle out front, the dome light switching on now and then as he works, maybe reporting in, she's not sure. Mads will most likely be able to cry herself into exhaustion, but Dad won't sleep tonight, Shaw knows that; not now that he knows everything she's learned from James and Brandy. The old man has been on and off the phone ever since, calling Stephen York, arguing for arrests that won't happen. Let Stephen try to reel him in with promises of safe haven.

Shaw opens her recents, knows Anders's number on sight; her stomach is so painfully cramped with tension and whiskey and not enough food that she slumps against the headboard with her knees drawn up, facing the dark mirror once again with its contrasting stripes of faint moonlight highlighting dust on the glass.

Anders doesn't answer. If he has any sense, he will have disposed of his smartphone by now, stopping the police from being able to roughly track his movements by pings off nearby cell towers. A generic voicemail robot invites her to leave a message. She sits dully, letting the recorded silence stretch on, then she plunges in:

"I know about the camp, Anders. You followed her for almost two years, didn't you? Probably pumped other people at church for information about our family, anything you needed. You're a stalker. You stalked, right? And waited for your moment. You must've sat outside the House of Pizza that last night . . . then followed James's pickup. You saw them let Thea out on the road. They made it so easy for you." She pushes her hand through her hair, leaving her fingers snarled there. "A little kid, fucked up out of her mind on booze and pills? And she would've recognized you, thought she was getting a safe ride home. Or did she even know what was happening when you put her into your car, you fucking—" Her voice breaks, and she lurches forward, pulling her arm back, ready to throw the phone, craving the release of a shattered, dark screen, killing the voice at last.

Finally, instead, she drops the phone, where it lands impotently in a snarl of blankets.

Shaw powers down, then, for an unknown time, the mostly room-temperature ice pack sliding off her hand, her chin sagging on her chest, her body leaning sideways in a sort of fugue against the propped-up pillows.

The ringtone draws her back. She sees by the glowing clockface that it's 2:48 a.m. Almost six hours have passed.

"I needed some time to debate," Anders says when she picks up. "Risk versus reward. Calling you back versus tossing this phone down a long, dark hole. Are the police tapping your phone?"

Her voice rasps out of her. "I don't know. Probably."

"I won't pretend to know much about all that. On television, they say that it takes a certain amount of time for the police to triangulate a caller's location. Such a satisfying word. 'Triangulate.' Anyway, my delight at hearing that you've finally managed to put your hands on a few of the missing pieces won out. So, good evening. How are you?"

Shaw swallows, runs her tongue over her furred front teeth, trying to stop her upper lip from sticking. "You tried to kill my family the other night."

"Now, don't exaggerate. That was only some of your family. And I was mainly trying to kill you."

"No, you weren't. If that was true, you would've rammed us. Or you would've tried to finish us off while we were stuck in that snowbank." She folds her arm across her chest. "What if you actually had killed me out there on that road, in a rollover or something? Then what would you do?"

Silence.

"What would you have done with the time you've got left?" She listens to his quietude. "I know that you're sick. I know that you've been going to that hospital for special treatment." She shifts position on the bed. "I looked over their website. They don't have an oncology department, so it's not cancer. What is it, then? Your kidneys?"

A sniff, a rustle of movement, as if he's reorienting himself. "Don't I wish. At least kidneys come in pairs. A person can live a long, healthy life with only one. No . . . over the past two years I've found myself in quite a predicament. An unjust one, really. I've never been a drinker. Always taken good care of myself. I even used to jog a little, in my salad days. And yet I find myself faced with this . . . failure." A blank moment of reflection. "It's stymieing to me."

"Yeah. Why, God, etcetera. Really makes you think." Shaw straightens a little more, rearranges the pillows for support. "Two years dates back to when you first started calling me. That's it, isn't it? You wanted somebody to know. Nobody, not even the cops, found out about your thin little connection to Thea. Hired for one summer to help teach a camp? The church probably didn't even keep paperwork on you."

"One week. One life-changing week in July 2005. Your mother forced Thea to go, of course. She even skipped with her friends one day, tried to sneak back in with the group during an outdoor trust exercise without anyone noticing. But I noticed. I promised to keep our secret. She thanked me."

Shaw shuts her eyes against it. "Father Joseph. He might've been one of the only people who could've recognized you, or even re-membered you from all those years ago, if anyone had ever asked the right question. Is that why you killed him? Or because you were angry that he never figured it out?" She waits. "Because how else could everyone appreciate how smart you are if you really did get away with making Thea disappear forever?"

"Not everyone. You."

"*Why?* Why me? Why does it matter so much to you?"

Abruptly, he speaks louder, more sharply. "You know, I'm afraid that I don't have patience for a phone survey just now. Being on the run has been rather stressful. I can't use my cards because the police might track them. I can't get a room. I'm afraid that I don't have the loving support system needed to remain a fugitive for long." There's a slight echo audible in the room where he is, his voice bouncing off a high ceiling, maybe down a hallway. "Then, I had an epiphany. Where's the one place where, when you have to go there, they have to take you in?"

"In your case? Federal prison."

"Come, now. You're not thinking hard enough. Perhaps a small hint. Not that you deserve it." He clears his throat, reads aloud, "'Shawnee. Four foot eight in March 1997. Almost four foot ten in December. Ooh . . . 1999 was a big year for you. Shot up nearly four inches by then, achieving your full height of Head Representative of the Lollipop Guild." He gives a sigh, maybe scooching down. "Thea was only slightly behind you. But then, you two were always so close in everything. I suppose the littlest Connolly is marked here somewhere—far, far below. . . .'"

Shaw feels a shock of cold. She knows right where he is. It's an obscenity and her tone reflects that, low, harsh, from the diaphragm: "What are you doing there?"

"At the moment? Enjoying all the comforts of home."

Shaw is off the bed in an instant, snapping on the lamp. "Is anyone else there?"

"I should think so. This is a family residence, after all. Fully stocked fridge, personalized wall calendar, little plastic food dish intended for a cat by the name of Patches. I do have some commentary on the living room color scheme for the lady of the house, but I'm afraid that she's indisposed."

Shaw drags jeans on with the phone squeezed between her shoulder and cheek, going for socks and a sweatshirt. "Have you hurt them?"

"No, never. Hardly ever. Well. The husband's taken a bit of a spill." Anders pauses. "I wonder what blood type he is. Hmm. Understand, those of us in need of regular transfusions are always on the lookout."

"What about the kid?" She's nearly shouting. "The little girl."

"I'm well aware of who you mean." There's another pause, more rustling of movement.

"Hello? Anders?" Shaw's eyes are wide, darting, seeing nothing until she hears the faintest sound over the speaker. A sniffling. Then a small voice, the words and their meaning lost in distance and distortion. But a child. No question of that.

Shaw makes an inadvertent sound, her gorge rising, squeezing her eyes shut for a count of five. "What do you want me to do?"

"Come home to me. That's all I've ever wanted. It's way past due. And I should warn you that if I see even the slightest sign of a police presence in the meantime, I will put an end to every life in this house. Even the damned cat. If I can drag it out from under the bed. And then there will be one last cleansing fire."

"I am not doing this."

"You had better, unless you'd enjoy seeing your childhood bedroom redecorated with arterial spray. Never challenge a dying man, Shawnee. You've got everything to lose. I have nothing."

Shaw turns uselessly where she stands, hyperventilating, no idea of what to do next, who to turn to, and the rage pours from her, her voice that of a stranger: "If I go into that house, you're not leaving alive, no matter what it takes."

"I like my odds." A muffled sound against the microphone. "I'll leave a light on for you."

She stands in her numbed state, realizing, only once he's gone, that he'd kissed the phone.

There's no time for anything beyond the most basic mechanisms of the lizard brain, negotiating a path out of the house without her family or the sheriff's deputy out front stopping her. Meaning she can't drive the Beast.

The last thing she needs is a cruiser tailing her with lights blazing as she tries to make it to Rishworth, to that little girl trapped with Anders in Shaw's house. If the cops try to negotiate a standoff with him, she has no doubt that they'll arrive to find a house full of corpses.

She needs only two things: the dog and the gun.

She goes around the boxes and Thea's strewn belongings to the safe in the closet and gets the pistol out, fumbling and cursing herself, loading the magazine, then stuffing the SIG Sauer into the back of her waistband like a woman sliding a sleeping rattlesnake against her skin.

Shaw goes downstairs softly, walking along the edges of the steps like she's trying not to wake the boys on Christmas Eve night, the flash of familiarity almost enough to buckle her. But now she can see the top of Dad's gray head, and the angle suggests he's out cold in the chair after all.

Aphrodite watches from her bed as Shaw moves quietly to the entryway and slides her feet into her boots, then pulls on her coat with a minimal amount of rustling, unlooping the leash from the last peg, holding it up for the dog to see.

Aphrodite stands immediately and crosses to her, heeling as if it's totally natural that they should be leaving the house together before dawn. They head down the hallway toward the kitchen door that lets out on the western side of the house, an easy fifteen-second walk around the corner of the house to the driveway, but instead they go right, jogging across the crusted snow of the backyard. Shaw hunches low, not sure if it's even possible for the deputy in the vehicle to hear the quiet sounds of their escape into the open pasture, but she knows the officer does periodic perimeter checks and she wants to be well away from here before one of those happens.

She doesn't dare turn on the overhead lights in the shop, instead using her phone's Flashlight app to locate the keys to Ryan's 1979 Ford F-250 pickup, urging the hellhound up onto the bench seat where the vinyl is cold and intractable, praying there's some gas left in the tank. Ryan used to keep gas cans on hand, but he may have moved them to his new shop by now, and the truck's been sitting in here unused for at least a year.

"Come *on*," she says under her breath, wincing as she cranks the key, any dread of a frozen or blocked fuel line banished by the partial turnover, and two tries later, the roar of the truck's engine.

The deputy will have heard it, most likely; there's no time. Shaw gets out and powers up the automatic bay door, running back to the truck and reversing out of the building with her arm slung across the top of the seat, Aphrodite slipping and sliding and bracing her paws to keep from falling into the leg space.

The truck handles stiffly, but she straightens out in the middle of the road, then floors it, refusing to look back, not for anything, not lights in the rearview of the pursuing cruiser or the all-night security lights of her house, maybe her dad and sister waking up, wondering where in hell she's gone, why she'd do something so crazy.

She'll be back. She has to believe that. She will live to tell.

21

S haw sticks to the back roads for a while, but the deputy never appears behind her. The truck has maybe a table-spoonful of gas to burn through before she's redlining it, but right when she's nearly sick from waiting for the Ford to start bucking and quitting, she comes upon a station with all-night pumps, where she puts in a quick half tank and nearly calls 911 three times before cursing, stuffing the phone back into her coat pocket, and leaning against the doorframe with her face pressed into her forearm. *Fuck.*

Aphrodite watches, panting, soaking up her human's anxiety, maybe even smelling Shaw's emotions, like they say dogs can.

Shaw gets back onto Route 15 and continues through the dark, passing only the very occasional car.

It's cold, still the wee hours, but dawn is brightening up the horizon, black crossing over to blue, the reflectiveness of the snow giving some luminescence to the streets of Rishworth as she pulls in to Pressman Street at just before four a.m.

The old house looks as it did before, the faint shapes of the porch swing and the plastic crate of toys discernable in the dusk. This time, however, there are two cars in the driveway, a small SUV and a compact. She imagines Anders's Charger is parked along the curb somewhere nearby, not close enough to be linked to this house if seen from the street. There is, indeed, a light left on for her over the front entrance, not to mention a glow behind the glass panes of the door, and another in the upstairs window, which is in what used to be Mom and Dad's bedroom.

Shaw waits, her shoulder and neck muscles rigid, gut churning, watching for any movement at the curtains, but nothing stirs.

She calls Anders. "I'm here." He doesn't say anything. "How do I know that you're not going to shoot me as soon as I walk through the door?"

"Because I don't like guns. Too abrupt. No sense of denouement."

Shaw pauses. "Have you hurt anyone since we talked?"

"I'm afraid that you'll have to come inside to find out."

Shaw closes her eyes, ends the call, then taps the emergency call option on her dial pad.

A 911 operator answers, and Shaw says, "A fugitive named Anders Jansen is holding a family hostage at 134 Pressman Street in Rishworth. He's a murderer and an arsonist. He told me that he's already hurt or killed the man who rents the place."

"Are you calling from inside the home?"

Shaw inhales briefly, lets it out. "Not yet."

Shaw hangs up, pockets the phone, takes her gun out of her waistband and slides it into her left-hand coat pocket—she's right-handed but it's still a throbbing claw from the beating she gave it yesterday—and then she goes stiffly around the vehicle to let Aphrodite out. Shaw hooks the dog's leash onto her chain collar, continually looking back at the house, checking for signs of life.

They walk up the short driveway, navigating around the cars, the gun a weight at her side, wondering how quickly she can grab it, if she's even capable of getting off a shot under pressure at a human being; wondering what the hell she thinks she's doing, whose reality this is, if this is another waking dream where she believes she's on track to find Thea, that her sister is down this road or this hall or down a long flight of stairs into dim mental clutter and confusion from which she'll wake at any moment, her hands cramped around emptiness.

She's at the door now, too fast but also achingly slow, Shaw lost in a muzzy sort of detachment as she watches her own hand from a distance, turning the knob, letting the door drift inward. It still smells like home.

The stairs and front hall are empty. Shaw crosses the threshold with Aphrodite and starts to push the door closed, but her attention is drawn by the fingers visible in the space behind the door.

She pushes it shut the rest of the way, looking down at the man stretched out on his side on the floor, one arm up, the other trapped beneath him. Young, late twenties, with blood in his hair and more pooled beneath his head, a broad dark stripe of it down the back of the gray hoodie he's wearing. Dad's tenant, the Hendricks husband, she's not sure of his first name. Completely nonresponsive.

Shaw's hand goes into her left pocket and grips the handle of the gun, poised to pull it free at the slightest sound, keeping the leash taut so that Aphrodite can't sniff at the blood, frustrated in her efforts to show her human that she found signs of death again. Shaw sinks down, never lowering her gaze from the hall and stairs, pressing two fingers against the side of the man's throat, hunting around until she thinks she feels something, maybe the slightest, thready pulse.

There's nothing she can do for him right now, so she moves toward the kitchen, still no noise in the house but the humming of appliances. She leans against the doorway, peering in, sure she'll see Anders sitting at the table or waiting in a corner. But there's no one. Outside the window above the sink, the blue light is growing.

The dog pulls toward the corridor again, not keening or growling or doing anything Shaw might've expected in an atmosphere with the corrosive emotional effect of mustard gas.

The cellar door is in here, but no way in hell is she going down the steps to that cobwebby, dirt-floored space, creepy under even every-day circumstances; she's always hated it, the vague, lurking shapes of the water heater and furnace, an old coal chute in the wall.

Still the dog pulls, so Shaw follows, going back down the corridor, Aphrodite invested in the blood and the motionless man. "No," Shaw whispers, jerking the dog back from him again, and that's when her peripheral vision discerns a human shape in the living room chair.

The lamps are off in there, but the dawn light through the window sheers gives him a silhouette: a head above a high-backed chair, a standing lamp beside him, and it's all so like the night that she waited up for Thea that, for a moment, in her panic, she believes that she's seeing herself, some shadowbox scene arranged to remind her who she and this place are to each other.

Then, the height of the person, the shape of the chair, different from that of her childhood, betray themselves, and a little air returns to her lungs.

Aphrodite's head dips low as she sights on him. The fur on her scruff lifts like metal shavings teased by a magnet.

"How I hate it when people hover in doorways." Anders's voice is a little hoarse.

Shaw's hand snaps out and hits the wall switch, blasting the room with light, revealing him there, gazing back, his limbs loose, knees planted apart. "Who are you, the Phantom of the Opera?" Her voice is shaking. "I'm not walking into a dark room, jackass."

The dog's growling now, the sound sawing in her chest, building as she watches Anders, smelling God only knows what piquant bouquet of emotions flowing from that quarter. He remains seated, sighing, watching Aphrodite. "You had to bring that thing along."

"Yup. Had to. I also brought a very abrupt gun. So, behave, now." Her mouth runs completely independent of her, nausea a stiff finger jabbed into the back of her throat, her gaze flicking around the room, which is different yet the same, Dad's old chenille couch against the wall but most everything else of decoration belonging to the tenants. "Where's the wife and kid?"

"Out of the way. I didn't feel that we wanted an audience to our conversation."

She jerks her head toward the man lying in his own blood. "He isn't dead yet. There's still time to help him, end all of this."

Anders's socketed eyes track her but otherwise his expression remains inert, as if she never spoke. "What do you think of my tableau? I had to drag the lamp over. And the chair leaves something to be desired, but I thought, in the dark . . ." He lifts the fingers of one hand, lowering them back to the chair arm.

Aphrodite now leans so far forward that Shaw's tension on the other end of the leash is the only thing keeping the dog from spilling over, locked in on Anders, her growling a steady ambient noise. "You look bad," Shaw says.

"You know, Shaw, I feel bad." He traces the line of the embroidered paisley pattern on the chair with one fingertip. "I missed a dialysis appointment because of you. Though, in truth, it's doing me very little good. The doctor said that in some patients tissue regeneration can begin after as little as one or two sessions." His imitation of a smile is tight, lips concealing teeth, the whites of his eyes yellowed. "Can't prove that by me. Let's face facts. I simply need a new liver."

"Well, a guy like you must have donors lining up at the door." His expression remains flat, the lenses of his glasses catching the lamplight. "You mad, babe?"

He snorts softly, his straight teeth revealed. "I abandoned the notion of never letting the sun go down upon my anger long ago."

"Yeah. You and me both." She shifts her weight. "Okay, here's how it's going to work. You're going to let the woman and the girl go. In exchange for them, you get me. Then you and I are going to sit right here while you tell me how to find Thea."

"Let me guess. The police will be joining us shortly."

"Oh, yeah. They'll be sending the SWAT. Major Crimes. FBI." She swallows. "You had to know that I'd call."

He looks at her for a long moment. "Well. What choice do I have?"

"Not a whole lot." She steps forward. "You're going to be straight with me about Thea or I will shoot you from the shins up until you tell me the truth."

"My oh my. You are tough. Broke the mold when they made you, hmm."

"*I want my sister back.*" The words emerge roughly, choked; she pulls the gun from her pocket, extending it so that the muzzle is level with his face.

His gaze flicks from the pistol bore to the dog. "You'll find both mother and daughter upstairs in the master bedroom. Sounds a little grand for a tenement like this, but you grasp my meaning."

"I'm not getting them. You are." Shaw jerks her head toward the stairs. "Go on."

"I'll warn you, I'm not strong. I've . . . been ill. Vomiting. This past week, with so little rest . . . it's taken a lot from me. I should go to a hospital."

"You were getting along fine when you followed me down the street."

"That was days ago." Anders presses his right palm down against the arm of his chair to boost himself up, and Aphrodite barks once, shrilly, her upper lip curled, trembling, above her canines; he stops, watching her. "May I stand?"

"Oh, by all means, asshole, you trot right up there." Shaw steps back, her arm nearly numb from being locked in place with Aphrodite's weight on the end of the leash, her injured hand pulsing plaintively for a break it can't afford. "At least have the decency to cover the girl's dad up before—"

His movement is reflexive, his left arm sweeping out with something tucked between his body and the padded chair, the slatting sound of a spray bottle meeting Shaw's ears a split second after the liquid has struck Aphrodite in the face.

The dog jerks, shrieks, and goes down as ammonia fumes fill the air. Shaw has only enough time to jerk the gun up before he pumps three times into her face, the first stream hitting her directly across the eyes before she can turn away.

Acid. Might as well be; her hands fly to her eyes, and she doubles over with a sound of pain and outrage. He got her, he fucking *got* her—the leash is gone from her hand, and Aphrodite's crying, the gun no more than a useless weight she can't let go of as she falls to her knees.

Swiping frantically to stop the burning and clear her vision— one eye can still open slightly—she catches a foggy image of Anders near the radiator along the far wall, dragging the dog across the floor, before Shaw's eyes seal with swelling and tears again.

A second later, his boot comes down on her shoulder, slamming her onto her side. Her head bounces off the floorboards; she screams, but rolls away, knocking into a piece of furniture and throwing out a blind side kick, which staves him off while she fumbles for the gun.

A savage grunt from him as he drives his heel down into the softness of her stomach. She cries out, rolls back, aims the gun at what she can't see, and fires anyway.

The shot explodes in the room along with a violent clank of metal. When she un-squints her good eye she sees the overhead light piece swinging, half of it dangling by wires, and a hole in the drop ceiling tiles.

Anders is gone; Aphrodite is gone. Shaw heaves herself to her feet, holding the gun with both hands, breath rasping out of her, her cheeks wet with involuntary tears mixed with ammonia.

She hears muffled sounds from upstairs, smothered screaming and crying, as well as the dog barking and thumping somewhere, a total madhouse. Shaw doesn't know where the hell Anders is hiding, but the kid's upstairs, so that's where she goes, angling her head to check out the landing, the short L-shaped hallway that leads to the bedrooms and bathroom.

She goes to Mom and Dad's old bedroom, pressing her back to the open door to see a woman lying on her side on the bed, her arms bent behind her with duct tape, moving to shield her child with her body at the sight of Shaw coming in. The girl, maybe four years old, long brown matted hair, is tucked in against her mother's core in a fetal position.

"It's okay." Shaw hurries to the bed; there's nothing handy to cut the tape with, so she rips at it with her teeth until she gets a tear started, the woman yanking her arms convulsively until she's able to untwist one arm and tear the tape from her mouth, then her daughter's. Shaw helps them both to their feet, where the woman scoops her girl into her arms. "Go, get out of the house," Shaw says. "Run down the stairs and out the front door."

"My husband—he hit him, stabbed him—I don't—"

"An ambulance is coming. Just get your daughter out of here."

Shaw follows them, one hand out to touch the woman's back, guiding, her eyes still burning horribly, the right one unwilling to open at all as they thunder down the stairs. Shaw stops on the second-to-last step, clinging to the railing as she watches them yank open the door and flee down the front steps. All the while, Shaw expects Anders to emerge, to stop them, but he never does.

Through the sidelights along the door, Shaw can make out the indistinct moving shape of the mother carrying her daughter down the driveway and across the street, where Shaw's blurred vision loses the ability to separate them from the dusk.

From down the hall, the thumping continues, along with Aphrodite's muffled barking. She's trying to get out of somewhere. Decision time: find the dog and hope she's in a condition to be of help, or find Anders, if he's still in the house. It's not a large place: kitchen, dining room, center stairway, living room on the other side, then the two bedrooms and bathroom on the second floor.

It's an easy guess where he'll most likely be. She reaches the top of the stairs again, this time continuing down the hall to the last bedroom, the one she, Thea, and Mads once shared.

Shaw goes to the doorway and sees him sitting on the edge of the mattress in what is now the little Hendricks girl's room. Funny; this is the larger bedroom of the two, most suited to be the master. Perhaps the small lingering details, the height measurements carved into the doorframe by Dad's penknife, the lavender-painted walls, whispered that this was meant to be a child's bedroom, and had been for decades.

This girl has her headboard pushed against the south wall, a big rainbow plush pillow knocked to the floor; anything beyond that is a swimmy blur to Shaw. Anders obviously sat here and listened to the sounds of her freeing the Hendricks family and did nothing.

Shaw stands with the gun hanging at her side, her adrenaline ebbing, her eyes throbbing dully in concordance with her pulse. "Why'd you let them go?"

Anders keeps his hands clasped. "I don't need them anymore. The girl was sufficient to get you here. Otherwise, they were an annoyance, what with all the whimpering and the pleading for their lives. You can only hear 'don't kill me' so many times before it loses all the endearing melodrama." His gaze lifts to her with another one of those small, inner smiles. "Hence the duct tape."

"You're out of time. The cops might already be here. They won't use sirens, pulling up to a house with hostages."

"Are you suggesting there may be snipers?" His voice is hushed mockery. "And tear gas?" His tone flattens again. "If they can roll any of those things out within an hour's timeframe in rural Maine, I'll eat your liver. Hold the fava beans." He passes his hand over his midsection. "I'm watching my fiber intake these days."

She struggles to form words like a drunk, her tongue a foreign instrument. "You promised. You promised me." She cocks the gun with some difficulty, determined never to look away again, never give him another chance to strip her defenses.

"Listen to yourself. 'Promised, promised.' You're a child. Has it never occurred to you that you simply stopped growing after you lost Thea? It's dreary and pathetic."

"You steal kids' lives. I'd say the pathetic crown goes to you, dickhead." Another sharp stab of pain in her right eye, and her expression contorts, fleeting thoughts of chemical burns and the fact that she needed an eye-wash station about fifteen minutes ago.

"Have you deciphered the meaning behind the fires yet?" He watches her. "I'm curious if you're capable of making the connections. It seemed so obvious."

She shakes her head slightly. "I don't see anything special. I never did."

"Highlights from 2005 into 2006. I watched Thea in all of those places. From afar. Sometimes from my vehicle, so she wouldn't feel self-conscious. Swimming with some boy at Lake Heron. Shopping with your mother. Lunch with her at a café, after. I must say, their relationship seemed strained."

Shaw adjusts her grip slightly. "You destroyed those places to draw me a map to Saint Anthony's?"

"I burned you a path to the answers you claimed you wanted so badly, yes. I kept hoping you'd attend one of the scenes—they were within your lab's district, after all—and I watched for you, but you never turned up. They always sent the man. At least, until the end."

He clears his throat, nods toward the street. "Do you know I used to sit outside—right out there—and watch this house? I watched your shadows move past the windows." He looks up at her sideways. "That was when I was in the full blush of my need for her, you understand. It always goes that way. Can't eat, can't sleep, all the old clichés. I must know everything. Her routine, who's in her life. The fervor is brief yet all-consuming. Because the simple truth of our lives is that there's only so much to know about anyone. Our days hold no more significance than a maze on the back of a cereal box. At a certain point, my need to . . . disrupt the pattern becomes more than I can stand." Another smile. "Particularly when opportunity presents itself."

Shaw aims the gun.

He looks back from beneath his brows. "Stop. Posturing. You won't do it. You need me too much. In fact, at this moment, to you, I'm the most precious thing in the world. Even more so than those blue-eyed boys of yours." He draws himself up in a stretch and stands. "Ryan was wise to take them when he did. I'd had designs on Casey . . . a simple snatch while he was waiting for the school bus, maybe . . . but was robbed of the chance."

"I don't have to kill you. I can start blowing little pieces off until you talk to me."

"So do it." He steps closer and she steps back, over the threshold onto the landing again, planting her feet, her chest heaving. "That is, if you're certain you're skilled enough to fire a bullet into someone without tearing open any organs or major arteries, sending them into shock, or killing them outright. Then again, I also may be more stubborn than you expect. What if you pull the trigger but I just . . . refuse?"

He closes the space between them, letting the gun bump the center of his chest. She's shuddering convulsively, adjusting her grip on the handle. "Then you've killed the only person who ever could've let you make amends with Thea. And your family. Allow you to compensate for failing them all so badly. I would think even a halfway interested person should be able to prevent their little sister from being violated and buried in the dirt the way Thea was."

"*Fuck you—*" Her finger squeezes the trigger.

He seizes it with his left hand and wrenches the gun to the side, trapping and twisting her finger inside the trigger guard. "If there's anything I can't abide, it's an uninspired vocabulary—" With a grunt, he chucks the gun behind him, lost to the room, his hands seizing first her trapezial muscles, jolting her, then grabbing her throat, his grip a band of iron.

Her eyes go wide, her mouth open, the pressure on her carotid arteries already cutting blood flow to the brain, but she's been here before, class after class, practice and muscle memory kicking in where reason can't—

She ducks her chin down against the dual thumb pressure on her trachea to create space, then brings her left arm between them, ramming down against his forearms with her bent elbow, at the same time twisting her whole body to the right with it, getting heavy, trying to break his grip.

They struggle—he's taller, stronger, but she's sturdy and well trained—and finally she's able to bring her knee up into his body a couple times, the last one landing near enough to his solar plexus to force some air out of him, make him let go.

Shaw hits him with a couple palm-heel strikes and lifts her knee into his groin, letting out a guttural cry as she slams her fist into his left eye, leaving him doubled over as she whirls and runs for the stairs.

Her feet hammer down the first four steps before he lands on her back, just drops on her, dead weight.

They hurtle down together in a tangle of limbs, Shaw crying out as the side of her head bounces off the edge of the step, and she bites her tongue, her mouth surging with blood.

They land hard on the entryway floor. Shaw's legs are caught under him, but in an instant, she's up on her elbows in an army crawl toward the open front door, spitting blood before she gags on it, giving an animal's scream as he catches her by fistfuls of her clothes, dragging her back, then onto her feet, jerking her around and propelling her forward with him by her coat and the back of her jeans.

"Come on." His voice is brutal, unrecognizable, and he's limping badly now, dragging her in a broken rhythm through the kitchen, past the scratch and scrabble of Aphrodite on the other side of the cellar door. "You want to know, I'll show you. I'll show you—"

Anders yanks the back door open, forcing her down the steps so hard that Shaw would've gone sprawling face-first onto the ground if it wasn't for his grip on her clothes. He marches her forward across the backyard, light enough outside now to discern the shed, the shape of the little girl's swing set.

Shaw tries throwing an elbow at him—he catches it, holds on—so she swings her left boot back to connect with his shin and scrapes her heel downward over his shinbone. He makes a muffled sound of pain, stumbles, and she wrenches free long enough to bolt, shouting, *"Help me!"* once into the small clearing and woods before he's on her again.

This time, it's a choke hold from behind. Within three seconds her face is suffused with blood, her teeth clenched in pain and the pressure of his forearm on her windpipe sealing off her air, her feet kicking back for another shin scrape, but her thoughts are lost in a white heat of panic because he's brought her out here to kill her, down in the snow, *no air—*

She grays out for who knows how long, seconds, the time it takes for the scraping of dried brambles against her legs to reach her detached senses. He's let off her neck a little, and they're at the property line, past the break in the fence, the thin strip of bushes separating their land from the blackness of the trees.

She lashes out again, not much strength left, kicking her legs, throwing her head back to slam his face with her skull. She's thrown down, rolling across the scant snow to land on her side, gasping, her cheek pressed to the rough, cold ground, for an instant savoring the chill before he presses his palm flat against the side of her face, his knee pinning her legs together so she can't wriggle out from beneath.

Anders leans close, his sour breath in her face. "You never even knew. Any of you—" His gasp of laughter is cracked. "Even with all your searches and posters and public cries for help, you never . . . even . . . *knew.*" Another gasping, sobbing laugh next to Shaw's ear, followed by a drop of hot blood from the blow she'd dealt his nose landing on her chin and rolling with gravity. "What's the expression? A home truth?"

Some of his meaning breaks through, and she stills, only her eyes moving back and forth, chest heaving, listening, letting him run with it. She's so close, right on the verge, some hazy vision of Thea discernible through the damaged miasma across her eyes, near enough to touch.

"That same night—the very *night*—I came here. I parked down the street"—he's stroking her hair now, snagging and ripping through the snarls in the back—"and I saw you. Another blond girl, sitting there in that window with the lamp on. All the while, your little

sister was in my trunk. I *almost* tried for you. The audacity of it—
going inside, seeing you turn, the fear in your face—oh, it appealed.
Imagine, when I found out later from the news that there was a
third daughter, asleep upstairs. What I had missed." More laughter
spills out of him, a flinching, convulsive act against her body, some
wellspring opened inside him—"But instead I chose caution, and I
hadn't been able to make up my mind until that moment, but then
I knew—sheer inspiration. The very thing."

Shaw's burned lens sees the translucent silhouette of Thea, hovering there, at the edge of the brush and trees, so still, never so still
in life, not that girl.

"I didn't have a shovel with me, so I had to come back. But I did.
Under cover of darkness. The ground was still somewhat frozen. No
small task, believe me. Couldn't have been six feet down—not even
close—so I always expected she'd be found—unearthed by animals
or time . . . but she never was." Sudden crushing pressure against
her head as he drives the side of her face against the icy snow, her
teeth digging into her inner cheek. "Feel her down there? Because
I do. Where was your close sister connection all these years you
were walking in this yard, living day to day, wondering *where is she.*
Hmm?" Jolting his weight against her with each word. "You never
even knew."

The disbelief rides a nauseating wave of horror. Shaw gives a
muffled wail, fumbling upward with her left hand, grasping one
of his fingers and yanking it sideways, wanting to hear that snap
of bone, making him the one to scream and finally curse, left no
choice but to jerk away from her—

She wriggles free, crabbing backward on her heels and palms,
gasping, blood on her chin, watching him where he kneels clutching
the hand with the sprained or broken finger, watching her with a
fixed and private sort of fascination. Inside her mind is a maelstrom,

sensing an energy from this ground that never existed until now, now that she knows that Thea's here.

"Why do you hate me so much?" Shaw's voice is small, broken, words escaping a swollen, damaged throat.

Anders rises slowly, still studying her, his face a passionless mask but for the gimlet eyes. "Because she called for you. When I had her . . . she screamed for you."

He lunges down for her. In that second—a fraction of—Shaw sees her window, and wrenches over onto her right hip to throw out a side kick, no time or proximity to fully extend her leg, instead hitting his kneecap at a forty-five-degree angle. She feels it, the tear, the give of the bone plate at the same moment that he screams—

She continues to roll to the right, barely avoiding him landing on her, then scrambling, wild-eyed, to her feet and running for the house—she's pushing as hard as she can but her body is wooden, her gait hobbled. Can't believe it when she hears him raving something at her and getting up, still coming—his uneven footfalls pounding after her—

Shaw stumbles up the back steps, doubled over, then through the open doorway and into the kitchen, landing heavily on her face and right elbow as he yanks her legs out from under her. She kicks back at him, crawling madly for the door in the far kitchen wall.

Shaw grabs the chipped porcelain knob and yanks it, rolling aside to crash into the table and chairs as the cellar door swings open under Aphrodite's weight, where the dog lands on all fours in a scrambling of nails on linoleum.

There's time for their eyes to meet, the dog and Anders, and Aphrodite never stops running. She goes from searching for balance to lunging within a span of seconds and strikes him full in the chest with her front paws. Snarling, she goes for the exposed flesh of his throat as he grabs her in a bear hug. They go down together, Aphrodite biting, shaking, impossible for Shaw to tell from her angle what the hellhound's got in her jaws, but Anders is fighting her, wrestling her, shoving at her head. The dog sinks her teeth into his hand—

There's a crash from the front of the house, shouts of, *"Police! Get down, get down—"* Shaw draws back against the table as an armed officer covered in black SWAT body armor and a helmet appears in the kitchen doorway, then another two at the open back door, assault rifles aimed first at her, then the scene of Anders being savaged by the dog.

"Okay, okay, okay," she says under her breath, sagging against the table leg as she raises her hands up higher, higher, watching the officers try to drag the dog loose.

22

Five days later, the property of the old house is taped off, the street closed to traffic. The Connolly family's story has been in heavy circulation around the state, even some national news outlets, so the press is swarming beyond the sawhorses, most of them staying in their vehicles to dodge the wind except for a couple intrepid cameramen crouching behind tripods to film official vehicles coming and going, the only footage they're being permitted while everyone waits to see what answers the day provides.

Shaw, Mads, the old man, and Ryan stand in a huddle in the driveway, which is as close as the state police will let them get. As the Connollys watch, an officer in an insulated black coat with POLICE printed across the back slowly pushes a wheeled ground-penetrating radar cart across roughly forty feet of area that has been cleared with the permission of the town, which owns the wooded lot behind their property, as well as by taking down a large portion of the fence Dad put up around their land when Shaw was a kid.

"You want a seat?" Dad asks Shaw, keeping his hand hovering close to her but not touching. "I stuck a camp chair in the back, just in case."

"No. I'm good." Shaw has a mild concussion. Her ribs are cracked, wrapped in bandages to ease the pervasive ache. Some of her organs are bruised. Her wrist is sprained, encased in an air cast, and two of her fingers are taped together to help heal the fractures she inflicted herself when she KO'd the steering wheel. Her throat and face show the evidence of having fought for her life, not to mention the speckling of finger-shaped bruises scattered in the places where he grabbed her, slammed her, tore a portion of hair free from her scalp. Her eyes are full of the three different types of medicated eyedrops the doctor prescribed to treat the alkali burns from the ammonia cleaner, keeping the swelling and tearing somewhat at bay while her corneas and lenses heal. It's not certain yet whether she'll suffer permanent damage. Here's hoping.

"Nobody's going to think less of you if you sit in the car and rest for a while, you know." Mads has an edge to her voice, also close enough to touch but not quite daring. "You've only been out of the hospital a few days."

"You should listen to her," Ryan says, staying slightly off to the side of Shaw, not so near as to be mistaken for the concerned husband, maybe, but present, much as he'd been since she'd texted him from the hospital upon admittance. Caring for the boys, keeping tabs on her recovery, staying quietly involved in the developments with Thea. "You've got nothing to prove—"

"Look, I'm not going to break. You guys ought to know that by now." Shaw won't take her gaze off the radar cart, which is able to scan up to ten feet of area as deep as thirty feet down in under a half hour, so they've been told; it's already been fifteen minutes. Shaw adds gruffly, "Sorry." This is how she's surviving, plugging along like a beat-up old packhorse, but having the boys in her cart is what keeps her going, helps her when a surge of panic comes out of nowhere and she has to close her eyes and focus on forcing the air into her lungs, reminding her body that it isn't under attack again, that home is safe, that her kids are right in the next room and as long as she can put her eyes on them, the earth keeps turning.

"We almost lost you." Mads stands with her arms folded tightly, hugging herself, the wind fluttering the fringe of her scarf. "We're allowed to worry, okay?"

Shaw continues to stand and watch. The officer is supposed to be receiving real-time responses on the display screen mounted on the handlebars, a 2-D map created by the sonar bouncing back from objects below the surface, searching for something that could indicate turned-over soil and human remains. Remains. Hope, grief, revulsion, a churning mixture that she's barely holding down. Fucking Christ, Thea. Right in their own backyard. If the Connollys are feeling overexposed right now, just wait until the Associated Press gets a taste of that headline.

"You remember the dress?" The words bolt from her and Mads glances over curiously. "You must. I know you say that you can't, but you remember prom night. She went with that skinny-ass senior, that gawky kid, but Thea's dress was sky blue and she actually looked like a girlie-girl that night. And you couldn't keep your hands off the material because it was so silky—"

"I sure do," Dad puts in quietly, his hands in his pockets, his gaze following the officer as he slows, checking the display, saying something to a nearby colleague who comes over to confer.

"And you said the thing," Shaw sounds like a little kid herself, quavering, insistent, "the other day, about putting your grubby little hands on her stuff, so you do remember. You must."

The officers crowd around the display, another two joining them, and the three remaining Connollys tense and move together imperceptibly, Mads's arms loosening as she speaks softly, distractedly: "She left her corsage on my bed. I found it when I woke up."

Shaw gives something like a laugh choked with tears, feeling Ryan's hand graze her shoulder but not quite rest there, and then she's walking forward, unbidden, toward the gravesite, catching Dad's hand and holding it, then Mads's, so that they cross the yard together toward the officer who's walking to meet them, Ryan staying behind and watching them go.

23

The Maine State Prison visit room looks a lot like what Shaw's seen on TV, a generally beige space within a gray place. Plastic tables with attached benches, visit officers overseeing the interactions between the inmates and their family and friends who take advantage of the one-thirty to three-thirty p.m. visitation hours.

It's a slow Sunday, by the looks of it, only a handful of other visitors here to see the cons, one woman crying audibly and leaning to touch foreheads with the heavyset fella she sits across from, a little boy of about two years balanced on her thigh, absorbedly dancing his stuffed cat back and forth on the tabletop.

Shaw slides onto the bench the officer directs her to and settles back to wait, her posture deliberate, determined not to betray her own anxiety. She'd carefully chosen her outfit of jeans, white blouse, wine-colored below-the-hip jacket, and ass-kicking boots. Not for him; for herself. To prove she's still who she always was, despite his best efforts. She saw the boys off to school as she'd been doing since the beginning of the lengthy leave Jewel had insisted upon, not just to recover from her injuries but to process the emotional repercussions of everything that had happened. The plan for the afternoon was to have Ryan pick Beau and Casey up after classes and bring them to his new shop, taking advantage of Beau's short break between winter and spring sports seasons to extort a little free labor: painting, cleaning up around the place to prepare for opening the business in one short month. In truth, it's just as much about giving Shaw some space later, after what she needs to do today.

It takes about ten minutes for a guard to bring Anders in. He isn't cuffed—she wasn't sure what to expect, this being her first time in the big house. She applied for this visit six weeks ago, checked in with the lobby officer when she got here, stored her purse in a locker, and passed through two metal detectors to be allowed entrance.

Anders wears a gray inmate sweatshirt over his orange jumpsuit. He moves slowly with a guard trailing him, but he's looking for her the moment he comes in, his gaze raking down the rows of tables, unblinking as he sinks onto the bench across from her.

The guard waits until Anders is seated, then steps back toward the wall, where he stands with his hands clasped behind his back; the officers don't seem to be taking any extra precautions or treating Anders like public enemy number one. Apparently, notoriety doesn't necessarily buy you any cred in a place like this, where having a rap sheet of hideous violent crimes is about as common as having a personal preference for cotton briefs.

Shaw and Anders lock eyes, neither speaking, but finally he moves his tongue in his cheek and says, "I would continue the staring contest, but they tend to take away one's privileges here if the rules aren't closely observed."

Shaw doesn't answer right away, taking in his yellowed skin, his eyes lost in valleys of shadow behind his glasses. He's thinner

336 o GILLIAN FRENCH

than when she last saw him at a hearing a little over a month ago, some of the most surreal and emotionally taxing weeks of her life. He's seven pounds lighter, at least, a gauntness to his neck and head as he sits there staring at her as if she's an unexpected bit of dark chocolate ganache he'd like to place on his tongue to melt. "I wasn't sure if you'd see me without your lawyer present," she says.

"You must've guessed that curiosity would win out. It's a trait we share." His gaze travels her, radiating an overt sexuality that she hadn't sensed from him before. She observes it mildly, with a numbness born of emotional turmoil, tragedy, a sense of hard-won absolution, and at least three burly guards between her and the predator. Perhaps it's a hunger not so much for a woman's body he's feeling, but for life, for access.

"I hadn't expected to see you again until the trial." He leans one elbow on the tabletop. "It's not every day that the one who got away comes for a visit, particularly not around a place like this. I've still got the love bites, you know." He brushes his collar back slightly, but she'd already noticed the fresh pink scar tissue visible down the side of his neck from Aphrodite's teeth, and more puncture wounds on his hands and wrists from trying to fight her off. "And a dreadful limp from those torn ligaments. Courtesy of you."

"Yeah, well, a girl's gotta do what a girl's gotta do, you know? It can't all be spa days and shopping sprees. So, the doc was able to hook that kneecap back on for you, huh?"

He gazes back, unmoving. "How's the family?"

"Believe it or not, I didn't come here to play catch-up with you. Though I am pleased to let you know that the guy who you tried to kill in my old house managed to pull through. It's kind of a miracle, really. He's back with his family now."

"There's nothing you can tell me about my case that I don't already know. I never miss the nightly news. I read everything the newspapers print about us. Those papers have been a saving grace, really. I give my cellmate the funny pages first and he promises not to bite my ear off while I sleep." Anders lowers his chin and his voice. "I saw that your father is filing suit against the Aroostook County Sheriff's Office, our former governor Mercer Brixton, and a developer fellow named Michael Bianchi. Alleging negligence, corruption, all sorts in the investigation into Thea's murder. He can't win, but I wish him luck all the same."

Anders flexes his fingers, as if tussling with a desire to do more with his hands than simply fold them on the table. "How did she look when they brought her out of the ground? Will you tell me that much?" He watches her face closely, the tight control there. "Was there anything left to speak of? She was so . . soft that night when I had her. It's difficult for me to imagine that reduced to—well, essentially a pile of bones?"

Shaw stares back.

"Ah. Icy silence. And speaking of bones, I've had some conversations with that state police detective friend of yours—York? He had lots of questions for me about the remains you found in Beggar's Meadow all those months ago. He seems to feel that I know something about them. It's a shame that the cause of death came back as inconclusive. I suppose we'll never know."

"Did you put her there, hoping that I'd find her?" Shaw takes in his look of amused disbelief. "I can't know how long you were stalking me. Or how many times you followed me into those woods. It strikes me as a real Anders kind of thing to do, leave a fresh kill out there where you know I search for my sister, get a hard-on from returning to the general area where you killed Thea."

"There's far-fetched, and then there's delusional. I'd say you've crossed the line."

"Yeah? I'll never stop trying to find out who she was. Or stop trying to link her to you." She leans a bit closer so as not to be overheard, sensing that the guard who brought Anders in is watching them closely. "Why the priest? You went out of your way to make sure Father Joseph didn't escape that fire. I still don't see the reason."

Anders holds her gaze, his lips together, bloodless.

"Come on. You said it yourself. You've got nothing to lose."

"If you must know . . . he didn't like me. Didn't approve of me." Anders pauses. "I gather he thought of himself as some great judge of character, and after one short week of working for Saint Anthony's, he basically invited me to move on. No offer of council or confession. Simply implied that he didn't think the parish was 'right' for me." Again, his fingers flex, dig into his palms. "Imagine that. A man of the cloth."

Shaw stares back at him, processing, summoning steadiness and resolve. "I really came here today because I wanted you to know what a good thing you did for us." His eyes tick back and forth, his expression slackening. "I know. You don't get it. You never will. But everything's changed for me now. All those years of not knowing . . . of wondering where my sister was, wanting so badly to bring her home. She was home. You brought her home, Anders. Thea was never more than a few hundred yards away from me and my dad or my baby sister all that time. Every happy occasion, every memory . . . in a sense, she was with us. So . . . after committing that selfish, disgusting act of stealing her life, you did us a favor. You think you've made fools of us. But that couldn't be further from the truth." Her voice fails for a moment, and Shaw focuses on replenishing oxygen to help keep her emotions in check. "We gave her an amazing memorial service. Hundreds of people came. Packed the house."

He swallows, the sound thick, dry. "If only I could've been there."

"I'd get used to missing out on things if I were you. More people care about Thea now than ever, and, still, nobody gives a rat's ass about you. Or ever did, huh? But then I guess that's your whole problem. At least in here, no more innocent kids are going to have to pay for it. See,"—and for this she leans closer than ever, close enough to see the tracings of red in the whites of his eyes—"you're going to die in here, and I'm glad. The jury is going to sentence you to life and then some for what you did to my sister, but that wonky liver of yours is going to quit long before that. Then they'll burn you down to a little pile of ashes, and drop you in a hole, and I'll be free to keep right on living." Tears are standing in her eyes, hot and bright. "Goddamn, do I love justice. Tastes like Pabst Blue Ribbon."

Anders sits still, an angle to his mouth, his hands now fisted on the table. "You never know," he says. "Cases like mine can have happy endings. A tissue regeneration could occur. I'm still receiving regular treatment. A donor could come through at any time at all, and I'll live to see them build causeways on the moon. I might even drop you a line now and then, over the years. Just to revisit old times."

"I think convicted murderers tend to land way down at the bottom of the donor list." She sits back, releases a shaky breath, and forces a smile. "I guess that's it. Have fun with your cellmate."

"If you think your troubles are over, you're mistaken." His words are sharp, rushing to fit them in before she can stand to leave. "What about that husband of yours? Hasn't come home to you, has he? And you're still too crass, too rude, too graceless to prove yourself at your job. You're a broken person and getting your sister's little bits and pieces back isn't going to change that." He exhales, lips drawing back from his teeth. "Holy God. You're the kind of thing I can't decide whether to kill or fuck. Or in what order."

The guard is approaching, catching wind of the conversation at last, and Shaw smiles harder, shaking her head. "My family's pain has been your life support for years now. I'm cutting you off."

She stands, looking Anders in the eye as the guard's grip comes down on his shoulder. Then Anders spits at her, the spray landing across her cheek. In the next second, he's slammed to the tabletop by the guard's heavy hand cuffing his neck, and she sees no more as she turns and walks toward the exit, refusing to wipe her face until she's out of Anders's sight.

Shaw retrieves her bag and goes into the parking lot, climbing into her car and dropping back against the seat with her eyes closed, just breathing for a while, the silence broken by the buzzing of her phone.

She wipes tears from her cheeks, answers without even glancing at the caller ID. "This is Shaw."

"Hi." It's Gauthier, with a long pause. "Is it okay that I called?"

"So okay that I'm tingling. Spit it out."

"Jewel says they need us at the scene over in Campton, and—she said it was okay if I called you. I know you've been on leave, but . . ."

"You're asking if I'm emotionally prepared to meet you there and pull some prints?"

"Basically. Yeah."

Shaw sighs, laughs, taps the framed photo of Beau and Casey dangling from the rearview, watching it swing and spin. "Does a bear go wee-wee in the woods?" She hears the pensive silence. "Don't answer that. I'll be there ASAP."

ACKNOWLEDGMENTS

My thanks go to my editor, Kelley Ragland, and the team at Minotaur for all of their hard work in bringing Shaw's story to readers, as well as for giving me a chance to live a dream by publishing in the adult crime realm. I'm so grateful for my agent, Alice Tasman, who has championed my writing for years, and who offered invaluable advice during the revision of this book. Onward!

I wouldn't be writing books at all if my parents hadn't encouraged my interest right from the beginning; thank you and love always to my folks, Jaci and Brent. A whole heap of love and gratitude goes to my husband, Darren, and our boys, who support me through all of the ups and downs of publishing, parenting, and life in general; thank you for putting up with me and giving me five excellent reasons to face the day.

ABOUT THE AUTHOR

Jacqueline Hall

Gillian French is an Edgar Award, Bram Stoker Award, and two-time International Thriller Award nominated author. Her previous novels, all mystery and suspense novels published for a young adult audience, include *Grit, The Door to January, The Lies They Tell, The Missing Season,* and *Sugaring Off.* She lives in rural Maine with her husband and four sons.